Peter Watt has spent time as a regular soldier and reservist infantry officer, articled clerk, prawn trawler deckhand, builder's labourer, pipe layer, surveyor's chainman, real estate salesman, private investigator, police sergeant and adviser to the Royal Papua New Guinea Constabulary. Peter has lived and worked with Aborigines, Islanders, Vietnamese and Papua New Guineans, and worked as a police officer in Asian crime and homicide units. He speaks Pidgin and Vietnamese and is studying German.

Flight of the Eagle is the final novel in his historical trilogy, the first two novels being *Cry of the Curlew* and *Shadow of the Osprey*. Peter is currently working on a novel set in Papua New Guinea between the World Wars. He lives in Tweed Heads, NSW.

Peter Watt can be contacted at *www.peterwatt.com*

D0949379

Also by Peter Watt

CRY OF THE CURLEW
SHADOW OF THE OSPREY

and published by Corgi Books

FLIGHT OF THE EAGLE

Peter Watt

CORGI BOOKS

FLIGHT OF THE EAGLE
A CORGI BOOK : 0 552 14796 6

First publication in Great Britain

PRINTING HISTORY
Corgi edition published 2002

3 5 7 9 10 8 6 4 2

Copyright © Peter Watt 2001
Map of Queensland by Mike Gorman

The right of Peter Watt to be identified as the author of
this work has been asserted in accordance with sections 77
and 78 of the Copyright Designs and Patents Act 1988.

Although inspired by real events, this novel is a work of
fiction. All central characters are creations of the author's
imagination and in no way reflect on any persons living or
dead. Racist language in the text does not reflect the
author's own views, but is intended to reflect the attitudes
and expressions of a particular time in Australian history.

Condition of Sale
This book is sold subject to the condition that it shall not,
by way of trade or otherwise, be lent, re-sold, hired out or
otherwise circulated in any form of binding or cover other
than that in which it is published and without a similar
condition including this condition being imposed on the
subsequent purchaser.

Set in 11/12pt Sabon by
Falcon Oast Graphic Art Ltd.

Corgi Books are published by Transworld Publishers,
61–63 Uxbridge Road, London W5 5SA,
a division of The Random House Group Ltd,
in Australia by Random House Australia (Pty) Ltd,
20 Alfred Street, Milsons Point, Sydney, NSW 2061, Australia,
in New Zealand by Random House New Zealand Ltd,
18 Poland Road, Glenfield, Auckland 10, New Zealand
and in South Africa by Random House (Pty) Ltd,
Endulini, 5a Jubilee Road, Parktown 2193, South Africa.

Printed and bound in Great Britain by
Cox & Wyman Ltd, Reading, Berkshire.

For my mother, Elinor Therese. With all my love.

ACKNOWLEDGEMENTS

A very special thank you to my wonderful mother and equally wonderful aunts, Joan Payne and Marjorie Leigh. Without their initial support this project would never have existed.

I would like to acknowledge the wonderful effort of my publishers in the United Kingdom, Transworld Publishers and the work of two people in particular: my editor Diana Beaumont and publicist Marina Vokos.

In the United Kingdom I would also like to thank Ian Wightman, Andrew Parker and Zoe Harris for their unstinting loyalty and friendship forged in cyberspace as a result of becoming Peter Watt readers. In Canada, Patricia Gowing and in the United States of America, Maureen Oblachinski.

As usual, my thanks go to the master of this genre Wilbur Smith, whom I had the pleasure to meet early last year in Brisbane, Australia. I have always hoped to present the colourful history of the Australian frontier in the same vein as Wilbur has done for early Africa in his novels.

In Australia my thanks go as always to my agent Tony Williams and all who work with him at the agency. And to Cate Paterson for the hours she spent helping me differentiate between *then* and *than*.

Colony of Queensland
1884

Kilometres

0   100   200   300   400   500

Torres Strait
Islands

CAPE
YORK

Gulf
of
Carpentaria

Palmer River

Port Douglas

Cairns

Coral Sea

Burketown

BURKESLAND

Townsville

Godkin
Range

Cloncurry

Bowen

Q u e e n s l a n d

BALACLAVA
RUN

Fitzroy River

Longreach

Barcaldine

Rockhampton

CHANNEL
COUNTRY

GLEN VIEW

Tambo

Brisbane
River

Toowoomba

Brisbane
Town

Uloola, behold him! The thunder that breaks
On the tops of the rocks with the rain,
And the wind which drives up with the salt
    of the lakes,
Have made him a hunter again:
A hunter and fisher again.

'The Last of His Tribe', Henry Kendall

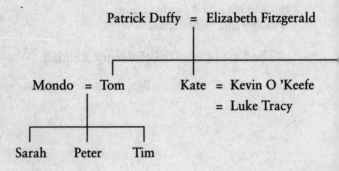

Patrick Duffy = Elizabeth Fitzgerald

Mondo = Tom   Kate = Kevin O 'Keefe
                                              = Luke Tracy

Sarah   Peter   Tim

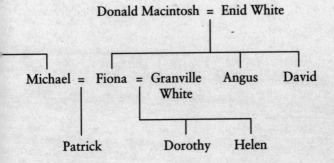

PROLOGUE

COLONY OF QUEENSLAND

It was a land as hostile as any the white man knew.

Vast spaces of lonely scrub and sand where the world's deadliest snake sheltered in the cracks of the clay pans during the blistering heat of the day and hunted the marsupial creatures by night. A land where a solitary Aboriginal hunter roamed in a tenuous existence with nature.

But Wallarie did not feel alone in this land. For he walked with the spirits of his people and the fact that he lived proved their existence. His life was indelibly marked by the waiting for the storm that would come to the world of men and change the unborn years ahead.

The warrior was now in his middle years and his long beard was shot with grey. His body was scarred and his eyes were fading with the progress of time. But despite his years he was still a warrior to be feared by the tribesmen he met in his long wanderings across the length and breadth of the Colony of Queensland. Nor was his reputation as a killer of white men forgotten on the frontier by the European settlers.

For Wallarie was now shrouded in the mythology of the frontier. He was now remembered as a spirit man who would come to snatch away little children – should they be naughty, nannies chided.

But this night he would sit cross-legged before his campfire and chant the songs of his people. The spirits of the land would listen as his fire crackled softly in the night and the ageing warrior would fall into a deep sleep. The spirits would come to him on the hush of the night wind to tell him things of the future as he slept by his fire. They would tell him of strange events unfolding: that the ancestor spirits had been disturbed from their long sleep and a vengeful storm was rising from the earth to lash the world of the white man. They told him that he must travel north to the lands of the fierce Kalkadoon warriors where he would meet once again with the blood of his past. He did not know what this meant but knew he must listen to the voices.

Wallarie – the last of his tribe – continued to dream his visions as the dingo howled mournfully in the desert night and the deadly taipan rose from the cracks of the clay pans to slither in search of prey.

When the sun came to the brigalow plains of central Queensland Wallarie left the cooling shelter of the ancient cave to trek once more north to the lands of the Kalkadoon tribesmen.

The
Storm Rising

1884

I

A young man of the Queensland Native Mounted Police squatted in the red dust of the plains. He was examining the faint outline of footprints as his colleagues sat uneasily astride their big mounts. His opinion was critical to the lives of the eight mounted troopers who had patrolled deep into the country of the greatly feared Kalkadoon warriors.

The police patrol had come a long way from their barracks near the frontier town of Cloncurry. To their front rose the craggy, dry hills of the Godkin Range whilst behind them the sparse bush and prickly trees of the termite nest dotted red plains. Only the buzzing of the pestilent flies and the swish of horses' tails disturbed the silence of the ever-present dry heat of the semi-arid lands of northern Australia.

Trooper Peter Duffy was a man living between two worlds. Half-Irish half-Aboriginal, he was the son of the bushranger Tom Duffy and Mondo, a woman of the Nerambura clan. He was in his early twenties and had inherited his father's well-formed physique and his mother's skin tone. He had the dark good looks that attracted coy glances from European women in the frontier towns while at the same time malevolent stares from their men. Despite his excellent grades at school and being raised in a European culture, he was forever reminded that he was a half-caste nigger by the whites around him.

When he had joined the Native Mounted Police in Townsville with his best friend Gordon James he was automatically designated as the tracker for the patrol whereas Gordon was able to acquire a commission as an officer. Gordon was, after all, the son of the famed Sergeant Henry James who had many years earlier helped disperse the tribes of the Fitzroy region.

That a contingent of the Native Mounted Police had killed his mother and father sixteen years earlier in Burkesland had initially troubled Peter. But loyalty to a best friend had overcome something that was a distant and very dim memory in the present reality of his youthful desire for adventure.

Peter gazed up at the distant line of ridges and had no doubt that the tracks led to the sanctuary of the hills. He did not like the situation. Every instinct told him the shimmering heat haze dancing on the craggy rocks of the ancient hills held death; it was in the very air itself. The silence was ominous – as if the spirits of the rocks had fallen silent to listen to the sounds of horses snorting and saddle metal jangling. Death was a buzzing sound in the young police trooper's ears.

'Well, Trooper Duffy, what do you see?' Sub Inspector Potter queried irritably from atop his mount. The long patrol in the saddle had played havoc with his haemorrhoids and the so far fruitless hunt for the elusive warriors made him sour around his men.

'Nothing good, Mahmy,' Peter replied thoughtfully, adding, 'I think the Kalkadoons want us to go in after them.'

'Rot!' the sub inspector snorted. 'Darkies don't have the white man's ability to plan a military strategy. I think you are being over cautious.'

Peter turned his face away so that the police officer could not see his expression of contempt for him. If only Gordon James, his boyhood friend, was commanding the patrol and not this pompous idiot. 'I think we should not go in, Mahmy,' Peter reiterated quietly. 'I think they are waiting for us.'

Peter knew full well that the police officer did not like him for what he was – a half-caste, the progeny of an abominable sin in the Lord's eyes.

The inspector had vigorously objected to his posting to his troop. *No, he wanted a full-blooded tracker . . . not some half-caste darkie!* But the half-caste had friends in the Mounted Police who insisted he be given the job as the patrol's tracker. They were now stuck with each other.

The European troopers cast nervous glances at their commander. They respected the young tracker who they jokingly said was 'almost a white man'. So when Peter advised not to go into the narrow, scrub covered gullies of the hills they listened. Like Peter Duffy, they had little respect for their arrogant commander who had until recently served with the British army in India.

The Aboriginal troopers of the patrol *knew* Peter was right and nervously fidgeted with their Snider carbines as they gazed at the slopes and hill tops searching for the dreaded Kalkadoon warriors. *This was not going to be a good dispersal!*

Inspector Potter swiped at the clouds of flies vying for the sweat on his face. He had already decided to ignore his tracker. The pesky Kalkadoons were badly in need of being taught a lesson and had speared their last white man. The troopers would go in.

If the Kalkadoons were waiting for them they were in for an unpleasant surprise up against the guns of the patrol. Their heavy wooden shields would not stop a Snider round from Queen Victoria's dispensers of justice in Queensland.

'Advance!'

Inspector Potter's order was delivered with a lazy disdain for all that smacked of commonsense.

Peter swung into the saddle and slid the police carbine from its scabbard. He rested the butt against his thigh. The hills seemed to scream a deadly silence. As loud as a scream from a dying man, he thought.

They rode in silence.

There was no nervous banter as they followed the tracks that Peter's keen eyesight could discern in the dry earth and the numerous footprints led them into a narrow gully bordered by rock strewn slopes.

Rocks big enough to conceal a man, Peter thought with mounting apprehension for what he could visualise unfolding. Rocks and scrub to conceal crouching men who had been trained as warriors from birth. Behind him the patrol followed reluctantly – except for Sub Inspector Potter, smug in his ignorance.

The sunburnt and sweating police officer shook his head. The bloody half-caste nigger was as gutless as he had suspected, he thought. No backbone when it came to dealing with primitive blacks armed with little more than sticks and stones. The matter of the man's timid behaviour was noted and would be duly reported upon return to the barracks at Cloncurry. In the mean . . .

He never did finish his monologue of censuring thoughts as he became vaguely aware of a strange swishing sound in the hot, still air of the narrow gully. A searing pain sliced through his groin and his mount suddenly reared in terrified agony as the barbed spears thudded into its flank. At the same time the seemingly deserted slopes of the hills were rent with the blood-curdling war cries from hundreds of Kalkadoon throats.

With a desperate yank on the reins, Potter vainly attempted to keep his mount on its feet, but the mortally wounded horse went down with a bone splitting crash, pinning him to the ground.

The men who showered the police patrol with rocks and the long hardwood spears were well over six feet tall and the plumage of emu and eaglehawk feathers piled on their heads gave them terrifying added height. Their faces were marked with bands of white feathers attached with their own blood and feathers also adorned their arms and legs. To the ambushed police troopers their surreal appearance seemed no less than an image of the demons of hell coming to claim their lives.

Potter clutched frantically at the spear in his groin. But the barbs of the spear were so designed that the spear could neither be pushed nor pulled once it had lodged. The Kalkadoon warriors whom he had sneered at only minutes before had lured him into the narrow gorge where they held the tactical high ground. The police patrol was trapped in a narrow dead-end gully without any chance to manoeuvre.

A spear-wielding warrior loomed above Potter who had lost his revolver. 'Die you white bastard!' the grizzled warrior spat and Potter was mildly surprised to hear his killer speak English as he clawed frantically at a spear impaled in his chest. Potter's eyes rolled in despair as he stared up at his killer. He had lost his patrol and now he was losing his life.

The warrior savagely yanked the spear from the dying inspector's chest while the last surviving troopers desperately attempted to disentangle themselves from their thrashing mounts and seek escape. But everywhere their terrified eyes fell they saw only waves of plumage-adorned bodies charging down the slopes from behind their rock and scrub cover.

Screaming taunts, the Kalkadoon warriors were on the troopers with lance-like spears to impale them to the red earth. With despairing screams for mercy, the troopers died under the blows of nullas and stone axes.

Razor-sharp stone knives slit open the bellies of the dead troopers as the warriors eagerly sought the kidneys of the men. They would eat the covering fat as a gallant gesture to the fallen warriors.

Wallarie turned his attention from the inspector at his feet to the last survivor – a trooper who stood alone and defiant, wielding his rifle like a club. The man had no chance, Wallarie thought, as a circle of Kalkadoon warriors taunted him with jeers.

Peter knew he was going to die and that he could not expect mercy from the men they had hunted so ruthlessly in the past. But he also knew that he would die fighting.

Had not his own father died as a fighting man in the rain-soaked hills of Burkesland those many years earlier? Had not his mother died from a bullet? Thus it was his fate to die like a man. His breath came in gasps as he sucked in the hot air to fill his lungs for his final act of defiance.

An older warrior armed with a blood-stained spear stepped from the circle of Kalkadoon taunting him. From the many scars that adorned his body, Peter sensed that the older man who confronted him was an experienced fighter.

Although Peter was prepared for death he hoped it would not be painful. He silently prayed to be brave when the spear pierced his body. In death he would show the Kalkadoon he was as good as any of their own warriors. Although Peter had learned to use the spear in close-quarter fighting the lance-like spear – and the way the

Kalkadoons used it – was different to the way he had been trained as a youth by the legendary kinsman Wallarie. The fierce tribesmen of the hills used the spear to stab rather than throw.

Wallarie wanted the police tracker to look into his eyes before he died on the end of his spear and the defiant police tracker made eye contact.

Tom, Wallarie thought in his confusion. He was gazing into Tom Duffy's eyes!

He hesitated and Peter could see an unexpected confusion in the scarred warrior's movements. Had he not seen this man before in a dream, Peter thought. Or was the man a real part of his life? The name, almost forgotten, came as a hiss to his lips.

'Wallarie!'

Both men lowered their weapons as they stared at each other in mutual recognition. A decade of the white man's years had passed since he last set eyes on the young man who was the son of his white brother in life. The enigmatic message of the dream in the ancient cave of the Nerambura echoed in the grizzled warrior's head. He had come north to meet the last surviving blood of his people in the next generation.

The Kalkadoon, who waited for the killing thrust of the strange Darambal man who had come to them from the south, muttered amongst themselves. *Why had the Darambal man lowered his spear before the hated enemy?*

Wallarie lowered his spear and stepped forward to acknowledge his kinsman.

2

Patrick Duffy, Captain of Queen Victoria's Imperial Army, stood oblivious to the cold sleet that drizzled monotonously around him and stared at the Celtic cross which bore the inscribed name *Molly O'Rourke*. The grave was overgrown with flowers that had blossomed in the Irish spring and would return to bitter weeds in the winter.

So this was the woman who, twenty-two years earlier, had delivered him into the care of his father's family in far-off Sydney, he brooded.

He stood ramrod straight at the foot of the grave and reflected bitterly on Lady Enid Macintosh's – his maternal grandmother's – account of the circumstances surrounding his birth: of how the old Irish nanny she had once employed had rescued him from his mother who would have sent him to one of the infamous baby farms of Sydney to rid her life of him. But Molly had rescued him and with loving trust placed him in the arms of his Aunt Bridget and Uncle Frank at the Erin Hotel in Sydney

It had been a traumatic night, so Patrick had been told, as it was the night that the Duffys had learned of his father's death in the Maori Wars of New Zealand. *A life taken a life given*, Uncle Francis had pragmatically philosophised.

Patrick was a tall and broad-shouldered young man and, except for his emerald green eyes, he was the living image of his father, Michael Duffy, in every way. His eyes were an inheritance from his beautiful mother, Fiona Macintosh.

But she was Fiona White, wife of Granville White, the man who part controlled the powerful Macintosh financial enterprises, a commercial empire which ranged from vast property holdings in England and Australia to shipping and merchandise enterprises in the Pacific, Asia and India. A financial conglomerate with its roots in England – and its tentacles snaking across the globe to the far reaches of the British Empire of Queen Victoria.

The young man's eyes glazed for just a moment as he reflected on Granville White. Ahh, but he would not dwell on the man who his grandmother swore was responsible for the murder of the uncle he never knew. For now he was on leave from his regiment to visit the village from where the Duffy family had fled – a mere six hours ahead of the warrant for the arrest of his paternal grandfather, or so he had been told by Aunt Bridget when he was a young boy growing up in the Erin Hotel.

Patrick sighed and pulled the collar of his coat against the bitter wind. An old woman with a tattered shawl leaned on her cane and intently watched the well-dressed young man who stood

28

silently at the foot of Molly's grave. 'Twas Patrick Duffy himself who had returned to his village, she wondered with superstitious awe as she watched the replica of another man from another time.

When she was a very young woman Mary Casey had known Molly and together they had baited the hated English soldiers occupying their country. And together they had vigorously pursued the handsome and wild Patrick Duffy for his attentions.

But the Protestant daughter of an Anglo-Irish landowner had caught the young rebel's eye and taken him to her bed. It was around that same time that the magistrate had sent his lackeys to arrest Molly for her rebellious acts and she had been transported as a fourteen-year-old girl to the fatal shores of New South Wales.

Mary Casey lived at the village presbytery as the housekeeper for the young priest, Father Eamon O'Brien, who was newly ordained and had come to replace Father Clancy. But Father O'Brien was not of the county born and was suspicious in his foreign ways. He was English educated and spent an unhealthy length of time visiting the ancient sites where the bloody practices of the Celtic priests, the Druids, were once performed. It was known that he even discussed the development of the True Faith in Ireland as some sort of integration with the ancient beliefs.

Mary shuddered. The ancient ways indeed! 'Twas a blasphemy! Her shudder, however, was not from the cold but a superstitious recollection of meeting the young man who had introduced himself politely as Patrick Duffy and had inquired of her where he might find Molly's grave. 'Jesus, Mary and Joseph!' she had uttered in her fear and crossed herself to ward off ghosts. He himself had come back from the dead from that savage dry land across the sea!

Patrick had been startled by her reaction to his inquiry. But he was not to know that he was the image of his paternal grandfather and that the old woman's fear rose from the root of her deep-seated Celtic superstitions. Without another word she had hobbled to the grave and pointed with her cane at the stone cross.

A wind flurry from the grey Irish Sea swept the cold sleet in swirls around Patrick's legs. He was not used to the cold. Years of soldiering in the far-flung campaigns of Queen Victoria's army in north Africa seemed to have thinned his blood.

Soldiering was not an occupation Lady Enid Macintosh had approved of for her only grandson after he had opted out of his studies at Oxford. She had vigorously resisted his desire to take a commission in the army but had reluctantly relented and agreed to his commissioning into a Highland regiment.

The life Patrick had yearned for was not that of a scholar but one which would satisfy his strange and inexplicable desire to travel and search for himself in the desolate places of the world. He had also been motivated by a desire to avoid returning to Australia and hence was forced to choose between two heritages. A decision either way would alienate him from one half of his blood.

As a young lieutenant he had seen his first

action at Tel-el-Kibir in Egypt. The campaign to protect the strategically important Suez Canal held by rebel Egyptian forces had been fought three years earlier and the echoes of the savage fighting still haunted Patrick's dreams.

The Egyptians had dug a huge trench across the expected path of advance by British forces under the supreme command of General Sir Garnet Wolseley and for seventeen blistering days Lieutenant Patrick Duffy had marched with his Highland infantry across the vast expanse of Egyptian desert until they faced the massive earthworks of their enemy. Cloaked by the desert's chill darkness, Lieutenant Duffy had led his kilted Highlanders under a canopy of crystal stars towards the enemy. As he had trudged beside his men his thoughts had drifted to what lay ahead – and what lay behind – in his life.

He had left Sydney at the age of eleven with his maternal grandmother, the formidable Lady Enid Macintosh, to live at the Macintosh London home. His entrustment to her patronage had been as the result of a pact formed between her and his guardian – Daniel Duffy – which had been forged years earlier in Sydney.

The young Catholic Patrick Duffy had been entrusted to the staunchly Protestant Lady Enid Macintosh with the seeming intention that he be educated at England's best schools. Her motive, however, was primarily ruthless; she intended to groom him to eventually take his place as the legitimate head of the Macintosh financial empire. He had Macintosh blood through his grandmother's side and would act as a counter to

Granville White – and even his own mother, Fiona White nee Macintosh.

But Lady Macintosh would never tolerate a Papist as head of the fiercely proud Protestant clan. It was her expressed view that, given time and exposure to an English education, her grandson would see the rationale underlying her beliefs.

Daniel Duffy had scoffed at the idea that Patrick would inevitably choose her religion. Patrick had been baptised a Catholic and a Catholic he would remain until death.

Enid had not counted on the young boy's natural charm and her own repressed grand-maternal feelings. Over time she had grown to love Patrick as closely as any mother could. He had filled the vacuum created by the death of her own beloved son David. Such was her fear of losing Patrick from her lonely life that she had not pressed his choice between his Irish Catholic and Scots Protestant world. One day the choice must be made if he were to take his rightful place at the head of the Macintosh empire. At least his time in the army of Queen Victoria would allow him to satisfy his wild Irish blood in the heat of battle.

As he marched with his men into battle Patrick knew that he had the love of Lady Enid on one hand and his Irish family's love on the other. Before him was the enviable opportunity to inherit one of the great wealths of the Empire – and the probable loss of the acceptance of Daniel and his family. For now, he grimly reminded himself, all that lay ahead of him was the chance of his own death or mutilation. At that moment his thoughts of past and future were devoured by the present fear as the Highlanders drew closer to the enemy.

Would he suddenly experience the fear of the coward and run? Would he freeze in the face of the terror and fail in his duty as an officer? Would he . . .

The horizon flared as if the sun were rising early and the soldiers marched in silence, wondering at the miscalculation of their officers in placing them so far out from the enemy positions before dawn.

Sir Garnet Wolseley had also wondered at the unexpectedly early dawn. But it had been pointed out to him that the astronomical anomaly was, in fact, the glow from the tail of a comet passing below the horizon.

Just before dawn sporadic firing from sentries forward of the Egyptian trenches snapped Patrick from his thoughts. Then the air was suddenly rent by the deafening roar of rifles flashing a wall of spitting fire in the dark. Wolseley launched his army against the unsuspecting rebel Egyptians. The flashes of rifles along the Egyptian parapet were point blank and the British bugles sounded the charge.

Patrick remembered later how the fusillade had come as a welcome relief from the accumulation of almost overwhelming fear. Jolted from the first seconds of frozen fear, the young officer's thoughts were of the task ahead.

He had roared for his men to follow him – and follow they did. With bayonets fixed and kilts swirling around bronzed legs, Lieutenant Patrick Duffy and his Highlanders swept forward with savage Highland screams of defiance.

In the savage melee of the hand-to-hand fighting

Patrick had lost his pistol but quickly retrieved a fallen Highlander's Martini Henry rifle. In the next fifty minutes of fighting he carved a bloody swathe through the Queen's enemies.

Attack ... counter attack. Screamed and garbled curses of friend and foe locked in life and death struggles; cries of men for mothers in many languages as they faced the inevitability of mortal wounds; a black face with teeth bared looming in the dark; savage killing ... thrust with the long bayonet and the agonised grunt as the bayonet found flesh. The Nubian clawing frantically at Patrick's face, feeling nothing but the savage exhilaration of killing lust. More faces and bodies until his red jacket was stiff with blood. He had roared the slogans of his savage Highlander ancestors and in the killing frenzy many had died on the point of his bayonet.

When it was all over Lieutenant Duffy was generously mentioned in Wolseley's dispatches for his leadership and personal courage. Brevet captain's rank was his eventual reward for the campaign to save the Suez Canal.

But months of campaigning in the deserts and exposure to the Nile's swamps had left him racked with malaria. It was still with him as he stood at the foot of Molly O'Rourke's grave. His military bearing crumbled and he swayed uncertainly

Mary Casey hobbled forward to help and found herself transfixed by a strange power behind the eyes that tried to smile off the fever.

They were the eyes of the Devil himself, she thought. Eyes that could steal the heart and maidenhead of a nun!

Patrick tried to shake off Mary's insistence that he go with her to the presbytery for a plate of hot soup but eventually acquiesced to her no-nonsense persuasion and followed her to the small stone annexe of the church where she ushered him inside and called to Father O'Brien.

Hearing her call for help, the priest quickened the mandatory prayers of his office and closed his missal to hurry to the tiny kitchen where he was confronted by the sight of a giant of a young man leaning on his frail housekeeper as she hustled him onto a well-worn wooden chair at the table.

'Father Eamon O'Brien,' the young priest said, as he thrust out his hand to Patrick, who he sensed was someone of importance given his bearing and expensive suit. When Patrick introduced himself the priest detected the accent of an educated man.

Mary Casey made herself busy warming soup – a thin gruel of stale vegetables and barley with a thin trace of lamb for flavour – in an old fashioned pot blackened by fires that could be traced back a century or more.

Patrick felt the warmth of the kitchen flood his body like the sun rising over the deserts of the Nile in the early morning. It was the warm feeling and ambience about the priest's kitchen that brought fleeting memories of a hotel kitchen in Sydney's Irish quarter. A place he had spent the first half of his life with his Aunt Bridget, Uncle Francis and Daniel's family.

'You are not from the village, Mister Duffy,' Father O'Brien stated as a matter of fact. 'You have an Irish name well known here, but an English accent?'

Patrick smiled at the observation by the young priest who also did not sound as Irish as he might have thought. In fact, he did not even look like a priest, but one who might have been at home in the hallowed halls of Oxford or Cambridge.

Eamon was thin and dark and wore spectacles. He had an intelligent and eager face that seemed to be questioning – even when his lips were still. 'No, Father, I'm not from here,' Patrick replied with a weak smile. 'And I may have an English accent, as you say, but I'm an Australian.'

'Australian! I did not know such a creature existed,' the priest said with a wry grin. 'But that might explain why an Irishman with an English accent would defend his identity in a land hostile to the occupation of these sainted shores.'

'My family came from this village back in the fifties. Patrick and Elizabeth Duffy were my grandparents on my father's side,' Patrick replied with some pride as he knew from the stories told in the Erin Hotel that his grandfather was a legend of sorts in his birthplace.

At the same time, as a soldier in Her Majesty's Army, he felt a little guilty at such pride. The rebellious Irish were a constant scourge of the Imperial forces. Their foolish thoughts of independence tied up valuable military resources.

'Ah, but you're not Patrick Duffy himself,' Mary Casey interjected with mumbled superstitious relief as she still harboured a slight fear that the man had come home to haunt the familiar places of his youth. 'God be thanked for that!'

Both priest and soldier cast puzzled glances at her strange statement.

Father O'Brien noticed Patrick's mystified expression and stepped in to extricate him from his confusion. He had a better understanding of the peculiar ways of his parishioners. 'So it would be a visit you would be making us, Mister Duffy,' he said. 'A pilgrimage, one could say.'

'I suppose that is probably the best description of why I am here.'

'I have heard of your grandfather,' Eamon continued. 'They say he fought the British army with Peter Lalor at the Eureka Stockade and was killed by the wild black people in Australia.'

Patrick wiped his face with his hand to rub away the sweat. The fever was not as bad as he feared it might be. 'Yes, that's true,' he replied. 'He was one of the rebel miners who stood with the Yankee Californian Revolver Brigade at Ballarat.'

'Then you will be welcomed in all the public houses here.'

'I doubt that, Father,' Patrick said somewhat sadly, shaking his head. 'I hold the Queen's commission in her army as a captain.'

The priest stared at his guest.

So that would explain why the man had been so deeply tanned by the sun, he mused. Soldiering in some far-flung and godforsaken campaign. 'The tradition of the Wild Geese is very strong in these parts,' he replied sympathetically. 'Many of the young men from the village have served, many under the Union Jack. I don't think it matters to an Irishman who he fights for, so long as he is promised a good donnybrook. But,' he added with a note of caution, 'it may not pay to announce to the world that you hold a commission. Your accent is enough to label you an Englishman.'

Patrick nodded. English, Irish, Scots . . . he had the blood of the Celts, Gaels, Angles and Saxons in him. Not to mention a touch of French from his paternal grandmother's side. That's what made an Australian, he mused to himself. He had held on to the identity of his birth and had even used his fists at Eton to defend the pride of his country although he had not seen it for many years. Maybe it was just his predominant Irish blood that made him so defiant of slurs about his colonial identity. But at the same time he was also fiercely proud of his Anglo-Scots ancestry.

Mary served the steaming soup to Patrick in a chipped china bowl. He glanced up at her and disarmingly said in a deep Irish brogue, 'Begorrah, Mrs Casey. 'Tis like me sainted old aunt herself would serve. God rest her soul!' And winked with a wicked smile that glittered with mirth.

Mary hooted with delight. 'Be away with ye, Paddy Duffy!' she said with the voice of a young girl, and nudged the handsome grandson of the man himself. 'You'd be takin' advantage of a good woman like meself next!' It was a familiarity that took the old woman back to another time when the young man's grandfather had swept her into his arms for a stolen kiss. Old memories in a new time.

'Ah but that I would, Mary Casey, except Father O'Brien might not approve.'

Eamon blushed and ducked his head at both his housekeeper's brazen response and the irreverent way Patrick encouraged her. Before Patrick could take a sip of the soup Eamon mumbled a hurried thanksgiving prayer for the food about to be consumed. He suspected that Patrick was not a practising Catholic as he had noted that the young officer had not been awed by his position in the village as the local priest.

'Where are you staying while you are visiting us, Captain Duffy?' Eamon asked.

'Down at the pub in the village. Bernard Riley's pub I believe it's called.'

'A distant relative of yours then,' Eamon commented. 'You have a lot of relatives in the village. Even Protestant relatives, since your grandmother was Elizabeth Fitzgerald. As a matter of fact I often visit with your dear departed grandmother's brother, George Fitzgerald. He and I share an interest in archaeology which I do not think my fellow Irishmen appreciate, do they, Missus Casey?'

''Tis not a good thing to be disturbin' the old places with picks and shovels, Father,' Mary growled as she stirred the soup in the big pot. 'The old ones should be left alone.'

'But that's superstitious nonsense, Missus Casey,' Eamon retorted, and Patrick detected a hint of teasing in his reply as the priest added facetiously, 'After all, Saint Patrick broke the power of the old ones and brought Our Lord to Ireland.'

Mary Casey did not reply but continued to stir the soup. She was as good a Catholic as any in the village but some things would never go away. Things that lived in the still grey mists beyond the village and were witnessed and sworn to by many a devout Irishman.

'You do not talk how I remember our Irish priests did when I was a boy growing up in Sydney, Father.'

Eamon smiled broadly although he was unsure whether it was a compliment or a rebuke. It depended on whether one was a devout follower of the True Faith. 'I grew up in England amongst Anglican Catholics and have travelled much of Europe,' he answered. 'But alas, my education in the broader world did not really prepare me for life as a parish priest in an Irish village. However, here I am as a mark of my vow of obedience to the Church.'

'Some would say English Catholics have no place in the Church of Rome,' Patrick baited with his own touch of humour. 'That English Catholics are as heretical as the Protestants.'

The priest beamed and took his glasses from his nose to wipe them.

'Ahh, Captain Duffy, I think you and I could have many a philosophical debate on many subjects. Cambridge old chap?'

'Oxford actually,' Patrick replied in his best affectation of English and broke into Latin. *'That we could, Father. Tacitus, the historian, was a particular interest of mine.'*

The priest raised his eyebrows at the young captain's fluency in the language of his Church. 'Do you also have an interest in Irish history?' he replied in English.

Patrick frowned. 'I'm afraid I know little of Irish history.'

'That's not surprising,' Eamon snorted. 'You received a classical *English* education. But possibly I could alert you to the prehistory of the land of your forefathers, Captain Duffy. If you had an interest in Tacitus then I could possibly intrigue you with the history of Rome's most serious rivals – the Celts.'

Before he could reply Mary Casey ladled another stream of steaming soup into Patrick's almost empty bowl then excused herself to shuffle off to attend to other duties in the small annexe that served as a presbytery.

When they were alone – and Patrick had finished his second helping of hot soup – Eamon continued with the conversation. 'I think if you are staying for a while I should take you to George Fitzgerald's place to meet him. He has a very good collection of artefacts we think date back to the age of the warrior heroes of Old Ireland. The Bronze Age, we amateur archaeologists call that time.'

'I would like that,' Patrick said. 'I think we can dispense with my rank. The name is Patrick.'

'I doubt that you are a religious man, Patrick, so call me Eamon,' the priest said with a warm smile. 'I gather that your lack of respect for titles is part of your colonial upbringing.'

Patrick laughed. 'Some things stay with a man. Yes, I suppose you are right. Australians all think they are as good as their masters no matter what their occupation or standing in society.'

'I see that the well-travelled Englishman Mister Trollope also noted the same thing in his travels in the colonies,' Eamon said with a smile. 'He was rather taken aback by the coachman addressing him as an equal.'

Into the late afternoon priest and soldier carried on a lively conversation on subjects of politics and history. Each of the two very different men, bound by education, warmed to the other's informal attitude. The priest produced a bottle of whisky and before the sun set in a grey sky both men had consumed three-quarters of the contents.

Mary Casey hobbled as fast as she could down to Riley's pub where she would spread the word on Patrick's arrival in the place of the birth of the great man, Patrick's grandfather himself. The news earned her an endless supply of whisky as she spun out the story to a spellbound audience of Riley's patrons.

Old men with pipes nodded sagely as they remembered the giant Patrick Duffy of the old days. They had been young men then but they vividly remembered the night the British troops came to arrest the big man and it was recalled that a sympathetic clerk in the magistrate's office had forewarned the Duffy family. They had only been short hours ahead of the arrest warrant and had taken the first ship out of port – which happened to be sailing for Australia, and not America, as Patrick Duffy had initially hoped.

When the grandson of the great man himself arrived back at the hotel somewhat the worse for wear after drinking with Father O'Brien, the patrons stared with a mixture of awe and pity at the young officer. Awe for the blood in his veins, pity for the fact that his blood had been diluted by that of the English.

In the confines of the smoke-filled bar Patrick politely nodded his greeting to the wall of silent faces that stared curiously at him before going to his room to snatch some badly needed sleep. And in his troubled dreams he would find himself back on the battlefield. But his moans and whimpers were lost in the Irish night as he tossed from side to side in a lather of sweat.

3

A day's ride east of the Kalkadoon ambush on the mounted police patrol Ben Rosenblum grunted as he raised a timber rail into position to complete his stockyards.

Ben was close to his thirtieth year and had finally realised a dream to own his own cattle property. It was not a grand place, just a single-room bark hut, stockyards and a corrugated iron lean-to that acted as a shed for saddles, tools and a few bales of hay. But he intended to carve out an empire one day for his young family and knew this with the optimism of his Jewish ancestors and their tradition of fighting the odds stacked against them.

Ben had once worked for the astute business-woman Kate O'Keefe and had shared the early years of Kate's rise to her considerable wealth. As a young teamster he had trekked the dangerous tracks to the Palmer River goldfields with her and together they had faced hostile tribesmen, floods and privation. Part of her unrelenting spirit to win had rubbed off on the young man who had spent the first part of his life in Sydney's tough waterfront suburbs. With Kate as his inspiration and guiding light, Ben had saved his money and the fruition of his thriftiness was the purchase of the property he had sentimentally named Jerusalem.

The name was a belated acknowledgement of his Jewish ancestry although he no longer practised as an orthodox Jew. Nor did he observe the dietary rules of his religion as the practicalities of survival on the frontier made this seem unimportant to him.

He had stepped further from his beliefs when he had been married by an Anglican priest to Jennifer Harris who had not been accepted as a suitable wife by his more conservative aunt and uncle, Judith and Solomon Cohen. It was bad enough that Jennifer was a Gentile but she also had a child outside of wedlock and, to confirm their worst fears, she refused to have her children taught the ways of Ben's religion.

Ben had first met Jenny on the Palmer River. She had been a grimy and malnourished young girl with a dirty and surly child in tow, the product of a terrible wrong. Jenny had been Ben's first love – and only love.

Jennifer had returned Ben's love with a spiritual more than a physical passion. Despite her reluctance to indulge in unrestrained passion he knew Jenny's love for him was as deep as a woman could have for a man and he was always patient. Kate had once hinted at terrible wrongs that had occurred to Jennifer when she was merely a child in Sydney but Jennifer never spoke of this – and Ben never asked.

When Ben heard the distant drumming of a horse at full gallop he checked the swing of the heavy hammer he was using to nail the railing of the stockyards. He cursed at the stress his adopted son Willie was putting his horse through and decided that he would have a few words with him.

'Ben!' Willie's call had a note of alarm not usual in the young man. At sixteen Willie had seen many terrible things in his life and as such it took a lot to cause him to lose his composure.

Ben straightened his aching back and watched Willie rein his mount across to the newly constructed stockyards still fresh with the sap of the trees oozing from cracks. The young man slid expertly from his horse to confront the tall, bearded man. 'Big war party of darkies camped out on the western boundary,' he panted as if he had run the four miles from the western boundary marked by the dry watercourse of Ben's property. 'Fifty, maybe a hundred,' he gulped with a mixture of excitement and fear.

'Any gins and piccaninnies with them?' Ben asked quietly. His casually asked question had a calming effect on the young man who felt a little ashamed of his boyish excitement in the face of adult calmness.

'Yeah, they got women and kids with 'em.'

'Then I don't think they're going to be an immediate threat to us,' Ben concluded. 'But we will take no chances.'

Willie nodded his agreement. He had absolute faith in the decisions of the man who he had slowly come to view almost as his own father.

Willie still did not know who his real father was as his mother had refused to tell him – or Ben.

''Bout time we had a cuppa,' Ben said as he hefted the hammer over his shoulder and turned to walk towards the little bark hut that was their home. Willie followed and hitched his horse to a rail outside the hut.

Inside the hut Jenny kneaded flour into a bread loaf. Sweat ran down her face in tiny rivulets and the bun she had secured to her head was falling apart. Time – and the rigours of the frontier life – had brought flecks of grey to her crowning glory of golden tresses. She no longer attempted to conceal a large strawberry birthmark on her face as she had long forgotten it existed.

Ben constantly told her that she was the most beautiful woman on earth even though she was sometimes self-consciously aware that her once slim waist had thickened since they had courted.

Rebecca, their youngest child, sat at the roughly hewn slab table kneading a small loaf in imitation of her mother. Although she was only four years old she could already cook. She glanced up at the two men blocking the light from the doorway, then returned to her task of getting the dough ready for baking.

'Where's Saul and Jonathan?' Ben asked trying to sound calm.

Jenny paused in her task and brushed aside the trickles of hair from her face – which left a dab of flour on her nose – and stared at her husband with a glimmer of concern clouding her eyes. 'Why? What's wrong?' she asked.

'Nothing. I was just wondering where the boys might be.'

'They took the dogs and went out in the bush to see if they could find some native honey.'

'I saw a bunch of darkies up on the dry creek. Did they go in that direction?' Willie asked.

Jenny's mouth gaped. 'I don't know. They just took off and said they would be back by dark.'

'They will be all right,' Willie said to soothe his mother's natural fears. 'Nothing will happen to 'em.'

Ben was also worried but he had faith in his two sons' alertness. They had been born in the bush and, although Jonathan and Saul were nine and ten respectively, they were independent in the ways of survival. Already they worked as men on the property and Ben respected them for their adult-like toughness. They could handle the cattle and were both crack shots with the heavy Snider rifle. Very rarely did they return to the hut without a kangaroo which would be shared with the five station dogs.

Rebecca felt the tension in the small hut and watched with wide eyes as the adults conversed. Willie could see her fear. He loved the little girl – almost as much as his mother – and placed his hand on her head to pat her fine locks of gold. She was very much like his mother in appearance and manners whereas his two half-brothers were much like their father. She glanced up at Willie with questioning eyes and was answered with a reassuring smile.

'I will ride out and find the boys,' Ben said in a manner that did not evoke any sense of panic.

'Willie, you can stay here and finish the yards while I'm gone.'

Jenny nodded. There had been a time many years earlier when he had said similar words and gone unarmed to warn the big Eurasian John Wong of the Aboriginal warriors' ambush on the track to the Palmer.

'Ben?' she said quietly, and with just the faintest trace of fear in her voice.

'I know,' he replied with a sad smile and the pair exchanged loving glances which cut short any need for words.

Ben took a rifle from a long wooden case beside their bed and slipped a box of cartridges into his pocket. He also strapped on the big Colt revolver Kate had presented him with on his first trek west with one of her wagons. Jenny retrieved the lead shot and powder flask from a sideboard. She loved the sideboard for its delicate woodwork carvings of flowers and leaves along its edges. It was one of the rare items in the hut that was actually shop bought although Ben had promised that one day she would have the best furniture in the colony.

Not that she cared for worldly goods as much as she cared for the tall, gentle man who was her husband. She had followed him across the frontier when he had walked beside the huge creaking wagons pulled by the stolid oxen and she had given birth to her sons in the shade of the wagons when her time came. Only Rebecca had been born in what was now their home on the property.

When Ben had completed his preparations for the search he turned to hug his daughter with a crushing expression of love and gently reached out to touch his wife's cheek. She responded by pressing her face into the broad, work-hardened hand. There were no tears in the parting, as tears might be an admission that she was worried for her husband and sons, but she closed her eyes briefly to draw in the scent of newly hewn timber and tobacco that lingered in the pores of his flesh.

Ben swung himself into the saddle and urged his mount forward with a gentle kick. As he rode past the stockyards and into the shimmering heat of the dry silent scrub he had a fleeting thought. It was as if the scrub were attempting to reclaim the hut for itself.

When he was gone from their sight Jenny took her daughter's hand and led her inside the hut. There it was acceptable for her daughter to see her tears. To be able to cry was the domain of women. Men bore their pain in silence.

The laughter of the women and children turned to cries of terror as they fled from the dry creek bed for the cover of the scrub.

Terituba scooped a spear from the cluster at his feet and faced the tall, bearded white man who had suddenly walked upon them. How could a white man take them so easily? He cursed as he prepared to fling the barbed weapon at the man walking fearlessly towards him along the creek bed. But the Kalkadoon warrior hesitated. If the white devil had penetrated the camping ground of his clan, then he could have as easily fired on them with the white man's terrible weapons that left bloody holes in their victims.

Terituba was not alone. Both young and old

warriors bristled a wall of spears uncertainly at the approaching white man carrying a bag in either hand. On the white man's hip was the gun that could be fired many times without a pause to reload like the long guns. But it was not in his hand.

'Let us kill him now!' a young warrior cried nervously to Terituba. 'Before he can kill us.'

'No,' Terituba yelled to his warriors. 'Not unless I say.' The warriors reluctantly obeyed. It would be so easy to shower the solitary man with spears that were waiting to taste blood.

Ben felt every nerve in his body tingle with the expectation of the bite of a barbed spear. He was gambling for more than his own life – he was gambling for the life of his two boys. He knew from their tracks that they would probably come home via the creek and stumble on the heavily armed party of Kalkadoon. So he was striking first, but with a gesture of friendship and not violence.

He continued to walk directly towards the tallest of the naked warriors who, he guessed correctly, had considerable influence amongst his people now gathered along the dry creek. He was a formidable figure of a man whose broad shoulders and barrel chest rippled with hard muscle.

Ben could see that the warrior fixed him with dark, unfathomable eyes as he approached. When he was about ten paces away Ben halted and placed the two bags on the ground. He stepped back and gestured with a friendly smile to the flour and sugar and waited with the cold fear of tension that turned his stomach into a mass of wriggling worms.

The dark eyes coolly appraised him for signs of fear – or madness. But neither seemed apparent and Terituba surmised the gesture was one of goodwill.

'Do not harm this white man. He means us no harm,' he called in a loud voice to his people. And Ben could sense the change in the atmosphere that seconds before had been loaded with deadly threat.

Women, children and old men drifted cautiously back from the surrounding scrub where they had fled. Terituba lowered his spear and strode towards Ben to examine the two bags on the ground. He knew flour and sugar as they had taken the delicious foods from a teamster's wagon after they had ambushed him a week earlier south of their present campsite.

Terituba prodded the sacks with the point of his spear and grinned at the white man. It was a signal all was well and the children were the boldest of the clan to approach. They reached out and touched the creature they had been taught to fear and who now smiled at them. In turn he was rewarded with shy smiles.

The women fell on the sacks and tore at the bags with the sharp points of digging sticks, squabbling with each over who should get the gift. Striking out with his nulla, Terituba waded amongst the women to bring order to the chaos. They fell back with screeches of protest but waited sullenly until he indicated who should be first to take a share. The men meanwhile stood back, trailing their spears and staring suspiciously at the white man. It was only the temporary benevolence of Terituba that kept him alive.

'Ben,' the Jewish cattleman said, pointing at himself. 'Me Ben.'

'Miben,' Terituba repeated and Ben smiled at his interpretation of his name.

'Terituba,' the warrior said, understanding that the white man had given his totem.

'*What meat is that?*' he asked.

But neither man understood each other's language and an awkward silence fell between them.

'Me lukim piccaninny belong me,' Ben finally said to break the silence. Terituba understood *piccaninny*. It was a word he had picked up along the trading routes between the widely scattered tribes of Queensland. A word the white men had brought with them and which had been adopted by the tribesmen.

Ben repeated the question, his hand shading his eyes as if searching for something. He pointed at himself. Terituba understood from the pantomime that the man was looking for his children and felt a natural sympathy for him.

'*I have not seen your piccaninny,*' he replied in the Kalkadoon language and, although Ben did not understand the answer, he noticed a sympathetic note in the man's voice. He nodded as if he understood and thrust out his hand to the Kalkadoon warrior chief who eyed the gesture curiously.

Terituba imitated the movement and Ben took his hand and pumped it twice as he thanked the big Kalkadoon. Terituba could only surmise the gesture was a greeting between men of equal stature. It was a strange feeling to be holding the hand of a white man who had not come to kill him.

Then the white man whose strange totem was Miben dropped his hand and turned away. The warriors raised their spears and rattled them threateningly at the back of the man walking from them. But Terituba called to his men to let the white man go unharmed and curiously watched as the man strode along the dry creek bed and the women went back to squabbling over the precious supply of sweet sugar and flour.

Would they meet again, Terituba thought idly as Ben disappeared into the shimmering heat.

When Ben reached his horse which he'd left tethered to a tree he suddenly began trembling with the effects of delayed fear. He leant against the rough bark of a yarran tree from which came the hard timber the Kalkadoon used to fashion spears and boomerangs. For Ben it was a source of fence posts and firewood.

He had gambled with his life and won on the premise that a warrior culture would respect courage and goodwill and knew now that he could go in search of his two young boys without fear of ambush.

By sunset Ben had relocated the tracks of his two sons who had fortunately taken a route bypassing the creek bed and the Kalkadoon camped there. The tracks led back to the hut so Ben wheeled his mount and headed for home.

As he approached the hut just on sundown the barking of the dogs was a welcome sound. The exuberant noise meant that the boys were home.

But his joy turned to a cold fear when he saw Willie stumbling towards him like a drunken shearer at the end of a seasonal pay cheque binge. Tears streamed down the young man's face which was contorted with an inconsolable grief.

With a sharp kick Ben spurred his horse into a gallop towards the young man and Willie screamed his name with the sound of despair that only death could bring.

4

The following morning Patrick woke to a beautiful summer's day.

The clouds had gone from the Irish sky and when he gazed blearily out of the tiny window to his room he saw the true colours of Ireland; a sea of green stretching across heather-like scrub and larch trees standing tall in neatly ordered copses.

In the distance beyond a sparkling blue lake he saw the most prominent feature of the fields: a tree-covered hill rising as a small but distinctive dome.

The tap at his door brought him out of his rapt gaze and before he could answer the door creaked open. A rosy cheeked young woman entered, carefully carrying a wide enamel bowl of hot water. She was about sixteen and the twinkle in her eyes bespoke the amusement she felt at finding the handsome young man in his long johns as he stood by the window. Patrick's twinge of embarrassment only seemed to amuse the young girl further.

'I'd be sorry for disturbing you, Captain Duffy,' she said, obviously unrepentant for catching the young officer in his underwear. 'But me father thought you'd be liking some hot water to wash up with.' Patrick blushed even more when he realised the girl was staring unashamedly at his groin. 'Thank you, Miss . . . ?'

'Miss Maureen Riley,' she replied as she set the bowl down on the bed. 'Bernard Riley would be me father.'

'Thank your father for me then, Miss Riley, for the hot water.'

'To be sure it was a *pleasure*, Captain Duffy, to bring the water to your room,' she said provocatively. 'And if there'd be anything else I . . . my father can do for you, it would be a pleasure.'

Patrick smiled at the young girl's open manner that verged on brazen. She was not beautiful, but pretty, in her plump and healthy appearance: flawless skin with a touch of red in her cheeks and raven hair tied back in a bun. Buxom but with a slim waist over broad hips.

Patrick had no illusions as to what she meant by *pleasure*. Here, in his room, stood the contradiction to the stifling mores of the Irish church. 'I will certainly keep your offer in mind, Miss Riley,' he said with a twinkle in his eye that would have been accepted by the young publican's daughter as serious flirting. Miss Riley was unaware of her own sensuality, however, and most likely would not have known what to do if Patrick had pressed the offer.

'You'd be going to visit George Fitzgerald with Father O'Brien today?' Maureen said, more as a statement than a question as she glanced curiously around the spartan but clean room.

'And at what time would that be?' Patrick countered facetiously.

'I don't know that,' she replied innocently, missing his gentle sarcasm. 'But I suppose that would be after midday as Father O'Brien has things to do until then.'

'Well then, I suppose I should get on with ensuring I'm ready to go with him after midday,' Patrick said as a hint for her to leave.

Although Maureen was forward she was not obtuse and she gave him a parting smile as she turned with an inviting swirl of her dress to leave the room.

As priest and soldier strolled along the country lane to George Fitzgerald's house Patrick was beginning to feel ill at ease with the idea of visiting his paternal grandmother's brother.

He knew the story of the elopement of his grandmother with his grandfather and how her father had threatened to kill the Papist upstart who had taken his beautiful daughter from his hearth. Such threats were taken seriously in a clannish land where memories of grudges never died.

The brisk walk was helping to clear his head and the summer's day was spectacular. The two men were an incongruous pair: the tall, broad-shouldered Patrick Duffy and the smaller priest who hurried to keep up with his long, measured, soldier's stride.

They came adjacent to the small dome-shaped, tree-covered mound Patrick had first viewed from the window of his hotel room. 'The hill? It doesn't look as if it belongs here,' he commented.

Eamon stopped to stare up at it. In the distance beyond the hill lay the unusually placid but cold Atlantic ocean. 'I think it was man-made. Possibly a burial mound for a great king,' he said as a tiny breeze caused his black cassock to flap around his legs. 'I think it even predates the Bronze Age. Mister Fitzgerald and I have often discussed an exploratory dig on it.'

Patrick did not see the figure until it moved. He shaded his eyes against the unfamiliar glare of the summer's sun low on the horizon. It was mid-afternoon and, without the cloud covering to keep in the heat of the day, the coming night promised to be crisp and clear. His training as a soldier in observing distant movement stood him well and he was able to focus on the figure. It was distinctly female. Even from the distance he could see the long auburn tresses flowing around her shoulders. On either side of her stood two huge shaggy grey hounds.

'It looks as if there is someone on the hill watching us Eamon,' Patrick observed casually.

'Has she hair the colour of fire?' the priest replied, and Patrick turned to him with a questioning expression.

'You can see her?'

'No,' Eamon answered quietly. 'But it must be Catherine Fitzgerald. She often haunts that queer place.'

'She has hair the colour of fire,' Patrick echoed as he turned to stare across the field at the girl. But just as he turned she disappeared along with the two hounds, into the trees. 'Ah, she has gone now,' he said with just a trace of disappointment.

'A strange girl,' Eamon commented as they turned away to continue their walk to the Fitzgerald house. 'She is a love child. Poor girl was born out of wedlock.' He paused, slightly embarrassed as he remembered the rumours he had heard after mass that morning. Even the breadth of the oceans that divided Australia and Ireland could not hold back gossip. It was rumoured Patrick himself was the result of an illicit union between Catholic boy and Protestant girl.

A silence fell between the two men for a short time. They both realised what had brought the absence of conversation until Patrick broke the embarrassed silence with a question. 'Who are her parents?'

'Her mother was George Fitzgerald's daughter Elspeth. God rest her soul. Her father, well, no-one knows as she never did say. She died just after Catherine's birth. George raised her.'

If ever there was a woman who could make Eamon forget his vow of celibacy it was Catherine Fitzgerald. Barely sixteen, she exuded a sensuality he had never before encountered. 'Ah, but she is a wild one,' he sighed. 'She is neither Protestant in practice nor of the True Faith. In fact it is said she is not even Christian but a pagan believer of the old ways of Ireland.'

There was something else Eamon could not quite understand but which disturbed him further. Something beyond the realms of all his religious training. He remembered the stories of the Morrigan, the Celtic goddess of war, death and procreation. And Patrick? He would be the handsome Irish hero Cuchulainn. It was a strange thought which he shook from his head.

Patrick was distracted by the flight of a raven that rose out of the fir trees on top of the hill where the girl had disappeared. Eamon was able to see the young man's eyes follow the flight and he shuddered. Had not the Morrigan turned into a raven and flown from Cuchulainn when they met? The warm mid-afternoon sunshine suddenly had a chill to it.

The two men continued to walk past apple orchards and raspberry bushes until they saw the imposing Fitzgerald manor before them. A huge stone house with many rooms, windows of stained glass and ivy covered walls, it was the house of established Irish gentry of considerable power and old wealth.

'Captain Duffy, your presence in the village has caused quite some speculation,' George Fitzgerald said, as he eyed with just a hint of hostility and suspicion Patrick standing beside Eamon. 'Some say you have come to resurrect the damned Fenians in these parts. That you come in the disguise of one of Her Majesty's officers in a Highland regiment.'

'Speculation breeds on ignorance, Mister Fitzgerald,' Patrick replied coolly, his eyes fixed on the man who had been brother to his paternal grandmother, Elizabeth Fitzgerald. 'I am *indeed* an officer of the Second Highland Regiment and no sympathiser to the Fenians.'

Eamon O'Brien shifted uncomfortably. It was obvious that old hatreds did not diminish with time and that the tall, gaunt man absorbing the heat from the gentle flames licking at the logs in the huge open hearth still held bitter memories. Had it been a mistake to bring Patrick Duffy to meet his distant relative? 'Captain Duffy is on leave from his regiment which may be sailing soon to relieve General Gordon at Khartoum, George. He has also served with Sir Garnet Wolseley at Tel-el-Kibir,' the young priest said to break the icy chill that had descended between the two men in the confines of the old library. He glanced from one to the other and could see they were men of equal standing: the squire of the Duffy village proud and straight; the young Australian erect and arrogant. But the mention of Patrick's military campaigns softened the animosity in the old man.

George Fitzgerald gestured to the old, well-worn leather chairs of his study. 'My only son was killed while serving as a captain during the Kaffir wars at Isandhlwana, Captain Duffy,' Fitzgerald said sadly.

He continued to stand with his back to the fire and made no further comment on the matter of his son's death. Patrick knew that some memories did not welcome elaboration and cast a cursory glance around the study.

It was a sombre place crammed with leather-bound books. In the dim surroundings with only a shaft of light illuminating a square of faded carpet at the centre of the room, it was hard to discern the subject matter of the volumes that lined the glass-covered shelves that reached to the ceiling. In the nooks of the library were stuffed birds: owls, pheasants, and an eagle with its wings raised, beak agape as if preparing to defend itself. On a wall was a sepia photo of a handsome young man in the dress uniform of a British infantry regiment, smiling enigmatically at all who entered the room. Patrick presumed it was a daguerreotype of the old man's son as the similarity between the two men was plain to see. 'I am sorry to hear of your loss, Mister Fitzgerald,' Patrick replied with genuine sympathy. 'I wish I had met your son.'

George Fitzgerald nodded stiffly and Eamon could see that some of the icy animosity towards the grandson of the man he had sworn so long ago to kill was slowly thawing. Old Fitzgerald was appraising his distant relative in a fresh light almost akin to respect. 'Is whiskey and soda your preferred drink, Captain Duffy?' the old man asked as he made his way across the room to an open roll-top desk crowded with sheaves of loose papers. 'I know it is Father O'Brien's.'

'Whiskey and soda thank you, Mister Fitzgerald,' Patrick replied.

George Fitzgerald shuffled papers aside to find a newly opened bottle of fine Irish whiskey and reached for the soda bottle on top of a bookshelf. He topped two crystal tumblers with the aerated soda water and passed one to his not altogether unexpected guests. News had spread fast from the village of the arrival of Patrick Duffy and George knew it was inevitable that they should meet.

It was rather ironic that the young man who now sat in his library bore the same name as the man who he had vowed to kill for the taking of his younger sister almost a half century earlier. She, the beautiful young daughter of a proud line descended from the Anglo-Norman invaders of the English King Henry II of the twelfth century.

Fitzgerald resumed his place before the hearth and raised his glass. 'The Queen,' he intoned. 'God bless her.'

Patrick responded to the toast. 'The Queen.'

He noticed that the priest raised his glass in the gesture of the toast but said nothing. 'Eamon silently toasts the expulsion of the British Crown from Ireland,' Fitzgerald said with a hint of mirth plucking at the corners of his mouth. 'We have often discussed the idea of a Republican Ireland and on many points we agree.'

Patrick was surprised at the old man's view and, as if reading his puzzled thoughts, Fitzgerald added, 'I *am* an Irishman, Captain Duffy, with as much claim to this land as Father O'Brien. Possibly more of a claim as Father O'Brien has spent most of his life in England. But I suppose, had he not spent his time travelling and being educated in foreign lands, then we may have not been able to reason as we do as educated and rational men.'

Patrick nodded politely. Somehow his exposure in his early years to a staunch Irish Catholic family had not prepared him for a Protestant Irishman declaring his Irishness.

'Captain Duffy has expressed an interest in learning more about the history of this county, George,' Eamon said brightly. 'No doubt to add to his understanding of the Fitzgeralds and the Duffys.'

Patrick had noticed that the priest used the old man's name in the familiar and guessed rightly they were firm friends – despite the difference on opinion over religion, and Ireland's political future.

'Then he has arrived at an opportune time, Eamon,' George replied. 'I am having a dinner for a few guests tomorrow night. Amongst my guests is Professor Clark who I have been corresponding with about our hill. He feels it may be well worth undertaking a dig.'

'We saw Catherine there on our way here,' Eamon said quietly.

Patrick thought he noticed a fleeting shadow of disapproval cross the old man's face. But Fitzgerald made no comment, except to frown. 'Catherine has probably as good a knowledge of the history of this region as her grandfather and I,' Eamon added, as if attempting to defend the girl's presence on the strange, dome-shaped hill. 'She is fluent in Gaelic and somewhat an authority on the old stories of the country. Especially those relating to the Celtic heroes and Druidic customs.'

'She neglects her French to achieve her fluency in *that* language,' her grandfather growled as he threw back the last drams of whisky and soda. 'I fear she has an unholy interest in the myths and towards that purpose she studies the old texts.'

Father Eamon O'Brien had to agree with his friend. The pagan ways of Old Ireland were steeped in savagery with dark sexual under-currents always present, a licentiousness of the warrior cult where the strongest took all they desired. As if conjuring the old gods by speaking of their existence in the mists of Celtic mythology, Patrick was suddenly aware of another presence in the room.

The pungent smell of dog and the sweeter scent of crushed flowers came to him on the whisper of a breeze. Catherine's barefooted entry into the library had been so silent that the men had not noticed the big oak door swing open behind them.

The two male hounds were impressive creatures, each two and a half feet tall at the shoulder with their long wiry grey coats giving them bulk. Patrick had heard of the legendary dogs of Ireland – the Irish wolf hounds – which had graced the halls of the Celtic kings. He remembered that they had been used to hunt wolves and deer, and the two that had accompanied Catherine certainly looked as big as any deer they might hunt.

The two giants padded across to the hearth and plonked themselves before the fire at George Fitzgerald's feet. 'Catherine, we have a guest Father O'Brien has brought from the village,' her grandfather said. 'Captain Patrick Duffy.'

Patrick rose, turning to exchange his introduction and was struck as surely as a heavy lead bullet from a Martini Henry carbine might fell him. Standing before him and framed by the ancient timbers of the doorway was the most beautiful young woman he had ever seen. Her fiery red hair unencumbered by combs or ribbons, flowed about her shoulders. Her milk white complexion was flawless and her deep green eyes almost glowed in the dim light of the library, such was their startling clarity. She wore a blouse in peasant European style – similar to those worn by gypsies – and her long skirt swirled around her ankles as she crossed the room. Patrick fought to recover his composure. 'Miss Fitzgerald, a pleasure to make your acquaintance,' he stammered. He was annoyed to see the flicker of haughty amusement cross her face. The damned girl knew she was beautiful! How many other men had she devastated with her beauty?

Catherine continued to hold his rapt gaze. 'I have been expecting you to come, Captain Duffy,' she said quietly with her faint smile. 'From the hill I saw you with Father O'Brien.'

'I also saw you, Miss Fitzgerald,' Patrick answered, recovering his composure. 'Then you seemed to disappear.'

'I can do that,' she answered, with a teasing note in her voice. 'Just disappear.'

Patrick knew that the perfume of the crushed flowers was a figment of his imagination but somehow it had heralded Catherine's entrance into his life. His life! What life? His thoughts were gloomy as the realisation struck him that within forty-eight hours he would be leaving the village to return to the regimental barracks in London and thence shipped on active service to Africa. He was on the verge of travelling to the deserts of the Sudan to face the savage warriors there and no life was guaranteed beyond the next battle. For a reason beyond his understanding he knew that he had just met the woman who he most desired in the world. 'Well, I hope you will not disappear tomorrow night, Miss Fitzgerald,' he said. 'Your grandfather has kindly invited me to dine with him.'

'Captain Duffy *must* wear his mess dress,' she said turning to her grandfather. 'Or he will not be allowed to dine with us.'

The old man smiled at her imperious order. 'My granddaughter's commands are rarely disobeyed, Captain Duffy,' he chuckled softly. '*If* you have mess dress with you, you are to present yourself accordingly at dinner. Decorations to be worn.'

'He has mess dress,' Catherine said knowledgeably. She had friends in the village and the inquisitive maid to the young officer's room had verified so. 'Redcoat and kilt.' Patrick raised his eyebrows questioningly at the young woman but she simply returned the question with a smug look of I-know-more-about-you-than-you-know.

'I shall wear my red dress,' Catherine said happily. 'It will complement Captain Duffy's uniform. I will be looking forward to you dining with us, Captain.'

Patrick smiled. He was aware of Catherine's frank appraisal of him. 'The feeling is mutual, I assure you, Miss Fitzgerald,' he replied. 'I shall be interested in Ireland's mythology, as much as its history. Father O'Brien informs me you are somewhat of an expert on the subject.'

'Mythology often has a basis in history,' Catherine said as she glanced at the priest. 'I dare say the exploits of your father over the last few years – as often narrated by the villagers here – will one day be part of our mythology.'

'I'm afraid your villagers have good imaginations, Miss Fitzgerald,' Patrick replied quietly. 'My father was killed fighting the Maori in New Zealand. That sad event occurred before I was born.'

'I know *you* must be right,' she said with a slight frown. 'The villagers *are* prone to tell tall stories in the public houses. It is part of the tradition in this part of the world. Still, many of the myths of old do have a basis of fact to them, Captain Duffy.'

Eamon had heard the same stories: of a big Irishman who went under many names. A man who had fought the Maori warriors of New Zealand and had fought in the Civil War of America. He had gone on to fight the Red Indians of the American West as well as fighting as a soldier of fortune in Mexico. It was said that the Irishman had one eye – the other lost in war – and was at least seven feet tall!

An Irish prospector returning to the Duffy village from the Australian Colony of Queensland swore on his mother's grave that he had once met Duffy in a place called Cooktown. That had been ten years earlier and he had called himself Michael O'Flynn.

'It is sad that the villagers are wrong,' Catherine sighed. 'A man such as the villagers describe would be well at home in the pantheon of Celtic heroes in this land.'

'If the rumours did indeed have a basis in fact, Miss Fitzgerald, then I am sure I would have known,' Patrick said with a grim smile.

'Well, Captain Duffy, I wish they were true, because I would have liked to have met the man you may some day become.'

With this wistful utterance she parted company from the three men and Patrick noticed the two huge hounds devotedly rise from their comfortable place in front of the fire to pad after her.

Patrick did not remember much of the

conversation that afternoon. He let Eamon and George dominate with talk about Professor Clark's intending visit. They discussed the possibilities of archaeological finds in a dig on the strange hill. Patrick's thoughts, however, were focused on the beautiful entity he had met.

Entity? Was such a word appropriate? he mused. Did not such a word best describe a goddess? And his thoughts drifted to the mention of the Irish mercenary, Michael O'Flynn. It was strange how this O'Flynn character could be linked to his dead father.

Eventually the conversation dwindled away as Eamon O'Brien reluctantly faced the fact of his office. He had confessions to take, cottage visits to the sick and elderly and a mass. Patrick bade his gratitude to George Fitzgerald for his hospitality and left with Eamon.

They trudged in silence towards the village. As they passed the hill Patrick glanced up as if expecting to see Catherine. But she was not on the hill, which was taking on a soft, dark glow as the summer sun slowly sank over the cold Atlantic ocean. The evenings were long in the Irish summer and filled with a magical hush, Patrick thought. And magic was in the aura that surrounded the beautiful young woman he had met briefly that afternoon.

Father Eamon O'Brien had been astute enough to notice the intensity of the exchange between Patrick and Catherine and brooded on a statement made by the young woman. He prayed superstitiously that its utterance had been merely a coincidence. Or was it that she knew exactly what she had said? '*I shall wear my red dress then!*' Had not the Morrigan worn a crimson mantle when she first encountered Cuchulainn?

Summer eves were also the time of the Druids whose pagan practice was deeply rooted in the mystical psyche of the Irish. Patrick Duffy had come to the village on the eve of the summer solstice.

5

Jenny's expression was a fixed mask of surprise. It was as if death had come to her as a total stranger even when she knew its arrival was inevitable.

In the tiny bark hut that had once been her proud home Rebecca whimpered. Her mother was dead but she did not know what death meant.

Sniffling back tears of grief, Ben's two boys stood behind their little sister while their father knelt by the narrow double bed holding his wife's cold hand and sobbing great splashes of silent tears that soaked the rough blanket covering Jenny's body.

From the moment he had seen Willie stumbling towards him Ben had known something terrible had happened to Jenny. Nothing else on earth could have caused the total despair he had seen in the young man's face other than the death of his mother. Now she had gone in an obscene and painful death to the deadly venom of a snake bite.

If only he had gone to the wood pile to fetch logs for the stove then she might be alive now, Willie anguished. But he had churlishly protested and in her anger his mother had gone in his stead.

The huge taipan had only been protecting her young when she struck with a blurring speed that was impossible for Jenny to recoil from. The syringe-like fangs buried deep in the unsuspecting woman's arm above her elbow releasing the toxin to travel its lethal course.

Willie had been at the table in the hut cleaning his revolver when he heard his mother's strangled scream and instinctively snatched up the weapon. As he bolted from the hut his first thought was that the Kalkadoon had launched an attack. Once outside, he realised that the revolver was not loaded and hesitated, torn between returning for the bullets, and reaching his mother.

But the fear for his mother's safety overrode everything and he sprinted with the empty gun to the wood pile. There he saw his mother standing ashen-faced, holding her arm. She stared at him with her mouth agape and he saw the huge brown snake's tail disappear deep into the stack of logs as it slithered away.

Without a word he had dropped the pistol to grasp his mother by her arms and led her back into the hut. Rebecca watched with wide-eyed confusion as her mother trembled uncontrollably in her shock.

Willie led his mother to the bed and laid her down gently as he searched frantically for the sharpest of the skinning knives. Rebecca started to cry when she saw Willie tear open the sleeve of her mother's dress and slice quickly across the fang punctures. Jenny stifled her cry of pain as the sharp blade bit deeply. She did not want her daughter to know she was in great pain. But the poison had done its deadly job and Willie's efforts were to no avail.

Jenny sensed that death was only a short time away and before she died she spoke of many things to her son. Of the love she had for him and her other children, of her love for Ben – and of the identity of Willie's true father. A fire came to Jenny's eyes and she recounted the terrible oath she had sworn as a thirteen-year-old girl nursing him as a squalling infant in a filthy rat-infested room in Sydney's slums.

Outside the hut Willie stared into the silence of the hot night and brooded on all that his mother had said to him before she died. His world had come apart in the awful speed of a striking snake and his thoughts were numb with loss and bitter with a terrible hate. She was torn from his life and her death left a wound that would never heal. But she had also left him with an oath sworn on all that was sacred.

His father's name was Granville White and he would confront him one day for the years of suffering he had inflicted on his mother as a child. A suffering so horrific that she could only bring herself to tell him as she died sweating and vomiting her life away. He had listened to the words of a terrified child as the drowsiness came to his mother and eventually turned to death. *Granville White, a fine gentleman from Sydney* . . .

He spat onto the ground as if to cleanse his thoughts of the very name and was vaguely aware of the taste of blood in his mouth. It was his mother's blood, that upon which he had sworn that he would settle one way or the other with the man who had sired him. He would confront Granville White who had so ruthlessly abused his mother and then cast her aside to fend for herself in a world where men used her body to slake the thirst of lust.

Oh yes, he remembered. The savage bites to her flesh when the drunken miners grunted like animals over her on the Palmer River goldfields. He remembered her screams of pain as they laughed in their lust and remembered her crying inconsolably in the rain and mud as they slowly starved to near death. She had begged scraps for him without thought of her own survival, such was the strength of a mother's love for her young. And only the kindly intervention of Kate O'Keefe had saved them.

'Willie?'

Young Jonathan stood holding an oil lamp which cast an anaemic light over his grief stricken and dirty face. 'What are we going to do?' he asked with the numbed despair of a ten-year-old boy confronted by the unthinkable.

'Ask Ben,' Willie snarled. 'He's yer father isn't he?'

'He's your father too,' Jonathan retorted with an uncomprehending frown for the unexpectedly savage tone of Willie's reply. 'I thought you might know what to do . . .'

'I know what to do,' Willie snarled as he snatched the lamp from his half-brother. 'Buggered if I know what you're goin' to do but I'm goin' to kill the bloody snake that killed my mother.'

Jonathan had never seen Willie so dangerously angry before. It was an anger like the beginnings of the fierce electrical storms that came on the hot and sultry days before the breaking of the dry season in the Gulf Country. An anger of silence expressed in the explosive crack of the lightning striking down the strongest of trees. He watched grim faced and frightened as Willie hurled the lamp at the wood heap where it shattered with a *woomph*.

The dry wood crackled as the burning oil spread the flaring fingers of flame and with a blind hunger the fire consumed the wood pile. The spreading ring of light crept outwards to silhouette the thin trunks of the surrounding silent trees as the fire rose higher and the thick smoke billowed with a sweet scent of the bush.

'Die you murderin' bastard,' Willie howled with a venom equal to that of the trapped taipan. 'Burn in hell!' But it was not just the snake that had taken his mother's precious life from him. For as the flames engulfed the twisted sticks of timber his thoughts were on a man whom he had never met but knew some day he would. And when that time came he knew that the fancy Mister Granville White should share the same fate as the creature writhing in agony trapped in the centre of the fire's heart.

Jonathan watched the wood pile turn to a funeral pyre for the snake as the inferno writhed in on itself and sent cascades of red cinders skyward like fireworks. He watched as Willie ranted obscenities into the night and yowled like a wounded animal.

Then suddenly Willie was gone. Swallowed by the depths of the vast scrub he ran blindly, sobbing for the pain that was in his body and soul.

Willie returned in the morning as the sun rose – an orange ball in the eastern sky above the stunted trees of the flat scrublands.

Rebecca ran to him and hugged his legs as he shambled across the yard towards the bark hut. He had always been her favourite brother as he was gentle and not teasing like Jonathan and Saul. She held him as one would cling to a life raft in a stormy sea but sensed that her beloved Willie was a different person to the one she had known the day before.

Ben had stood as a gaunt spectre under the shade of the tiny sloping verandah roof that provided a cooling shelter to the front of the hut. He had watched his daughter run to Willie across the dusty yard and greet him with her love and watched as the young man stopped to stroke the mass of yellow curls that came to his waist.

'Becky! Go and put the billy on,' Ben asked the little girl before turning to call back into the hut, 'Jonathan, Saul. Go and fetch some wood for the fire and help your sister.'

The children responded eagerly to their father's orders as they were the first words they had heard him utter in hours and were thankful for direction in a time when the world had come to a sudden halt. Although the terrible grief was in him, so too was the firm and gentle guidance of a father.

The sadness was not a surprise to Rebecca who knew tears had a place in life. For it had been her alone who had often witnessed her mother's tears when the men were absent at their work. Tears that her mother cried for the loneliness of their existence; tears for reasons unknown to Rebecca when her mother held her tightly in her lap as if she was frightened she might lose her only daughter to a monster that came in the night to snatch her away. And sometimes tears of happiness which welled when her father stood awkwardly in the hut grasping a bouquet of wildflowers.

'Willie,' Ben said gently. 'You and I will make a coffin for your mother. A good one.'

Willie nodded. Yes, a good one for his mother he thought, to sleep under the dry red soil of the desolate lands. 'We will bury her this morning beside that tree she planted last year,' Ben continued. 'The one over there,' he said, and indicated the lone sapling struggling to establish its domain amongst the hardy scrub trees.

The sapling was a pepper tree. Jenny had been given the seeds before Ben and she had left Townsville to take up their selection. With loving care she had been able to raise a bed of seedlings. But despite all her care only one of them had survived to be replanted. The struggling tree had been precious to her as the mature tree would one day provide a spreading canopy of shade, a place sought by man, bird and animal as a refuge from the blaze of the summer sun. But now it was a place for Jenny to sleep for as long as the tree existed in life.

'I'll dig the hole and you can make the coffin,' Ben added gruffly. 'We've got some timber in the shed that will do.'

He was having trouble keeping his grief in check but knew he had responsibilities. Jenny would not have wanted him to allow his feelings to cause him to neglect their family.

'Now?' Willie asked softly. He was reluctant to commit the body of his mother to the ground where he knew she would be permanently taken from his sight.

'Now!' Ben snapped. He was in no mood to be questioned. 'Sorry, Willie,' he checked gently, placing his hand on the young man's shoulder. 'I . . .' He faltered. With Jenny gone he had no words to fill the emptiness that existed between them. 'We'd better get going before it gets too hot,' he concluded gruffly.

Before the sun rose high above the flat scrub Jenny was laid gently in her grave. Rebecca knelt and placed a posy of dry wildflowers on the fresh earth mound and then stood back to shelter in her father's shadow.

Jonathan and Saul also stood beside their father while Willie stood alone a short distance away, staring at the dark red earth.

No words were said over the grave, just silence for the memory of a living, laughing, crying, scolding, loving woman who had been mother and wife to her family. No tears, just dry red eyes exhausted of salty moisture. No feeling, except numbed shock and inconsolable grief. No sound but the lazy buzz of flies and the distant lonely cawing of a crow.

Stones would be placed on the earth to provide a shield against the dingos but that was a task to be done when the sun lost its bite in the late afternoon.

Jennifer Rosenblum, aged thirty, mother of four and wife of Ben Rosenblum for ten years, would forever sleep in the shade of the pepper tree she had nurtured against the perils of frontier life. In time the tree would grow and its roots fold loving fingers around the remains of the woman whose body now provided its nurture.

That night Ben sat by the grave of his wife and spoke to her. He idled through the night in a conversation that was conducted as if she were sitting at the table in their hut darning a sock or sewing a new dress for Becky. He talked of inconsequential things that were the grist of love between a man and a woman.

And there were silences in his monologue as he paused to listen to the familiar sweetness of her voice that existed only in his mind. He remembered her desire to see her children get an education, something she had never had herself. She especially wanted Becky to find a life away from the loneliness of the frontier.

Ben talked on softly and the tears rolled down his whiskered cheeks to soak his thick, bushy beard until he finally fell into a deep sleep of exhaustion.

6

The dinner served at George Fitzgerald's table was a sumptuous affair. But Patrick had lost his taste for roast venison. Nor was he attentive to Professor Ernest Clark's colourful and rather risqué anecdotes on the savage Celtic practices of old Ireland. He was also reluctant to allow himself to be drawn by Sir Alfred Garnett into an account of his experiences at Tel-el-Kibir and he only exchanged a few words of polite conversation with the magistrate James Balmer, who sat on his left, and with the Norrises, who sat opposite him.

Captain Patrick Duffy was preoccupied with brooding thoughts and his retreat into self-imposed silence could almost be described as churlish. From what he could glean from the conversation that flowed with the wine, Henry Norris had considerable holdings in Welsh coal, English railways and Birmingham steel. Although it was obvious Norris was a man of great wealth he did not have the acquired manners of old wealth. His roots in the back streets of Newcastle still appeared in his mannerisms and speech.

Further down the table Sir Alfred Garnett and his wife Lady Jane tended to dominate the conversation. At least Sir Alfred did with his talk of fox hunts and thoroughbred horses. When Sir Alfred was not attempting to thus engage the dinner guests, he berated the magistrate George Balmer on the scourge of the lingering Fenian threat to life and property in the county. Patrick took an instant dislike to the loud, garrulous knight of the realm on account of what he represented to the Ireland of Patrick's Catholic ancestors.

At the end of the table, seated next to Sir Alfred and his wife, sat the Reverend John Basendale and his wife Tess. The Reverend Basendale was the vicar from the local Church of Ireland and a frequent dinner guest of George Fitzgerald. It was not as if George found the man interesting – he was a meek and colourless man in comparison to Eamon O'Brien – but he could at least deliver the traditionally acceptable Church of Ireland form of grace. The minister and his wife smiled dutifully at Sir Alfred's stories but did little else.

Along Patrick's side of the table sat the distinguished American Randolph Raynor and his pretty wife Ann. He and his wife were guests of Sir Alfred, as were the Norrises. The American had investments in railways and cattle in his own country and it was obvious that the common interest of the Raynors and Norrises transcended continents. Randolph Raynor was a tall, well-built man who spoke softly but carried an air of authority about him like a military cloak. This was not surprising; he had served in the Civil War as a young colonel in a militia unit of the Northern forces of Mister Lincoln.

Beside Ann Raynor sat the Norrises' daughter Letitia. Now eighteen, she had blossomed into a very attractive young lady – and a very eligible catch for some worthy young man of good (and wealthy) stock. Her raven hair and dark eyes contrasted with her milk white complexion that was highlighted with a hint of rouge. It was obvious from the moment she had set eyes on the tall, broad-shouldered young captain wearing the uniform of a Highlander that all men in her life would mean nought should the dashing British officer ask her to elope with him.

Letitia was a prudish snob who did not like Catherine. She considered her as too free in her ways and thus not a lady. Or was it that she felt deep jealousy for the way all men stared with undisguised admiration for the girl with flaming red hair and flashing smile? She sulked in petulant silence as she toyed with her food and snapped irritably at one of the old women servants who placed a dish before her. Letitia was not happy having been seated away from the handsome Captain Patrick Duffy.

At one end of the stout oak table sat George, presiding over the dinner, with his beautiful and socially accomplished grand-daughter at the far end, facing him along a row of candles flickering in their silver candelabra. The soft, yellow glow highlighted the costly jewellery worn by the ladies around slim throats and dangling from dainty earlobes.

The same soft glow reflected off the polished

brass buttons and badges of Patrick's resplendent uniform. The gentle glow also highlighted the faces of the guests and flashed off the crystal goblets raised as the guests sipped excellent French and Spanish wines. George Fitzgerald tapped the goblet in front of him with a silver spoon to silence the babble of voices for a moment.

Patrick rose, as did the other guests, and glanced down the table. Brett Norris stood as tall as Patrick himself and carried the arrogant air of one born to wealth. He leant to whisper something in Catherine's ear just before George Fitzgerald proposed the toast to the Queen and, in deference to his American guests, the President of the United States of America, Mister Grover Cleveland. Catherine giggled and placed her hand on the handsome young man's wrist while her lips pressed close to his ear. The intimacy of her gesture did not escape Patrick's notice. He mumbled his response to the toasts as social protocol required, resumed his seat and stared morosely into the dark coloured port in his crystal goblet.

Brett Norris was the son of Henry and Susan sitting opposite Patrick and had been conveniently seated on Catherine's left. Patrick was fuming with jealousy. He had not considered the possibility of some other man intruding on his short time with the beautiful woman whom he had so recently met.

When the dinner was over the guests rose from the table and broke into cliques – the men to sip port and smoke cigars, the ladies to take tea and coffee or sherry. The men would continue talk of investment opportunities, game shooting, fox hunting and salmon fishing, while the ladies gathered in a huddle to gossip of scandals in the county, fashions in London and holidays in the south of France.

Patrick selected a good Havana from a silver box and leant to light the cigar from the flickering flame of a candle. From the corner of his eye he could see Catherine standing very close to Brett Norris and laughing softly at something he said.

Patrick feigned to ignore their intimacy and strode after the men into an anteroom adorned with paintings of rural life, portraits of past Fitzgerald men and women and paintings of fine, thoroughbred horses. Tea and coffee pots steamed on a silver salver set on a polished teak sideboard. Further along was a crystal decanter of good port and rows of small glasses.

Patrick poured himself a port and was about to join the circle of men when he heard his name called. He turned to see Letitia Norris approaching him with a hopeful smile.

'Miss Norris,' he acknowledged politely with a smile and a nod of his head.

'Captain Duffy, I'm afraid I was denied the pleasure of your conversation during dinner,' she said, gazing up into the emerald eyes of the Australian. They were beautiful eyes, the eyes of a poet. Like the eyes of the romantic Lord Byron whose tragic life was not unlike the one this soldier led. A man destined to fight for the Queen in exotic places and dream of her with unrequited yearning. 'I was hoping I might have the opportunity to engage you now,' she sighed as Patrick glanced across her bare shoulders at Lady Jane Garnett holding court with the women. He noticed the disapproving expression on Letitia's mother's face. Soldiers were not fit company for her daughter, not even officers, whose pay was not sufficient to keep her daughter in the style to which she was accustomed.

Despite the pursed lips and scowl from Susan Norris, Patrick chose to indulge in some harmless flirtation with the young woman who, he could see, was smitten by him. Besides, Catherine was not the only pretty young lady in the room.

Letitia continued to gaze into his eyes with her wine-moistened, rose-bud mouth partly agape, revealing tiny perfectly set teeth. But Missus Norris was a determined lady. She swept across the room to rescue her daughter. With feeble protests Letitia desperately sought a way of remaining in the company of her latter day Lord Byron but her mother's will was stronger and she led her daughter to the court of Lady Garnett to indulge in proper social intercourse.

Patrick smiled ruefully for the opportunity lost to make Catherine jealous. But things did not go unnoticed by Catherine who realised she also had competition for the captain's attentions. It was a thought galling to her that he might even find the prudish Letitia Norris in the slightest bit interesting, and with a deliberate gesture of defiance she took Brett by the arm and swept across the room towards Patrick.

He noticed Catherine approaching with Brett Norris on her arm, her red dress clinging seductively to her body and accentuating her hourglass figure. Her hair was piled on top of her head in a crown of whorls and she wore an emerald necklace around her pale throat. The gems caught the colour of her eyes perfectly and Patrick felt a surge of desire for her.

'Captain Duffy, you did not have an opportunity to meet Mister Brett Norris when you arrived,' she said sweetly, with a smile which concealed the take-nothing-for-granted-about-me expression in her eyes. 'Brett, this is my grandfather's guest, Captain Duffy.'

The arrogant smile on the son of the English industrialist imparted its own message. 'A pleasure to make your acquaintance, old chap,' Brett said, without attempting to offer his hand. Not that this was practical as Patrick held a cigar in one hand and a port glass in the other. 'Catherine has told me a lot about you over dinner and I gather you are some sort of hero. I see you even have a couple of medals. What are they for, old chap?'

Then and there Patrick wished his competitor for Catherine's attentions was before him in the desert at Tel-el-Kibir dressed in the white uniform and red fez of a Nubian rifleman where he could bayonet the bastard! 'For service at Tel-el-Kibir in '82,' Patrick growled. 'A bit for the old Empire, old chap.'

'Rum show, so I have heard,' Norris replied. 'Killed a lot o' darkies yourself then?'

Patrick noticed that the young man had taken on the affectation of London's aristocratic fops and appeared to have little of his father's roots in the way he spoke and acted. And he, with a petit bourgeoisie background – a term Patrick had

87

picked up in the readings of some obscure German Jew by the name of Karl Marx he had skimmed through whilst in his first year at Oxford.

It was not as if anyone would probably remember Marx in the years to come, he had thought then. There had been so many social philosophers expounding their views in the last few years. But the description of petit bourgeois seemed apt for the man now standing before him at Catherine's side. 'Yes, we killed some, we killed a lot at Tel-el-Kibir,' Patrick replied softly as for a moment his memories were transported to that terrible dawn of fear and death.

'Probably an easy thing to do when the poor beggars you are fighting have no chance against British arms, what!' Brett said with the hint of a sneer.

Patrick's hackles rose like those of a fighting dog. It was clear that the man was attempting to bait him in front of Catherine.

'Maybe we didn't kill as many of those poor beggars, as you call them, as your father's coal pits kill Welsh miners.'

Patrick's blood affinity for the Celts of Wales. had flared and the hint of a sneer disappeared from Norris's face as he realised that he had pushed the Highlander officer just a bit too far. Although he prided himself on the social status that his father's financial situation gave him, he realised that nothing protects you against a man who has lost some of his fear of violence in war. Catherine had followed the exchange and she too realised the green eyes of the Australian had a cloudy look that was animal dangerous.

'I say, old boy, that was not called for. I think you should apologise immediately,' Brett Norris bluffed.

But somehow it sounded more like the bleating of a sheep to Patrick's ears. 'If you will excuse me, Miss Fitzgerald,' Patrick flashed a savage and cold smile, 'I think I will join the gentlemen for port and cigars.'

He did not see the frown of annoyance flit across Catherine's face as he strode away, his kilt swirling around legs muscled by miles of forced marches as an infantry officer. He was not playing the game the way she presumed he would!

'Surly uncouth lout, that Captain Duffy,' Norris said loud enough for Patrick to hear as he walked away. 'He is a disgrace to the Queen's uniform.'

But Patrick ignored the taunt and joined Professor Clark as Catherine cast Brett a withering look.

'Captain Duffy is to sail to Egypt very soon,' she hissed. 'And will probably be facing great peril again. I rather think you were being a bore with your talk.'

But Brett Norris only smiled at Catherine's rebuke. He had regained his composure. 'The man has no class,' he sneered. 'And I suspect no real means of private income.'

'You know nothing of Captain Duffy,' Catherine flared in defence of Patrick who was now standing with his back to them.

Brett could see where Catherine's attention was directed. 'Ladies might be infatuated by the likes of such men, my dear young Catherine,' he said.

'But they have enough practical sense to marry men like me. Men who will inherit wealth and power and who can provide the luxuries they so much yearn for in their years ahead.'

Catherine felt the breath of pragmatism blow softly in her ear and remained silent. *Yes. A woman did have to be practical when it came to the future.* But this was the present – and she was acutely aware that she was a woman who loved the romance of life, as much as the luxuries of wealth. At her elbow was a devilishly attractive young man who would do anything for her. In the circle of men stood Captain Patrick Duffy who she could easily give herself to. The choice was hers alone and she replied softly, 'It may be possible I am not the lady you think I am.'

'Catherine, come and join the ladies and let your young man alone for a moment,' Lady Garnett commanded rather than requested. 'I am sure Mister Norris has a point of view to add to the conversation of the men.'

Catherine normally did not find the small talk of the women interesting but Lady Garnett's imperious invitation gave her the opportunity to part with Brett Norris's company and be alone in her thoughts. 'Thank you, Lady Garnett, I would *love* to join you,' she answered. 'Possibly you might relate your experiences in the south of France to me. One day I hope to visit the Riviera and take in the sunshine.'

Miffed at Catherine's subtle rebuke, Brett Norris idled over to the circle of men to join his father. At least he could talk confidently in such distinguished company of power and wealth.

More than the uncouth and arrogant Captain Duffy could with his limited world of soldiering!

The cool summer's eve held the mists of magic – at least it felt that way to Patrick when he bid his host good evening and stepped into the open air. Or was it that he had drunk too much port and was feeling the romance of the land of his Irish ancestors? Despite his last glimpse of Catherine in the company of Brett Norris, he was determined not to let the bitter memory spoil his last night of leave in Ireland.

'Would ye be likin' a lift back to the village, Cap'n Duffy?' the coachman asked from the seat of the gig. He had been hired by George Fitzgerald to ferry the Reverend and his wife from the vicarage, as well as pick up Patrick from Bernard Riley's pub. Between visits to the kitchen of the Fitzgerald manor for fine table scraps and some alcoholic refreshment he had waited patiently while puffing on his battered pipe for the guests to leave.

'No, but thank you. I think I will walk home tonight,' Patrick replied politely. 'It will do me good.' *There would be a lot of walking ahead when he reached the Sudan's arid and rock strewn deserts with their craggy hills . . .*

'Very good, Cap'n Duffy, and top o' the eve'n to you then.'

7

The twitter of bush birds, and the snort of a horse being saddled in the soft light of the predawn, were now familiar sounds to Kate Tracy.

Kate Tracy, sister of Michael Duffy, had once been known as Kate O'Keefe. In Sydney at the age of sixteen she had married a shiftless handsome son of Irish convicts. A marriage motivated out of infatuation for the man who would leave the young girl almost destitute and pregnant at Rockhampton when he ran off with the wife of a local publican. That had been in 1863 and Kate had not seen her estranged husband until she visited his grave at Cooktown twelve years later. But her ill-chosen marriage had put her on a path north to the untamed Colony of Queensland and eventually to amassing a personal fortune through bullock teams transporting sorely needed supplies to the people of the frontier.

Approaching her fortieth year she was now one of the wealthiest women in the colony and although she could afford a lavish lifestyle she lived modestly with her prospector husband Luke

Tracy in their rambling house in Townsville. The frontier and its people had ownership of her soul and the desire to return to Sydney was long gone.

'Just about ready to go,' she heard her husband's gentle American twang. 'Figure I should be into the hills before sunset,' he added.

Kate unconsciously reached out to touch the old scar on his face that marked the point of an English soldier's bayonet – a scar that reminded all of his stand with the American miners at the Eureka Stockade over thirty years earlier. She had since married the man who had continued to love her through the lonely years of his life prospecting at the edges and beyond of the Queensland frontier. The tall, taciturn Luke Tracy had always carried his love for Kate as he struggled through the tropical rainforests of North Queensland, trekking the wide arid plains of scrub tree in the west and into the ancient dry hills of central Queensland. He was a scarred veteran of the Stockade of '54 when he stood and fought as a young man with the California Independent Ranger Brigade against the redcoats on the goldfields.

'I know,' she replied, hoping she would not cry at his departure west on his journey to the little frontier town named in honour of the ill-fated explorer Burke. 'Have you spare ammunition?' she asked.

The tall man standing over her smiled reassuringly as he stroked her face with a callused hand. 'You needn't worry 'bout the Kalkadoon,' he said. 'I'll be riding well north of their territory.' He ran his hand down to her swollen belly. 'I'd be more worried about you, Kate,' he added. 'This time you've got to look after yourself – not go worrying about the business. Let the people you employ look after things.'

Kate nodded and forced back the tears. It was the pregnancy, she told herself, that had made her so emotional lately. The terrible spectre of two babies lost still haunted her. The first lost had been a son who had died hours after he was born and was buried at Rockhampton. She had been seventeen at that time and the father of her child had been Kevin O'Keefe, her first and worthless husband, who had deserted her on the eve of their son's premature birth.

But Luke had been there to provide a strong shoulder to lean on in the weeks and months following. It was then that she knew she loved him but dared not expose herself to the pain of admitting her love was for a man who saw only lonely places where gold might be. The American prospector had seemed to be one of those men fated to ride out and die in one of those forsaken parts of the frontier. She wanted the man who would share her life to be with her – not always riding out of her life.

Ten years past she had finally admitted to herself that she would rather risk losing him than not having him in her life at all. And that was when she also proposed marriage to him in a miner's tent outside the goldfield's port of Cooktown.

A child was born eight months after they had been formally married but the baby girl died from a fever six months later. Her grave was one of many at Cooktown where Kevin O'Keefe, Kate's first husband, also lay buried. But his death was the inevitable outcome of living a life steeped in crime.

The death of their daughter had caused Kate to retreat grief stricken from the world. But Luke had been with her and his quiet strength had nursed her through the self-recriminations. What had she done to cause the baby's death, she had asked herself. Could she have done something to prevent it?

Luke had reassured her that death on the frontier was not always explainable – nor should one blame oneself. His pragmatic advice came from personal experience as he had many years earlier lost a wife and child to fever. At that time he had ridden the Queensland frontier alone with his grief and often similarly questioned himself under the vast panorama of southern stars. As there was never any answer he came to learn that the grief must have a natural end. It was this blunt pragmatism he was able to eventually convey to Kate.

Years later she now carried their baby. She sensed that this time God would be kind and deliver them a heathy child who would grow to inherit all that she had fought to obtain in life.

'I know God will look after you, my husband,' Kate sighed, realising the tears would not be constrained by her conscious efforts. 'I pray that you will return home as soon as you can to hold our baby.'

Luke noticed the tears and felt a surge of love for this beautiful woman who had honoured him with her unconditional love in spite of his wandering ways. 'I'm not much at being a good

Christian,' he said quietly, pulling her to him in a gentle embrace. 'And I don't think God takes us old Yankee prospectors seriously when we make Him promises when the chips are down. He kind of knows we stray a bit but I will make you the promise that I will be there when the baby is born. I know God will be on your side to make sure I am.'

Kate sensed his gentle mocking of her strong Catholic beliefs. Luke was a man more in harmony with the beliefs of the Aboriginal people of the vast lands beyond the towns of the Europeans. She often mused to herself that this might be because the purpose of his life was to dig in the earth to find his precious gold. That the earth held the secret to life itself.

Although he was in the early years of the second half of his century on earth Luke was still tough and capable. His trip to a property near Burketown he felt was essential – although Kate did not. Luke had heard a rumour that a new breed of cattle was being shipped from Asia. It might be the tropical north's answer to the tough conditions that killed cattle from the south. His interest in cattle breeding had been a result of his years of self-imposed exile as a cowboy in the Montana territory just before his return to Queensland for the Palmer River gold rush.

Kate had unsuccessfully argued for him to remain but saw the look in his eyes that told her he was still trying to prove he could be a stable businessman and be part of her enterprising life. It was really his love for her that had caused him to set out on the journey – a way of showing her that it was not gold that ruled his life but a need to help Kate's ventures. She relented and they now stood in the paddock behind their house as he completed his tasks for his departure.

'I'd better be going,' Luke said gruffly as he reluctantly turned away from Kate. 'Sun will be up soon and it looks like it's going to be a hot one.'

Kate let him slip from her arms and he strode to the horse waiting patiently for the chance to leave the fenced paddock. With years of experience he swung himself into the saddle and pulled down on the reins to wheel away. Kate waved and he acknowledged her wave with a broad smile. Then the bush swallowed him as he rode away.

Kate lingered for a short time in the paddock as the early morning shadows touched the dry grass. He would keep his promise she told herself. He would be with her when their baby came.

Kate was to farewell a second person that day.

The hoofbeats of a horse, the clink of bridle metal and the heavy clomp of boots on the verandah told her that young Gordon James was visiting. The sounds were familiar as Gordon often visited – not to see Kate but Sarah.

'Good morning,' Kate said, addressing the young, grim-faced police officer at the door. 'I . . .' She did not have a chance to finish her words as Sarah bounded down the stairs to stand at her side.

'Gordon!' she exclaimed, as if surprised. 'Why are you visiting so early in the day?'

Gordon's face reflected his pleasure at seeing Sarah but he did not smile. 'I came over to say I may be away for some time. Maybe months,' he replied. 'I have to ride to Cloncurry. We got word that Inspector Potter's patrol was ambushed and that he is dead along with nearly all his men.'

Both Sarah and Kate paled.

'Was Peter with him?' Kate asked in a whisper. She had never approved of her nephew – whom she had raised as she would her own – joining the Native Mounted Police. But she knew the bond between Gordon and Peter had been stronger than her concern for Peter's choice of careers.

'Peter is safe,' Gordon reassured. 'It was he who rode back to Cloncurry to tell us what happened.'

'Thank God,' Kate whispered.

'I just came over on my way out to say goodbye.'

Kate glanced at her niece and noticed that she was impatient to be alone with Gordon. 'Would you like to come in?'

'Ah, no thank you, Missus Tracy,' he mumbled. 'I had better get going. They want me in Cloncurry as soon as possible to organise an expedition to hunt down Inspector Potter's killers.'

'Then I will leave Sarah to wish you a safe journey and know that you go with my fondest regards. When you see Peter please tell him that he has our love and prayers.'

'I will,' Gordon replied and added, 'I would ask a favour before I go, Missus Tracy.'

'I hope that I may oblige,' Kate answered, with just the faintest trace of reservation in her expression.

'I was hoping that you might look in on my mother from time to time. She is not always well.'

Kate's expression instantly softened. 'That does not require a favour,' she replied. 'Your mother remains one of my dearest friends despite my expressed feelings towards you convincing Peter to join your damned police.'

Gordon glanced with a touch of guilt at a space beyond Kate but his guilt dissipated when he noticed Sarah step past her aunt. Kate fell silent. It seemed like only yesterday that Gordon's father had brought a chubby little girl to her, along with her brothers Peter and Tim. Now she stood as a young woman beside the man whose frequent visits were her reason for the day existing. They were a striking couple, Kate reflected. He, dashing in his neatly pressed Native Mounted Police uniform, with his knee-length boots and pistol at his side. She, with her striking golden skin and jet black hair flowing past her shoulders. Kate knew that the exotic beauty of her niece had been noticed by more than one or two eligible young men around town but her eyes had always been for the son of Henry and Emma James. It had been that way since they had left the innocence of their childhood behind and realised it was the attraction between a man and a woman that they had for each other. Gordon was in his twentieth year and Sarah a year younger. At that age passion ran deep and commitment for life was a presumption. Kate left the young couple alone to say their farewells.

Gordon took Sarah's hands in his own. 'I don't like going and being away from you,' he said. 'But I have to do my duty.'

Sarah felt the warmth of his hands and the

calluses brought about by his years of horsemanship. 'You know that my wish is that you and Peter were not part of the Native Mounted Police,' she said gently. 'You know how I feel about them.'

Gordon looked away. His own father had been present when the Native Mounted Police had hunted and killed both her parents years earlier.

'That was a long time ago,' he said. 'Things are different now.'

Sarah did not answer his statement as she knew the argument that would follow. Instead, she preferred to separate Gordon, the officer of the police she hated, from the man she loved with a passion. 'If we are ever to be together,' she said quietly, 'then you will have to choose me over your love for your bloody police.'

Gordon looked into her eyes and saw the fire of her convictions. He knew she had good reason to hate his job. 'I love you more than anything else in this world,' he replied lamely, although he also knew that he loved his job as a leader of men living a life of adventure away from such dreary jobs as clerks in stores or tellers in banks.

'Words are cheap,' Sarah flashed. 'I would be yours if you proved your love by giving up the Mounted Police.'

'I came to tell you of my love,' Gordon pleaded. 'But all you do in return is rebuff my words with your insistence. Sarah, it is not an easy thing that you ask. My father was a policeman and I honour his memory by being one myself. I even owe my commission to his memory.'

Sarah could see the pain in his eyes and wished that it was not so. Especially as he was riding away for such a long time. But she also knew the ghosts of her parents would forever divide them as long as the man she loved remained with the force that had killed them. She let her hands slip from his and turned her back on him. 'Please be careful,' she choked, tears welling in her eyes. 'I cannot say anymore to you than that.'

Gordon watched her walk away and felt the turmoil of the parting.

'Sarah,' he called, but she did not respond as she closed the door behind her to go to her room where she would watch him ride from her life.

Kate watched her niece stumble up the stairs and guessed what had transpired in the parting. She heard Gordon depart and listened at the bottom of the stairs as the muffled sobs echoed in the house. Kate sighed and began to make her way up the stairs to Sarah's room. Why was it that love was never easy, she questioned. Would it be as hard for Sarah to find love as it had been for her?

Later in the day Kate realised her promise to Gordon.

Emma lived alone in a cottage at the edge of town and when Kate announced her arrival she was ushered inside with hugs and exclamations of joy. As Kate's business interests expanded she had less opportunity to visit and chat. For a moment she felt apprehension when she disengaged herself from the embraces to gaze at Emma. She noticed the dark rings around her friend's eyes and how much her once flame-red hair had greyed. Emma was growing old and the observation only reinforced their shared past.

'You must join me for tea,' Emma said. 'I insist.'

'I wish I could but I must return home before dark,' Kate replied. 'I just wanted to see how you were coping with Gordon's departure.'

Emma smiled sadly and turned to lead Kate into her tiny kitchen. 'More that I should ask you how you are faring,' she said. 'You must be very close to your time.'

Kate unconsciously placed her hand on her swollen stomach. 'Yes, very soon from the way he kicks.'

'So you feel it will be a boy,' Emma said, as she poured hot water into a china teapot.

'Well, if it isn't a boy then it is going to be a very strong girl.'

Emma laughed and for a moment Kate saw the young girl she had first met over fifteen years earlier – a vibrant, fun-loving girl just off the boat from England who had loved, married and buried Henry James. At least buried him in her memory as his body was never found.

Both women had been close but in recent years Peter's decision to join his boyhood friend riding with the Native Mounted Police had put a wedge in the friendship. It had been Emma's support for Peter's decision that had rankled Kate. She perceived Emma's obtuse attitude as being blind to Peter's best interests in favour of supporting his happiness above all else. After Peter foolishly enlisted, Kate had found excuses to visit less and less. But their friendship prevailed and Kate often missed the easy company and conversation they had always shared.

'I think that it was not a good idea for Peter to

follow Gordon,' Emma said, as she poured the tea for them.

Kate glanced at her friend with a start – it was as if she had read her mind! 'I have always thought that,' she replied. And the barrier that had been the wedge between them seemed to crumble.

'I was blind to how unwittingly my support for Peter to be with Gordon might place Peter in danger,' Emma said. 'Gordon told me how fortunate Peter was to survive that terrible massacre of Inspector Potter's patrol.'

'It is more than that,' Kate said quietly. 'Peter could lose his soul if he continues with the Mounted Police. They were, as you may remember, responsible for the deaths of his parents in Burkesland back in '68.'

Emma winced and Kate knew that it would be better to drop the subject lest it open a fresh wound between them. It had been Emma's husband who had been with the patrol that hunted Peter's parents and was eventually responsible for their deaths. Kate had not held Henry James accountable as he had proved earlier in a hunt that he would have prevented the deaths had it been within his power to do so.

'I wish we could go back to that year and change everything,' Emma said in a whisper edged with tears. 'So much tragedy seemed to come to us both from that year on. I would like to remember how it was when we were younger and living down at Rockhampton. Do you remember the picnics and how we all used to sing around your piano? Henry had such an awful singing voice . . .'

She trailed away and the tears flowed. Kate

reached across the table. Emma grasped her friend's hand and with the other swiped at the tears. 'Oh Kate, I have this terrible feeling in my stomach that we have not seen the last of the tragedies in our lives,' she gasped. 'I feel that we may lose those close to us very soon.'

Kate gripped Emma's hand reassuringly. 'I pray that the curse that has come to us has run its course. We have good health and we have our children.'

Emma withdrew her hand and stood to wipe away the tears with her apron. 'I pray that you are right,' she said, with an attempt at a smile. 'Maybe Peter will see that it is in his best interests to return to Townsville and work with you in the company.'

'I pray he does,' Kate said without much confidence. She knew her nephew placed great stock in friendship. That Australian concept of mateship.

The two women chatted until the tea was cold and when Kate at last departed she did so with Emma's words of foreboding echoing in her memory. Superstitiously she placed her hand on her stomach and uttered a prayer to the Virgin Mary. *Please Mother Mary, protect all those born – and unborn – in my life.*

8

The cool night air helped clear Patrick's head as he set off along the road from the impressive Fitzgerald manor. His footsteps echoed loudly in the eerie silence that was broken only by the hoot of an owl hunting nocturnal mice.

After he had walked a half mile along the road he could see in the distance the sombre outline of the tree-covered dome, outlined by the soft light of an almost full moon. It was foolish, he knew, but he still strained to see if Catherine was standing on the summit.

On an impulse he cut across the field towards the dome-shaped feature and in a short time, after wading through a sea of grass wet with the early dew, the hill loomed over him. From the copses of trees on the hill where a low creeping mist had gathered, the scent of firs wafted to him, a rich, antiseptic perfume.

As he stared up at the grove Patrick felt the mist swirl around his bare knees with its cold damp fingers. Why was he contemplating a climb to the summit? He frowned and shook his head. Maybe he just wanted to see why the mound had such an appeal to Catherine.

The climb was not difficult as the hill was not very high and the dark firs enveloped him in hushed and brooding silence until he reached the summit. At the top the firs retreated from a small clearing of stark white, flat stones.

Limestone, Patrick thought, as he entered the mysterious circle. And obviously man-made as they had a distinctive, geometric pattern which was almost concealed by the grass that struggled to break the lines and circles designed by some ancient race of people.

Patrick stood expectantly at the centre of the stones from where he could see, through a gap in the trees, the moon as a silver slivered path across the cold still Atlantic sea. But he was bitterly disappointed as the mystical experience he half-expected to occur did not eventuate. Instead he felt only a coolness creep up his legs – and a loneliness enter his soul.

The silence of the hill was broken by the sinister sound of dead fir needles crackling. Patrick slid a dirk from inside his long sock, a practical weapon of first resort. The huge shape padded towards him with a low, threatening growl and Patrick crouched with the dagger in his hand.

A wolf! No, not a wolf. A wolf hound!

'Lugh! No!'

Catherine's command brought the big dog to a halt and it propped obediently, awaiting the next command. Patrick relaxed and in the dim light of the moon glimpsed Catherine as she emerged into the clearing holding the hem of her long red dress up from the dewy grass. Behind her followed the second of her huge hounds and Patrick eased the knife back down the side of his leg.

Catherine dropped her hands away and the hem of the dress fell around her ankles to fall on a flat white stone. 'You did not bid me goodnight, Captain Duffy,' she said quietly. The big hounds padded to the edge of the clearing where they took up positions staring into the copses.

'I could see that you were rather preoccupied with Mister Brett Norris,' Patrick replied tersely. 'I doubted that my absence would mean much either way to you. We hardly know each other,' he added with a growl of his own.

'In this place you and I have known each other for thousands of years,' she answered softly, staring up at his face shadowed in the moonlight. 'Reaching back to the time this mound was built. In this place you were Cuchulainn and I, I was the Morrigan,' she concluded with a whisper.

'Who was Cuchulainn?' Patrick asked.

'Oh, a legendary warrior of old Ireland. He slew many enemies, just as I suspect you have. He could do anything he wanted. He was a man who was also the son of the Sun God. But then the Christians came and killed his memory.'

'And the Morrigan, who was she?'

'The goddess to whom Cuchulainn owed much of his success in war.'

'Did they love each other?'

Catherine averted her gaze and sighed. Then she stared up at him and said sadly, 'I think you should some day return to Ireland to find that answer, Captain Duffy. It is written in the old texts kept by the monks in their musty archives.'

Patrick gazed into the eyes made dark by the night and wondered at the vision standing before him. She was no longer the sophisticated young woman of the dinner party but the enigmatic girl he had first met standing barefooted in her grandfather's library. 'I promise you I will,' he said. 'That is, if you are not otherwise occupied by Mister Brett Norris's company.'

'He is a dear friend who would like to marry me.'

'And you?'

'No. At least not for a long time.'

Patrick felt his hopes deflated by her last statement. So the English fop still played a role in her life? Or was it that she still played games with his feelings? 'I don't know when I will be able to return,' he answered, feigning disinterest, as he was not going to play the game by her rules. 'A lot can happen on a battlefield.'

'You will not be harmed, Captain Duffy. The Morrigan protects you.'

'I'm not your Cuchulainn, Miss Fitzgerald. I'm just a simple soldier of the Queen who takes the same risks as every other soldier in the fighting,' he said as he tore his eyes from hers. 'But I will return to Ireland. If only to study the history of this country and learn more about myself.'

'And not to see me?' she asked.

'That is a question without an immediate answer,' he replied, turning to stare out over the Atlantic. 'A question only you will answer with time and consideration as to what is truly important in life.'

'And what is important in your life, Captain Duffy?' Catherine asked as Patrick turned to her again. 'The search for yourself here?'

Patrick was stunned by her perceptiveness. She could almost be the damned Morrigan she thought she was. Her uncanny knack of seeing inside his soul was disturbing. It was a place that belonged to him alone. 'A decision I must one day make, but either way I lose,' he replied bitterly, adding, 'A search for a truth as to how a mother could deliberately send her baby to a place of death.'

'Your mother?' she asked gently.

He nodded.

'We have a lot more in common than you think, Captain Duffy. Except that I never knew who my father was. At least *your* father has a name and is already a legend in this part of the country.'

'I'm afraid your villagers have him confused with someone else,' Patrick said with a bemused smile spreading across his face. 'Although it is rather flattering to think that my father has been attributed with this Michael O'Flynn's rather colourful reputation.'

'There is magic in this place, Cuchulainn,' she said seriously. 'And you should open your heart to it. Then one day you *might* find that your father *is* Michael O'Flynn.'

Patrick's soft laughter warmed the cool air of the clearing and impulsively he touched Catherine's face with his hand as one would a naive child. 'Do you know, Miss Catherine Fitzgerald, that I could almost believe what you say because you bring the magic to this place.'

Her hand gripped his wrist. '*Believe*, Patrick!' she replied fiercely. 'Believe you will find yourself in your father and that one day you will return to this place. It is very important.'

Stunned by her fierce conviction Patrick struggled for thoughts and words. He suddenly drew her to him. His lips sought hers with a savage and explosive hunger and she flung her arms around his neck.

Her response was equal to his own. The mutual desire had smouldered between them from the moment they had met and now the intense spark of passion became an all engulfing fire in Patrick's body. But Catherine pushed him away with half-hearted whimpers of 'No, not now'.

'I loved you from the very first time I saw you standing on this hill, Catherine. I don't know how I could have loved you then. All I know is that I did. Maybe you are the Morrigan but you will not tell me how the story ends.'

Catherine took deep breaths before answering and the two big wolf hounds rose and padded menacingly closer but she waved them away. Unsure, they sat on their haunches and continued to watch Patrick with suspicion.

'Come back when you have finished your search and I will tell you how the story ends,' she said once she had her feelings under control. She stepped back from him at an arm's length as her eyes dropped to the front of his kilt. 'You certainly have the prowess of Cuchulainn,' she said cheekily and Patrick blushed at her brazen observation. 'I fear you carry the *gae bulga* under your kilt, Patrick Duffy,' she continued with a gentle laugh of admiration.

'What is a *gae bulga*?' Patrick was embarrassed by her gentle teasing of his rather uncomfortable condition. He had never known a woman to talk so openly about such matters.

'The *gae bulga* was a Celtic spear with many barbs. It was a terrible weapon. When it pierced the body it could not be withdrawn because the barbs would open from the shaft. And, in your case, very much like the swelling of my hounds' shafts when they service a bitch.'

Patrick's shocked expression at her explicit descriptions only amused Catherine and encouraged by his embarrassment she continued to add to his discomfort. 'Oh, do not appear so shocked, Captain Duffy. A man of your experiences must appreciate that a girl growing up in the country sees many things. It is all part of our education on life.'

'Well . . .' he spluttered. 'I know of such things. But they are not things one would expect to be discussed in mixed company.'

'We are alone, Patrick, and I feel I can be myself with you,' Catherine said quietly as she stared out at the sea. 'I should return to Grandfather before he notices my absence. I'm afraid he is not altogether happy about me seeing you. I had planned to sit by you at dinner but Grandfather insisted I sit at the end of the table next to that horrid sister of Brett's and Mister Norris himself.'

'I wish you could stay longer. I've hardly had a chance to get to know you.'

'When you return, Patrick,' she said, touching his face gently with her hand. 'But before I go I have something I would like you to carry with you always. Something that will remind you to return to Ireland.'

Patrick gazed after her as she left him standing in the centre of the flat stones. At the edge of the trees she stooped to retrieve something only as big as her hand. She brought the mysterious object to him and placed it in his hand. In doing so she curled his fingers around the object. 'Promise me you will always carry Sheela-na-gig with you wherever you go,' she said. 'But also promise me you will not look upon her until you have reached the privacy of your lodgings at Riley's pub.'

'I promise,' Patrick replied, slightly confused by her gesture. 'But what is Sheela-na-gig?'

'She is a goddess who even predates the Morrigan. I found her one day when I was a young girl exploring the mound. But I hid her until now. I was afraid she would be taken from me by Grandfather for his collection.'

Patrick felt the cold stone object in his hand and could make out the outline of a human-like figure. In many ways he knew the ancient goddess in his hand was as mysterious to him as the girl who reached up to kiss him. Her kiss was gentle and lingering. Neither wanted to break the strange magic of the moment. But the moon was low on the horizon and soon it would be very dark on the hill.

'Be careful, Captain Duffy,' she whispered close to his ear and her breath was sweet on his cheek. 'I will offer prayers to Sheela-na-gig to protect you in those dangerous places you must go.'

Reluctantly Catherine tore herself away and, without looking back, walked with the two huge hounds through the thickets of fir down the slope.

Patrick turned the stone over and over in his hand and although he was curious he kept his promise not to examine the ancient artefact until he was in his room. What might the stone relief reveal to him in the light of his room? Would it reveal the spirit of Catherine Fitzgerald to him?

His dormant superstitions told him he should leave the place before the faerie people came to take him for all eternity. Or was it that a faerie girl had already stolen his heart for all eternity on the sacred hill of the Celts?

The moon was waning as he walked briskly back to the village. The air had cooled considerably and the village was asleep as his footsteps echoed in the narrow, winding, cobblestone streets. Only the yapping of a dog from somewhere in the village accompanied him to Riley's where an irritable Bernard Riley opened the door of the hotel to allow the young officer to enter. Patrick thanked him but Riley waved off his thanks with a grumble as he shuffled back to his room in his nightshirt.

In his room Patrick placed a candle on a sideboard to examine the object and in the circle of dim light thrown by the candle he saw for the first time the Celtic goddess Sheela-na-gig. 'God almighty!' he swore softly, although with a certain amount of reverence, as the shadows of the dancing candle flame brought the little figure to life. 'No wonder she hid the thing!'

For Sheela-na-gig was the goddess of fertility and she stared up at him with an enigmatic smile on her face.

Lying on her back with her legs spread invitingly wide, she held open her out-sized vagina with her hands extended from behind her knees. The vagina was swollen with physical desire and he stared at the figure transfixed by its primeval posture of anticipated pleasure and procreation.

It was as if in the little goddess of pre-Christian times he was seeing the basis of the true soul of the people of his Irish blood: a race of men and women immersed in the sensuality and uninhibited lust of sex. But this deep, unbridled sensuality had been channelled by religion into the zealous prayers and observances of Holy days.

As Patrick stared at Sheela-na-gig he felt he understood a little better that part of his Celtic self that was wild and free.

'Thank you, Catherine,' he whispered in a choked voice. 'You are my goddess . . . and it will always be so. No matter where I go I will adore you on the shrine of your body and soul.'

He then packed the little goddess in the deepest and darkest corner of his travelling bag and, sighing, sat on the narrow bed to remove his boots and gaiters. Once he lay down Patrick's thoughts drifted into dreams. The turmoil of the evening merged with strange dreams of a hill on the other side of the world. Not a hill he had ever seen personally but one described to him by his grandmother, Lady Enid Macintosh. A sacred hill of an ancient race of people slaughtered on the Macintosh property Glen View over two decades earlier. Somehow he could visualise the dry craggy hill as if he had visited the place himself and in his dreams the hill became the fir-covered mound of the Celts. Two sacred sites of two peoples whose pagan spiritual beliefs had no place in modern thinking.

When he awoke Patrick remembered the dream as vividly as the moments he had spent with Catherine under the waning moon. Maureen, the innkeeper's daughter, was at the door of his room and the pub was bustling into the day's activities.

He rose from under the warm blankets still fully dressed and Maureen entered the room without inquiring whether or not it was an opportune time. She placed the bowl of hot water on the narrow sideboard. Patrick thanked her and she left reluctantly as he set his feet on the floor to change from his mess dress into more comfortable civilian travelling clothes.

After a hearty breakfast of bacon and eggs, Patrick made a final visit to Father Eamon O'Brien and Mary Casey. They talked briefly, expressing regret that they did not have more time to sit and talk of subjects they had in common.

Mary Casey gave him a self-conscious kiss on the cheek and a quick affectionate hug as she bade him God's protection in the coming crusade against the infidels of Islam to save poor General Gordon. She was able to forgive Patrick for his strange Protestant beliefs as he was engaged in the common Christian fight against the evil Moslem heathens.

Aboard the coach taking him to Belfast, Patrick glanced back at the little village nestling on the shoreline of the cold Atlantic. It seemed as if nothing would ever change the ancestral home of his Irish blood. It was a timeless place.

He thought about what had been. He had found a magic place and an ancient Celtic goddess in the living form of a beautiful young woman with fiery red hair. But his thoughts became gloomy when he thought what lay ahead. Desert, Dervishes and probable death for many in the coming war to relieve General Gordon at Khartoum. The promise that he had made to Catherine to return to Ireland seemed impossibly far away. *'Be careful, Captain Duffy.'* Her parting words echoed in the hiss of the rain beating down on the clattering coach. *'In those dangerous places you must go.'*

9

The melodious warble of magpies woke Ben at
dawn. He had not noticed the chill of the early
morning as he slept but was aware of it now as he
uncurled in the dust and sat up. He shivered and
rubbed himself.

Slowly he rose to his feet and gazed across the
yard at the hut where he could see little Becky
staring back at him, her hand shading her eyes
against the rising sun's orange glare.

'Daddy?' she called when she saw her father
striding towards her. 'I have made breakfast for
you.'

Ah, but she was so much like her mother, he
thought with a surge of paternal love. While she
lived Jenny would always be with him.

'I spoke to your mother last night,' Ben said as
he sat at the table with the pannikin of bread and
dripping in front of him. 'I think she would have
agreed that Willie take you all to Townsville to
stay with your Aunt Judith and Uncle Solomon.
Then Willie can return to the property,' he added.

The younger boys cast each other shocked

expressions. It was inconceivable to even consider leaving their home at such a time. They were needed here and not in a town where freedom was restricted to streets and houses! But they wisely made no sign to protest other than in the frowns clouding their faces. Becky stood at her father's shoulder. Her bottom lip quivered. *She was losing her father too!*

Ben saw the tears welling in her eyes. He drew her to him and placed her in his lap. His arms wrapped around her and he could smell the earthy sweetness of her thick tresses. His heart ached for the decision he had reluctantly made to send away his children. But more was at stake than Jerusalem alone. 'It won't be forever,' he said gently. 'Just for a couple of years until things change here.'

'What things?' Saul piped up in a confused voice. 'What things change? Mum's dead and we're old enough to know that, Dad. You need Jonathan and me to help you run the place. Send Becky . . . but not us!'

'I said for a couple of years,' Ben growled at his son who had always been the more daring of his two boys. 'A couple of years for you all to get a decent education and make up your own minds as to what you want to do. Stay in Townsville or come back here to help me and Willie run the place.'

'But we don't need to go to school to know how to run the place,' Saul continued, undaunted. 'Me and Jonathan do our work around here already as good as Willie. You don't need schooling to handle the cattle. You can teach us all we have to know.'

'You do need an education,' Ben snapped. 'It's something your mother always wanted for you. She always wanted you to learn how to read and write and I have to honour her wishes.'

Honour her wishes, Willie brooded. Honour her wish to exact vengeance on the man who had caused her life so much pain as a child. He leant forward, his elbows on the table top. 'Shut up, Saul, and listen to what your father says.'

Saul's face flushed with anger as he swung on him.

'He's not *your* father,' Saul flared. 'I heard what Mum said to you before she died. So you can go to hell.'

Ben's face drained of blood at his son's retort and the crack of his backhand caused Saul to topple from the bench at the table. 'Never say that again in this house,' Ben whispered hoarsely, as the white hot anger choked him.

Shocked by the speed and savageness of the strike from his father, Saul lay sprawled on the hard-packed earthen floor holding his hand to the swelling redness of his cheek. 'A man don't need to be natural born to be a son.'

In those words, Willie suddenly felt a surge of love for the man who had been his mother's husband. Until that moment he had never truly accepted Ben as his father as he had always been a competitor for his mother's attentions.

'Never again, Saul,' Ben hissed to emphasise the seriousness of the warning. 'It would have hurt your mother more than you will ever know to hear you say what you did just then.'

'Sorry,' Saul mumbled as he returned to his

place at the table. He could taste blood in his mouth where a tooth had cut the inside of his cheek and was partially satisfied to see that his father was trembling with regret for the pain that he had inflicted on him in his explosive fury.

He is a tough one, Ben thought. The sort of boy who would grow to be the natural inheritor of Jerusalem some day. But in this thought alone he felt guilt for the dismissal of Willie who should, by his position in the family, be the son chosen to inherit the property. *Blood was thicker than water* crept uncomfortably into his mind.

'When do yer want me to leave with the kids?' Willie asked quietly, and Ben was grateful for the question.

'Tomorrow. You pack all you need to take the track from Cloncurry to Townsville. I'll give you a letter explaining everything to Solomon and you can pick up supplies in town on your way to see them. Make sure you take a good supply of shot and powder with you.'

'We take the dray?' Willie asked and Ben nodded.

Jonathan had remained silent throughout the altercation between his father and his defiant brother and had even given Saul a reproving look when he'd sat back down at the table after having been sent sprawling. Although he was as reluctant to leave his father and the property as his brother, Jonathan also felt a guilty twinge of relief.

He still had vague memories of his first years of life in Townsville where there were so many wonders and delights denied to them on Jerusalem. So many other children to play with instead of the gruelling work of the property And books he would learn to read. No, life for a couple of years in Townsville would not be so bad. Besides, the Cohens had a lot of money and didn't have to work as hard as their father.

The next morning Willie harnessed the best of the horses to the dray and packed the supplies they would need for the long trek to Townsville: flour, tinned beef, sugar, tea, bags of water, a rifle and ammunition, canvas sheet for shelter and a bag of chaff for the horse. They took little else as there was little else to take.

Both boys sat in the dray with Becky beside Willie, hugging her sole toy, a doll Jenny had made for her from scraps of dresses. Her golden locks were greasy and tangled with neglect as her hair care had been a loving chore Jenny performed.

Willie cracked a stockwhip and the dray rumbled across the yard and past the newly built stockyards. The heavy, iron-rimmed wheels raised a low cloud of fine, red dust that trailed like a plume.

Shading his eyes with his broad-rimmed hat, Ben stood by the stockyards and sadly watched the dray disappear into the scrub. He could see the boys gazing back at him with grim set faces and he watched as Becky turned to wave the hand hold-ing the doll. It was at that moment he felt that his heart might physically break and he choked back the tears he thought he no longer had in him.

When they were out of sight he turned to walk to the grave of his wife. He stood with his head bowed and spoke to her, explaining that they would return one day as the people she had always wanted them to become. The silence of the vast bushland echoed in his ears as he strained to hear the rumble of the dray or the crack of the whip. But he heard nothing except the twitter of the tiny bush birds flitting in and out of the brush in search of insects. For the first time in many years he was truly alone.

No, not alone! Jenny would always be with him in the laughter that might some day return in the form of his daughter as a young woman.

Ben stood by Jenny's grave for an hour, unaware of the many dark eyes that watched him from the concealment of the scrub. Eyes of warriors who, as they crouched in the shadows of the bush with spears fitted to woomeras, had also watched the passing of the dray.

But the spears did not fly to pierce the flesh of the white people. For Terituba recognised the man who had walked fearlessly amongst them and brought them flour instead of death. Terituba signalled to his party of warriors to move on and leave the white man to grieve in peace. For he respected this man and his death would serve no purpose. There were other white men to hunt until they were either killed or left the land of the Kalkadoon.

Silent as moving shadows, the Kalkadoon war party slipped deeper into the scrub to hunt and return to their clan camped at a waterhole north of Jerusalem. Soon they would join the other Kalkadoon clans in the basalt hills to plan strategies to drive the invaders out.

*   *   *

Willie had not turned to look back at the bark hut. He had not looked back at the place where his mother was buried because he wanted to remember her as a living being and not something as part of the earth. He knew he would never again return to Jerusalem. He could never be part of the land owned by Ben as he had always known that the land would go to either Jonathan or Saul. He would deliver Ben's children to Townsville and seek a way of life that would eventually take him south to the place of his birth – Sydney. And when he finally got there he would honour the oath he had made to himself after his mother's death. He would kill his real father.

10

Gordon James's dark eyes and jet black hair were the features that first struck the observer and, although he was not exceptionally tall, his commanding demeanour made him appear so. His clean shaven face was tanned a golden hue as a legacy of the long hours he had spent in the saddle leading patrols of Native Mounted Police on forays against the last remnants of Aboriginal tribes who deigned to resist the white squatters.

Dressed in his uniform jacket and with his riding trousers tucked into knee-length boots he was an impressive sight as he stood with his back to the plank trestle bar of the Cloncurry hotel and eyed his audience: squatters and their stockmen, teamsters, selectors, prospectors and a few of the merchants who worked closely with the bushmen. Tough and uncompromising men dressed in the rough working clothes of their trades: moleskin trousers, bright shirts, wide-brimmed hats and knee-length boots. They carried guns on their hips and cradled rifles in their laps. The mostly bearded men stared back at the young police officer with just a hint of contempt and hostility while outside the hotel dogs snarled and snapped at each other, disputing territory.

The squabbling dogs were watched by a gaggle of bearded men who lounged under the shelter of the verandah of the hotel. These patrons of the hotel had decided the meeting inside was of little interest to them and amused themselves with snide comments on the lack of ability of the Native Mounted Police to disperse the pesky Kalkadoon in the district. Their comments were intended for the ears of the two uniformed police troopers who also lounged at one end of the verandah, waiting for their commander to finish his meeting inside.

Other than the ruckus created by the mangy dogs there was little movement along the wide and dusty main street of the frontier town. The hot midday sun had driven most living creatures under shade. Only a lone dray rumbled down the street and its occupants did cause some curious on-lookers to stare at them as they passed, heading for the general merchandise store. Two young boys, a young girl with yellow hair, and a surly looking young man at the reins.

Inside the bar the men packed together, some sitting, some standing, muttering amongst themselves and continuing to stare at the officer who made a loud cough and tapped the bar with the base of an empty gin bottle. The improvised gavel gained their attention and he introduced himself by rank and surname and thanked the men for answering his call to the meeting. Then he launched directly into his introductory speech. 'I know the treacherous murder of Inspector Potter has filled you with all the abhorrence that such an act will elicit in good men,' Gordon James piously intoned to his audience. 'But I promise you I will take all steps necessary to bring to heel the darkies responsible for the crime.'

The audience were men who had heard it all before from the far-off government in the distant capital of Brisbane Town. *Another shiny arsed trap who had all the answers to the almost daily increase in Kalkadoon warfare in the Cloncurry district!*

'You and whose army?' a squatter sneered as he sat with his arms folded over his ample paunch. 'The black bastards will lead you down the garden path before they rip yer guts out and eat yer kidneys.'

His observation was backed with head nodding and low growls of agreement from the audience, cynical that such a young man could be a better policeman than the older, experienced policeman who had been led into an ambush and killed.

'Give the man a fair go, Harry,' someone drawled from the back of the bar in a broad American accent. 'His old man was Henry James.'

'Never heard of 'im,' the podgy squatter snorted.

'You wouldn't, Harry,' the American added facetiously. 'He was a local man.'

The reference to the former Victorian farmer's newness to the district put him in his place and brought a snicker of laughter from the old timers of the frontier who were tired of the irksome squatter's continuous bragging of how better the Colony of Victoria was to that of Queensland.

'Yeah. You tell him, Commanche Jack!' another voice called from the men packed into the bar.

Gordon was grateful for the American's support. It was interesting to hear that his father was still a man whose formidable reputation existed in the memories of the tough men of the frontier. 'Mister Jack, I gather your name indicates you have some experience fighting the savages of your land?' the young police officer queried.

Commanche Jack pushed his way forward through the throng of frontiersmen. 'Nigh on twenty years, Inspector,' he replied. 'They even prettied up my face one time so the wimmen would like me more.'

He was a short stocky man who Gordon judged to be in his middle years but who carried himself like a man twenty years younger. Gordon was impressed by his scarred face. Here was a man who knew his business when it came to dealing with savages, he thought as he appraised the American settler. 'Then you might be of considerable help to me in the future,' he said. 'I plan to organise a patrol to hunt down the recalcitrant darkies and bring them to justice and I will need the assistance of such experienced men as yourself to swell the depleted ranks of the Native Mounted Police.'

'A posse you mean, Inspector,' Commanche Jack said with a wry grin. 'Sure, I'll ride with you.'

'We don't have posses in the colonies,' Gordon commented with an embarrassed cough. 'Such oddities appear to be peculiar to you Yankees, I'm afraid.'

'Whatever you want to call it, I'll be in it,' the

American answered with a grin that revealed tobacco stained teeth. 'I'd like to get me a darkie scalp while they're still around fer the gettin'.'

The men who had come to hear the young inspector of the Native Mounted Police hooted with laughter. The American's eagerness to join the hunt for the dreaded Kalkadoon gave them heart. *Surely they could bring the problem to a resolution with Snider and Colt.*

One man who had personal experience with the well-disciplined battle tactics of the Kalkadoon sat quietly to one side of the young inspector, listening to the exchange of views on how best to beat the warriors who lived in the range of hills north of Cloncurry. He was Trooper Peter Duffy.

Peter sat unobtrusively in a chair with his Snider carbine butt down on the floor and its barrel pointing towards the ceiling. Dressed in his uniform with a bandolier of cartridges slung across his chest, he had been selected to accompany Gordon to the meeting. This had pleased Peter, as he and Gordon had grown up together. His boyhood friend and now police commander had arrived in Cloncurry under orders to take command of Sub Inspector Potter's badly demoralised remaining force of troopers. But he had little time to speak privately with Peter when he arrived.

As boys growing up in North Queensland they had spent truant weeks living with the wandering tribes of the Cooktown region and had at one stage gone on walkabout with the wild Kyowarra tribesmen as far as the Normanby River. That was when Gordon's father had trekked after them to bring them back and only Wallarie's intervention had saved the former Native Mounted Police sergeant from certain death.

Peter smiled to himself as he contrasted his own life in the Native Mounted Police with that of his best friend. It was an ironic smile. Gordon should have been the tracker and he the commander. He was, after all, much better educated than Gordon and Gordon's skills of tracking in the bush were much better than his own. Gordon had learned well from the Aboriginal teachers who had introduced them both into bush lore, whereas he had paid more attention to the teachers who taught in the Townsville school.

When they joined the Native Mounted Police Gordon had automatically been granted rank whereas Peter had been relegated to the barracks as a trooper. It was nothing personal, Gordon had explained with some awkwardness. But he was a darkie and therefore not as smart as a white man. His tactless explanation had not rankled Peter who had grown used to the position in life that his part-Aboriginal blood bestowed on him. And besides, his father had been Tom Duffy, the notorious bushranger, Gordon had added as if attempting to take Peter's thoughts off the misfortune of his birth.

'You ever hunted Kalkadoon before, Inspector?' a lean, bearded teamster asked directly. 'They's a cheeky lot. They'll take yer bullocks and eat them in front of yer and bare their arses at you at the same time. They's not like any other darkies I've known on all my years haulin' supplies in Queensland. 'Fraid of nothin' these Kalkys.'

'I must admit, sir, that I have not hunted Kalkadoon. But I fail to see how your darkies are any smarter than others I have dispersed in recent times around the Cairns district and further north.'

'Maybe that's what Inspector Potter said,' Commanche Jack cautioned, and heads nodded agreement to his quietly spoken statement. 'Maybe he thought he was dealin' with them India men. I know'd from my own country that the Mescalero Apaches ain't Arapahos an' fight different. What you got here is a kind of Mescalero and he ain't no peaceful reservation Injun. No, sir! What you got here is somethin' you ain't dealt with before, Inspector. You got a colonial Mescy on your hands.'

'I bow to your sage advice, Commanche Jack,' Gordon replied graciously. 'But a well-trained and disciplined contingent of Her Majesty's Native Mounted is a match for any warlike tribe in all the colonies. Or former colonies of the Crown for that matter.' His pointed but light-hearted jibe at the Yankee's rebellious political history brought a smatter of laughter from the audience and a wide grin from Commanche Jack.

'Mebbe so, Inspector. Mebbe so,' he replied good humouredly.

The rapport between the tough and experienced Indian fighter and the young, relatively in-experienced police officer, brought a tacit acceptance of Gordon from the others in the room. He sensed he was winning them over slowly to accepting his role as overall commander of the expedition to track and disperse the Kalkadoon.

'Well, gentlemen, I believe there is little else to discuss at this point except to tell you that I intend to hold a meeting here in two weeks' time at the same hour. I would urge you all to be here so that I can go over my plans for the expedition we will mount to rid us of the Kalkadoon problem once and for all.'

The men muttered amongst themselves and nodded agreement to the meeting as they rose from their chairs. Gordon turned to Peter still sitting in his chair. 'Trooper Duffy!'

'Sah!'

'We shall depart and return to the barracks now.'

'Sah!'

Peter followed Gordon out of the hotel and into the heat of the afternoon. Gordon slipped off his kepi and wiped his brow. The sweat had not altogether been caused by the stifling heat in the hotel bar. The two troopers who had been lounging around the front of the hotel waiting for the boss to come out smartened their demeanour at his approach and saluted their officer.

They unhitched their horses and as Gordon swung into his saddle he said quietly, 'Come over to my office after evening drill, Trooper Duffy.'

'Sah!'

'Good man! We have a lot to talk over,' he added with a conspiratorial wink that thawed the stiff formality that had existed between them ever since Gordon had arrived at the barracks. Not that there had yet been time to sit down and discuss the old days as Gordon had been met by deputations of frightened settlers and concerned townspeople as soon as he had arrived from Townsville.

They wheeled away from the hotel and rode with stiffly erect backs down the main street. Their disciplined appearance was greeted with smiles and waves from those few people who were sheltering from the sun on the verandahs of the shops of the town.

Word had gone around that the son of Henry James had taken command of the troop and many of the old timers still remembered his father's considerable reputation as a disperser of the native tribes down south in the Kennedy district. If'n he was 'alf as good as h's old man then there was some 'ope of dispersin' the pesky Kalkadoon, they generally agreed.

II

Horace Brown watched the little steam lighter chugging towards the wharf. He leant on his cane with one hand and shaded his eyes as he peered across the muddy creek as the boat weaved between the wooden hulled coastal traders, making its way to the wharf. The day was mild and a clear blue sky promised good weather. This was fortunate, as on rough days passengers being transported from the steam ships anchored in Cleveland Bay often arrived in open whaleboats soaked and without their luggage.

Others also stood waiting on the wharf but hardly took notice of the lonely figure of the little Englishman who occasionally removed the spectacles from the end of his nose to wipe them on the sleeve of his jacket.

Horace was hardly noticeable to those about him because he could best be described as a non-descript man – a distinct advantage in his profession. For unobtrusive people made the best intelligence agents; they drew little attention to themselves or their occupation of gathering information and turning it into useable intelligence. But Horace – Remittance Man to those who made his acquaintance, and spy master to the passenger he waited to greet – had little time left working for Her Majesty's Foreign Office. A fact he was acutely aware of as the cancer ate at his body and sapped his life. How long? Six months at the most he guessed.

He hobbled painfully forward as the few people on the wharf pushed their way towards the boat that now steamed into the wharf. His rheumy eyes searched the passengers on the lighter for the distinctive figure of the tall, broad-shouldered man with the black eye patch and was rewarded with a glimpse of him standing like Ulysses watching for his Penelope amongst the mixture of Chinese and European passengers the lighter transferred from the ship out of Singapore. 'Ah, dear boy!' he sighed with tearful happiness to himself. 'You have finally come home from your odyssey in the Orient.'

Michael Duffy was far from a boy. In ten years' travelling the Orient he had used other names and nationalities to stay one step ahead of the men who would rather see his espionage activities permanently curtailed by his violent demise. Although in his mid-forties, his body was hard with muscle and his remaining blue eye blazed with energy even though his once thick, brown curling hair was now shot with grey. It was still in the style of his younger days, worn just above the collar of his immaculate white starched shirt. He also wore a fresh black eye patch over the eye socket where shrapnel from Confederate artillery had taken his eye in the Civil War between the States of America. His clean shaven face was tanned and smooth without any sign of ageing and his rugged good looks still turned the heads of ladies of all ages.

'Mister O'Flynn, dear chap,' Horace said as he gripped Michael's extended hand as he stepped ashore. 'It is so good to see you well.'

Michael was taken aback by the gaunt man whose eyes bravely attempted to shine for him. He had last seen Horace in good health: a robust and portly man addicted to opium and young Chinese boys. But the man before him looked nothing like the person he had left to travel to the Far East. The transformation left Michael speechless for some seconds and he felt an unexpected wave of pity for the man who had ruled so much of his latter life with the ruthlessness of the obsessed. 'Horace, you old bastard! How the devil are you?' And he suddenly regretted asking such a tactless question as it was obvious to him the man was seriously ill.

'Well enough, Michael. Well enough.'

Michael could have sworn that the tough and ruthless man who had survived the Crimean Campaign of '54 and played a dangerous game of intrigue with his German adversaries in Asia and the Pacific was on the verge of tears. To break the awkward moment Michael placed his arm around the shoulders of the smaller man and steered him down the wharf towards the town.

'From your dispatches I gathered things became somewhat risky from time to time, old boy. I hope not too risky,' Horace said as he walked slowly beside the big Irishman. 'I was often worried you might let your wild Irish passion get you into trouble.'

Michael snorted with amusement at the Englishman's concern. 'You mean you were concerned you might lose me,' he replied. 'And have all that trouble recruiting someone else to do your dirty work.'

'Not true, old boy,' Horace retorted with indignation. 'I've grown rather fond of you over the years.' Michael did not know whether to believe him. The man was both ruthless and sentimental.

Once off the wharf Michael was amazed at how much Townsville had grown since he had last seen it in '75. It was still a town of tin and timber but there were also fine public buildings of stone and brick. The great red rock hill reared up from the town itself to dominate the view inland and the streets were lined with gas lights. They were a short walk from the newly built Excelsior Hotel into which Horace had booked him when Michael noticed that, although the town had grown, the unpleasant smells of the cesspits remained.

He carried only one bag. It was battered and had seen much service in its travels but he had never considered replacing the old carpet bag; it symbolised his life. For all that was necessary to his existence he carried in the bag: his razor, a brace of Colt revolvers, two changes of clothes and a faded photograph of an unsmiling little boy staring with serious eyes at the camera. The photograph had been given to him by his sister Kate Tracy. It had been sent to her from Sydney by their Aunt Bridget prior to the boy sailing for England. The photograph was Michael's most treasured possession. It was of his son – now known as Captain Patrick Duffy of Her Majesty's military expedition to the Sudan. A son who was unaware that his father was even alive.

In a short time they arrived at the hotel. Michael signed in under the name O'Flynn. In the Colony of New South Wales he was still wanted for a murder that he had not committed. In his long years as a mercenary soldier he had killed many men who probably had not deserved death. But the only killing he had done purely in self-defence was called murder by the authorities of that southern Australian colony.

Michael's room had access to the front upper verandah where the view took in the muddy waters of the creek he had crossed to reach the wharf from his steamer. He could see the tall single spars of small wooden boats moored along the shore. A pleasant breeze played along the verandah and there was a sense of peace about the place. North Queensland was fast becoming home to him for many reasons. Here lived his sister Kate and her husband, his Yankee friend, Luke Tracy. Here resided the man who controlled his life and managed his pay. And here, too, he was not wanted for murder.

Horace had arranged for a bottle of cold champagne to be brought to them on the upper verandah and both men settled back in comfortable cane chairs facing out to the street. Horace raised his glass in a toast. 'The Queen. God bless her!'

'Saint Pat. And damn the British to hell!' Michael responded.

This irreverent response to the toast had become a long-standing private joke between them. They threw back a good mouthful of the cold, fizzy wine and settled into the chairs to stare vacantly into the blue sky beyond the railing, both men deep within memories that the shared ritual stirred in them.

'I should have shot you that night in Cooktown back in '74 when we first got to know each other,' Michael growled softly, and Horace chuckled at the recollection of confronting the dangerous, wily Irish-American who was in a rum-induced sleep.

'If you had you would never have got to see the exotic Orient. Or settled scores with Mort,' he replied. 'Or picked up that rather lucrative reward from Cochin China from the princess's eternally grateful family.'

'Maybe,' Michael pondered. 'Or maybe I would have had a life as a painter of beautiful landscapes instead of living constantly with the fear of someone putting a bullet in me.'

'You have done a lot for Her Majesty's Empire in the last ten years, Michael. That must count for something in your life.'

'I had little choice, Horace,' Michael retorted. 'You and your contacts in the colonies made sure of that. But that's all finished now. I'm home and no more of the past.'

Horace fidgeted with the cane and tapped the end with his fingers. He cleared his throat as he leant forward in his chair. 'Not quite, dear boy. Von Fellmann is back and I believe he is behind a second expedition to claim New Guinea for the Kaiser's empire.'

Michael stared at the timbered floor of the verandah. 'I came home to find what's left of my life, Horace. I came home to leave the ghosts of my past in other countries. I've had enough.'

'What would you do here, Michael? You have no real savings so you cannot retire to the life of a painter. Work for your sister? Work in a store, keeping ledgers of accounts? Do you think you could live like that after all you have done and seen? Do you think my contacts *could* protect you from that knock on the door in the middle of the night and some policeman with a warrant for your extradition to New South Wales to answer a charge of murder?'

'You mean *would* protect me against arrest, not *could*.'

Horace did not answer. He knew Michael was right. Once his usefulness to the profession was finished so, too, was any need to keep him out of the clutches of the law. 'Not my choice, dear boy. If it was within my power I would not be asking you to do this one last thing,' he apologised sadly. 'But after this I give you my word that the Crown will find a way of showing gratitude and repaying you for services rendered faithfully to the Queen. God knows you deserve some kind of reward for all that you have done.'

'Why not recruit someone else for the job?' Michael asked.

'Because a situation is unfolding in Sydney where your knowledge and talents will be best employed.'

'Sydney! Jesus, Mary and Joseph!' Michael exploded. 'That's the last place I want to go. If the traps are going to catch me then Sydney is the most likely place on earth. Why doesn't the bloody British government just annex the damned place themselves?'

Horace leant back in his chair and pursed his lips with an expression of annoyance. 'Because we have stupid men who refuse to listen to wiser men,' he replied. 'We have men in London, like Lord Derby at the Colonial Office, who advise Gladstone that the resolutions of the Intercolonial Convention held in Sydney a couple of years ago are the ravings of naive colonial premiers about the possible threats to future defence in the Pacific to Australia. Gladstone does not believe that Bismarck intends to annex New Guinea. He has even gone one step further to reassure the Germans that he has no intentions of acting on the resolutions for British annexations proposed by the Sydney conference. That is why.'

Michael was well aware of the Englishman's concern towards German imperial interests in the Pacific. Although his colleagues in the Foreign Office still looked towards France as the natural threat to English interests, Horace had been a lone voice nagging them about the rapid expansion of the German military machine in Europe. He could see years ahead to when Germany would have established trading posts in its annexed territories – which could easily be used to support future military operations against strategic British interests. To Horace the drive for imperial annexations was a dual drive for military supremacy in the inter-national chess game of strategic moves. The political leaders in Australia held the same views.

Horace had dedicated his very life to thwarting

the Germans in the Pacific. Michael Duffy's fluency in the German language had been an extremely valuable asset in Horace's undeclared war against German covert operations. The man who opposed Horace was Bismarck's intelligence chief in the Pacific, Baron Manfred von Fellmann.

Michael sighed and poured himself another champagne. 'If you know the bloody Germans are going to annex New Guinea why do you need me in Sydney?' he growled. 'It's obvious those fools in London aren't particularly interested in what happens out here.'

'They would be *if* I could prove von Fellmann is organising an expedition with the intention of seizing the northern half of New Guinea and the surrounding islands,' Horace replied quietly. 'But I have no proof. All that I know is that he has suddenly returned to Sydney as a representative for a German trading company and claims that he is setting up an expedition to go to the islands to indulge in trading with the natives.'

'That's possible, you know,' Michael interjected lamely. 'It's been over ten years since he last tried to get his hands on New Guinea. And he might be like me, a man who wants to find some peace in his last years of life. Trading in the islands can be very lucrative, you know.'

Horace laughed softly and shook his head. 'I doubt that the Baron ever required a contingent of German marines to protect him. Not the hero of the Franco–Prussian war.'

'How do you know he has marines with him?' Michael asked suspiciously. *Was it a ploy by Horace to justify sending him south?*

'We have both been military men, Michael. It is easy to recognise fellow soldiers – even if they do pose as German merchants.'

Michael could not argue with Horace's point. If the Prussian was in Sydney with a contingent of marines he was obviously on a covert mission of some kind.

'You realise, of course,' Michael said, 'that von Fellmann probably still holds somewhat of a grudge from my mission to blow up the *Osprey*.'

'I know all that. But I think you will find a way to renew your acquaintance with certain key people around the Baron.'

Michael flushed with a realisation. 'You mean Penelope, don't you?'

Horace nodded. 'Not only the Baroness, but also her lover of many years.'

'And who would that be?' Michael asked with an edge of jealousy.

Although he knew that Penelope was a woman of unlimited passion for the pleasures of the flesh and had taken many lovers, memories of her golden hair cascading on silk sheets, her milky white skin bathed in a sheen of perspiration, her body arching with her desire when he entered her came to him with bittersweet recollection. In all his travels and in all his years no woman – except possibly Fiona – had ever matched the beautiful wife of the Prussian aristocrat in the act of un-bridled coupling. And he had known many women's bodies in his turbulent life.

'Fiona White. Your son's mother,' Horace said softly.

His revelation caused the champagne flute

destined for Michael's lips to remain hanging in mid-air. 'Fiona!' The name came as a soft hiss from his lips. Fiona was Penelope's lover! He had no reason to doubt the Englishman's intelligence. Horace was rarely wrong.

'An interesting situation,' Horace said quietly, 'if I must say so myself. And you, the link between both women.'

'Penelope is in Sydney with Manfred?' Michael asked.

'Yes, she is staying at their house they keep on the harbour. I have reason to believe she spends a lot of time with Fiona while Manfred gets on with organising his mission. And from what I already know we have little time to send you south before he completes his plans to sail from Sydney. But you will have enough time to visit your sister before you leave,' Horace added kindly. 'I know you have a lot to catch up on concerning your son and family in Sydney, so I will leave you with the bottle and be on my way. I will see you here tomorrow at ten in the morning.'

He rose stiffly from his chair and stretched his back. The pain was through his whole body now and he badly needed the opium to help him forget the future and the painful reality of the present. 'This will be the last time for us both,' he said softly. 'I promise you that with my very life. You know, Michael,' Horace said in parting as he leant heavily on his cane, 'if you ever get to grow old and write your memoirs, they would make interesting reading. Especially with regards to your acquaintance with the ladies in your life.' He sighed a deep sigh and continued in a sad voice,

'But men like you and I do not have the same privileges of old generals retired to the comfort of their libraries to reminisce about the battles they fought. The battles we have fought over the years can never be told. We carry our memoirs in our heads, memories of good men and women who have died so that others might live in a secure peace. And I suppose it will always be so for us, and for those who follow us in future times – and future undeclared wars – for the information that keeps us one step ahead of our "friends". Until tomorrow, dear boy.'

Michael stared after the little Englishman hobbling along the verandah on his cane. He had little to show for his life, Michael brooded, except the many scars of old battles in foreign lands that marked his body; of memories of good and bad times, of terror and laughter. Of a family in Sydney who had buried him so long ago and to whom he could never reveal his existence for fear of the scandal it would bring down on them.

But he did have a son! A son who he had met briefly in Sydney for just a few minutes. At the time he had not known that he was talking to his own flesh and blood. Now all he had was the chemical image on a faded photograph of an eleven-year-old boy. What sort of man had he grown to be?

Michael was aware of the pact made with Lady Enid Macintosh and his cousin, Daniel Duffy. Kate had told him all as confided to her by Daniel. And Michael had to agree the deal was of personal benefit to his son's future. Where else could he get the best education in the world than England?

With whom else other than the powerful and wealthy Macintoshes could he have access to a financial empire rivalling the biggest in the colonies?

But a fundamental issue had to be resolved by his son alone – an issue that was more important than all the fame and fortune the Macintosh name could grant. He must never forget that he was born a Duffy and would die a Duffy. Part of being a Duffy meant retaining his allegiance to the Church of Rome and to deny either his name or religion was to deny his father.

Ahead of Michael now was the possible re-acquaintance with the woman who was the mother of his son. And there was also the prospect of meeting Penelope and her husband, Baron Manfred von Fellmann, one of the most dangerous men Michael had ever encountered in his violence-filled life. Ah yes, all this was ahead of him, and life was not a guaranteed thing in his own dangerous existence.

12

'Troop will stand at attention. Aaaa ... ten ... shun!' Gordon James drilled his men relentlessly on the dusty parade ground at the police barracks. The troopers' arms began to ache as they shouldered carbines, sloped arms and brought the carbines to the state of present. Gordon wanted to push the physical and mental resolve of his men to the point where they no longer thought of themselves as human creatures capable of feeling pain or distress. He had learned his technique of drilling men when he was a boy watching his father as barracks sergeant drill his troopers.

'That trooper there!' he bawled as he detected one of the white policemen waver. 'Third from the right. I haven't given the order for the attention yet. As a matter of fact I might even go for my evening supper and when I return give the order.'

All the troopers groaned softly lest they be heard. The way the new boss was driving them they half believed he would carry out his threat and leave them for an hour in the painful position. The wavering trooper cursed to himself for allowing the upstart bastard to see him fidget.

'Keep your eyes straight ahead. Don't blink unless I say so!'

The tableau of human statues waited patiently for the final order to stand at ease, thus releasing the tautness of stretched muscles. But the order did not come and the troopers remained frozen at attention. The officer who tortured their resolve was ominously silent. Then his voice came to their ears like the hiss of a snake warning of its impending strike.

'I know you think,' he said, 'that the Kalkadoon are noble warriors who rule this country, who can strike at will and send you all scuttling back to the barracks to sit around like old women bemoaning the hopelessness of it all. Well, this is my first meeting with you as a troop and, as you can see, no glorious speeches as my way of introducing myself. Just this drill and a lot more to follow. And at the end of two weeks I promise you that you will be glad to go out and disperse the darkies and I also know that you will be the best Mounted Troop in the colony if not Her Majesty's Empire at the end of two weeks. Staaand . . . at . . . ease. Too bloody slow! We'll do it again until you are all able to get yourselves together.'

They came to the attention and stood sweating with the setting sun in their faces. Men squinted to focus on the figure silhouetted against the orange ball, as Gordon had deliberately placed his men with the sun in their faces. He could see their discomfort but gained no pleasure from it. 'Second trooper from the left. Yes, you. Where is Sergeant Rossi?' he barked and the second trooper from the left pulled a puzzled frown and made a move to seek out the barracks sergeant who had been exempt from the drill. 'Don't look for him, keep your eyes straight ahead,' Gordon bawled. 'Tell me where Sergeant Rossi is now.'

'Not here. Sah!' the trooper responded as he stared into the fiery orange ribbon of light that stretched along the western horizon. Black swirling stars clouded his eyes and as he fought to clear his vision the trooper suddenly saw a second figure to the left side of the officer and standing ten paces away. It was Sergeant Rossi! 'Sergeant Rossi is to my front, sah!' he replied somewhat sheepishly.

'If Sergeant Rossi had been a dirty big Kalkadoon, trooper,' Gordon said in an almost conversational and compassionate tone, 'with a dirty big spear, then you would probably have been a dead man by now. And that would mean I would have to write home to your dear mother to tell her lies about your sobriety and respect for the weaker sex. For a God-fearing man as myself such a letter could send me to hell. But I would have at least the consolation of finding you there.'

Gordon's short speech on the drinking and whoring reputation of his white troopers, and the comparison of size of the very short Italian sergeant – who had once fought against Garibaldi – with the giant Kalkadoon warriors, brought a snicker of laughter from the troopers standing at ease. *Maybe the new boss might be all right.*

Gordon let the snicker of laughter go unchecked. He knew he had to give a little to get a lot from them in two short weeks, and he also knew instinctively that he was winning them over, as he had the squatters and townspeople earlier that afternoon. Sure, the Kalkadoon might have them frightened. But as far as he was concerned the tribesmen were little different to any others he had dispersed in the past. 'The lesson I hope you have just learned from my question concerning Sergeant Rossi's whereabouts is obvious to you. If it's not then I will tell you. When you are tracking myalls beware of letting the sun blind you in the late afternoon. Keep your eyes always away from the setting sun or else the thing you thought was a black tree trunk might suddenly move and spear you. Sar'nt Rossi!'

'Sah!'

The barracks sergeant hovering nearby came stiffly to attention and snapped a smart salute.

'Your parade, Sergeant.'

'Sah!'

'Give the men drill until the sun is below the horizon, Sergeant,' Gordon said softly to the little Italian with the huge moustache that curled with wax at its ends. 'Then make sure their carbines are cleaned and ready for inspection before they retire tonight. I will inspect them at nine o'clock sharp.'

'Sah!' The ends of the moustache bristled with efficiency as he stepped back and saluted Gordon, who returned the salute with the lazy affectation of officers.

'Paaraade. Aaaa . . . ten . . . shon!'

As Gordon walked away from the troopers to return to the office that had once been Sub Inspector Potter's he felt the wave of satisfaction that comes after a good drill session. Yes, he had learned well from his father how to handle men. Ah, but that he could do the same with Sarah Duffy! As Gordon walked away Trooper Peter Duffy watched him and wondered at how things would be between them now.

After the evening meal Peter marched over to the office occupied by Gordon. He knocked at the rough-hewn, timber door and announced his presence. A muffled voice granted him permission to enter and Peter stepped inside. Gordon was sitting at a plain desk scattered with paper.

He glanced around the tiny office to see an old picture of a young Queen Victoria on the wall behind Gordon; a fly-specked surveyor's map of the district was pinned beside the obligatory depiction of the reigning monarch, and on a peg behind the door to the office hung Gordon's belt and pistol.

He could see Gordon had been drafting requisitions for supplies and writing reports on the situation as he had found it upon his arrival in the town. Peter stood at attention as Gordon dabbed his pen in an ink bottle and scrawled his signature at the end of a requisition. He did not look up to greet Peter's entry but continued to sign the report. Finally he said ominously, 'Haven't you forgotten something?'

Puzzled, Peter frowned. 'I don't think so,' he said slowly as he cast his thoughts about for what he may have forgotten. He was dressed in the uniform as regulations required.

'You forgot to salute when you came in, Trooper Duffy,' Gordon said. He placed the pen aside and looked up at the young policeman standing loosely to attention before him.

'Sorry, Mahmy,' Peter replied as he stiffened and saluted.

Gordon was not wearing head cover and returned the salute as protocol required by sitting stiffly in his chair with his hands on his knees.

'That's better,' he said less formally. 'As much as we have been friends for years I know you will understand that discipline must be maintained regardless of the personal relationship that may exist between us.'

'I understand, Mahmy,' Peter replied formally to hide the hurt he felt for his longtime boyhood friend's apparent coolness towards him.

'Take a seat, Peter, and stop calling me Mahmy. Only the charcoals in the troop address me as Mahmy.'

'I'm half-charcoal, sir,' Peter replied with an undisguised bitter edge as he sat stiffly on the government issue chair in front of the desk. 'Maybe I should address you as Mahmy half the time.'

'In this office and outside this office you call me sir. I know that is hard for you but we both belong to Her Majesty's constabulary and we knew the rules when we joined.'

Peter could not bring himself to acknowledge the rebuke. So this was how things would be between them from now on. Gordon had changed dramatically. His martinet behaviour was so unlike the larrikin boy Peter remembered growing up with. They'd been as close as any brothers. When Peter became aware of the subtle and disturbing changes early in their enlistment, he speculated that Gordon's behaviour was driven by his friend's need to eclipse his legendary father's reputation. It was as if the son were out to prove himself a better man. Peter shook his head. Henry had been a man who he had looked up to in lieu of his own father's absence. He was certainly no martinet and now Gordon's formal reprimand to an old friend simply reinforced Peter's opinion. Gordon had become a horse's arse.

'I've read the report you submitted on the massacre of Inspector Potter's patrol while I was at Townsville,' Gordon said quietly. 'Damned thing to happen to a fine officer, so I've been told, or was he such a fine officer?' The question was delivered with the two men's eyes locking and Peter realised that in his own way Gordon was reaching out to re-establish a trust between them. His request to comment on the conduct of an officer was one not normally made of mere troopers.

'He was a bloody fool,' Peter answered. 'He had no idea of how good the Kalkadoon are at fighting on their own lands.'

'Our lands,' Gordon corrected. 'The lands the Kalkadoon occupy have been legally leased, or purchased, by the men who we are here to protect.'

Peter did not reply to his officer's view on the matter of ownership. He was confused himself as he was a member of the Native Mounted Police and thus a representative of the Crown. But he was also half-Aboriginal and it was this half that secretly sympathised with the plight of the tribesmen who he also hunted. Although he had received the best education his aunt Kate Tracy could buy for him, white society still considered him a darkie, a nigga or part myall. As a trooper, he was a half-caste charcoal.

'I would like you to elaborate,' Gordon said reasonably, 'on why you considered Inspector Potter's decision to go into the hills in pursuit of the Kalkadoon a mistake.'

Peter leant forward in his chair. 'Inspector Potter underestimated the Kalkadoon. He treated them as inferior fighters and that cost him and the patrol their lives.'

'But you survived, Peter. How?'

The question took Peter unawares. He had never included his contact with Wallarie in any report. How could he alone survive such a cleverly executed ambush?

'Wallarie saved me,' the young trooper answered softly. 'He was with them.'

Gordon winced as if slapped in the face. Wallarie! The warrior who had taught them both the ways of the Darambal people when he and Peter had been boys. The sorcerer who had so cunningly eluded the Native Mounted Police for years and had become part of the frontier folklore. The man whose very name and existence carried the mystique of an ancient curse on his father. The being which was both friend and foe. 'Wallarie is alive?'

Peter nodded and Gordon stared down at the desk as he gathered his thoughts and feelings. He had been locked in a terrible turmoil of indecision but was now clear as to what he must do. His duty to the law went far beyond any personal feeling he may have had for his old mentor in the ways of the indigenous people. 'When we capture him he will no doubt be tried and hanged for the crimes he committed when he rode with your father in Burkesland those years past.'

'You cannot capture a spirit man,' Peter said softly. 'No-one will ever capture Wallarie.'

'He may be many things but I fear that your darkie half clouds your judgment,' Gordon said with an edge of anger. 'Wallarie is *still* only just another blackfella wanted for the murder of white men.'

'He was your friend once, and saved your father when he had good enough reason to let him die on the spears of the Kyowarra. Do you not remember that day when we were kids?'

'I remember,' Gordon struggled. 'But we have a duty to the law of this colony and you must always remember that too if you want to take your place alongside us.'

'Alongside *us*?' Peter countered. 'Not *with us*. No, not with us, because despite all my education, and the fact that half my blood is a whitefella's blood, I will always be a blackfella to you. Just like the way you think about my sister.'

'Shut your mouth before you say something you might regret,' Gordon flared. Peter had touched on a subject that made the young officer most vulnerable. 'Just drop the subject about Sarah now. I'm warning you as a friend and not as your superior officer.'

But Peter was angry. So angry that even if the warning had been directed from Gordon as his superior officer it would have still gone unheeded. The matter of Gordon's desire for his beautiful sister had festered in Peter for some time now. The three had grown up together and Sarah had been equal to them in the rough and tumble of children's games. But as they grew older Peter had noticed the change in his sister's attitude to Gordon. She began to avoid the rough games of the boys and Peter became aware that his younger sister acted strangely around his best friend. When he was old enough to experience the effect the opposite sex had on him he became aware of what was behind her behaviour towards Gordon and he was also acutely aware of where it might go. Now he was angry enough to bring the matter to a head and release the poison between them.

'No. I won't shut up. I'll tell you just how it is with us blackfellas. My sister is a lady who can do something with her life. She has brains and a lot of eligible blokes around Townsville will "forgive" her for being half-caste. In fact, they would marry her. But she mopes around, hoping that some day you will ask her to be your wife, except you are frightened that if you marry her your chances of promotion in the Mounted Police will be a lot less if it is known you have a gin as your wife. No, you will end up using her to satisfy your own needs and, in time, cast her off to marry some respectable white woman. Then my sister will be just another darkie gin around town giving herself for a cheap drink. She . . .'

Gordon sat trembling, white with rage behind his desk. *Peter had gone too far!*

'You don't know what's between Sarah and me,'

he interjected with quiet fury. 'You might be her brother, but you don't have any idea what my plans are concerning her.'

'Do you?' Peter snarled.

How had the situation come to this? Had it always been the real reason for their meeting? Had the issue of Sarah's future really been the reason to talk privately? Had all else that transpired in the office been a mere formality?

As Gordon glared at Peter sitting across from him the guilt that touching on the truth elicits in a man's face was obvious. All that he had said concerning his attitudes to Sarah were true! Yes, he wanted her. But at the same time he was pragmatic enough to realise what could happen to his career should he profess his love to the beautiful young woman! 'I . . .' He struggled to find words and was no longer an officer talking to a subordinate but a man defending himself against the bitterness of a brother who loved his sister. He leant forward and raised his hand as if to ward off the piercing glare of his boyhood friend. The room shrunk away as they were together again laughing and loving the bush they grew up in, Peter teasing him over his sister's obviously amorous attentions. He fought to find words in his defence and was saved by the urgent rap on the door. Gordon recovered his composure and sat up in his chair. 'Who is it?'

'Sar'nt Rossi, sir.'

'Come in.'

The door opened and the Italian police sergeant entered the room in an agitated state. His dark eyes bulged and his moustache seemed to bristle.

He was so agitated that he forgot to salute. Gordon overlooked the lapse in protocol as he accepted his senior non commissioned officer as a naturally excitable Latin.

'Scusi, sir, but a blackfella 'e bringa message to barracks.'

'What blackfella, Sergeant Rossi?' Gordon asked, in an attempt to calm the little sergeant down.

'A blackfella no trooper know but say might be a Darambal man.'

Gordon exchanged a sharp glance with Peter who appeared as equally surprised at the apparent tribal identity of the Aboriginal messenger.

'Wallarie?' Gordon hissed and Peter raised his eyebrows and nodded. *It could be no-one else!* 'Where is the blackfella now?' he asked as he rose from his chair.

'He go away,' the sergeant answered. 'He talka to a charcoal trooper, Trooper John, before he go, tell him that when you ready the big chief of the Kalkadoon ready to fight you. He say the big chief of Kalkadoon not 'fraid of white man. He kill alla troopers whoa come lookin' for him.'

'Very good, Sergeant Rossi,' Gordon acknowledged calmly. 'Now get the troopers to saddle up and go and catch the blackfella who brought the message to us.'

Sergeant Rossi rolled his eyes and shrugged his shoulders. 'Black troopers 'fraid of the Darambal man. They say man a debil debil. They say he turn into a baal spirit.'

'You tell the charcoal troopers that the Queen pays them to hunt baal spirits along with live blackfellas who have the cheek to threaten me. Is that clear, Sergeant Rossi?'

'Sah!'

'Good. Then go and get the men to saddle up. Scour the northern approaches to the town as that's the most likely route he would have taken to get here from the hills.'

The sergeant saluted smartly, turned on his heel, and went directly to the barracks to rouse his troopers. When he was gone Gordon excused Peter with a wave of his hand and he slumped back into his chair behind the desk.

'We won't catch him,' Peter said as he opened the door to join the troop in the hunt for Wallarie.

'Why shouldn't we?' Gordon snapped irritably. Somehow the fact that the Darambal warrior had chosen to deliver the threat from the Kalkadoon chief had an ominous ring to it, like a bell chiming doom. Or was it that there was a link with the man who now stood in the doorway and his sister? They were, after all, half-Darambal.

'We won't catch him because Wallarie knows our white ways. Remember, my father taught him.'

With the parting barb Peter closed the door behind him leaving the officer alone with his hidden fears. Sarah and Wallarie. Love and a shattered friendship.

13

Willie and the children felt awkward standing on the wide, polished timber verandah of Solomon and Judith Cohen's expensively comfortable home. They were covered in the dust of three weeks' travelling to Townsville and Willie felt out of place as the Cohens lavished attention on the three children of Ben and his mother.

Judith knelt to brush away Rebecca's straggly locks. Willie stood self-consciously aside, twisting his broad-brimmed floppy hat in his hands once he had solemnly shaken hands with the Jewish merchant whose chain of businesses now spread across real estate, transport, stocks and shares as well as the stores he and his wife had established in the rapidly growing towns of the Colony of Queensland.

When Judith turned her maternal attentions on the two boys Solomon stepped in to defend their masculine pride from the silly outpourings of a doting woman.

'Oi, but the boys are too grown up for such things,' he said as he ushered them to comfortable chairs on the verandah. 'Look how they have grown since we last saw them, Judith.'

Tears of joy welled in the tall, dark woman's eyes as she continued to fuss over little Rebecca who lapped up the attention and the clean, luxurious surroundings of the sprawling Cohen house. It was set amongst well-watered gardens of imported and native trees and was an oasis in a town that had ruthlessly cut down its trees to provide timber for building and fuel.

The four travellers were grateful for the cold milk and sandwiches a maid brought to them on a silver salver and suddenly Willie remembered Ben's letter. He rifled through his trouser pockets to locate the folded sheets of paper with his free hand and when he found the letter thrust the dirty and crumpled paper towards Solomon. 'Ben gave me this to give to you,' he mumbled, biting hungrily into the delicious freshly baked bread.

Solomon retrieved his reading spectacles from his waistcoat pocket to read the childish scrawl of his wife's nephew as Willie and the three children devoured the sandwiches. They were a pleasant change from tinned beef and the occasional kangaroo they'd shot for the cooking pot whilst on the long trek from Cloncurry across the seemingly endless plains of desiccated grass and dry trees.

Rebecca sniffled as she ate and wiped her nose with the back of her hand. Jonathan reached over and pulled her hand down with a little reproving scowl. It did not pay to look like ignorant country kids in the midst of town people, he thought. Judith suggested that they might buy them some ice-cream later in town and the undreamed of luxury made the children's eyes pop with impatient anticipation.

Even Saul's reaction, which had been suspiciously reserved until the offer, was that of a kid who had forgotten for a moment the harshness of life on Jerusalem. Ice-cream was a mere fantasy on the long, hot days in the bush. Although he had never tasted it he had a fixed idea what its cold, creamy taste would be like.

Solomon read the letter and carefully folded it. 'It will be good to have the laughter of children around here, Judith,' he said as he patted Saul on the head affectionately. 'With our Deborah in Europe.'

Children! Saul thought angrily. He was no bloody child. No, he would return to Jerusalem as soon as he got the chance. Jonathan and Rebecca could stay but his place was with his father riding the bush and mustering the small herd of cattle.

'You will stay with us, Willie,' Judith said as she guided Rebecca along the verandah towards the servants' quarters located at the rear of the house in a miniature replica of the main house itself. In the laundry the little girl could be scrubbed and dressed in one of Deborah's old dresses that had been carefully stored by Judith for sentimental reasons. Her daughter had grown to be a lithe, dark-eyed beauty whose voice was enthralling the audiences of Europe in the great opera houses. And her fame as a singer had spread to the Americas where she was destined to tour within months.

Sometimes Judith would take out the carefully

stored little dresses and stare at them. How had the time gone so fast in her life; one day a rowdy little girl playing rough games in the Queensland dust with equally rowdy frontier children, then the next day, a sophisticated young lady performing for the crowned heads of Europe. Judith had always known fame and fortune was her daughter's destiny.

Scrubbed, and outfitted in one of Deborah's childhood dresses, Rebecca's brothers hardly recognised their little sister who scowled at their teasing grins. But the grins quickly faded when Judith said firmly, 'Your turn next Jonathan and Saul.'

They cringed at the assault on their manliness. How had it come to the tall stern woman ordering their lives like they were little boys? At least these were Saul's thoughts, if not his brother's.

'I don't want Missus Tracy meeting you in your present grubby state tonight when we dine with her,' Judith said as she gripped the bar of soap in one hand and grabbed for Saul's collar with the other.

Willie also washed and changed into the clean working clothes that Solomon presented him with as a gift from the store. He gratefully accepted the clothes and now sat at Kate Tracy's table gazing at the woman who, although bordering on her fourth decade, remained as serenely beautiful as the woman he and his mother had first met on the Palmer goldfields ten years earlier. She was a woman of great beauty, unfaded by time and toil. But she also had a compassion that had not been diminished by power, prestige and her rise to a vast fortune. Next to his mother, Kate occupied the most important role in the young man's life.

Willie could not help noticing the heavy swelling of Kate's pregnancy. So she looked as if she might finally realise her greatest dream, he thought. To have her own child. He was aware of the tragedy that stalked Kate's life.

'Willie, help yourself to as much lamb as you like,' Kate said kindly. 'I suppose it will be a change from all the beef you have been living on at Jerusalem.'

'Thank you, Missus Tracy,' he replied softly.

Kate cast him a look of sympathy. The poor boy was suffering for the loss of his mother in a suffocating cloak of silent grief. Kate understood death. She had experienced so much in her own life. Her father murdered by the then Native Mounted Police Lieutenant Morrison Mort on the orders of the Scots' squatter Sir Donald Macintosh. Her eldest brother fatally shot by a trooper from the same police years later in Burkesland. And the death of her own babies. She had learned to come to grips with their untimely deaths. But not with the memories.

The dinner in the elegantly spacious house that was the home of Luke and Kate passed in a kind of subdued politeness. But the death of Jennifer hung over the meal. Willie sat silently at the table, picking at his food with a fork while the Cohens and Kate discussed their mutual business arrangements and future plans for expansions as if conducting a general meeting of directors. Together the unlikely union of Irish-born woman and English-born Jews had proved to be extremely lucrative and together they had prospered.

The links between Kate and the Cohens went beyond mere financial considerations, however. Their relationship was more like the closeness of family. It had been Kate's guiding hand that had steered Judith's sister's son Benjamin Rosenblum to learn the tough ways of the Queensland frontier and eventually invest for himself in a large tract of cattle country north of Cloncurry. And through Kate, Ben had first met Jennifer Harris who would become his wife and bear him three children.

As the Cohens shifted from business to gossip about rival entrepreneurs Kate noticed Willie's melancholy. She had helped rear the young man as a boy when Jenny had worked for her as a nanny to the children of her dead bushranger brother, Tom Duffy, and his Darambal wife Mondo. As orphans the children had been placed in Kate's care and grew up with the best education and all the love of a good family.

Kate had always considered Peter and Sarah as she would her own. She sighed when she thought about Tim. Always a strange boy, he had simply disappeared one night three years earlier. The note he left on his bed said he was going out west to find work. Since then nothing had been heard of him. Nor had there been any messages to his brother and sister.

Kate reminded herself to talk to Willie as soon as she could get him alone. And she wished Luke was with her to share her thoughts on the young man's grief.

'Ben has written a letter asking us to keep the

children until he is able to get on his feet,' Solomon said, interrupting Kate's thoughts about her husband. 'He has not specified a time for them to return to him.'

'That could be a good idea while the myalls are rampaging in the district,' Kate replied, bringing her thoughts back into line with the conversation across the table. 'He could hardly leave the boys and Rebecca at the house while he was off working the cattle.'

'He had *me* to help him,' Willie said softly. 'But it would have been hard to look after Becky.'

'Quite right!' Solomon replied with an embarrassed cough and realised that he had been guilty of excluding Willie as a member of the family.

'Hasn't Luke gone west to Burketown?' Judith asked Kate with just the hint of concern for her friend.

'Yes, he rode out a week ago.'

'Won't his travels take him close to the Kalkadoon country?'

Kate had not wanted to dwell on the possible danger her husband was exposing himself to. She had tried to convince him to take a boat to the Gulf town but he only smiled and kissed her on the forehead with reassurances that he was more than capable of looking after himself. 'Luke's a tough old dog,' she answered confidently.

But a haunting memory of an almost forgotten conversation with Judith came back to her. It had been many years earlier when Kate had been hurt and angry with the tall American. They had been in Judith's tiny dining room in her house at

Rockhampton and the subject of men like police sergeant Henry James and the American prospector had been raised by Judith – men whose fate was a lonely and forgotten grave in the vast plains of the western frontier. *No memorials to such men*, Judith had commented and Kate had felt the chill of an omen for her American. Now she shuddered with repressed fear. 'Luke will return in good time,' she said, as if to convince herself, and Judith nodded her agreement.

When the dinner was over the Cohens made ready to leave in their buggy with Ben's children. Willie had ridden over to Kate's house on the dray horse and so lingered to chat with Sarah who had engaged him before he could swing into the saddle and ride away.

Kate waved from her verandah as Solomon flicked the reins to the buggy and the fine-looking harness horse stepped out. She turned her attention to Sarah and could see her pretty niece talking to Willie. Kate regretted that she had not had the chance to speak to him after dinner but the Cohens had promised ice-cream and the shop would soon be closing.

He swung himself into the saddle and rode after the buggy that bumped and swayed down Kate's tree-lined driveway. Sarah waved after him, turned and walked towards the verandah. Kate thought how beautiful Sarah had become. Tom and Mondo would have been proud of their daughter, she thought as she watched her approach with a frown clouding her dark face that had the exotic sheen of her mother and the fine features of her father. Her full lips, slightly agape as she frowned, revealed ivory white teeth. But the most startling feature the young woman possessed was her light blue eyes. Many men had trouble accepting that the beautiful and desirable woman was in fact of Darambal blood when they gazed enraptured into her face. Her long dark hair was piled in a tight bun on top of her head and she walked with the easy grace inherited from her mother's people. 'Is something wrong?' she asked as Sarah climbed the three steps to the verandah.

'Why do you ask?' Sarah said.

'Because I could see you frowning.'

Sarah paused and turned to gaze at the horse-man who rode after the buggy. 'I wanted to tell Willie how sorry I was to hear of Jenny's death, Aunt Kate,' she replied. 'And he said it didn't matter. He is acting very strange.'

'People have different ways of protecting themselves from the pain of grief. I suppose Willie's answer is his way. He loved his mother very much.'

'I know,' Sarah said turning back to her aunt. 'But he also said that he was going to find his father and settle with him. I said, "Do you mean Ben?" and he said, "No, my real father." Then he said to me that he was never returning to Jerusalem.'

Kate once again felt the old demon of fear. His real father! So Jenny must have told her son about Granville White. No good could come with the revelation about the man who Michael said was in one way or another an evil and dangerous man in his own right! She would ask Michael's advice on the matter when he came again to visit her that evening.

Already her big brother had won the heart of his niece Sarah, who had swooned with girlish infatuation when she first met her legendary uncle the previous day on a brief visit. *Ah, but her brother could charm women of all ages!*

The sun raised its soft and peaceful glow along the western horizon above the still bush. Flocks of screeching pink and grey galahs wheeled overhead, causing Kate to glance skywards. Where would Luke camp tonight? By some waterhole, thinking of her? Or had he reached the safety of a homestead?

She dismissed the thoughts that had come to worry at her mind and glanced down at her niece's feet. Kate frowned as she could see that Sarah was not wearing shoes as a young lady should, a remnant of her childhood that lingered. 'Go and put on your shoes, young lady,' she said firmly – but not harshly. 'Your uncle Michael will be here soon and he just might think his niece is not all that grown up,' she added. The young woman pouted when ordered to put on shoes but beamed at the mention of her newly met uncle who had promised to bring her a present.

Sarah skipped across the verandah, causing Kate to smile. Not quite a woman, she thought wistfully. But no longer a little girl tagging after her brothers and Gordon James anymore either.

14

Inside the cavernous merchant depot of Wong &
Sons the visitor was transported by the scents and
sights to the Orient itself. Due to his time spent in
Cochin China, Shanghai, Hong Kong and
Singapore Michael Duffy was familiar with the
fragrant herbs and exotic spices. In fact, stepping
inside the cool, cavernous shed that was piled to
the roof with crates, jars and cedar boxes came as
a relief from the fetid smells of Townsville's
sewage.

Michael adjusted his eyes to the dim interior of
the depot and focused on a solidly built Eurasian
man, arguing with a smaller Chinese man. The
Eurasian, as tall as himself, was berating the other
in the Chinese language and had not noticed
Michael enter his store.

'Hello, you son of a turtle,' Michael said loudly.
The Eurasian swung his gaze on the man who
would dare question his parentage with the old
Chinese expression of insult. 'And begorrah it's a
grand day for the Irish. Even half-Irish chinks,'
Michael added to his insult.

'Michael Duffy, you old bastard!' John Wong roared and completely forgot the Chinese merchant he had been taking to task over his exorbitant demand on the price of ginger. 'You're still alive!' In great strides the son of an Irish mother and Chinese father closed the distance between them and gripped Michael's shoulders with his huge hands. With a silly fixed grin of happiness he stared into Michael's face. 'How the bloody hell are you?'

'Still alive, despite friends like you and Horace Brown in my life,' Michael replied with an equally stupid grin of his own. 'Bejesus, John, you've grown fat living the life of a prosperous merchant.'

'And I intend to get fatter, you worthless bastard,' John growled fondly in response to Michael's observation on his thickening waist line. Although just thirty years old he was beginning to show the physical signs of a contented middle-aged man. 'So forget any suggestions that I might help you and Horace Brown out on some hare-brained scheme.'

'John, John!' Michael replied with feigned hurt for the rebuke from his friend. 'Would I visit an old mate to ask any favours except you find a bottle and we share it for old times' sake? And none of that cheap rice wine either.'

John released the grip on his friend's shoulders and turned his attention to the Chinese merchant who stared curiously at the big European with the black leather patch over one eye. John said something to the merchant who scowled and broke into a torrent of Chinese that caused John to respond with a growl, 'And the same to your ancestors too!'

Then he turned to Michael and led him to the back of the store and into a tiny room cluttered with ledgers and odd jade curios from the exotic East. He motioned to Michael to sit down on a crate jammed against the wall and rifled through his ornately carved teak desk to find the bottle of gin he kept for emergencies such as Michael Duffy turning up in his life. He then located two small bowls into which he poured the fiery liquid. He raised his bowl. 'Cheers and God bless Saint Patrick and my illustrious Chinese ancestors,' he intoned with a grin spreading across his handsome face. Michael responded by throwing back a good mouthful of the clear, spiced liquid. 'So when did you get back?' John asked cautiously. 'Have you been to see Kate?'

'Yesterday,' Michael answered. 'I will be seeing her again later this evening.'

'Have you seen Horace Brown yet?'

'Yes, but he looks pretty sick.'

John nodded gravely. The little Englishman often visited him to sit and talk in Chinese. Their friendship was based on mutual professional links to the past – links that John hoped to keep well and truly in his past as he got on with the job of building up his importing business from the proceeds of a ransom for the return of the beautiful Cochinese girl to her family years earlier.

Horace had kept John informed of Michael's life in the Far East. At least he'd told him as much as he thought it was safe to tell. Lately Horace's visits had become less frequent as the cancer took a greater grip on him and the opium John supplied had less effect.

'I don't think he will see the year out,' John said in a sombre tone. 'A passing of an era in our lives, old friend.'

'The bloody Foreign Office will soon find a replacement,' Michael said bitterly. 'The bastards don't really care about him.'

John raised his eyebrows. He could have sworn that Michael was growing attached to the Englishman who had so often placed his life at risk. 'So what are your plans for when he is gone?' he asked. 'You know that you will always have a place here with me.'

Michael smiled sadly at his friend who sat leaning forward behind his desk. 'Thanks, old friend. But I have to see what happens in the next few weeks before I go making any plans.'

From his answer John knew Michael's life working for Horace Brown had not finished and he guessed why Michael had come to see him. 'I have a lot of responsibility here, Michael,' he countered before Michael could broach the subject. 'I can't help you in whatever you've come for.'

'Ahh. You know me too well,' Michael replied with a sigh. 'I did come here to ask for your help, as you obviously knew I would.'

John's expression clouded. Commonsense dictated that he avoid any professional relationship with the Irishman, but loyalty tugged at his conscience. He owed much to his friend: his present prosperity and his beautiful Cochinese wife who had borne him two healthy sons and a daughter.

'What sort of help?' he asked in a weak voice as he knew the eye fixed on him bored into his soul and sought the roots of true friendship.

'Nothing especially risky,' Michael answered, bringing the bowl to his lips with both hands. 'Just a trip south to Sydney to expand your business. That's all.'

It sounded so simple yet John knew full well everything in his friend's life had an element of risk. 'And the bloody rest,' he growled, annoyed at how easily he had committed himself to helping the soldier of fortune.

Or was it that John missed the wild days of living on the edge and hated admitting that to himself! He had a family and thriving business and his wife would never understand even though she would obediently accept any decision he made as she was, after all, the dutiful wife on account of her Confucian heritage. But his children were growing up with minds of their own, a problem they inherited from their European blood and contact with the unruly European children with whom they mixed. They, too, would object to him going away.

Not only was his family the centre of his universe, John was a respectable businessman who had gained a place in the social circles of Townsville. He had a membership with the local horseracing club and owned a stable of horses himself. He was also respected for his astute knowledge in picking thoroughbred winners for the track and was the link between those European businessmen trading with the Chinese community and establishing the lucrative links in the Far East. The Chinese community in Townsville respected the big man for his intimate knowledge of their ways. John now stared at Michael silently as he weighed up the involvement that could cost him his life.

'Horace thinks the Germans are going to annex New Guinea,' Michael said quietly. 'This is our last job. I promise.'

'So why go to Sydney? You could get yourself hanged down there.'

'No choice. That's where von Fellmann is.'

John had never met the Baron but he knew a lot about him from what he had been told by Michael – and what he knew chilled him. The Prussian was a ruthless man. 'Then if the traps don't get you von Fellmann will,' he commented sarcastically. 'Or someone like him.'

'That might be so,' Michael mused. 'But no-one lives forever. Only the memory of who we were lives on in our children and their children.' The echo of something he had said before resounded silently in the tiny office. Michael shifted uncomfortably in his chair. Would his own son ever remember him?

'Damn you, Duffy, you bastard!' John swore. 'You know I will back you. When do we leave for Sydney?'

Michael grinned at his old partner. 'As soon as you have lied to your wife about your reasons to sail to Sydney. I've already purchased your ticket.'

When Michael arrived to visit his sister, his niece Sarah was not disappointed with the gift that he had promised. She gaped at the beautiful dress and made little noises of surprised joy. It was the finest dress she had ever seen! For Kate he had brought a volume of poetry by the Australian poet Henry Kendall entitled *Songs from the Mountains*.

Sarah gave her uncle a crushing hug to thank him and then skipped away to try on the dress. She would find an excuse to be wearing it next time Gordon came home on leave.

When she was gone Michael followed Kate to the front verandah. There they could relax in the cooling evening breeze and share a bottle of rum. Kate was no stranger to the drink. She had worked the tough tracks with the bullock wagons and a tot of rum at the end of the day lifted her exhausted mind and body beyond mud and dust.

She gazed lovingly at the big man lounging in a chair on the verandah and thought wistfully of all the terrible things he must have seen and done in his tormented life. His youth was gone and his dreams to pursue a life as a painter almost forgotten. Oh Michael, my poor darling brother, will you ever find the peace you so much deserve, she thought as she watched him gazing into the soft shadows of the warm night. 'You know you still have the beguiling ways about you that broke Aunt Bridget's and my heart when we were young,' Kate said as she took a seat beside her brother. 'The young ladies who worked for Uncle Frank fighting over you. My lady friends begging for an introduction.'

Michael laughed softly at his sister's flattery. 'That had to be a long time ago,' he said with a grin. 'Not much call with the ladies for a one-eyed battle scarred man in the autumn of his life. A man without a respectable job and not much love either,' he continued quietly. 'Just the occasional snatch of paid love in some Chinese brothel.'

His frankness did not shock his sister. She sensed that she was one of the few women in his life to whom he could feel free to express his thoughts. 'You can settle down and leave the past behind. There is always a job here, as you know,' Kate prompted gently. 'Luke thinks you are one of the finest men he has ever known. God knows why when you almost got him killed twice,' she added with a touch of exasperation.

Luke and Michael had worked together for Horace Brown to foil the Germans annexing the southern part of the New Guinea island. Then they'd mounted a rescue expedition for the Cochinese girl held by Morrison Mort.

'Wish I could, Kate,' Michael sighed. 'But I have one more job to do before I could even consider your generous offer.'

'It's that evil little Englishman again, isn't it?' Kate spat as she realised her brother was a long way from finding peace. 'And I hope you haven't come to recruit my husband for whatever he has planned for you.'

'I've done with the recruiting, Kate. I only need John Wong and he has agreed to go with me to Sydney.'

'Sydney! Are you mad?'

'Probably,' he replied as he raised his glass and held it up against the rising moon. 'But I have a need to confront my past as well as doing what needs to be done.'

Kate stared at her brother in the dim light of the

verandah, watching the shadows of his face to see if he had changed expression. His identity as Michael Duffy was one of the worst kept secrets in the Colony of Queensland, she thought with growing alarm. Surely the rumours of his existence would have filtered to the police in Sydney by now? 'By confronting your past, I suspect you mean seeing *Missus* Fiona White,' she said with the emphasis on the married status of the woman her brother had first loved.

'Fiona. Yes,' he said dreamily as he continued to stare through the glass at the huge yellow moon. 'And others.'

Kate had sworn to her brother to keep the fact of his existence a secret from all other members of the family. As far as they were concerned he had been buried and the mourning had been done with. Kate had disagreed with him but remained true to the oath she had sworn. 'It might be better that you leave the past behind,' she warned gently. 'When they are disturbed, matters of the past have an ugly way of changing the present in ways we might not like.'

'That's for me to discover, Kate,' he answered firmly to deter any further sermonising on the subject. 'But I won't be taking any stupid chances that might put myself or John at risk. No, I have a job to do that just happens to mean I have to confront certain aspects of my past. And yes, Fiona is one of those aspects, but not through choice.'

'Whatever you do always remember you have a son you will most probably meet one day,' his sister reminded him. She knew what her wild brother was capable of. 'I doubt you would want him to lead the life you have now.'

Michael threw back his head and laughed. 'A bloody British officer! My son is a bloody British soldier. What would Da say if he were alive and knew his grandson was wearing the uniform of his old enemies? And you worry about him finding out about *my* life!'

'That's not what I meant, Michael,' Kate said quietly. 'And it seems fate has conspired to lead him on a path not unlike your own violent destiny. Don't you think it is strange that your son should choose to be a soldier?'

'I always wanted to be a painter, Kate,' Michael reminded her as he swilled back the contents of his glass. 'Not a bloody soldier of fortune.' She could see the moon soften the shadows on his face and could also see the pain of a lost life in the glow as he added, 'He must have got his disposition for soldiering from his mother's side of the family.'

Sarah appeared on the verandah in the new dress. It accentuated each graceful curve of her blossoming body and she pirouetted as the dress swirled around her ankles. Michael smiled. It was strange that the young lady should turn out to be such a pretty, graceful creature given that he fondly remembered his brother as a lumbering and awkward oaf. Must have got the beauty and grace from her mother, he thought as he made genuine expressions of admiration for how beautiful she looked as she stood in the moonlight. The rum was soothing his troubled thoughts of the future as he sat with the only real family he had.

When Michael bid his farewell later in the

evening to go to the ship that would sail for the south, Kate could hear the curlews calling to each other in mournful wailing cries and she shuddered with superstitious dread. Were not they the spirits of the dead roaming the night? Had this not been a day of ill omens?

The hammering on the Cohens' door woke all in the house. Solomon rolled on his side and groaned. Who could be calling at this unearthly hour in the morning, he thought as he groggily forced himself into a sitting position in the bed beside his wife.

'Judith!' Distress was evident in the sound of the woman's voice from the verandah.

'Kate, is that you?' Judith answered as she pulled a shawl around her shoulders. She was out of bed before her husband and almost fully awake with the awareness that something must be terribly wrong for Kate to disturb them at such an early hour. 'Is something the matter?' she called as she fumbled for a kerosene lamp and lit the wick. The pale light flickered into a steady, anaemic glow and Judith could hear the confused mumbled voices of the boys as they came awake in the sleep-out. She made her way to the front door to see Kate pale and trembling with a fear Judith had not seen in her friend's face for many years.

'Oh, Judith, something terrible has happened to Luke.' The words tumbled from Kate's lips before Judith could utter any words of her own and impulsively she placed her arm around Kate's shoulder to usher her inside to the dining room. Willie stood behind Solomon and the two men stared through bleary eyes at Kate who had apparently come straight from her bed as she still wore her nightdress.

'A terrible dream came to me tonight,' Kate whispered hoarsely as she stared vacantly at the yellow flame of the lamp. 'I feel that my darling Luke is dying in some terrible and lonely place.'

Judith did not attempt to dissuade her friend with reassuring words. Kate had always had the unsettling gift to know such things. Instead she held Kate to her as if the gesture might take some of the pain from her friend onto herself. 'The muddy water. I saw the muddy water and that crow again. I . . .' Kate paused and struggled to describe the chilling dream in words. How did you find words to describe feelings that were physical and yet not real? 'I heard Luke call me from a long way away. He said that he loved me, even beyond the death he was facing. I . . .' Then she ceased speaking and began to sob.

The two men stood awkwardly on the edge of the room, helpless in the face of the unknown and unacceptable. Only Judith seemed to understand Kate's strange insights. Solomon's eyes met his wife's with a questioning look. She motioned with her eyes for the men to leave them alone.

Willie followed Solomon to the kitchen where he lit the wick of a lantern. Neither man said a word as Solomon slumped into a chair. From the dining room they could hear the murmur of the two women's voices and sobbing. So much pain and suffering in the world, Solomon pondered. It was just a matter of waiting for Judith to tell him what he should do to help when she was ready.

A tall grandfather clock chimed four times. Three-quarters of an hour before it could boom five times they heard the scrape of chairs and the front door close. Judith came to the kitchen. The two men both looked to her expectantly.

'Kate has gone home to try and rest for a while,' she said simply in a tired voice. 'Willie. You will go to Kate's house at dawn and help her prepare for a journey to Burketown.'

'To Burketown!' Solomon exploded. 'But she is almost at her time of confinement.'

'I know,' Judith replied holding up her hand to quell any further protest from her husband. 'I have tried to talk her out of going but she insists she cannot leave Luke out there. It is something she must do.'

'Well, she can't go alone,' Solomon growled. 'That would be foolish in her state.'

'She won't be going alone,' Willie said quietly from the end of the table. 'I will go with Kate and look after her.'

Judith cast an appreciative glance at the young man. 'I know she will be safe with you, William,' she said softly. 'God will protect both of you.'

Solomon stared at his wife with an expression of wonder and disbelief. Wonder for her acceptance of Kate's lunatic decision and disbelief that God alone would protect a very pregnant woman on the long and perilous track west to the Gulf. Then he glanced at Willie and saw the fire of the fanatic. Oi but God had some strange people working for Him!

15

Soon the sun would rise across the silent, scrub covered plains. A good time to die, Luke Tracy mused as he gazed east. Propped with his back against a tree he finished the last entry in the leatherbound journal Kate had given him. The gift was an attempt to encourage him to record the many things he knew of the Australian bush – and his colourful life as a prospector who had sought gold on two continents as well as his adventures when he fought the British at the Eureka Stockade alongside Kate's father. But the journal had remained empty, except for what he had written as the closing chapter of his life.

The words he now wrote were simple and full of love. No regrets but one: that he would never hold their child in his arms or again roam the bush of his adopted country and teach him or her its ways. But a man paralysed in the legs was of no use to a woman as active and passionate as Kate, Luke thought, with a deep and despairing sadness.

His horse lay dead only yards from where he had dragged himself to the shade of the tree the day before. Startled by a wallaby bursting from almost under its hooves the big thoroughbred had panicked and reared. Horse and rider had crashed heavily to the ground.

The horse had thrashed its legs and whinnied pitifully. As Luke had recovered his senses he realised in horror that the fall had broken his back. He was able to use his arms, but from the waist down there was no feeling.

He had been able to drag himself across to his horse and use his Big Colt pistol. The shot was clean and the horse died a quick death. With great difficulty Luke released the saddlebags by cutting loose the straps before dragging them to a bumbil tree where he propped himself to wait.

It was only a matter of how death would come to him. It had been almost twelve hours since the horse had thrown him and he knew that the chances of somebody finding him were as remote as the area he had deviated into. He'd decided to follow a likely trace of gold. Old habits died hard, he snorted in frustrated anger as he knew his search had taken him well off the track to Burketown.

But even if he was found by some traveller or prospecting party he knew it would only be his corpse they would come across. For Luke Tracy had already decided that he would take his own life. He would rather die than live out his life as half a man! He would not burden the woman he loved more than his own life. Better he be found dead than have to look into Kate's pitying eyes.

When would he pull the trigger of the revolver that lay near to his hand? On the next sunset? Or when the dark came to visit as a friend, covering a man's eyes from the harsh beauty of the limitless horizons of the ancient continent? No, he did not want the darkness to be the last thing that he saw. He wanted to take with him the splendid vision of a flaming orange sunrise.

Tears flowed as he thought about Kate and the child she carried within her body. God gave and God took away, he thought. Kate's religion forbade the taking of one's own life. The mortal sin of despair, she had once told him. But Luke's was the spirituality of the dark peoples who had roamed these ancient lands. Maybe in the next life he would be a spirit of this country, a spirit of the rocks that held the yellow metal which had ruled his life.

He closed the journal in his lap and carefully wrapped it in a spare shirt Kate had insisted he take with him on the trip. He slipped the package inside a saddlebag and secured the straps. He did not want scavenging animals to disturb the last words to his wife. One day someone was bound to find his bones and the bags hopefully still intact and Kate would know how much he loved her from these simple scribbled words.

The sun was little more than a glowing rim through a gap in the sparse trees of the plain when Luke Tracy lifted the revolver.

'Goodbye, my darling Kate. I will love you even in the next world,' he whispered softly.

The booming echo of the gun rolled across the plains.

16

Two weeks out of Townsville and the birthing pains came to Kate. Willie heard her cry of distress as he rode ahead of the dray and turned to see her bent over on the seat, gripping her swollen stomach with both hands. With the reins trailing free the dray horse plodded forward, raising tiny puffs of dust on the dry, almost treeless plain. 'Jesus,' he swore savagely as he tugged down on the reins of his mount to wheel his horse back to the dray. She was obviously having the child, he thought in a panic. Out here, of all bloody places! Miles from the next settlement.

'Help me down, Willie,' Kate gasped and gave a grunt of pain as another contraction racked her body. Her waters had broken and she knew her time had come.

Willie flung himself from his horse to reach up and assist. When he had helped her down she propped herself against the only place that offered shade – against the wheel of the dray – and continued to pant as the waves of pain rolled over her. 'What'll I do, Missus Tracy?' Willie asked in a despairing voice as he squatted on his haunches in front of her. 'I only ever delivered cows before.'

She gave him a weak smile of gratitude for his offer and she saw the expression of absolute fear in his face. 'Just let nature take its course. Set up a camp for us. That's what you can do.'

'Right,' he mumbled and scanned the plains seeking the trees that might mark a creek line or waterhole. But there were no trees growing distinctively together, only the occasional stunted one struggling for life in a sea of desiccated grass on the distant horizon. They were deep in the same country that the ill-fated Burke and Wills expedition had traversed almost a quarter of a century earlier, eventually claiming the explorers' lives.

Kate brought her knees up and reached under her long dress to drag down the cotton bloomers she wore. It weren't right that a man be present at such times, Willie thought self-consciously. Maybe better that he at least ride on to Julia Creek settlement to see if a midwife was there.

'Get me the water from the dray,' Kate gasped weakly. 'I have a terrible thirst.'

Willie scrabbled amongst the supplies and found a large bottle of water. He handed it to her and Kate swigged in great gulps. The heat and exertions of her labour had left her parched with thirst.

'Might be better I ride to Julia Creek and find a doctor or midwife, Missus Tracy,' Willie said when she handed the bottle back to him. 'Not much I can do here, 'cept set up camp and make you comfortable.'

'How far is Julia Creek?' she asked.

Willie scratched his head as he gazed westward. 'Maybe only a few hours' hard ridin',' he answered, his knowledge of the track coming from the trip he'd made with Ben's children along the same route weeks earlier.

Kate could see that his suggestion was really a plea. He would not desert her but his feeling of helplessness in the face of her labour left him with only one real alternative. She thought about his offer and decided that he was right. He might just fetch back a midwife or doctor in time for the birth. 'Maybe you could give it a try,' she replied and saw the expression of relief flood his face. 'But first just get me a few things from the dray before you leave.'

He collected the items Kate asked for and spread them where they were close to her reach: a clean man's shirt she had brought for Luke for when she found him, a small phial of laudanum for her pain and the water bottles. He also placed a sharp knife and reel of twine beside her, only realising their significance once he had done so. She was preparing to deliver the baby herself.

Kate watched Willie ride away at a gallop until he became a shimmering image that twisted and melted in the mirage-like haze. It would be dark in a few hours and she prayed that the baby would come while she had light to see what she was doing. The contractions eased momentarily allowing her to relax and calmly assess the situation. She knew she must keep her baby clean when he came. He! Why was it that she thought of her baby as a son when she could not possibly know? Was it that God was merciful in his own way, granting her a male life for the one she knew He had taken from her?

The flies came to pester her with their tormenting feet tickling her face and their droning buzz in her ears. Theirs was the only noise in the otherwise eerie silence of the plains – and virtually the only movement.

Ah, but there was one other with her! She gazed up to the azure, cloudless sky to see a giant eagle drifting on the thermals. A majestic wedge-tailed eagle soared in search of carrion or prey and kept her company in her lonely world.

But the soaring eagle was not the only company she had. Kate did not see the dark figures of the tribesmen approaching from across the plains as a clan of nomadic Aboriginals followed the flight of the eagle to the dray.

The horse raised its head from nuzzling at the dry grasses and stared at the shimmering line of people slowly wending their way towards them. He snorted when their strange scent reached him on a tiny zephyr-like breeze but Kate was only aware of their presence when she thought she heard the murmur of human voices through the buzzing of the flies that crawled all over her.

She tried to turn and scan the plain but the effort caused her pain and the voices seemed to stop when she groaned with the shock of the pain. She closed her eyes to try and block out her agony. When she opened them she gasped with sudden fright at the unexpected sight of the tall, skinny warrior standing over her with his spears grasped in his hand. But when she stared into his bearded face she saw a kind expression of sympathy and not animosity. She smiled and the nomad returned the smile.

He turned to call over his shoulder and an Aboriginal woman appeared to kneel beside Kate and cluck with maternal sounds at her distress. Then the Aboriginal spoke to Kate in a language she did understand! 'By jingo, Missus, goodfella we painum you, my word. Bigfella bird he bringum message to blackfella.'

The significance of the man's words was lost on Kate as the contractions became sharper. She was now in full labour but she had many eager women's hands to help her bring her son into the world.

And so Matthew Tracy was born in the shimmering heat of the late afternoon. Covered in the red earth and with bits of stick and grass adhering to his birth slicked body, the squalling baby was passed to Kate's breast by her Aboriginal midwife. The woman beamed a broad, white toothed smile at the shared pleasure of a new life brought into their harsh and arid plains.

Willie returned later that evening. Exhausted from his hard ride, he brought back with him the wife of a shanty keeper and her son, a gangly youth who drove the buggy conveying her.

Willie had seen the tiny campfire on the plain and it had guided them in the dark to the dray. He virtually fell from the saddle when he saw Kate nursing her infant son. She appeared well but her long tresses of dark hair hung lankly about her face.

She smiled weakly at her visitors who stared at the pair propped by the big wheel of the dray. 'I had help,' Kate said hoarsely and gazed down on Matthew Tracy with an expression of complete serenity. 'But my helpers have gone back to the bush.'

'Darkies?' Willie asked in awe. 'Some black-fellas help you?' Kate nodded and Matthew thrust his head from side to side in his way of telling the source of his sustenance that he had enough for now.

The wife of the shanty keeper knelt beside Kate and admired the baby which appeared to Willie merely as something wrinkled and ugly. Only a woman could find a kid so appealing when they looked like that, he thought, and shook his head. His laughter pealed across the plains and he whooped for joy as he slapped his thigh with his broad-brimmed hat. Kate was well and she finally had the baby she had wanted for so many years!

The visitors remained for the night. In the morning they left to return to Julia Creek. Kate thanked them but the woman roughly dismissed her thanks with embarrassment. She didn't think she had done a favour, merely what any person would do hereabouts when called on.

Willie harnessed the dray horse. Rifling through their supplies he noticed most of the flour, sugar and tea were missing. Kate told him she had given the food to the Aboriginals in gratitude for their kindness. He growled that the gesture was too extravagant but Kate answered that they had enough to return to Townsville.

The young man was surprised at her decision, but relieved at the same time. She had her baby to think of and the long trip ahead would tax the strength of a fit man, let alone a mother weakened by the rigours of childbirth.

But Kate was not thinking of her strength which she knew could have carried her on in search of her husband. She knew that the search was futile because her beloved husband was certainly dead. He had come to her in the early hours of that morning, whilst they had slept in the fading glow of the dying fire. He had stood on the plain and smiled gently on her and their sleeping baby. In her mind she heard his drawling, gentle American voice telling her to return to Townsville. Her search for him was futile, he told her, for he lay in a lonely place that no man would find for many years. He also told her that when they did eventually find his bones, his words of love would be there to reach out to her in the distant years ahead. Then he smiled and walked away from her across the plain towards the western horizon. He was gone and only his memory remained in Kate's dreams.

Kate had woken in the early hours and saw the meteorite blaze its brilliance across the darkness of the western sky. 'Luke,' she whispered as tears choked her plea for him not to go. For a long moment she watched the night sky as her quiet sobbing racked her body.

Exhausted by the long and hard ride, Willie meanwhile had slept soundly nearby, curled under his blanket. When Matthew woke and began to cry Kate lifted him gently from the shirt to place him on her breast. His crying had stopped as she rocked him, continuing to gaze at the beautiful canopy of stars overhead. She talked to Luke in her mind until she was weary and at last a peace descended from the stars to wrap her gently in the mysteries that lived beyond the science of men.

Willie saddled his horse and swung himself into the saddle. They had set out to find a dead man but had found a new life instead, he thought somewhat philosophically. Now it was time to take Kate back to her home and for him to go in search of his own life.

He could not go south to Sydney without money or supplies. He would work his way south with one of the cattle drives, or even get a job as a driver with the Cobb and Co coaches that now crisscrossed the colony. Eventually he knew he would confront the man who was his father and kill him.

The eagle soared above the tiny plume of dust that trailed behind the dray and the lone horseman heading into the rising sun. While at a campsite on the northern plains of the Gulf country, a nomadic people sat in the shade of the trees of a creek discussing the birth of the white baby who had been born to fly with the eagles.

Thunder and
Lightning
1885

17

South of the great Nubian desert, and north of the
mystical mountains of Ethiopia, a soldier curled in
a foetal position. He lay in a bed of sand and in
his exhaustion was oblivious to the desert chill
of the night – or the night noises of an army at
rest: the soft murmurs of men whispering their
thoughts and fears to friends who could not sleep;
the camels, mules and horses restless as if sensing the
excitement that was like an electric presence
in the newly arrived contingent of volunteers from
the Australian colony of New South Wales.

It was fortunate that there were such sounds as
they helped muffle the tiny, child-like whimperings
of Captain Patrick Duffy. Under an uninterrupted
canopy of twinkling Sudanese stars his body might
have been asleep but his repressed fears came in
the night to haunt him and he twitched and turned
in his troubled sleep. For the moment he was a
long way from the reality that would come to him
harshly in his waking hours: blistering deserts and
sudden, obscene death. For the moment he was in
a world of Celtic mists where a beautiful and

195

naked red-haired goddess lay on a bed of wild-flowers. Her ivory white legs were spread enticingly apart and a full moon caused the exposed rose petal swelling of her womanhood to glisten with her lust. A naked stranger stood at her feet as she beckoned with sweet, throaty words ... *I am Sheela-na-gig* ... *enter my body and slake the heat of your desire.*

But the stranger turned to gaze with a triumphant and malevolent smile. *It was Brett Norris!* Patrick watched helplessly as Norris lay on top of Catherine and entered her body with the *gae bulga*. She turned to smile, a distant smile of erotic detachment. She moaned with pleasure and clung with her legs to his back as he entered her and his was the seed she took into her while Patrick watched helplessly with a fear for the fate that was more terrible than death – the loss of his goddess.

'Captain Duffy, wake up, sor.' *She was gone* ... 'You feelin' unwell, sor?' a concerned voice asked. 'Not a touch of the fever would it be?' Patrick slowly opened his eyes to focus. Private MacDonald was bending over him with an expression of concern.

'Thank you, Private MacDonald,' he mumbled. 'I just had a bad dream.'

'That's orright, sor,' the huge Scots soldier replied with a sigh of relief in his thick Glaswegian burr. 'This place be a place of nightmares.' Patrick pushed himself into a sitting position and rubbed his eyes as the burly Scotsman placed a mug of steaming tea in his hand. 'Get this into yor, sor, help clear yor head.'

Patrick accepted the tea with gratitude and sighed. 'What time is it?' he asked as he took a tentative sip of the strongly sugared brew.

'One o'clock, sor. The Brigade Major says we are to join Captain Thorncroft and the Tommy stalks on the left flank for the advance.'

'Damn! I was supposed to see the B.M. at ten o'clock last night,' Patrick said and came immediately out of his sleep-induced torpor. 'You should have woken me.'

'Hoot, mon! Major Hughes told me not to,' Private MacDonald said soothingly. 'He said you deserved a wee sleep.'

Private Angus MacDonald had been assigned to Patrick as his batman while he was on secondment to the New South Welshmen from his posting with his Scots' Brigade. The giant soldier had fought beside Patrick at Tofrick ten days earlier when the Dervishes had surprised Brigadier General Sir John McNeill's infantry at an improvised defensive enclosure. Tofrick was only a short distance from the bustling port of Suakin on the Red Sea and the attack by the fierce desert warriors had taken a heavy toll on the defenders. It was only beaten off after ferocious fighting with bayonet, rifle butt and bullet and at one stage in the fighting Patrick had been felled by a bullet that had passed cleanly through the muscle of his left upper arm at the shoulder.

He had been locked in hand-to-hand fighting with two white-cloaked tribesmen armed with spears and shields when the shot had felled him. His revolver had jammed and he vividly remembered a spear poised above him to deliver the fatal thrust. Then he heard the sweet sound of an enraged Scot in a full killing rage. He remembered also the blood that sprayed him as the butt of a rifle being swung like a club crushed the Dervish's head in a single blow. And from that moment on the big Scot formed a bond with the young captain who he had always respected for his natural warrior abilities. It was a bond understood by soldiers regardless of rank. Although the captain had an Irish name it was rumoured he was half-Scot anyway and this helped endear the tough Glasgow-born soldier to Patrick.

And now they were returning to the scene of the bloody battle. Patrick had requested Private MacDonald as his batman for his secondment to the *Tommy Cornstalks*, as his native-born colonial countrymen were called by the British troops. The nickname was in deference to the noticeable greater height and lankiness of the colonials compared to their British-born cousins. For the Tommy stalks, the Sudan Campaign was the first time they had served alongside British and Imperial forces as an official contingent. Admittedly, only the Colony of New South Wales had supplied a small force of infantry and artillery but both were acutely aware that they represented the country of Australia as a whole.

In the early hours of the morning the bivouac stirred into life. The New South Welshmen would get the chance soon to show their well-experienced British soldier cousins what they were made of.

Patrick stood and brushed himself down. He no longer wore the kilt as he had at Tel-el-Kibir. The

British army had finally learned the lesson of camouflage and the khaki uniform they now wore in the field was designed to blend with the surrounding dry and rocky countryside of the Sudan. Although the Australian contingent had marched off the ships wearing red jackets and blue trousers, they soon exchanged their ceremonial uniform for desert khaki. Tea, coffee and tobacco juice had been used to stain the otherwise white belts, straps and pith helmets and they now blended with the huge army of Imperial and British troops.

Patrick adjusted the straps and pouches of his marching kit and slipped the revolver from the flapped holster. He quickly cleared the weapon's mechanism of sand and carefully reloaded each chamber. 'Lead on, MacDuff!' he said to Private MacDonald who pulled a face in the dark.

'It's Private MacDonald, sor.'

Patrick grinned and shook his head. It was obvious the big Scot was not a reader. But that did not matter; his brawny arms and roared slogans of the MacDonald clan in the heat of battle counted for far more in the Sudan.

The two soldiers had little difficulty finding the left flank of the ten thousand strong army camped in the desert. Both men were seasoned campaigners whose knowledge of many bivouac layouts instinctively guided them through the throng of camels, mules and horses which were tended by a small army of camp followers. The army of Sir Gerald Graham was formed into a giant rectangle, the dimensions of which were approximately two hundred by five hundred yards. To all intents and purposes it was the same British square formation that had stood against the terrifying might of Napoleon's cavalry at Waterloo.

Inside the human enclosure of rifle and bayonet armed soldiers, the camp followers went about their business of securing loads of water, rations and the accoutrements of a Victorian British expeditionary army: the officers' personal mess kits, canvas covered ambulance wagons marked with the distinctive red cross, fodder for the pack animals, medical supplies, veterinary equipment for sick animals and the quartermaster's jealously hoarded bits and pieces to be issued as replacements to careless soldiers.

Patrick came upon the New South Welshmen drinking ration issued cups of coffee. They were easy to find in the dark. He only had to navigate towards the distinctive accent that, fed on sunshine and copious quantities of mutton and bread, had grown in its own peculiar way. It was strange for him to hear so many of the drawling voices in the Sudanese night. Gentle memories of his childhood flooded him with nostalgia for the mild Sydney winters of sunshine and even the sweet, pungent smell of burning eucalypts in the dry hot summers as the bushfires blazed around Sydney. Too long he had lived amongst the English in the snow and sleet of the long northern winters. Too long away from the sights, sounds and smells that were peculiar to the land of his birth. Not even the magical Celtic mists could ever take the place of those experiences that had happened far across the

Indian ocean in a land both new and very old. 'I'm looking for Captain Thorncroft,' Patrick asked a soldier he could see silhouetted against the starry horizon.

'He's probably with Lieutenant Parkinson. Over there, mate,' the colonial replied cheerfully as he pointed towards a huddle of men in conference nearby.

'Officer present,' Private MacDonald growled from behind Patrick. He was not going to tolerate colonial bad manners.

'Sorry, mate, I mean, sir,' the colonial replied, not sounding repentant for his failing to recognise Patrick's rank. But Patrick only grinned at the man's impudence; it was a refreshing change not to have a soldier tip the forelock to rank.

When Patrick and Private MacDonald were out of hearing, the colonial soldier turned to his companion to continue discussing the possibilities of engaging the Dervish leader Osman Digna's forces within the next twenty-four hours. Digna was an ally of the charismatic Mahdi who had led the tribesmen in the holy war against the British. The Dervishes had sacked Khartoum months earlier and the charismatic General 'Chinese' Gordon had been slain.

What had initially commenced as a British expedition to relieve Gordon had now become a punitive exercise. Gordon had never been a favourite of the British prime minister, Gladstone, but the British press agitated the public to pressure Gladstone's government into sending a force in support of the man who had achieved nigh on sainthood in the eyes of the people. *Gordon Pasha* could not be left to stand alone against the Moslem infidel. To the British public, the force that had been despatched to the Egyptian territory of the Sudan was a modern crusade to defend all that was virtuous in Victorian England.

But to the two colonial soldiers drinking coffee and talking in the night, the moral indignation of outraged civilians safely ensconced in Britain meant little to men who would have to face the lethal brunt of battle. Their hushed talk was centred on what might occur during the next day in their lives and not the values of a holy crusade. Practical talk of where they would next eat, how far they would march under a blazing sun, and how well their rifles would stand up against the arms of the Mahdi's warriors.

A second soldier, who had remained silent when Patrick had approached, was a big man equal in size and strength to the Scot who had growled at them. He was not a young man and only his contacts with the flamboyant Catholic politician in Sydney, William Dalley, had ensured his enlistment in the Australian contingent. But such influence with the premier of the colony was not beyond the reach of an Irish policeman who walked the beats of Sydney Town. For such a man might get to see and hear things that the good citizen did not. And in doing this make uneasy friends in high places and gain access to the ear of the premier. Constable Farrell's intimate knowledge of the comings and goings of the city's gentlemen to houses of carnal pleasures had helped him out of a delicate situation involving stolen grog and into a conveniently timed expedition far across the sea and away from embarrassing questions being asked around Sydney. He was now Private Farrell and the English officer who had spoken to them had stirred a queer feeling. It was as if he had met the man before – or someone very much like him.

Private Farrell listened to his fellow soldier chat on but he was staring intently at the officer framed against the night sky. The former policeman was puzzled. Why should the English officer who he had not clearly seen in the dark remind him of someone from his murky past?

'What do ya reckon, Frank?' the other asked.

Francis Farrell turned to stare at his mate. 'Reckon about what?' he said, as if returning to the conversation from the backstreets of Sydney. 'I didn't hear you.'

'Yeah, I know. You were staring at the officers.'

'Just thought I might have met that bloke before,' Farrell replied as he swilled down the last of his coffee. 'But it's not likely,' he said in a distant voice. 'Maybe just someone who from a long time ago reminded me of him.'

Someone a long time ago . . . Somehow the tiny connections seemed to have a root in a long past violence. A wrong done and never rectified.

'You are rather late, Captain Duffy,' Thorncroft said, much as a schoolmaster would reprimand an errant schoolboy. 'Colonel Richardson has joined with the right flank.'

Patrick almost apologised for his apparent tardiness in arriving with the left flank but checked himself. He was not late. Reveille had been set for one o'clock and the brigade major had briefed him he was to join the colonial force then. 'I will see Colonel Richardson when the sun rises, Captain Thorncroft,' he replied mildly, dismissing the haughty attitude of his military counterpart. '*My* B.M. was exact in that regard.'

'Well, you could have paid *our* commanding officer the courtesy of meeting him tonight rather than waiting until the morning,' Captain Arthur Thorncroft persisted peevishly.

It was Private MacDonald who defied all military protocol to step to the defence of his officer and his quietly delivered interjection took both officers by surprise. 'Beggin' yor pardon, sor, but Captain Duffy was wounded at McNeill's Zareba a wee few days back and hasn't had much sleep since. So I'd be thinking he needed some and so did the Brigade Major.'

Thorncroft was above average height but the huge Scotsman towering over him made him feel small and the reference to Patrick being wounded in the heavy fighting at Tofrick – which now appeared on military maps as McNeill's Zareba – was intended to put the pompous colonial officer in his place as a soldier who had yet to prove himself in action. The point was not lost on Captain Thorncroft; he had never seen any active service in his career as an officer in the colonial militia of New South Wales.

'Thank you, Private MacDonald,' Patrick said warmly for the fierce loyalty exhibited by his batman. 'I'm sure Captain Thorncroft understands. Why don't you see if our colonial brothers have a spare cup of coffee before we fall in for the advance?' Patrick continued. 'I'm sure they wouldn't refuse you.'

'Sor!'

MacDonald lumbered into the night, seeking out the distributor of coffee to the troops. He knew Captain Duffy was going to have words with the upstart colonial officer and did not want him to be a witness. Could be that he was going to give the wee mon a physical lesson in manners, he thought with a grin.

When he was gone Patrick turned to his counterpart. 'You and I seem to have got off on the wrong foot, Captain Thorncroft. And as we have to work together I will apologise for missing the opportunity of meeting with Colonel Richardson. I believe he has had distinguished service with the British army.'

Indignant as he was, Thorncroft could not help fall under the charm of the liaison officer sent to them from the brigade headquarters. This was not to say that he liked the man but his graciousness in offering the apology had to be accepted.

'That's all right, old chap. Apology accepted,' he said. 'I'm sorry to hear that you were wounded. Where did they get you?'

'The arm. Bullet passed through cleanly. Did no serious injury,' Patrick replied, although he still felt pain in the arm. The Dervish bullet had cut open the flesh without fully penetrating and he had been careful to keep the wound clean as disease was rife in the Sudan. The wound was healing satisfactorily but promised to leave an ugly scar for life.

He had been forced to argue with a captain

from the field ambulance that he was fit to immediately rejoin his men after they treated him. But the brigade major had intervened to transfer him to headquarters and then detach him as a liaison officer to the newly arrived Australian contingent. He explained that Patrick's experience in African campaigns would be invaluable in assisting the colonials. Major John Hughes had been a captain at Tel-el-Kibir when Patrick was a lieutenant and the two men had become good friends.

Patrick knew full well that his friend was attempting to keep him out of the action at least until his arm healed and as liaison officer he would be forced to keep close to the staff of Colonel Richardson and away from leading at the front as was his usual practice.

'Well, all going to plan we should have the privilege of engaging the Dervish,' Thorncroft said happily. 'Looking forward to seeing some action.'

Patrick made no comment but turned to stare out at the flat horizon. The stupid man would soon change his mind if he got to the stage of looking into the dark eyes of a Dervish intent on killing him.

'Any advice, old chap?' Thorncroft asked. 'Before we engage the Mahdi's men.'

'Just find the biggest Scot you can, and stand beside him when the fighting starts. Oh, and keep your revolver clear of any sand. That's about all I can tell you that's of any help for now.'

Hours later Patrick felt lost without his regimental comrades around him. Instead, he marched alongside the eager but raw troops of his native land in the still, chill night of the Sudanese desert.

Beside him strode the big Scot, humming sentimental ballads of his homeland. Other than the clinking of metal on metal of the soldiers' kits and the occasional protesting bray of an army mule, there was little else to hear on the silent march south. Their boots squelched in the sand, creating an eerie sound.

At least not having command of troops gave Patrick a chance to think about other things than the welfare of men who trusted in his decisions. He found his thoughts continually drawn back to the dream that had haunted him only hours earlier. Why had Catherine not answered any of the many letters he had written to her? Was it that she had found the attentions of Brett Norris more to her liking? He sighed. Almost nine months and not a single word from her. Nothing! Instinctively he patted the ammunition pouch strapped to the belt at his waist. Sheela-na-gig lived there and she had kept him alive as Catherine had promised.

The little stone goddess lay at the bottom of the pouch under spare rounds of revolver ammunition. He smiled when he had a fleeting image of some soldier going through his pouches should he be killed in action. What would he think finding such a lurid icon in the possession of an officer?

A wild animal called in the distance, a chilling howl. Jackal? Hyena? Patrick did not know but its lonely call caused Private MacDonald to pause in his song before he began to hum again.

Another three months of silence from Catherine

would make a full year without Patrick knowing what she was doing. His lonely, bitter thoughts echoed those that had plagued soldiers for thousands of years, thoughts which would continue as long as men went away to fight and others stayed at home with the women. Ah, but it was the cruel nature of a woman's wants, he thought. He did not agree with many of his fellow officers who maintained that a woman did not desire carnal pleasure, an opinion based on personal experience in the arms of a pretty young seamstress when he was at Oxford for his short sojourn as a student. She had seduced him and her uninhibited pleasure in his arms had shattered all the things he had been told about the lack of pleasure a woman derived from the sexual act. She had shown him how to touch her in a way that increased her pleasure. God! How beautiful those moments had been in her tiny, damp room above her father's shop. Sixteen years of age and Cristobel was her name, he remembered. And she had been madly in love with life and him, but had died from a burst appendix while he was away with his regiment in Scotland.

Across the early morning sky a meteorite blazed a trail of tiny fragments. Its appearance brought a murmur of admiring comments from the men who had seen it. 'We had a comet at Tel-el-Kibir,' Patrick said softly, and Private MacDonald ceased humming his tunes. 'We thought it was a bad omen at the time. I suppose it was for the poor devils who died that day.'

'Yes, sor, I suppose it was,' Private MacDonald answered dutifully.

'Do you have family, Private MacDonald?' Patrick asked, and the big Scot bowed his head. 'I dinna know sor. I left a wee bonnie lassie at the dock two years ago. She promised she would wait but I have not heard one word from her since.'

'You and me both, Angus,' Patrick replied, and the use of the soldier's first name seemed natural. It was a rare moment when the military barriers fell away between superior and subordinate in the strict discipline of the army, but for the moment they were just two young men a long way from home and cloaked by the darkness of the early morning.

'Have you got a bonnie lassie waitin' for you when we return then, Captain Duffy?' the Scot asked sympathetically, sensing his officer had a need to talk.

'I thought I did.'

Patrick sighed sadly before both men lapsed into silence as the might of the British army advanced on the scene of their last bloody battle against the Dervishes.

'God almighty!' Captain Thorncroft gagged as the stench rose from the earth.

The blistering sun had cooked the decomposing bodies of men and animals that had lain in the desert for almost two weeks. Vultures bloated with the abundance of rotting flesh from the British, Dervish and the pack camels killed at the Tofrick enclosure hopped and flapped into the azure sky to wheel in spiralling circles overhead.

Some of the vultures ignored the army that had marched on the scene of the desperate fighting and continued to rip flesh and entrails from the bodies that were black but no longer swollen, as their flesh had been long pierced by the cruel beaks and the expanding gases released.

Patrick stood beside the colonial officer and took no pleasure from his discomfort at the sight and smells of the battlefield. Even he had trouble keeping in his stomach the tea he had drunk hours earlier. Dazed soldiers walked amongst the dead whose hastily buried bodies had been exposed by animals and the shifting sands for all to see. Others stood back and forced down the tinned meat and bread they had been issued for breakfast.

Angus MacDonald was glad that the bodies of the British soldiers were no longer recognisable. The ravages of decomposition and the scavenging birds and animals had made sure of that. He did not want to see any friend who he had laughed with, whored with, or got drunk with in this state.

But one man did not react to the hellish spectacle in the same way as most of his comrades. As a policeman working the poor districts of Sydney, he'd had many years' exposure to the sight of death in all its most hideous forms, and over the years he had built a shell of immunity to the demise of human life.

As he spooned greasy meat from a tin, Private Francis Farrell's attention was on the tall, broad-shouldered young British officer who stood alongside Captain Thorncroft. Farrell stared at Patrick who had detached himself from Captain Thorncroft and now stood alone gazing past the battlefield in the direction of the distant ruined village of Tamai which had been razed a year earlier by British troops after a major battle with the Dervishes. And it was near the ruins of the Egyptian village that the advancing force were expected to encounter and fight another major battle with the Mahdi's men.

The former policeman from Sydney wiped at his neatly trimmed beard as the fat dripped from his spoon. Now that he could see him in the blazing morning light, the man definitely reminded him of someone.

Private Angus MacDonald was striding towards the captain holding a chunk of bread and a mug of water. 'Hey! Jock!' Farrell called softly to the Scot as he passed him.

Angus acknowledged the call and turned to stare at the man almost as big as himself. He had recognised the Irish accent. 'What would you want, Paddy?'

'That boss of yours, what would his name be?'

'Now why would you be wantin' to know, mon?'

'Because I'd be askin' a civil question, boyo. And my sainted ancestors fought for Bonnie Prince Charlie at Culloden. That enough reason for a haggis eatin' Gael?'

At first Angus had bristled when he heard himself addressed as Jock but he could not help but smile at the Irishman's explanation as to why he should answer his question. Angus' ancestors had also stood with the Jacobites against the forces of British redcoats and their lowland Scots' auxiliaries on the terrible battlefield. 'God bless yor sainted grandmother for providing a well-needed service for those brave laddies at Culloden, Paddy,' he answered with a wicked grin.

But Francis Farrell was not to be outdone by any big, hairy legged Scot and retorted with a twinkle in his eye. 'Me sainted grandmother used to bounce me on her knee and say, "Francis, me boy, the reason those Highlanders lost to the bloody British at Culloden was because they didn't have the strength left when I'd finished with them."'

Angus chuckled. 'Captain Duffy be yon officer, Paddy,' he replied with a grin. 'I hear he was born in Sydney Town.'

Patrick Duffy! No wonder there was a familiarity. How often had he had a drink with the big German Max Braun at Frank Duffy's Erin Hotel and bounced young Patrick on his knee! Frank Farrell shook his head in utter amazement. 'Young Patrick Duffy in the bloody uniform of a British officer,' he muttered as he continued to shake his head. 'Who would have ever dreamed? And what would the big man, Michael himself, think about his son being a bloody British officer!'

Angus could not hear the Irishman's mutterings and was impatient to get breakfast to his captain. The Irishman looked as if the sun had got to him already. 'See you around, Paddy,' he said with a nod of his head. 'Might be we could share a wee dram or two sometime. Keep your bog Irish head down when the fightin' starts, mon.'

'You look after your boss, Jock,' Francis replied as he came out of his state of amazement. 'I knew his father and a finer man you would never meet,' he added once the Scot had departed.

Patrick Duffy! Sure and he was the image of his father at that age, Farrell mused as he watched the Scot march across to Patrick. And would young Patrick have come across his legendary father in his travels?

Over ten years had passed since the former policeman had last seen Patrick. There was some matter of his maternal grandmother, Lady Enid Macintosh, taking the boy to England, for his education Farrell remembered. Something about his inheritance. Old Frank Duffy had been very tight lipped about the circumstances which his own son, Daniel Duffy, had arranged. But Daniel, being the good lawyer that he was, let little be known of the mystery surrounding Patrick and his connection with the wealthy and powerful Macintosh name. Ah, but he would talk to the young Patrick when the opportunity arose, Farrell thought, tossing aside the empty tin and wiping his hands on the side of his trousers. Right now, however, he would have given anything for a cold drink back at the Erin Hotel.

The order to fall in and resume the advance across the shimmering hot sands was issued. For the troops, the order had not come too soon.

Patrick crossed the advancing square to make his introductions to Colonel Richardson. The sun was almost directly above them and little shadow was cast by the men and animals below. The forced march was going to be an ordeal and he wondered how the colonial volunteers would fare under the conditions.

By the time the army came to rest that night, however, Captain Duffy would feel pride for the stamina of the men from the country of his birth. Only three collapsed senseless. But not until the late afternoon.

18

The tiny puffs of dust beneath the horses' hooves swirled to form a large, red cloud that trailed like a plume behind the combined column of thirty or so men. They galloped across the sparse scrub plain dotted with knee-high termite nests. Sub Inspector Gordon James led his column, following the guide from Sergeant Rossi's patrol, which had been operating close to the distant low hills of the Godkin Range.

The guide had been despatched to find Gordon's column and lead them to a creek where Sergeant Rossi was presently located. It was the first time the Italian sergeant had reason to call on his senior officer in the four months that they had been scouring the plains north of Cloncurry in their search for the Kalkadoon war parties.

When they finally reached the line of trees that marked a meandering creek, Gordon reined his horse to a halt and flung himself from the saddle. He strode towards his sergeant who was standing with a small party, staring at the corpses of three white men stripped naked and swollen black.

From the mutilations to their bodies it was obvious that the three men had died violent deaths.

'Kalks,' Commanche Jack grunted as Gordon joined the semi-circle of police and frontiersmen staring at the bodies which lay on their backs at the edge of the creek where a deep, rock waterhole trapped a last reservoir of dirty green water. 'Ripped 'em open to take their kidney fat to eat,' he added as he squatted to get a closer look at the bodies covered in clouds of flies buzzing in thick, noisy clouds around the wounds. 'Looks as if'n they went for a swim an' the Kalkadoon jumped 'em,' he continued as his experienced eyes took in the scene. 'Don' pay to take a bath aroun' here.'

The sickly sweet, unpleasant stench of the decomposing bodies caused some of the watching men to gag.

'Get them buried before sunset, Sergeant Rossi,' Gordon ordered with a wave of his hand. 'And see if the myalls left anything that might identify who they were.'

The sergeant picked a handful of his troopers who quickly began to dig out a large single grave.

While the troopers sweated with bandannas over their noses, Gordon called a meeting of his expedition leaders as they stood or squatted in a semi-circle around the young police officer. Some of the men smoked pipes, their Snider rifles close at hand. Others just stood with thumbs tucked in belts slung with a variety of pistols. 'This,' Gordon said indicating with his finger to the three dead men awaiting burial, 'is the first sure sign since this expedition set out from Cloncurry that the myalls are in large enough numbers to dare attack a party of white men. It appears to me from what I have been told by the black trackers that the Kalkadoon are retreating back to their mountain bases.'

'Don't make sense the Kalks would bottle themselves up in the hills, Inspector,' Commanche Jack drawled as he idled in the dust with a stick. 'They's fight like the Apache. Hit an' run the homesteads with us chasin' 'em all over the scrub in every direction. Jus' don't make sense for 'em to head fer the hills.'

'A good point,' Gordon answered. 'But I feel that they are just bold enough to think they can take us head on in a fight. They think they are drawing us into ground of their choosing. But they have underestimated the power of the carbine.'

'Mebbe so,' Commanche Jack grunted. 'Mebbe so.'

'And that is their fatal mistake, gentlemen,' Gordon continued. 'Because what we need is to be able to pin them down in one place and let our rifles secure a lasting peace in the Cloncurry district. Tomorrow we begin the final stages in the dispersal of the Kalkadoon. Sergeant Rossi?'

'Sar!'

'Your column will ride with us tomorrow. From now on we will scour the valleys and hills to the west of our present position as a single force. We will endeavour to secure the ridges so denying the myalls any vantage points to rain rocks and spears down on us.'

'Some of them hills are bloody high, Inspector,' a bearded squatter commented, an edge of disbelief in his voice. 'We're not going to get horses up all them hills.'

'You can bet that the Kalkadoon have worked that out for themselves. So we take particular note of such hills and surround them. If the myalls are on top then that is where they will die. Are there any further questions that need answering at this stage?'

The leaders of the parties shook their heads. *The young inspector seemed to know his business.* 'I dare say that I don't have to warn you to be particularly vigilant from herein,' Gordon said in parting to the men. 'I feel that the myalls here are quite capable of launching an attack on us in the night. So keep sentries posted around your campsites.'

All had to agree with the young officer. Especially once they saw the naked and mutilated bodies of the three luckless men tumbled into the shallow grave nearby.

They rejoined their comrades who had commenced preparing their campsites for the coming night. Battered billies for boiling water for the tea and cast iron camp ovens appeared from the packs the spare horses carried.

The horses were hobbled to graze on the dry native grasses and men agreed to what watches they would stand through the night. Packs of greasy, dog-eared playing cards were produced out of saddlebags for the odd game or two to help while away the time. The reality of the three dead men buried nearby had not unduly disturbed the tough frontiersmen. Death was a common enough event in their hard lives.

Night came to the expedition's camp, first as a gentle, beautiful orange light and then as a dark velvet cloak studded with crystalline diamonds.

Trooper Peter Duffy gazed across at Gordon James sitting alone by his small fire sipping tea from a mug. Over the long weeks of fruitless patrolling neither man had attempted to bridge the widening gulf of their dying friendship. The only thing they had in common now was Sarah – for Peter a loving concern of a brother for his sister's future; for Gordon a desire for a woman of mixed blood and a turmoil as to what he should do about his feelings for her.

Gordon gazed up at the stars and remembered the Aboriginal belief that they were the spirits of the dead. There were so many stars that a strange thought occurred to the young police officer. Would the skies be filled with many more before the expedition returned to Cloncurry? Three days earlier, boomerangs and spears whirred through the haze of the mid-afternoon, raining down amongst his column of horsemen.

Gordon had rallied his troopers and auxiliaries after the first onslaught to chase after the Kalkadoon who had flitted like shadows amongst the sparse trees of the plain. His reaction was based on the premise that the ambush was a sporadic affair. As such, the party had galloped at the warriors, his troopers and frontiersmen fanned out in a rough semblance of a charging cavalry.

But suddenly he had found another party of Kalkadoon warriors waiting to ambush his exposed flank. This time the spears found targets amongst the confused attackers. Two horses went down riddled with spears. The charge had ended in a melee, both horses and men breaking into confusion and panic as they fled in all directions. The warriors jeered at their retreat. Only Gordon's leadership had been able to rally his men, and turn a panicked flight into an orderly withdrawal.

When they had regrouped, sweating horses shivered and trembling men grinned sheepishly at each other. How easily they had underestimated their opponents, Gordon thought as he searched the plain for the Kalkadoon who had seemingly disappeared into thin air. It was a mistake he would never make again to underestimate the fierce and intelligent tactics of these warriors. Inspector Potter had underestimated them, and paid with his life.

On a hill top deep in the range of low round hills to the west of the Native Mounted Police campsite a seasoned warrior also sat alone by a fire and poked at the glowing embers with a stick.

Wallarie moodily watched the fire spirits dancing in a shower of sparks, fleeing into the night sky to join the twinkling spirits of the heavens. But he was not alone for long as he was joined by a broad-shouldered young warrior of the Kalkadoon.

Terituba had heard tales about the Darambal sorcerer who had travelled from the south to join them. It was said that the Darambal man knew much about the ways of the white men and had once befriended one who also had been hunted by the white tribes and the hated Native Mounted Police. The Darambal warrior had quickly learned the language of the Kalkadoon and been accepted as an advisor to the war chief.

Terituba sat cross-legged beside Wallarie and gazed into the glowing embers.

'When the white men come to us we will wipe them out,' he boasted to Wallarie who he knew had advised the Kalkadoon strongly against retreating into the hills. 'Here they will be trapped in the hills and their horses of no use to them on the steep hillsides.'

But Wallarie remained silent and continued to gaze at the fire, ignoring the proud young warrior's boast. They did not truly know the persistence of the white troopers as he did!

'We have the river to give us water and food,' Terituba continued. 'We have the rocks to shower on the enemy from our hills and we have killed a leader of the black crows before. They do not have the knowledge of the land as we do.'

Wallarie finally broke his silence. He could no longer stand the arrogance of the younger man. 'The man who leads the black crows is a white man who knows the land,' he said quietly. 'I know this.'

Terituba stared at Wallarie with surprise. 'But he is only a white man. How could he know the land as we do?' he sneered.

'Because he has lived amongst the Kyowarra for a time, and learned many things that we know. His father killed my people, until only I was left to tell you. He is a killer of all black people of the land. I know this because I know the man called

Gordon James just as I knew his father before him.'

Terituba sat and listened as the older man uttered his words and felt the chill that came with the magic of a divine revelation. After a short while he rose to his feet and left Wallarie alone by his fire. The sorcerer was surely a man to be shunned or killed, he thought as he walked away.

When he was alone again Wallarie pondered on the coming of Gordon James to the hills with his horses and guns. Peter Duffy was with him. Peter, son of the big white man Tom Duffy and Mondo, Wallarie's blood relative. Peter was coming to kill his brothers who stood against the hated troopers of the Native Police.

A dingo howled from the depths of a valley. The old warrior glanced with dark eyes into the flames of the fire and saw things there. He crooned the songs of his people, songs that only he now remembered, until the dreams came. And when the dreams came the spirits of his people reached out to him across the vast plains of scrub, red earth and broken hills.

In his visions the spirit of the hill told him what he must do to save the memory of his people. Wallarie tried to protest but the voice of the spirit was strong and changed shapes to frighten him. Finally the Darambal warrior conceded to the wisdom of the ancestors. He sighed in his troubled sleep as the dingo howled to its kind in the God-kin Range.

19

Michael Duffy bit the end off his cigar and spat the nipped section into the water that lapped gently against the rock wall of Sydney's Circular Quay. Passengers disembarking from the ferries bustled past him with barely a glance. He took his time in striking a match. He was in no hurry. He would savour the rich taste while he waited patiently to meet the man Horace Brown had contacted in the von Fellmann matter.

Paperboys peddled their trade, shouting to the passengers hurrying by in a language as unintelligible as that of an auctioneer. Horse-drawn trams and hansom cabs waited at the busy focal point of Sydney's link with the world. Steam ships lay at anchor in the many coves of the harbour city and sailing skiffs owned by the wealthy skipped the waves.

Michael idly watched the ladies in their long dresses that sprouted ungainly bustles. Men sported top hats and frock coats. He remembered similar scenes when, in his youth, he and his cousin Daniel had caught the ferry to Manly

Village on the other side of the magnificent tree-lined harbour. It was there that he had first met the beautiful daughter of the powerful Scots squatter Donald Macintosh. But Fiona Macintosh was now Missus Fiona White and married to the man who had been responsible for the terrible turn of events that had thrust him into the violent world of mercenary soldiers.

Michael felt strangely at peace – even with the ever-present threat of his identity being disclosed to the police and the thought of the dangerous task that lay ahead of him – in the familiar sights and sounds of the city of his youth.

'Mister Duffy,' the deep, cultured voice behind him said as he continued to gaze across the water of the cove. 'It has been some time since we last met.'

'Major Godfrey. I see you are well,' Michael said with some shock at recognising a face from his past. The last time he had met the military man had been over ten years earlier when the major had introduced himself at Baroness von Fellmann's afternoon party. They had talked about Colonel Custer and Michael had expressed his view that the Boy General would be in trouble if he ever confronted a united Indian front. Although the British officer had scoffed at this view Michael had proved to be right. In the intervening period George Armstrong Custer had perished with his troops at Little Big Horn. 'Mister Brown informed me that you would be my contact in Sydney and somehow that did not surprise me.'

The older man smiled wryly. Although George

Godfrey wore the fashion of the day, frock coat and shiny top hat, his bearing was that of the professional soldier: ramrod straight back, bending only at the neck to look down on the world of civilians. 'Do not draw the conclusion that I am in the same profession as my dear friend Horace, Mister Duffy. My occasional work assisting him has been my duty as a soldier of the Queen. Any favours over the years have been motivated by a desire to see the possible enemies of Her Majesty foiled in their devious attempts to gain advantages over our imperial interests. I am a retired Colonel and have a small holding at Parramatta that is now my preoccupation in life. This will probably be the last time I will be assisting Horace in his work.'

Michael smiled to himself at the former English officer's quickness to disassociate himself from Horace Brown. *Intelligence work was not the occupation of gentlemen, as he had been told by Horace once.* 'That too is also my hope, Colonel,' Michael said, deferring out of politeness to the other man's title. 'This is definitely my last mission for the bloody British Crown.'

'Understandable sentiments for the son of an Irish rebel,' Godfrey said. 'But obviously not a sentiment shared by your son, who I believe is with the Sudan expeditionary force at the moment.'

'You know a lot about me, Colonel,' Michael growled. 'What do you know about my son?'

Godfrey knew a lot about Patrick but he was a man not prone to telling more than he thought necessary. Not even to the young man's father. The former British officer had worked for Lady Enid Macintosh for some years and had watched Patrick grow to become a man any father could be proud of. That is, if he did not object to Patrick's ties with Queen Victoria's imperial interests.

'I have been reliably informed that your son is one of the finest officers to serve Her Majesty,' he offered. 'And apparently he has a taste for that working-class sport of bare knuckle boxing which I believe he gets from you.'

'He got that from Max Braun, not me,' Michael replied as if dismissing the matter. But he felt a secret pride in his son's link with his working-class background. 'Max taught him to fight, just as he taught me when I was much younger.'

'He must have been a very good teacher,' Godfrey commented. 'From what I have heard, your son is unbeaten champion of his Scots' Brigade. And from my personal experience of serving with those hot-headed kilt wearers, that is no mean feat. It's just a pity your son does not know more about the considerable accomplishments of his father in the good cause of Her Majesty.'

Michael stared with his good eye at the slightly taller man. 'He doesn't even know I'm alive,' he snorted bitterly. 'And besides, I am not particularly proud of working for English interests.'

'He is bound to find out one day that you are well and truly alive,' Godfrey said, returning the stare. 'Your existence is one of the worst kept secrets I know of.'

'So it seems,' the Irishman mused. He looked away and turned his gaze to The Rocks. It was still a seedy place that the good citizens of Sydney shunned. Its tenements and alleys appeared to wear an air of decay and despair like a dirty and torn mantle. 'Hopefully not as well exposed in New South Wales as it seems to be in Queensland.'

'Hopefully not,' Godfrey sighed. 'It would not pay to have a man's reputation questioned in regards to associating with a wanted felon such as yourself, Mister Duffy. But let us not dally with small talk. Small talk is not the grist of old soldiers such as you and I.'

The ferry passengers passing by the two men paid them little attention. They could be two gentlemen discussing the chances of a thoroughbred at the Randwick racecourse. Or the current threat the Russians posed to the security of the colonies due to their alarming moves in Afghanistan, the spectre of the Russian bear lumbering southward as it sought control of the gateway to India having emerged as a real threat to the British Empire in the vulnerable colonies of Australia. Already the conversation on many citizens' lips in the harbour city was of a possible strike by the considerable Russian naval force at England's vulnerable Pacific colonies. It was being mooted that the colonial volunteers who had sailed from the very quay where Michael and Colonel Godfrey now stood should be recalled to defend the city against the possible dreaded appearance of Russian warships in the harbour.

They might have been surprised – had they been privy to the conversation between the two men – that they were not discussing an immediate Russian threat but rather a long-term German threat to the security of the colonies.

Michael listened in silence as Colonel Godfrey outlined the support that was being provided for him and John Wong in their quest for information concerning Otto von Bismarck's intentions to seize Pacific territory for the Kaiser. At length, they parted company with a handshake.

Michael lingered by the water, puffing on the cigar and contemplating his next move as he watched the streaks of gold appear on the oily waters where the sun kissed the harbour. He would return to the office below the cramped residence he shared with John Wong. The lease had been paid for by the resources of Horace Brown and was located on the waterfront at one end of the cove where it had a clear view of ships coming and going. Ostensibly it was an office for import and export to the Oriental markets in China. But it was also an ideal base to monitor the activities along the waterfront where the right people could be nurtured to talk of things important to intelligence.

Michael pondered on the most difficult aspect of his mission: not the danger he was exposing himself to with a possible confrontation with the Prussian aristocrat, but what would happen when he met with Fiona? He puffed at the last of his cigar and flicked the stub into the water.

20

Captain Patrick Duffy was preoccupied with just staying alive for another day of the desert campaign. The British expeditionary force had completed a gruelling march across the blistering desert sands to arrive at the heights above the village of Tamai. Men hastily built a Zareba of stone and earth on sundown while aerial observers in a gas air balloon drifted above them to watch the manoeuvring of the Dervish army in the distance beyond the ruins of the village. A report was scribbled and dropped to the ground from the balloon's basket where it was snatched by a waiting runner who took the message to General Graham's mobile headquarters: the Dervishes were retreating to hills away from the advancing British army. The news would have cheered most but it did not cheer General Graham. He desired a decisive engagement with the rebels in a set piece battle and the fleeing warriors of the Mahdi were denying him that opportunity.

Standing alone on the forward perimeter of the defences, Patrick did not feel the same relief as many of his fellow soldiers for the Dervish retreat. Their exposure to the battlefield at McNeill's Zareba had dampened their enthusiasm for war, although they would not openly admit to this amongst themselves. Patrick knew too well that none of them would get an undisturbed sleep that night. His experiences in the Sudanese campaign had made him aware that raiding parties would creep back in the night to snipe and harass them. They might even possibly launch a full-scale attack on them. They were a brave and fanatical enemy who, in the holy war against the invading British puppets of the Egyptian government, held the belief that death granted them a place in heaven.

Patrick stood observing the sweating soldiers gathering rocks amongst the stunted copses of mimosa bush on the rugged, bare hillsides. Behind him the native camel handlers of the commissary tussled with their obstinate animals as they unloaded their cargoes of military supplies for the night's bivouac. As Patrick observed the army digging in and preparing for any possible attack his eyes swept the surrounding hills. Dust rose as a thin film to filter the setting sun in a scene that was deceptively peaceful. The picquets were posted and stood gazing out through the arcs they had been assigned. Patrick was pleased with the preparations. He knew the craggy heights gave the army an advantage against any attack.

'Yor think they will be comin' tonight, sor?' Private MacDonald asked as he joined Patrick. 'Or do ye think they have decided to run?'

'They will be back,' Patrick replied as he gazed

down on the ruins that had once been a village. He could see evidence of newly constructed mud houses amongst the ruins. 'It will only be a matter of degree.'

'I was hopin' for a wee bit o' sleep tonight,' the soldier grumbled. 'So are our Tommy Cornstalks. The march wore them out.'

'I don't think they would sleep, even if the Madhi's men leave us alone,' Patrick mused. 'They appear eager to prove themselves in battle and, I suspect, will be kept awake by their personal fears.'

Private MacDonald knew precisely what his officer meant. Men who had never been in battle would lay awake locked in the personal fear that their courage would fail them when the killing started. *Would they run away?* It was strange that officers never seemed to feel fear, the private soldier mused. They always made a point of being at the front of their men in battle, at least the junior officers. Captain Duffy was like that. No sign of fear when the fighting started.

But little did the private know the terrible fear all officers experienced before a battle. It was a fear they could confide in no-one – not even fellow officers – that they too might lose their courage and run. For Patrick the cool soldier's facade under fire hid his very real fears as a man who wanted the chance to live and love.

At the forward edge of the Zareba toiled Private Francis Farrell. He hoisted a large stone and slammed it down on top of a small wall that had begun to form a landmark. The work of building a low redoubt against attack was an unexpected and unwelcome surprise to the exhausted troops after the gruelling march. But that was the way of armies . . . march, work, stand guard and march again. Somewhere in between, the army allowed you to eat so that you could march, work, stand guard and march again. Rest and sleep were luxuries an advancing army issued when the commander was satisfied his enemy had been defeated – and only then.

Private Farrell glanced up from his work and saw Patrick Duffy standing with his back to him, gazing out at the village of Tamai. Maybe this would be a good time to make himself known to the man who he could plainly see was the Patrick Duffy he had once bounced on his knee at the Erin Hotel. He would tell him of his father and of what a fine man he was. Tell him how he still lived and hoped for the day they would meet.

The big former Sydney policeman straightened from bending over to push the rock into position. He felt his head swim. There were black spots floating before his eyes.

He groaned as he slumped to the hot earth. *Get him to the field ambulance!* He heard a voice call from the end of a long tunnel and strong arms lifted him from the earth. Too bloody old to be running around with the boys, he thought. Stupid idea to volunteer in the first place. It took four brawny soldiers to carry his limp body to the medical staff who were placed with their wagons at the centre of the defences.

The demented ramblings of the colonial soldier struck down by the sun made little sense to the medics who bathed his forehead and neck with cooling water . . . *something about Captain Duffy from the Scots' Brigade*, the surgeon major overheard. *Something about him being alive and innocent!*

The surgeon major knew Patrick Duffy and wondered why a colonial soldier should be raving about his innocence. Maybe he would mention the matter to Patrick when he next saw him. But for now his patient was dangerously ill and the army surgeon had seen more soldiers die from illness and disease than he had seen die of battle wounds.

In the night the Dervishes came, as Patrick knew they would. Sniping shots from outside the defensive perimeter sent men scattering out of the light of campfires. Orders bellowed by senior NCOs, cursing men scrabbling for rifles, the braying of a mule startled by the rending of the night routine – sounds that no longer caused Patrick any great alarm. So they were not in for a night attack, he thought with some relief. Or else they would not have announced their presence with sniping. 'You probably will get a wee sleep tonight, Private MacDonald,' Patrick said to the Scot who gripped his rifle and groped for his bayonet in its scabbard on his belt. 'The Mahdi's not coming tonight.'

The sniping was answered with a volley of rifle fire from the outer defences and the artillery guns that trundled with the army roared out, hurling high explosive shells in the general direction of the incoming sniper fire until the snipers' rifles fell silent. Inside the relative safety of the Zareba the men could rest in the knowledge that their guns would keep the enemy at bay. Throughout the crash of rifle and artillery fire Patrick lay on his back with his hands behind his head staring up at the beautiful canopy of crystalline stars. Ancient points of brilliance that showed all their magnificent lustre to the harsh and desolate places of the planet.

It was a strange time to think about Catherine Fitzgerald when death could come from an unseen Dervish warrior firing blindly into the redoubt. As a liaison officer he found himself with little to do than think about her. The brigade major had conspired with the brigade commander to rest him so that he could fully recover from his wound. He had only to report twice a day to his headquarters, a short distance away, where Major Hughes told him the same thing each time: 'Just keep an eye on the Tommy stalks, Captain Duffy. Give them any advice you think they could do with. Oh, and report regularly to the aid post so that he can have a look at your wound. That's about it, old chap.'

'Catherine, why do you not answer my letters?' Patrick sighed softly as the exhaustion of the hard march crept over him like a suffocating blanket and lulled him into his loneliness. Would the tormenting dream creep to him again in the night?

'Sorry, sor?'

'Nothing, Private MacDonald. Just thinking.'

Patrick gazed at the stars and watched as the constellations slowly wheeled across the velvet black night sky. He did not remember going to sleep. Sleep was like death. It was a nothingness to his conscious being, an oblivion.

Through the long hours of the night the braver of the Dervish snipers returned to fire random shots into the mass of British troops huddled behind their walls of rocks, rifles and bayonets. Only one fatality was recorded for the night: a soldier accidentally shot dead by an officer who mistook the man for a Dervish warrior. But the random firing did not disturb Patrick's deep and dreamless sleep – the exhausted sleep of the seasoned soldier.

Private MacDonald pushed a steaming mug of coffee and a handful of hard biscuits in his face. 'Mornin', sor and happy Easter,' he said cheerfully. 'Major Hughes told me to tell you to see the surgeon major before we move out this mornin'.'

Patrick pushed himself into a sitting position and rubbed the sleep from his eyes. 'Good God! Is it Easter already?' he asked.

The big Scot grinned down on him cheerfully. 'Good Friday, sor. But no hot cross buns.'

'That would be expecting too much.' Patrick grinned as he sipped from the mug of steaming coffee. It tasted good as the batman had ensured it was well-sweetened. 'But it might not be a good Friday for the Mahdi's men if we catch up with them today.'

'No, sor, it might not.'

When he had finished his breakfast Patrick quickly shaved, using the last dregs of his coffee to wet his face. The sugar was sticky but the razor's blade left his skin clean. Water was precious and the captain wondered why he should not grow a beard like many of the soldiers around him. It would have helped dispense with this morning ritual and save time.

When he had finished shaving Patrick scooped up his canvas webbing of straps, belt and pouches that lay in the sand within arm's reach of where he had slept during the night. He froze with shock. During the night a sniper's bullet had passed a fraction of an inch across his sleeping body to bury itself in the pouch where the little goddess resided. Superstitious horror swept him. *Was Sheela-na-gig injured?*

With trembling hands he opened the pouch to peer inside. She lay unscathed at the bottom of the pouch, under the spare rounds for his revolver. 'So we are both still together, little goddess,' he whispered as he touched the enigmatic smile on the Celtic goddess's face with his fingers. Your silence is no less than that of the Morrigan herself, he thought wistfully. Was it that Catherine had found another?

Under the canvas of a field ambulance wagon, Private Farrell lay in a coma. The surgeon major examined him and frowned. The man's condition was not good. He should be sent back to a hospital at Suakin, Major Grant thought with some concern. But they were deep in enemy territory and the sick and injured would have to remain until General Graham was satisfied the Dervish warriors were not capable of interdicting his lines of communication to their rear.

Major Grant remembered the man's delirious ramblings before he slipped into his coma during the night. The Irish colonial volunteer seemed to know Captain Duffy from the Scots' Brigade. The major could see the young infantry officer striding towards him across the square. 'Patrick, old boy. Come over here,' he called. 'There is a colonial here who has been using your name rather a lot, for some strange reason.'

Patrick greeted the surgeon. He was a good friend from their many games of chess together in the officers' mess. He stopped at the rear of the wagon beside the surgeon and peered down at the face of Francis Farrell.

'Do you know him at all?' the surgeon major asked.

'I don't think so,' Patrick replied with a slow shake of his head. *But there was something vaguely familiar about the man.* 'Who is he?'

'Private Francis Farrell from the New South Wales contingent.'

'Constable Farrell!' Patrick exclaimed. The memories came flooding back: soft summer evenings sitting in the backyard of the Erin Hotel in Sydney; old Max and the big Irish policeman swapping stories and drinking Uncle Frank's grog; laughter and Patrick sparring with the big policeman as Max urged him on in his thick Hamburg accent full of English words a little boy should not hear, or use. Suddenly here in the Sudanese desert, on the edge of a possible battlefield, was a link with his past in Sydney. A rich Irish past full of love and friendships.

'Ah, so it seems you know the man,' Major Grant said. 'Apparently he was a policeman, at some time in his life then.'

'Sydney,' Patrick answered as he stared stunned at Farrell's pale and fevered face. 'He was a good friend of the family. He and Max were my teachers in the art of boxing a long time ago.'

'So I have the honour of tending to one of the men who taught you the manly art,' the surgeon major said with a wry smile. 'Obviously a good teacher, from what I've seen of your abilities in the brigade matches.'

He had witnessed Patrick's prowess in the boxing ring on occasions. Patrick represented his brigade against other units in the army and had a fearsome reputation as a winner. The surgeon very rarely had to tend to Patrick after a fight – just his opponents.

Hailing from a Scots' regiment that boasted hard men, Patrick's place as the best fighter in the regiment was no mean feat. His fellow officers found his interest in boxing somewhat peculiar when their interests ran to horses and cards. But they also held fierce pride in their fellow officer's prowess in a sport that was normally the craft of the working classes. The young captain was prepared to take the punishing blows of any soldier who wished to match himself in the ring against one who hailed from the upper classes.

'Get this man well, Harry,' Patrick said softly. 'He and I have a lot of catching up to do. At least ten years' worth.'

The surgeon nodded. 'Now let's have a look at your arm, old boy, or you won't have much of a future fighting for those damned mad Scots of yours.'

Patrick stripped off his shirt and while the surgeon examined his wound Patrick stared at the very ill Irishman lying on a stretcher. This was a day of strange and frightening omens, he thought.

21

Fiona White – nee Macintosh – was meeting with the woman whose love for her had not faded with time or distance. Penelope – also known as the Baroness von Fellmann – was still a beauty whose looks had not faded with time. Her golden tresses showed no trace of grey and her voluptuous figure still retained the hourglass appearance of her younger days – albeit with just a little help from the rigid stays of tight fitting corsets.

Fiona's own dark beauty also remained although her ebony tresses were flecked with silver. Her startling emerald green eyes glowed with a vitality which was heightened by the presence of her cousin. Together in the drawing room of Penelope's lavish house the two women provided a distinctive physical contrast. Fiona's slighter figure, dark hair and ivory coloured skin contrasted with Penelope's golden skin and her sensual fullness of figure. Penelope's azure blue eyes gazed into the emerald green of Fiona's with a love that neither woman had experienced in a long time. Not for at least three years, when Fiona had visited the von Fellmanns' estate, in Germany.

She had travelled with her daughters, Dorothy and Helen, to Europe from England where the two young women, in their late teens, were to finish their education. Fiona had chosen Germany as she knew the girls would have Penelope and her husband Manfred to watch over them, which was of extreme importance.

Granville White had destroyed any semblance of a marriage after molesting his own daughter. Fiona had even attempted to kill her husband when she discovered what had been occurring with Dorothy in their library. As her attempt had been unsuccessful, she had settled for estrangement, and her return to Australia was merely a business interlude before she returned to Germany, and Penelope's bed.

Manfred knew of his wife's affair with Fiona and he had even arranged for them to stay together at a hunting lodge which he owned in Bavaria. He did not fear losing his wife to Fiona as he knew that his wife also loved him. Equally, but in a different way.

Granville White was also well aware of his wife's infidelity with his sister. But his acceptance of the situation was now based on indifference. Or was it helplessness? The affair that had started many years before between the two women had stripped the man of any hope of a natural love between husband and wife. But not only had he lost his wife, he had also lost his two daughters. Fiona had vowed that he would never see them again.

The two women sat chatting about the education of Penelope's twin boys, Otto and Karl, who were almost ten years old, and of Fiona's own daughters' progress in the expensive German college for ladies. The talk of children inevitably raised the ghost of a young man Fiona had lost to her own mother. Her son, Patrick Duffy.

'Have you seen him since your mother took him to England?' Penelope asked gently, and reached out to hold her cousin's hands in hers.

Fiona smiled sadly. The question hurt her with a pain that had never left her life. Although the mention of her estranged son's name evoked the bitterness of decisions made, she had a need to talk. 'After I visited you and Manfred in Prussia I visited my mother's family in England. I wanted to see Patrick at his school at Eton . . .' She trailed away and a tear splashed Penelope's hand.

'Did you see him?' she prompted softly.

'No. I was afraid that he might greet me with the hate for me that my mother has poisoned him with,' she replied in a whisper, and looked away.

Penelope allowed the silence. She knew there were no words that could ease the pain of a mother losing a son twice in her life. Once, when she had reluctantly given up her son at birth and a second time, when she was forced to choose between the deep and abiding love she had for Penelope and the return of her son. She had decided to retain Penelope's love. It was a cruel choice her mother had forced on her and Fiona had to live with the agonising consequences.

Finally Fiona withdrew her hands from Penelope's and wiped away the tears from her eyes. 'I even went to Eton and talked to his masters. They were very nice and told me that Patrick was at the top of his classes, but just a little bit unruly, and had almost been expelled from school for his insubordination. They said the senior boys were wary of him as he was prone to thrashing them if they attempted to impose their will on him.'

Penelope smiled and broke into a merry laugh. 'He certainly has taken after his father,' she said, realising that Fiona was speaking with pride of her son's past rebelliousness. 'I could never imagine Michael bowing to fagging if *he* had been at Eton.'

At the mention of Michael's name Fiona's own smile faded. 'Have you seen Michael?' she asked.

And Penelope also ceased smiling. 'No, not for many years. But Manfred often curses his name. He has told me Michael has been working against the Kaiser's interests in the Orient. For that horrid little Englishman Horace Brown.'

'Did Manfred say when he last knew of Michael's whereabouts?' Fiona asked softly. Although she loved Penelope she had never been able to forget the passion of the young Irishman who had opened the door to her deep and, until then, repressed sensuality.

'He thinks he was in Shanghai last year. But Manfred's contacts lost him there,' she answered, and took her cousin's hands in hers once again. 'Michael Duffy is like some beautiful big cat with nine lives.'

'Nine lives is a limited number,' Fiona sighed. 'From the little I know of him from you he must have used at least eight. I pray that my son has the same luck as his father.'

Michael Duffy had always been a haunting presence between the two women. Penelope felt twinges of guilt whenever she was with her beautiful cousin in bed. Guilt that she had shared her body with the only man Fiona had ever truly loved. But she consoled herself with the conviction that Michael's tormented and dangerous existence put him beyond the reaches of a normal life. He was a man who would always be forced to seek snatches of temporary love in the brief moments he spent in many women's arms. His dangerous life had little to offer beyond the sun that rose in the mornings when he left a woman's bed. And it had been his very love for Fiona that had forced him into the lonely life he now led. 'I'm sure Patrick is blessed with his father's luck,' Penelope said as she knew Fiona was thinking about her son's welfare in the war being fought in the Sudan. 'He has already survived a campaign with the army in Egypt.' Better he was in Sydney, Penelope thought. Even if it meant being with his grandmother whose unrelenting bitterness towards her own daughter was preferable to the uncertainties of a battlefield.

'I wish I could just see Michael once more,' Fiona whispered hoarsely. 'Oh, if I just had the chance to talk to him, he might be able to tell Patrick I did not willingly send him away when he was a baby, that circumstances conspired against me and I made a choice I thought was right at the time. I truly believed Molly would find him a loving family to live with.'

'She did,' Penelope said gently. 'She took him to Michael's family where he was loved.'

'I know that now,' Fiona replied, and the haunted look came to her eyes. 'But I fear my mother has poisoned my son's mind forever. She has told him that I intended to send him to a baby farm.' She paused and the haunted look took on a savage edge. 'And it was *she* who told Molly to send my son to one. She must have known the unwanted babies were disposed of by starvation or other means.'

'Your son will return some day to Sydney,' Penelope reassured. 'And I am sure you will have the opportunity to tell him the truth then.'

Fiona tried to smile at her cousin's soothing words but her smile turned into a bitter look. '*If* he ever returns to Sydney I fear he will have to fight another war,' she said bitterly. 'Granville plots to see that he is not able to take his place in the family.'

'I doubt that he could do that,' Penelope replied. 'Your mother has quietly declared that Patrick is your son and no doubt has the proof to back her claim to his rights.'

'She has, but Granville has threatened to fight her in the courts to disinherit him.'

'Surely he has no grounds to do such a thing,' Penelope scoffed. 'No doubt she has the Duffys as witnesses in her case. And you?'

Fiona lowered her eyes and it dawned on Penelope that she did not want to answer the question. 'You are going to remain silent?' she asked, and Fiona nodded. 'Why remain silent concerning your son's identity? I doubt that the threat of scandal would deter you. So why remain silent?'

'I have come to an agreement with Granville,' Fiona answered. 'I have given my word that if I remain silent he will not pursue the matter in court. But if he does, then I will break my silence and acknowledge Patrick as my son.'

'But my brother will still have Patrick as his rival under the terms of the will,' Penelope said. 'I cannot see why he should accept the agreement, knowing my brother as I do.'

'I agreed to signing over my share of the inheritance Father left me,' Fiona said, and her cousin cast her a horrified look.

'Granville will then have a third of the estate,' Penelope said. 'And if your daughters side with their father with their shared third when they turn twenty-one he will have the majority of the shares. He will then be the undisputed master controlling the Macintosh holdings.'

'I know,' Fiona replied softly as she contemplated her momentous decision that had changed the fate of the Macintosh name. She had granted control to Granville who had schemed for years for such control. Now the prize was within his unscrupulous grasp. But the signing over of the shares did come at a monetary expense to Granville. His credit with the banks was stretched as a result of the transfer.

The ramifications of her cousin's decision were not lost on Penelope. Under the terms of Sir Donald's last will and testament he had generously left his sole remaining child a third of the companies. Another third was left to be divided between her heirs, his grandchildren, and the final third of the estate to his wife, Lady Enid.

Dorothy and Helen's shares were being managed by a trustee company until they came of age. But Sir Donald had not anticipated an illegitimate grandson when he dictated the terms of his will. Lady Enid, however, had already put in motion the plan for Patrick to take up his share, a minor but critical share that would give Enid the majority edge over her hated son-in-law – at least until Dorothy and Helen came of age when it was possible the balance of control over the Macintosh financial empire could tilt back to Granville.

Penelope realised her cousin's foolish decision had been made as a gesture of maternal love for a son who would have nothing to do with her. She had signed away the very inheritance that was hers to a man they both knew was capable of doing anything to achieve his aims. Ironically though, in the signing over of her shares to Granville, Fiona had struck a blow against her mother. Enid would now see her own ruthless dreams of the companies remaining with the male blood of a Macintosh heir shattered. Although Patrick would never be in a position to control the family empire, Fiona knew he would still be provided for in a comfortable manner for the rest of his life. If nothing else, her estranged husband was a very astute businessman who would ensure the companies prospered.

Penelope had trouble digesting the news concerning her brother's possible control of the companies. The realisation of his extended power burnt her stomach like acid and she reflected bitterly on the man who had abused her so many years earlier. In winning Fiona's love she had struck her own blow of revenge by taking her from his bed. But that had not been her primary aim. She had always genuinely desired her cousin in a way no man could understand.

22

Before the sun could savage the British army forming up in its monolithic square which was edged
with rifles and bayonets, the order was given to
advance. Horses of the escorting cavalry neighed
and snorted and the gun carriages of the artillery
rattled into motion as they moved forward. Mules
left with their handlers at the Zareba brayed calls
to those of their cousins who carried on their
backs the squadrons of Bengal Lancers, fierce,
hawk-eyed men wearing the distinctive turban and
sporting bushy beards. The dust rose up from
under the boots of ten thousand infantry soldiers
who shouldered arms to march on Osman Digna's
warriors in the hills beyond the ruins of Tamai
while a small force of soldiers was left behind at
the fortified camp to protect the precious supplies
of the commissary from a sneak attack.

Located at the rear of the British square,
Captain Patrick Duffy and Private Angus
MacDonald trudged forward with the New South
Wales infantry. In a cloud of dust, and under a
blazing sun, they advanced through the silent,

deserted ruins of the mud houses of the village. Around them were signs that the village had been used as a base of operations by the Dervishes.

The army did not stop, but continued to advance on the parties of warriors who they could see filling in water wells as they retreated. The enemy remained tantalisingly out of range of a major engagement and General Graham was frustrated at not having Osman Digna hurl his army at his mobile fortress of human flesh. His faith in the iron discipline of his well-trained and seasoned troops was unwavering and he knew a decisive battle now with Osman Digna could possibly bring the Mahdi to heel. But his hope that the fuzzy haired warriors might be savaged by bullets, bayonets and bombs on his square appeared to be disappearing as fast as the retreating Dervishes who fully realised that their spears, shields, swords and antiquated muskets – backed by all the fanatical courage of religious fervour – would not guarantee a victory.

Digna's commanders used instead guerrilla tactics, denying the land's most precious resource of water to the invaders while they sniped from the cover of the rocky hills.

In dashing forays the fierce Bengal cavalry squadrons galloped forward in an attempt to encircle the Dervishes before impaling them on the tips of their long cavalry lances. The accompanying gunners of the artillery unlimbered their field guns with the highly trained and precise movements that had been drilled into them on the more peaceful gun parks of England. The guns boomed and hurled the heavy explosive projectiles into the hills where they exploded in sprays of shrapnel balls.

Cheers rose from the ranks of infantry whenever they could see the columns of earth and smoke rising in the hills as dirty tufts to then wither and die in the air. From the front ranks facing the retreating skirmishers the British fired controlled volleys into the hills. Smoke, dust, noise and the inevitable desiccating heat of the arid land rolled over the square as it stood temporarily still to allow the rifles and guns of the army to seek targets.

Patrick's experienced ear detected the small whizzing sigh of returning fire as the Dervish bullets fell in the square, spent in their over-stretched range. A colonial soldier behind him, thinking his comrade had punched him in the shoulder, cursed angrily Then he realised he had been hit by a stray bullet from the Dervishes and his anger turned to amazement. He was wounded! Another suddenly yelped and hopped a few yards before he, too, realised he had been shot in the foot.

Comrades snatched up the wounded men and carried them to the medical wagons. The square was given the order to continue the advance but struggled to hold its shape as it moved through the broken ground of the covered mimosa hills.

Patrick cursed softly at the order. They may as well return to the Zareba on the other side of Tamai. It was obvious that the fuzzy wuzzies – as the British had nicknamed the Dervish warriors for the black mops of hair piled on their heads – were not showing any signs of falling for General

Graham's wishes. The advance could go on forever – and the army march forever, or until it ran out of supplies or morale. No, Patrick concluded, a different approach was required to fight this kind of war where the enemy nipped at the heels of the giant with painful bites that sapped resolve.

As if reading his thoughts Private MacDonald growled, 'I dinna think all the marchin' will do us any good, sor. Might as well be back at Suakin rogerin' their women folk.'

Patrick grinned. He was thinking more of strolling the narrow streets of the white-washed mud and stone buildings of the port city on the Red Sea and searching for African artefacts in the bazaars. His brief acquaintance with Catherine had introduced him to an interest in archaeology.

'I have to admit you might be right, Private MacDonald,' he answered, and dutifully cautioned as was expected of an officer. 'Except the venereal diseases of this part of the world can do more damage to us than the bullets the fuzzy wuzzies are firing at us now.'

Angus did not reply. He had his own view on life. Soldiering on active service certainly made a man careless of the morrow which might never be after a battle gone wrong and the best thing about the kilt was that it must have been invented for soldiers in a hurry to snatch carnal pleasure without the cumbersome fumbling of Sassenach trousers. Only a soldier hopelessly in love with the doe-eyed girl he left behind would utter such a cautionary statement, he thought. Or a married soldier who feared the wrath of his wife more than he feared death itself!

Near the end of the day's gruelling advance, and skirmishing with the retreating warriors of Osman Digna's army through the arid hills beyond Tamai, the order was given to about face and withdraw to the logistics base at McNeill's Zareba. They were returning to whence they had advanced from earlier that day and, although it was apparent that the eager colonial volunteers were disappointed with the outcome, they also looked forward to the cool of an evening tucked within the defences and a good night's sleep.

All had not been lost. Honour had been satisfied with the drawing of colonial blood and, with the sound of war still ringing in their ears, they turned about and marched along the same route as they had advanced. On the return they saw smoke billowing over the last of the standing buildings of the village at Tamai. Graham had ordered its total destruction. It would be a lesson to the Dervishes, proof that the British army could go anywhere at anytime. With stoic acceptance the retreating Dervishes watched the soldiers fire the village and saw their homes burn then crumble under the weight of the flames. Eventually the British would go and they could return to rebuild. It was, after all, the Will of God, that such things happened.

They had no sooner returned to their own hills when Patrick found himself summoned to brigade headquarters. To furnish a verbal report on the conduct of the colonial volunteers, he surmised.

But when he arrived at the tent of Major Hughes, to whom he regularly reported, he noticed that the officer had a worried expression on his face. Major Hughes had been in a deep discussion with the artillery colonel who had commanded the guns that had fired that day at the retreating enemy. 'Captain Duffy,' he said, as Patrick threw a reasonable salute for the benefit of the artillery colonel. 'Colonel Rutherford and I have just been talking about you.' Patrick was mystified. And the colonel's grave look was disconcerting. 'The colonel was commenting on how you gave his best fighter a thrashing in the ring at Suakin last December. He feels there should be a return fight for the sake of the artillery's honour. A chance for the gunners to redeem themselves.'

'I feel, sir, that your gunners redeemed themselves today from what I was able to observe,' Patrick replied gallantly.

The colonel smiled at the flattery. 'They did well,' he replied. 'But I fear we fired a lot of shells for little return.'

'Colonel Rutherford has an idea on how his guns might get the maximum return on their expenditure of ammunition, Captain Duffy,' Major Hughes said conspiratorially. 'And I agree his idea has a lot of merit. But it involves somewhat of a personal risk to whoever should volunteer to undertake the task. How is your wound progressing?'

'The wound has never been any bother, sir,' Patrick replied cheerfully, and unconsciously flexed his arm to prove so. 'Not much else I can do with the Tommy Cornstalks, sir. They seem to be performing admirably well considering it's their first campaign.'

'Good show,' the major said absent-mindedly, staring out at the setting sun. Clearly he was still troubled by whatever the artillery colonel had suggested to him concerning a special mission.

The brigade major brought his attention back to Patrick. 'I have to put the idea to the brigade commander for approval. But I think he will give it, considering his frame of mind at the moment.'

'General Graham must be feeling as frustrated as the Tommy stalks,' Patrick suggested. 'They want to get at the Mahdi's men in a decisive battle, too.'

Major Hughes nodded and Patrick realised whatever the artillery colonel had suggested might achieve the commander's aim as well as the ambitions of the eager colonial troops. 'At night the fuzzy wuzzies creep in close to the Zareba to snipe us,' the major said. 'We bear the sniping and leave the night to them to virtually move about at will. But, as any soldier knows, even Dervishes must have a place to fall back on before the morning comes. And it appears that they have probably grown rather arrogant about their ownership of the night. A well-trained soldier just might be able to locate that forming-up point, then report back to the guns on their position for a precise bombardment on them. Catch them while they are sitting around scratching their arses and congratulating themselves on a good night's harassment of us. Do you have any ideas on how the mission might be achieved, Patrick?' he asked using his first name fondly, for the man he knew would not hesitate in volunteering for the dangerous task.

Patrick sighed and turned to glance out at the hills before answering. 'I would reconnoitre ground in front of our defences for a likely position to take up. The ground would be a position most likely used by a sniper firing on us.'

'If so,' Major Hughes cautioned, 'then the chances are high that you might bump into any Dervish who should use the cover of night to take up that position.'

'I could take care of that, sir,' Patrick replied quietly.

The brigade major knew it was this critical factor in the mission that only one of his officers was truly capable of. And this young man had a proven record of coolness in the madhouse of killing that was battle. Besides, his physical strength was unsurpassed in the brigade.

Hughes nodded. 'I have no doubts that you could, Captain Duffy.' The artillery colonel nodded in agreement at the B.M.'s choice of officer for the mission. He had seen Patrick defeat his best fighter in a punishing match with his strongest gunner in the inter-unit fight at Suakin. 'I will seek the brigade commander's approval then,' Major Hughes sighed. 'In the meantime you can get on with your reconnaissance, Captain Duffy, and prepare yourself for the job. I will have word back to you before last light whether you will go ahead or not, but at this stage, I think you would be advised to liaise with Captain Thorncroft to have the picquets aware of your movements on the perimeter. It would not do if they shot you. Not with the vital information you will carry for Colonel Rutherford.'

'Sir,' Patrick replied, saluting the brigade major and the artillery colonel. 'If there is nothing else I suppose I should use the little time I have to prepare.'

'Yes, Captain Duffy, I agree.'

'Good luck, Captain Duffy,' the colonel said warmly. 'Your intelligence just might deliver the fuzzy wuzzies a parting lesson in good manners. And I hope to see my gunner give you a sound thrashing when you return to fight him back at Suakin.'

As Patrick walked away from the brigade head-quarters to join Private MacDonald who was preparing their evening meal, he passed by the ambulance wagons where Private Francis Farrell was being treated. It would be good to talk to the man who, he now remembered more and more, was like some distant uncle in the close circle of Irish immigrants to the Colony of New South Wales.

Those days had been an innocent time when he believed Daniel Duffy was his real father and Michael Duffy, his long dead uncle. The truth of his parentage had been explained to him as a young lad and his maternal grandmother, Lady Enid Macintosh, had also explained his mother's apparent treachery.

But what had originally grown out of Lady Enid's need to use the boy as a weapon against the duplicity of her own daughter and son-in-law had developed into a genuine, doting love of the stern woman for her grandson. His natural charm had beguiled the matriarch who held precious the

Macintosh bloodline and the boy was granted all the privileges of English society; Patrick had taken to his life with the ease of his noble blood.

The surgeon major greeted Patrick warmly. The white apron he wore was spotted with the blood of the soldiers' wounds he had tended to. No, Private Farrell had not as yet recovered sufficiently to rejoin his company, he replied to Patrick's question. Patrick thanked him and then parted company to carry out a survey of the ground in front of the perimeter of the Zareba.

Angus wondered at the strange expression on the young captain's face as Patrick squatted in the dust to accept the mug of coffee he passed to him. The mission had been cleared by the commander and he was to move out at last light. He had quickly briefed his batman. Angus knew what the expression was. He had seen the same look on the faces of men before battle. Men who believed their luck had finally run out.

'You'll be needin' this,' Angus said softly as he presented an item he had long hoarded.

Surprised, Patrick accepted the lethal knife. Designed by the American of the Alamo, Colonel Bowie, the weapon's fame had spread to the far corners of the earth, to any place where fighting men required both a sharp point and razor fine cutting edge. 'Thank you, Private MacDonald,' he replied gruffly. 'Better than the English steel they issued us.'

'That it would be, sor,' Angus winked conspiratorially. 'The Sassenachs have no appreciation of the broad blade.'

Patrick turned the knife over in his hand. He hoped that he would not be close enough to his enemy to have to use it. Somehow he had more faith in the protection of Sheela-na-gig.

23

The hills appeared smooth and round, like an old crone's molar teeth. It was as if the Godkin Range had chewed at the blue skies for so long that they were just plain worn out with age. But a few of the low hills were chipped along their summits, with small lines of rocky cliffs where they had bit on the occasional hard cloud. It was into the hills in the late afternoon that the expeditionary force of police and bushmen rode in search of the Kalkadoon.

Gordon James led the column while Peter Duffy rode with an uneasy eye on the sparsely scrubbed, concave slopes of the hills baked dry under the harsh sun. He had passed this way before and vividly remembered how the Kalkadoon warriors had risen from the ground from behind the barest of cover to ambush them. And he was not the only member of the current patrol to ride with an eye cocked warily on the surrounding silent hills. Ahead of the column rode the scouting trackers of the Native Mounted Police, rifles balanced across their saddles.

As Peter rode he reflected on the gulf that had to some extent always existed between himself and the man who led the expedition. At first in their early years it had been as a small crack which had widened, however, when they joined the Native Mounted Police. His Aunt Kate had attempted to talk him out of joining the ranks of the very people who had hunted his mother's people into almost total extinction, the same force that was eventually responsible for the death of both his parents.

Peter often had recurring nightmares of his mother staring at him with lifeless eyes from the flames of the campfire as the fire licked and sizzled her flesh. In his nightmares she was still alive but helpless in the flames as she pleaded to him with soundless words. If only he knew what she was calling to him. What was she asking him to do?

Why had he remained in the force when his friendship with Gordon was no longer something he could consider a part of his life? Now he was certain that this would be his last patrol. He would resign when they got back to Cloncurry. From there he would return to Townsville to work for his Aunt Kate. Gordon James could go to hell.

The hushed silence of the bush was shattered by the sound of a gunshot and the echo rolled off the hills from somewhere up ahead. Troopers snatched carbines from saddle-buckets and frontiersmen thumbed back hammers on their single shot Sniders. Gordon James raised his hand for a halt and called to his police riding ahead to keep a sharp lookout. All in the mounted force felt the gut wrenching fear of ambush as the hills seemed to close in around them. Frightened eyes scanned the slopes for the movement of shadows.

'Look to the hills,' Gordon roared unnecessarily as every eye was already staring up at the summits, searching frantically for sight of the dreaded warriors.

Horses pranced nervously and men taut with fear swore curses to relieve the tension. But nothing happened until an Aboriginal trooper burst through the scrub to rein his horse in beside Gordon. 'Mahmy! Catch 'im blackfella gin long creek.' The trooper's dark eyes rolled, revealing a smoky whiteness. 'Kill 'im one fella gin.'

Gordon spurred his mount forward and signalled for the troop to follow. They rode until they reached the river where, on the sandy bank that led down to a deep rock-pool, an old Aboriginal woman cowered under the gun of a European trooper. A twine dillybag lay beside her, from which spilled freshwater mussels.

Further along the bank lay the body of an old Aboriginal woman spreadeagled by the impact of the projectile that had taken her in the back and shattered her spine.

'What happened?' Gordon asked the trooper.

He was one of the recent white recruits who Gordon did not like or trust and was standing over the terrified old Aboriginal woman cowering at his feet. 'Came on 'em in the creek,' he replied, viciously prodding the old woman with the barrel of his rifle as she wailed with terror for what she knew was inevitable. 'Called on 'em to stand in the name of the Queen,' the trooper continued. 'But they decided to run. Got the one over there, boss.'

'So I see, Trooper Calder,' Gordon said from the vantage of his horse. 'Good shot considering the distance.'

The trooper beamed with pleasure for the praise from his commanding officer. Commanche Jack sidled his mount up to Gordon and stared down at the old woman curled on the ground in a foetal position. He was chewing tobacco and rolled the twist in his mouth. 'What are yer gonna do with her, Inspector?' he asked and spat a long brown stream of tobacco onto the sand between the two of them.

'If I let her go she will go straight to her people and tell them where we are,' he replied quietly. 'That leaves me with little choice.'

'They's already know where we are,' Commanche Jack said as he leant on the horn of his saddle and gazed thoughtfully up at the summits that reared from above the thicker bush beside the river. 'Know'd where we was the minute we rode into these hills.'

'How do you know that?'

'Mescaleros, Kalkadoons. All fightin' people,' Commanche Jack replied, rolling the remaining tobacco in his cheeks to savour the nicotine. 'They'd be watchin' us right now. Probably discussin' what yer gonna do with this here darkie lubra.'

Instinctively Gordon glanced up at the tops of the hills surrounding the river valley and the American chuckled. 'You ain't gonna see 'em, Inspector. That's the whole idea of a good fightin' man. He knows more about you than you do about him.'

'Well,' Gordon replied ominously, glancing at the old woman cringing in the hot sand. 'If they are watching then they are going to learn a lesson concerning the fate of those who resist the Queen's law.'

'You gonna shoot the darkie?' Commanche Jack asked quietly. He caught Gordon's gaze. 'You could let her go.'

'I'm not an executioner,' Gordon replied. 'You, or one of your party, will have to dispose of her.'

The tough American straightened in the saddle. 'Not me, Inspector. I signed on to fight Kalks. Not shoot old darkie wimmin. You want her shot, you do it yerself.'

With a gesture of disgust the American spat a stream of tobacco into the sand, barely missing Gordon. He wheeled his horse aside to ride back to his men. Gordon scowled and swore under his breath. If the seasoned Indian fighter was not prepared to execute the woman, who would? 'Trooper Calder!' Gordon knew the man had a reputation for callous indifference towards life and although he had only been on one dispersal Gordon had been sickened by the man's obvious relish for killing Aboriginal women and children.

'Sir!'

'Take one of the patrol with you and *help* the darkie gin down the track a bit,' Gordon said quietly. 'I think you have a good idea what I mean.'

'Yes, sir,' the trooper replied with an evil grin. He prodded at the old woman with his rifle, causing her to wail piteously as she curled defensively into a ball. 'Duffy, you half-caste bastard. Quit starin' an' help me with yer cousin here,' Calder snarled. ''Elp me get 'er up on 'er feet.'

Peter slid from his horse with an easy movement and without a word he gripped his rifle and strode across to the trooper who had slammed the butt of his carbine into the petrified woman's back. The spectacle of the terrified woman curled on the sand had triggered a distant memory of his mother. *What had she called to him?*

Peter stayed Calder's arm as he made ready to hit her again. 'We aren't going to get her on her feet and out of here if you keep hitting her,' he said.

The trooper glared at him with the eyes of a savage animal but reluctantly conceded to Peter's advice. 'Yeah. You get 'er on 'er feet,' he snarled. 'Or drag the black bitch, if yer 'ave to.'

Peter heaved the woman to her feet and her eyes met his briefly. What she saw was a strange compassion and although she trembled with terror she felt less frightened than before. With gentle words Peter coaxed her away from the mounted horsemen.

Calder followed, his carbine slung carelessly over his shoulder. He turned to glance over his shoulder and wink at Gordon James who stared stonily at the backs of the two troopers disappearing in the scrub. 'A good distance away, Trooper Calder,' Gordon called. The further away the better, he thought, as if the distance would divorce him from what he knew was about to occur.

'Yer doin' a good job there, Duffy,' Calder said, as he followed Peter who half-supported and half-dragged the Aboriginal woman through the bush adjoining the river. 'Looks like yer got 'er thinkin' she's gonna be let go.'

Peter did not reply but continued to help the woman through the bushes until they emerged in a clearing adjoining a section of the river where it widened and flowed between jutting reefs of rocks.

'This'll be far enough,' Calder said and brought the rifle off his shoulder. 'Get 'er to make a run across the river on them rocks.' Peter let the old woman go and she fell to the ground in terror. He knelt and with calm, friendly words coaxed her to her feet.

With tentative steps she tottered towards the river and the path of reefs that spanned the rapidly flowing eddies where she broke into an unsteady hobble. Calder slid the sights on his rifle to fifty yards, tucked the butt into his shoulder and took a sight on the old woman. 'See if I can get a second darkie with a single shot,' he muttered above the gentle bubbling sound of the river. He closed one eye and breathed in slowly and was releasing his breath when he felt the muzzle of Peter's carbine bite behind his ear.

'Pull the trigger and I'll blow your head off, you white bastard,' Peter hissed as the trooper froze. 'Unload the gun very carefully,' Peter commanded.

He watched with grim satisfaction as the old woman reached the far bank where she disappeared safely into the scrub. She could have been my mother, he thought sadly. Just an old woman whose only crime was being Aboriginal. But now she had been given the right to be with her people and live out her life as God had intended.

'You half-caste bastard,' Calder spat as he opened the breech of his carbine and ejected the unfired round. 'Mister James will have to be told you let the darkie bitch go.'

'Isn't that what he told you to do, let her go?' Peter replied with feigned innocence.

'You know what Mister James meant as well as I did,' the furious trooper replied as he lowered his rifle. ''E never intended the black bitch to leave 'ere alive.'

'To kill her would have been murder,' Peter said quietly. 'So you should be grateful I stopped you doing something you might have been sorry for if it ever got out.'

Shaking with rage Calder stepped back from Peter who by now had lowered his rifle. Calder's fury, however, was such that had his rifle still had a bullet in the chamber he would have preferred to kill his fellow policeman. 'You know, Duffy, you don't even talk like a darkie,' he hissed glaring at the young man who faced him. 'You don't even act like a blackfella.'

'Maybe it's because *us* blackfellas are smarter than you white shit,' Peter replied. He had never felt more in control than this moment but knew that his decision to save the old woman's life had placed him on one side of his bloodline.

'We go back an' I report what you did here, Duffy, yer finished,' Calder snarled.

'We will see,' Peter answered quietly and turned his back contemptuously on the trooper who was still fuming with frustration for having an unloaded rifle.

*   *   *

'I didn't hear any shot,' Gordon said to the two men standing at his stirrup. 'What happened?'

'Trooper Calder's gun misfired, sir,' Peter replied before Calder could answer. 'She got away before I could get her in my sights.'

'That right, Trooper Calder?' Gordon asked suspiciously and Calder shifted uneasily from one foot to the other. Never dob in anyone to the bosses, echoed in his mind.

'Like Trooper Duffy said, boss, bloody gun misfired.'

'Get Sergeant Rossi to have a look at it when we camp tonight,' Gordon growled, dismissing the two police troopers. 'Join the troop.'

Gordon scowled as the two men walked over to their horses. He knew when men were lying. He also had no illusions that Peter could be trusted. It was only inevitable that he would eventually revert to his blackfella blood. But for the time being he dismissed his reflections on his former friend's loyalty to the Native Mounted Police and thought about the present situation. If what Commanche Jack said was true about being watched by unseen myall warriors they would have to find high ground for the night campsite. High ground that gave them the advantage, should the Kalkadoon decide to launch an attack on them in the dark. 'Sergeant Rossi,' he bawled down the line of horsemen strung out through the bush on the river bank. 'Get the scouts up the hill over there. Make sure no-one else has taken up residence before us.'

The sergeant acknowledged the order and relayed it to the troopers.

Peter swung himself into the saddle and turned to glance at Calder. The man returned his look with a sneer. Peter reminded himself to stay clear of the man who clearly had murder on his mind. He reined away to join the patrol and prayed that the old woman had found her people. He also prayed that Gordon would not find the Kalkadoon. For if he did, the young tracker knew that his former friend would show no mercy to the men he hunted.

24

Divested of his webbing Patrick breathed deeply to steady his nerves as he sat cross-legged, watching the sun disappear below the horizon. He tried not to think beyond the next few hours.

When the sun was gone he gave Angus a friendly slap on the back as he bade him goodnight. The big Scot shook his head as he watched the young captain swallowed by the darkness. The bonny lad had the look of a dead man about him, he thought sadly.

Patrick passed through the outer guard perimeter post where Captain Thorncroft was personally briefing the sentries on Patrick's mission. It was important that a nervous sentry did not shoot the returning officer in the early hours of the morning. Otherwise the cold-blooded courage required to carry out the mission would come to nought. Thorncroft whispered Patrick good luck in his mission. Better him than me, he thought as Patrick disappeared into the hostile desert.

* * *

A clear sky and the shadows of the silent, rock strewn gullies was Patrick's surreal world as he crawled on his belly towards a tiny knoll of stone. His hands and face were blackened with charcoal, which helped conceal his tanned flesh, but he still felt acutely aware that his khaki uniform stood out like a beacon in the night. He only carried his service revolver, a pocketful of spare rounds and the bowie knife.

He had carefully selected his route to reach the knoll which he had identified as an obvious place for a sniper to take up. It had a commanding position outside the effective range of the defenders in the fortified camp, but it was close enough to deliver random harassing fire. And now the knoll was in sight, silhouetted against the vast star studded skyline of the hill. But would the position already be occupied? Very carefully he slid the knife from inside his boot gaiter and rolled the blade on its side. A thrust from the bowie to the chest required the blade to penetrate in such a way that the blade could slide between the ribs and not be deflected by the tough connecting cartilage. In his other hand he gripped the butt of his pistol which was attached to his uniform at the end of a lanyard.

It was an eerie and frightening feeling to be so far from the Zareba. The only sounds he could hear now were those of the desert: the yipping howl of a jackal calling in the night; the flutter of some nocturnal bird seeking or escaping its prey or hunter.

Crawl slowly and avoid dislodging loose stones, Patrick forced himself to remember. Take your time. Sheela-na-gig is protecting you.

Then it suddenly dawned on him that the little goddess was still with his webbing. This was the first time they had been separated in the campaign. The dreaded thought went through his body with a shudder of primeval fear. He was without the talisman he had grown to firmly believe kept him alive.

He lay still and considered returning to the safety of the Zareba. Nothing made sense anymore. The panic welled up in him threatening to send him into an uncontrollable quaking fear. No. He had come this far and he knew there was no turning back. It was a stupid and illogical thought for an educated man to believe unseen forces guided one's life. That a stone idol and the words of a beautiful girl could keep him alive!

On the skyline, mere yards away, the rock moved! *No, not the rock, but the head and shoulders of a man.* So his extreme caution had been justified.

Patrick lay very still, his eyes barely above ground level, watching the Dervish sniper moving about in the dark with little concern for his security. He knew that he must neutralise the sniper and take his place on the knoll and from there he could slip off and follow the other snipers to wherever they rejoined the main body of their supporting base area. Once identified, he could double back and provide the coordinates for the guns to range on and then the artillery could deliver a concentrated bombardment. Not only would the bursting shells of the guns deliver to the enemy a reasonably good lesson, but also show them that approaching a Zareba at night could be fatal.

The head and shoulders merged with the rock on the knoll as the warrior rested his long, flint-lock rifle ready to fire his first shot into the British camp. His thoughts and concentration would have been on the possibility of his shot finding a target amongst the British as Patrick uncoiled from the cooling earth with the speed of a striking snake. The sniper died with the knife plunged into his chest. His gasp of pain was the last noise he made as he crumpled to the ground.

Patrick reefed the knife from the dead man but he did not have a chance to congratulate himself on his highly successful ambush. He was acutely aware that he was not alone.

Shadowy figures rose out of the earth from all around him. Ten, twenty, maybe more warriors rose, shocked by the sudden appearance of an evil spirit of the desert that burst with lethal fury amongst them. They had been squatting silently behind the sniper's knoll waiting to disperse to their own positions in the hills when Patrick had struck.

'God almighty!' Patrick cried in despair as he turned to face the unexpected threat, instinctively flinging up his pistol to fire blindly into the mass of warriors only yards away.

Stunned by his unexpected appearance, the Dervish warriors reacted slowly. Two of Patrick's wildly fired rounds found targets in their ranks and the men grunted in pain as they crumpled. When the pistol was empty Patrick spun on his heel and sprinted down the knoll towards the desert, away from his own lines.

Only the forward picquets heard the very faint

popping sounds drifting to them on the still night air – and they dismissed the rapid volley as some mad tribesmen firing off their guns in the hills. They did not bother reporting the matter in the morning; they had been more interested in the sniper fire that came from closer quarters during the night, plunging uncomfortably close into the Zareba.

In the morning Private Angus MacDonald realised that the young captain had not returned. Major Hughes sent out a scouting party of Indian cavalry to reconnoitre the path that Captain Duffy had taken. They rode onto the deserted knoll and a cavalryman noticed the many blood stains in the earth. But there were no bodies – nor any sign of Captain Duffy.

When they reported the matter back to the brigade major he nodded and turned away from the bearded soldiers astride their big horses. The brigade had lost their finest junior officer and he had lost a friend.

General Graham had issued his orders to return to Suakin that day as the brigade major transmitted a telegram to Lady Macintosh informing her of the tragic news that her grandson was officially listed as missing in action. His telegram would be followed in due time by a letter of condolences for her loss, for although Patrick was listed officially as missing rather than killed in action, Major Hughes held little hope for the young captain's survival. If the Dervishes had not killed him then the desert soon would.

As they marched away from the hills of Tamai

for the port of Suakin, Angus carried the webbing slung over his shoulder and remembered Captain Duffy's last request before he went off into the night. He had told him that under no circumstances was he to open the pouches of his webbing, and when he had reached the Red Sea, he was to throw the webbing into the waters.

Angus had not questioned the request. He knew a man facing death made such strange requests. But Captain Duffy had explained something to him that was stranger than the unusual request. He had said he thought the webbing might drift on the currents of the ocean to Ireland where it would be found by the Morrigan. Angus had not asked who the Morrigan was but he suspected that the webbing contained something very precious that no man had a right to know about. But he would not have to dispose of the webbing in the Red Sea, Angus told himself with an unshakeable belief. Captain Duffy would claim it soon himself when he rejoined the brigade.

As the army fell back on the port city of Suakin Private MacDonald held tenaciously onto Patrick's webbing. He should have handed it back to the quartermaster but that was not necessary. Captain Duffy would want it back when he returned, the brawny Scot reasoned and the quartermaster tentatively agreed.

25

As the sun set below the tops of the hills the troopers and frontiersmen set about establishing their campsites. Sentries were posted and the horses hobbled for the night as firewood was gathered and bedrolls laid out.

Although the scene appeared deceptively serene all the men of the expedition harboured their private fears. They knew they were deep in Kalkadoon territory in the Godkin Range and the night could easily be rent with the bloodchilling war cries of the tribesmen. The talk around the campfires during the evening was subdued and few men lingered in the circles of light that were cast in the dark.

Peter sat alone, away from his fellow troopers. Word had spread to the others of his treacherous act and now he was shunned by men who had once respected him. But he was not alone for long.

Calder lumbered across from his campfire to stand over him. 'The boss wants to see you, darkie,' he sneered. 'Get your black arse over there now.'

Peter rose and casually brought up his carbine with the barrel pointed at Calder. The gesture was not lost on Calder. He backed away in fear. But he was a tough man and spat at Peter's feet. 'You an' me going to settle up one day, Duffy,' he snarled. 'You can bet on that!'

Peter ignored his threat and strode across to Gordon who was sitting on a log, hunched over his fire with his coat around his shoulders. The evening chill was beginning to creep into the still night air of the mountain range.

'You wanted to see me, sir?' Peter asked in a flat voice.

Gordon gestured for him to sit down. 'I just wanted to talk to you, Peter,' he said. 'I think we have to clear the air between us.' The fire that framed Gordon's face flickered in an uncertain expression. Peter sat with his rifle between his knees and waited. 'I have a good idea that you stopped Trooper Calder from carrying out my request this afternoon. You may have done the right thing.' Peter blinked with surprise but did not comment. It was obvious Gordon had much on his mind. Gordon continued staring into the flames as the fire crackled softly. 'I've never shot down darkies who weren't resisting before,' he said quietly. 'Never shot down gins and piccaninnies, unless it was an accident. My father never agreed with shooting darkies unless it was necessary ... so my request this afternoon was wrong.'

'She got away,' Peter lied. 'Trooper Calder's

carbine misfired.' He would stick to the story, protect the original lie.

Gordon glanced up at him with a sudden shift of anger in his face. 'You and I know that's not true so drop the bullshit,' he flared. 'No matter what happened you probably saved me from some unpleasant questions if someone had got drunk and talked about the incident later on.'

The subdued talk of men beyond the campfire drifted to them. In the far distance some unknown animal squealed as an unidentified predator took its life. Dingo, owl, native cat – who knew? Both men paused in the conversation to listen. All noises in enemy territory were suspicious; it could have been some form of call between the Kalkadoon.

Gordon swung his attention back to Peter and continued, 'You might have prevented a bad situation developing for us by your actions. But, at the same time, you have forced me to decide to send you back with the resupply party to Cloncurry tomorrow morning. I'm sorry, but your loyalty is in doubt and now your continued presence is bad for the troop's morale.'

'Yes, sir,' Peter answered. 'But you are wrong about questioning my loyalty. Despite what happened this afternoon I was ready to fight the Kalkadoon. I just wasn't ready to murder anyone. Not even for you.'

Gordon did not reply. He picked up a mug of tea beside his boot and sipped the hot beverage. 'That's all, Trooper Duffy,' he said softly as he stared into the darkness. 'You can go.'

Peter rose and walked back to his fire where he

sat down heavily So, it was all over. He felt no regrets.

At piccaninny dawn the men came awake as the sentries shook them from their sleep. They ate hurried meals of cold damper bread washed down with hot tea and as soon as they had saddled their horses Gordon called a briefing for his patrol commanders concerning the route they would take that day. He had decided to follow the river valley south having calculated that, if they were going to locate the main base of the Kalkadoon, it would most probably be in the higher and more rugged hills which posed natural fortresses against a mounted attack. He also guessed that the tribesmen would locate themselves close to a good supply of water, and the river valley pointed like an accusing finger south.

Peter Duffy swung himself into the saddle and joined four heavily armed frontiersmen who had been tasked to return to Cloncurry for extra supplies. Gordon had not disclosed the reason Peter was riding with them and they accepted him as an extra escort.

By the time the sun kissed the valley floors the column of troopers and bushmen auxiliaries were slowly weaving their way cautiously through the thicker scrub adjoining the river bank.

In the south the Kalkadoon tribesmen waited for their enemy. They had stockpiled extra spears, boomerangs and nullahs on the hill tops they had chosen to fight from. Their tactical decisions would have pleased any European general of the day but their decision to stand and fight did not please the wily old Darambal warrior. He had vainly attempted to persuade the supreme war chief of the Kalkadoon to return to waging the successful guerrilla tactics of hit and run.

When Wallarie gazed around the hill tops at the men who proudly stood with backs unbent he felt a deep sadness and honour to be amongst the warriors who had dared to stand and fight. Could such audacity not prevail in battle?

The runners came to the hills with messages from other hill tops further north. They reported that at the present rate of advance the white man would be on them in a day. Wallarie squatted in the dust of the hill and crooned a song for the young men who boasted of deeds to be done in the coming battle. But they ignored his Darambal song for the dead as he sat cross-legged on the craggy heights, gazing north into the thick scrub and tree-lined valley below and wondering if he would ever see his kinsman Peter Duffy again. Perhaps they would meet in the Dreaming.

26

The silence of the hot mid-afternoon was shattered by the bloodchilling war cry of the Kalkadoon. A whispering shower of spears sang their lethal song and the swish-swish of boomerangs whirred death in the air.

'At them, lads!' Gordon cried above the shots and shouts from his column of troopers who milled as the deadly wooden weapons fell amongst their ranks. But they rallied quickly under Gordon's calm leadership and spurred their horses forward at the fleeting shadows in the thick scrub of the narrow river valley.

Please God, Gordon prayed, that Sergeant Rossi and Commanche Jack would react to the situation as he had briefed them to.

The naked Kalkadoon warriors fled before the mounted charge as it crashed through the spindly scrub. But suddenly the fleeing warriors propped and turned to face the charge with fresh spears fitted to woomeras. A second shower of hard-wood spears whistled through the mid-afternoon air and a trooper screamed as one of the deadly barbed spears found flesh. He toppled from his horse as he grappled vainly at the slender shaft protruding from his thigh.

If Sergeant Rossi and Commanche Jack were not in position they were all dead men, Gordon thought frantically as he twisted to fire his revolver at the dark figure that had suddenly appeared at his stirrup. The warrior fell back and his spear clattered to the ground.

On the left flank of Gordon's patrol the massed warriors appeared like weeds to surround the troopers who had ridden recklessly into their ambush. The air was full with spears and boomerangs flying from two directions as the warriors joined with the ambushers who had waited patiently for the troopers to pursue them.

It appeared to the Kalkadoon that the white man had learned nothing of their tactics. The patrol was hemmed in by the thick scrub and the Aboriginal giants were able to engage them in close quarter fighting. It would be rifle butt and pistol against wooden shield and nullah.

The trapped troopers sought desperately for escape but the fleeting shadows became a massed wave as they surged forward from the vulnerable left flank of Gordon's patrol. The Kalkadoon came at them from the front, leaving the trapped patrol of fifteen troopers pinned against the river on one side as the warriors encircled them with whoops and battle cries of imminent victory. To be unhorsed in the melee meant certain death and the trooper who had been speared in the thigh knelt on the ground firing, loading his carbine with a desperation born of this knowledge.

Dear God! Gordon prayed with dying hope for the plan he had so carefully planned. Save us! His revolver was empty and he lashed out at a warrior whose body was partially covered by his wooden shield. The man fell back and was saved by his shield which took the brunt of the pistol as Gordon swiped at him. He was grinning triumphantly and Gordon suddenly experienced the meaning of raw fear. He was seconds from being unhorsed by five other Kalkadoon who had joined the fight to finish him off. There was no retreat and the circle was closed on the troopers who fought their own battles for survival.

The grinning Kalkadoon warrior swung his stone axe in a low arcing movement and the sharp edge of the hand-chiselled head caught Gordon a glancing blow in the calf of his leg. He hardly felt the pain; his thoughts were focused on a fighting retreat and he was no longer even aware of his carefully laid-out plan in his concentration to survive.

The rolling volley of shots came from behind him as Gordon frantically pulled down on the reins of his mount to drag her out of the semi-circle of Kalkadoon. They were attempting to close with him with shield, stone axes and lunging lances of wood as he became vaguely aware that the semi-circle had disintegrated. Above the increase in the blasts of carbines and pistols he could hear the roars and shouts of Commanche Jack's troop of horsemen as they descended on the flank where the tribesmen had waited in ambush. Above the din of gunshots, screaming men and cries of mortally wounded warriors he could hear the distinctive accent of the American urging his men on.

The skirmish had turned into a desperate battle of survival for the Kalkadoon who were now themselves caught between the troopers and the sudden appearance of the white bushmen riding down on them with guns blazing. With a desperate courage the tribesmen fell back, although they continued to fight in a disciplined manner.

Commanche Jack's pursuing horsemen hesitated in the face of the Kalkadoon's determined and orderly retreat. With adrenalin spent and reason returned, they broke off the engagement to fall back out of range of the deadly missiles that still filled the spaces between the trees.

Gordon's hand trembled so badly that it caused him to drop a couple of rounds of his pistol as he attempted to reload. It had been too bloody close, he thought as he used the ejection rod under the barrel of his Colt to eject the empty cartridges. He was vaguely aware that the warrior with the stone axe who had wounded him lay face down a few yards from where he sat astride his horse. Blood trickled from a gaping wound in the man's shoulder.

Gordon's horse snorted and shifted under him and suddenly the fallen warrior was on his feet. The wounded man was far from beaten and with a loud cry the Kalkadoon lunged at Gordon's horse, snatching at the trailing reins. The crack of the rifle coincided with the wounded man gasping with pain and toppling forward. The top of his head was blown away in the split second it took the heavy Enfield .577 bullet to strike him.

'As tricky as Injuns,' Commanche Jack said from the cover of the bush. Even as he rode towards Gordon he was reloading his rifle with a fresh round. 'Good thing fer you, Inspector, I was ridin' past.'

The tough American slid from his horse and pointed his rifle at the man lying face down in the red sand. 'These darkies are as ornery as any Apache I ever had cause to meet,' he said as he cautiously approached the corpse. But, from the state of the warrior's shattered head, it was obvious that he was dead. 'Fight even when they should be dead. Now a man like that takes a lot o' beatin'.'

'You took your time,' Gordon snarled ungratefully. 'They almost had us.'

The former frontiersman of the American West tipped his hat to the back of his head and stared up at the police officer glaring down at him. 'We had a mite trouble with our hosses on the slopes getting to you. Lucky we even got to you when we did.'

Gordon had not anticipated this problem of the second column traversing the slopes of the hills on their left flank. He had predicted accurately that the Kalkadoon ambush party would hit them from the left when they went after the warriors whose task it was to lure them into the trap. And in accordance with his prediction he had briefed a column under the command of Commanche Jack to push their horses up the slope and then descend on the ambushers' rear.

But the relieving column's going had been hampered by loose rocks and small cliffs impeding their route. It had been fortunate for the relief column that the Kalkadoon had been preoccupied with annihilating the troopers of Gordon's patrol and thus had not noticed the slow advance of horsemen to their rear.

When Sergeant Rossi brought his patrol into the ambush site Gordon was stunned to see that many of the bushmen were nursing wounds. The little Italian's face reflected the shocked expression of one who was aware how close he had come to facing his Maker. Gordon had left his third column as a reserve force. It was only to engage the Kalkadoon on his orders and he had not been able to order the reserve force in! What had happened?

'Theya cumma outta the bush,' the sergeant said in a flat and weary voice. 'Theya almost killa us. Alla roun' us. This way, thata way . . .' His voice trailed away and Gordon could see a thick smear of dark blood on the sergeant's hand when he gesticulated. Clearly the Kalkadoon had appeared suddenly in the midst of the reserve force of horsemen trailing Commanche Jack's forces.

'Where did the main body of the myalls come from when they attacked you, Sergeant Rossi?' Gordon asked, although he already had a good idea.

'Behind us. Theya cumma behind us. Some attacka from the side.'

Gordon nodded knowingly. The Kalkadoon had not only laid an ambush on their advance but had been stalking them as well. It was a credit to the hunting skills of their enemy that they could have launched such a large scale attack on his expedition without disclosing any sign of their positions prior to the clash. But such an attack also signified to Gordon that he was very close to the main base of the warrior tribesmen.

Weeks of patrolling the hot and dusty red plains of the Cloncurry district in search of the elusive warriors were coming close to the time of a decisive confrontation. Always the Kalkadoon had been able to ride the patrols ragged as they dashed from one reported incident to another. It had seemed to Gordon a pattern had emerged of a well-coordinated series of strikes by the tribesmen intended to wear down his punitive expedition in frustrating, fruitless follow-up actions.

Gordon had finally realised the pattern used against him was intended to wear his men down. Instead of riding from one reported skirmish to another he had deployed his force into a sweeping screen of horsemen patrolling westward across the plains. They had zigzagged north and south so that the mounted and heavily armed force might be seen by the small raiding parties roaming the scrublands in search of unwary travellers and lightly defended homesteads.

Unwittingly the Kalkadoon had fallen for Gordon's tactic of herding them back to their defendable rocky fortresses in the Godkin Range to the west. Unwilling to be cut off by the roving patrols of troopers and bushmen from their women and children, the Kalkadoon had retreated slowly south.

Over the weeks Wallarie had listened to the reports filtering into the hills with the runners returning from the war parties. He had realised with growing concern that the Kalkadoon were being herded like stock. And, like stock, the Kalkadoon were being massed for slaughter.

He had put his views forward but was ignored by both the council of Elders and the Kalkadoon chief. Although the Darambal man was respected for his knowledge of the white man, the Kalkadoon felt that he over-estimated the ability of the troopers to effectively engage them on their own lands. Could it not be that the white men were being led with the same blind confidence that had brought about the massacre of Inspector Potter's patrol? Did they not outnumber the mounted force whose horses were useless on the steeper slopes of their fortress-like hill? And what enemy could come against the stockpile of weapons they had on the hill tops?

But now that the furious bursts of gunfire that had rolled as echoes in the hills had ceased, the warriors stumbled, wounded and bleeding, into their hill top camps. Women wailed and children cried for those who did not return. The Elders muttered amongst themselves. Had the Darambal man been right?

Terituba was one of the more fortunate survivors of the ambush that had gone terribly wrong for the Kalkadoon. Stricken by the loss of friends and relatives, he staggered from his desperate climb to the top of the hills and collapsed with exhaustion. A short distance away Wallarie sat cross-legged, by a fire, fashioning the barbs of his newly made spear. 'The black crows tricked you,' he said calmly to the young warrior panting for breath as he lay on his side in the crumbled rock of the hill top. 'They scattered you with their horses and guns.'

Terituba raised himself into a sitting position. The wailing of the women was terrible in its intensity. He searched the weeping mass for his wife and two sons. He could not see them and remembered vaguely that she had gone with the women, early in the morning, to the river to search for food. His sons were too young to join the young men as they had not yet been initiated into the tribe. They had gone with the other boys in search of goannas and small wallabies with their spears and nullahs.

Terituba felt a dread for his family's safety, knowing that the white men and their black troopers were advancing as an unstoppable force along the river. What if they should fall on the women and children down in the valley? 'It is not like before, Darambal man,' Terituba finally answered, holding his bearded face in his hands. 'They fought us from all sides. Their guns killed many of the fighting men.'

Wallarie continued to chisel with the sharp stone at the end of his spear. 'Their leader is cunning, as I have warned you, Kalkadoon man,' he said quietly, without looking at Terituba. 'He will not stop until you are all dead. He is not like his father who I once knew. He is proud and wants to prove he is a man like his father. But he is not his father. He does not have the same spirit. His father learned *not* to be proud of killing my people. That was before his spirit left his body.'

The younger warrior listened to the words of the Darambal man and no longer sneered at his perceived timidity. For Terituba had a taste of what the Darambal man had warned and he did not like the bitterness of the blood in his mouth. 'We will show the white man Gordon James that he cannot defeat us when he comes to our lands,' he said fiercely, as conviction surged through him with the recovery of his physical strength. 'We will do to him what we did to Inspector Potter.'

But even in his bravado the Kalkadoon man remembered the terrible power of the guns. Men were flung into the earth with gaping wounds and the horses were able to dance away from grasping hands endeavouring to unseat the riders. A worm began to eat away at his confidence to defeat the whites. But he would not let a Darambal man see his doubts and he would not betray the creeping fear he felt. The Kalkadoon were like the fish dammed in the traps they built in the rivers. No. A man must fight to protect the lands that he held sacred.

Terituba knew that his people were possibly facing the same fate as the Darambal man's people. To not resist the invaders surely meant loss of the traditional lands. To resist could mean the loss of a people. Either way, one without the other, was death to the spirit. They were left with only one alternative now that they had allowed themselves to be trapped. A final and decisive battle, the outcome of which would be critical to the very survival of the Kalkadoon.

The Kalkadoon warrior rose to his feet from the earth that was his by birthright. He stood unbeaten and uncowed to face the north from whence his enemy advanced.

27

'Five troopers wounded. Two seriously with spear wounds. Seven of the accompanying party of bushmen wounded. One with a serious wound from a boomerang.' Gordon James read off his list to the force of grim faced troopers and bushmen gathered around him, their rifles and carbines close at hand. 'Well, gentlemen,' he said, glancing up from the notebook in his hand. 'That is about the extent of our casualties at this moment. We have been fortunate not to have lost anyone so far. And today we inflicted a blow against the Queen's enemies. I suspect the Kalkadoon are licking their wounds right now. But I also suspect, despite the defeat they suffered here today, they are far from beaten.'

Men nodded agreement and muttered amongst themselves. They had a grudging respect for the warriors who demonstrated an intelligence in warfare normally reserved for European armies. One or two of the bushmen had served in Britain's colonial military expeditions against the tribes of Africa and gave unexpected compliments to the bravery of their present foe: here was a fighter who knew how to employ tactics and terrain to the advantage of himself. A foe who could stalk them with the stealth of long training and strike, then withdraw with all the discipline of a British square withstanding the assault of a superior force.

'What's yer plan, Inspector?' Commanche Jack asked, chewing on his endless supply of tobacco and crouching on his haunches with his long-barrelled Enfield as a prop.

Gordon cleared the earth in front of him with his boot and, using a twig, drew a map in the red soil. It showed the river valley and hills to the south as he imagined they might be. He snatched up a handful of river stones from the sandy beach adjoining the nearby river and included them in his sketch. When he was finished the men at the briefing huddled closer. 'We are here,' he said poking at the sketch. 'The stones represent the hills to our south.' He turned and pointed at the line of summits that ran north-south and poked above the scrub trees.

'According to my estimations the enemy will be holed up on one of those three largest hills you can see to your front,' he said, and the men glanced up at the hills. The afternoon sun blazed brightly off the rocks and men shaded their eyes with their hands as they surveyed the deceptively peaceful country for signs of Kalkadoon occupation. They saw none but they expected little else with the knowledge they had now painfully acquired of the Kalkadoons' ability to conceal themselves. 'We will camp here for the night and at first light send out small patrols to ascertain which hill the main force of the Kalkadoon are occupying. When this has been achieved the patrols will return and we will assemble for an assault on them.'

'You mean attack 'em?' a bushman questioned, whistling through his teeth. 'What if'n we can't get our horses up the hill? That would mean we'd have to go at 'em on foot. Don't like that idea one little bit, Inspector.'

'We would have cover,' Gordon reassured as he could see the idea did not appeal to many of the bushmen. 'A spear will not go through rock.'

Horse, gun and rider were a unit that gave them the edge on the Kalkadoon. From a horse they could fire, retreat, reload and fire again. The horse gave them the capacity to stay out of range of the deadly wooden missiles but on foot retreat was severely limited.

'What guarantee we would have cover?' another bushman asked in a concerned voice. 'Maybe the hills the Kalks are on are as bare as the hills we passed coming this way. Just a few trees and nothin' much else.'

The gathered bushmen nodded more vigorously and the muttering became louder. They were all volunteers and could withdraw their services.

Gordon had the answer. 'If we don't finish this now and retreat back to Cloncurry the myalls will think they have beaten us. If that happens, then the weeks we have been hunting them will be a waste of time and they will renew their attacks in the district. Their chief issued a challenge for us to dare and come after him. Well, here we are. We have no other choice than to finish this fight once and for all. If we don't, then you will not be able to sleep safely in your beds at night. Your women and children could be brained by a nullah. The Kalkadoon will keep on spearing your stock until you have nothing left to stay for.'

Even the men who had asked the questions nodded agreement. Gordon could see the tough bushmen would come down off their horses if they had to. They would fight, but so, too, would the warriors defending their lands. 'I am sure we will have the cover we need. I suspect the Kalkadoon will have chosen a hill with plenty of cover for himself,' he added as a balm for their fears. 'Our guns outrange their spears. We will keep it that way when we attack. We will work to cover each other as we make our advance against them as we did successfully today.'

His final attempt at reassurance was not entirely convincing. Many of the men gazed around the scrub at the Kalkadoon bodies and realised that they had also taken casualties in the savage skirmish and Inspector James's own trapped patrol had almost been massacred. They fully knew what had occurred had merely been a delaying skirmish and not a full-pitched battle.

When he had finished his briefing and issued his orders to the patrols that would seek out the Kalkadoon stronghold the following day, Gordon watched the men amble away to set up campsites. Sergeant Rossi had his orders to organise the care of the wounded and to arrange for an escort party to take the more seriously wounded men back to Cloncurry.

Gordon remained standing by his map. He

slipped his '73 army model Colt revolver from his holster to complete the task his trembling hands had failed to achieve before. He now loaded the gun with ease and his hands no longer shook with his fear. Once it was loaded and gripped in his hand he felt again its awesome power to take life. His decision to press the advance on the Kalkadoon was an important one in the colony's short history, he knew. To lose against the Kalkadoon with the force he had mustered could be a turning point in the way the government pursued its policies of opening up territory for settlement. Should they be defeated in battle then public pressure might force negotiation with the ancient and traditional landowners.

No, he was not going to be the first representative of the Crown in the Colony of Queensland to be defeated in a major battle with the Aboriginal warriors. But if he was to ensure total success, his victory had to be a final, crushing defeat of his enemy.

He slipped the revolver into the holster on his belt and gazed at the summits of the larger hills of the range to the south. They were out there waiting for him. No doubt, they also realised the significance of the outcome of one last, decisive battle. Not in political or historical terms, but for the very survival of their tribe.

Gordon had a feeling that his old mentor of his boyhood, Wallarie, would have been proud of the way he had learned the killing ways of the Kalkadoon. Or would he now be cursing his very existence?

28

The telegram boy was awed by the size of the house with its lush gardens. From the front door he could see the magnificent harbour below and his astonishment was only broken when a maid opened the door to chide him for not using the tradesmen's entrance. She snatched the telegram from the impudent boy. It was addressed to Lady Enid Macintosh and the maid handed the telegram to her on a silver salver where she sat in the library poring through business correspondence.

The library doubled as Lady Enid's office as she now ran the family companies in reluctant conjunction with her son-in-law Granville White, whose office was in a building in Sydney's Bridge Street. But from her home Enid was able to monitor and decide on those matters affecting the future of the prosperous conglomerate.

She was approaching her seventies and her once jet black hair had faded to a pure white splash of snow piled on her head. Her skin remained relatively youthful looking and her trim figure was like that of a woman twenty years younger.

Stern and unsmiling, Enid thanked the maid and when she had left stared at the telegram with a rising fear. She instinctively knew that it contained bad news and her hand trembled when she read the brief but sharp words on the paper. *Captain Patrick Duffy officially listed missing in action. Letter to follow. Major Hughes B.M.*

In the simple military expression lay the loss of the only person she had grown to love after the death of her son David. Soldiers do not simply go missing, she thought in her shock and disbelief. It was the army's way of saying that he was dead and that they could not find his body.

The maid heard the strangled cry and hurried to the library. Without knocking she burst into the room and was shocked to see Lady Enid sitting so very still and pale in the huge leather chair behind the teak desk. It was as if the woman was dead but still remained breathing! Doctor Vane would have to be fetched.

Michael Duffy gazed at the electrotype reproduction of a long dead Roman general's gold and silver plate. He wondered with idle curiosity just how much the original now held in some European museum would be worth in monetary terms. The original had been excavated from a dig at Hildesheim, near Hanover in Germany, where it had lain in the earth for fifteen centuries. Buried by the retreating Roman legions during a time when the fierce northern warriors had exploded from the dark forests of their lands to sweep south towards the heart of the Roman Empire, bringing about that time in history known to European scholars as the Dark Ages.

The choice of meeting place with Colonel George Godfrey was rather apt, Michael thought, as he stood pondering on the link with the past. The warriors who had forced the Roman general to hide his prized plate might once again sweep across modern Europe. Not as undisciplined warriors wielding swords and spears, but as highly trained and disciplined troops, armed with the latest Krupps weapons of mass destruction. Not this time a threat to the Roman emperors – but a threat to the British Empire of the English Crown.

The newly opened museum in College Street opposite the magnificent Hyde Park in Sydney's very busy heart, held collections of natural and techno-logical history to rival famed international exhibitions of a similar kind. Exotic stuffed animals, birds and fishes from all corners of the world, brought the Australian public a step closer to the dwindling number of wild places on the planet. Steel railways were pushing into steamy jungles and across the vast and lonely plains of Africa and the Americas, taking carriages loaded with immigrants, scientists, tourists and entrepreneurs with them.

'Good morning, Mister Duffy,' the voice at his elbow said, and Michael turned to greet Colonel Godfrey who stood gazing at the plate nestled behind its glass case. 'A magnificent replica of Roman beauty, is it not?'

'Nice to have the original over the mantelpiece,' Michael replied with a smile. 'Would be worth a small fortune.'

'I dare say you are right,' Godfrey commented, and hooked the furled umbrella he carried over his arm. The weather outside the confines of the museum was brewing for one of those short but sharp thunderstorms that often ripped through the city. 'How far have you progressed with your inquiries in the last few days?' the colonel asked as the two men walked slowly away from the exhibit towards a wooden bench set aside for weary visitors.

'I've confirmed the men working around the Baron's ship are, as you and Horace suspected, Imperial marines,' Michael said as they took a seat. 'My German was fluent enough to convince them I was sympathetic to the Kaiser's ambitions to spread the advantages of German culture to this part of the world.'

Michael had noted where the marines drank when they were not with the supposed trading ship moored in Sydney Harbour. He had ingratiated himself in their company as an Irishman who happened to oppose all things English and explained his fluency in their language by inventing a German mother from Hamburg. With the ready flow of strong alcoholic spirits the German tongues loosened and he had been able to pick up bits and pieces of useful information.

'And what of Mister Wong's efforts?' Godfrey asked. 'Has he had any success?'

'He's established contacts with the Chinese in Sydney,' Michael replied and stared at the polished marble floor of the museum. 'Even found one of his countrymen who delivers vegetables to the Baron's house. The man has a good relationship with the servants there who keep him up to date on gossip.'

When he glanced up, Godfrey could see the pained expression in the big man's eye and had a good idea why the revelation of gossip in the house would cause it. Horace Brown had confided all in a report to him prior to the mission being undertaken and the report included Fiona's relationship with her equally beautiful cousin, the Baroness Penelope von Fellmann.

'When will you make contact with Missus White?' he asked gently.

'Day after tomorrow. It appears from what John has learned from his contact that Missus White will be staying at the Macintosh cottage in Manly Village and I suspect that she will be also meeting the Baroness there.'

'What will you do?'

'Meet with her and solicit her assistance with blackmail,' Michael replied bitterly. 'If there is no other way.'

The colonel nodded and a silence fell between the two men. They watched the parade of ladies and gentlemen file past the exhibits.

Godfrey sighed and broke the silence. 'Your work with Horace is finished, Mister Duffy,' he said quietly and Michael looked sharply at the other man as if not believing his ears. 'Horace telegraphed,' Godfrey continued, 'to inform me that the mission is over.'

'Over? What's happened?'

'I don't know, old chap,' Godfrey answered. 'But Horace will tell you himself when he arrives next week. He left Townsville just after I received his telegram last week and I am as much in the dark as yourself. In the meantime you will be paid until

Horace terminates your longstanding professional relationship with him.'

'Then why ask me all the questions about the Germans?' Michael asked with a frown of annoyance. 'You could have told me the mission was off when we first met.'

'I had my reasons,' Godfrey said, staring straight ahead. 'Your work with my friend Horace is over but I think a man like yourself will be interested in undertaking a job for another dear friend of mine. A job that will reimburse you more generously than what Horace has been paying you in the past.'

'What job? And for whom?' Michael asked suspiciously.

'That,' Godfrey sighed, 'I am not at liberty to say at this particular moment. But I will ask you one question before we go any further with this conversation and you can either accept or reject my offer.'

'Ask the question,' Michael growled.

'To what extent would you go to find your son?'

Michael felt a chill creep into the museum. 'What do you know that I don't, Colonel?' His breathing had stopped.

'Apparently you are not privy to the news of your son being reported missing in action. I'm sorry.'

'The Sudan?'

'I'm afraid so. It appears he was on a reconnaissance mission for the army at some place called McNeill's Zareba when he went missing and from what the army can tell me it seems he must have clashed with a band of Dervishes beyond the lines. They did not recover the body. So he is officially missing in action until they have substantive proof of his death.'

The terraced walkways of the spacious hall of the museum closed in on Michael. Patrick missing in action, presumed dead! His son was the only part of his life that was created out of an act of love. 'What does my son's fate have to do with the job you are offering me?' he asked, barely above a whisper.

'The person who has an interest in hiring you is a dear friend and has been recently made aware of your availability to carry out a trip to Africa and my ability to have letters of introduction prepared for you for the general staff of the army at Suakin. We both feel you have more than a financial interest in finding Captain Duffy, or at least confirming, either way, his fate.'

'Who is *that* person, Colonel?'

'All in good time,' Godfrey replied. 'But first your word that you will accept the offer I have made on behalf of my friend.'

'You bloody well know I would go in search of my son. Money or no money.'

'In that case I will meet you at Central Station at seven o'clock in the evening at the main entrance. We will go from there in my carriage to meet my friend and discuss the matter.'

'You aren't going to tell me who your *dear friend* is before then?' Michael asked irritably.

'All in good time,' Godfrey repeated. 'I am sorry you had to learn of your son's fate in this manner, Mister Duffy. I know that you have had no contact with him. But I also know he is your son and always will be.' Michael stared with a vacant eye at the marble floor as the colonel rose from the seat stiffly and glanced around. 'You will need time to think,' he said gently. 'You can inform Mister Wong he is no longer required in Sydney. I believe he has a family and rather prosperous business in Queensland and so no doubt will be pleased to return home.'

He unhooked the umbrella from his arm and absent-mindedly prodded the marble floor with the metal point. 'You are a fortunate man to be able to command the loyalty of Mister Wong,' he added as he made ready to walk away. 'I believe he would follow you to hell if you asked him.'

'We have been to hell together, Colonel,' Michael said quietly. 'I would never ask him to go with me to that place again. It is only a place where I go.'

'Yes. I believe you do,' Godfrey said sympathetically and cleared his throat. 'I will bid you good day, Mister Duffy.'

As Michael watched the colonel walk away he wondered who had a vested interest in ascertaining Patrick's fate. Who had access to knowledge about his own identity and how? 'Granville White!' he hissed between clenched teeth. Was Granville White the *dear friend*? It made sense that White would have friends at Victoria Barracks. If this was so, he knew he was in great danger. Was it that the traps would be waiting for him? Was it that Granville White desired to ensure his completion of a mission he had set out to achieve over twenty years earlier when he had hired the thugs to kill him?

Paranoia was an inevitability in this world of

treachery and deceit and only his comrade-in-arms, John Wong, could be trusted deep in enemy territory. Was it a coincidence that the colonel had told him John's services were no longer required?

Michael felt as if he was walking in a valley with his enemies enjoying the advantage of the hills on either side. But at the end of the valley he could see Fiona smiling sadly at him. He sensed that her need to talk about the fate of their son was equal to his own. At least now he could go to her without the threat of blackmail. But the thought of the meeting with the colonel the next day caused Fiona to fade from his vision. Was he walking into a trap set by the utterly ruthless man he had sworn to avenge himself on one day?

'You leave tomorrow, John,' Michael said firmly to the big Eurasian sitting opposite him in the dingy office that had been a front for their operations against von Fellmann. Not that the office would have fooled a careful scrutiny by anyone acquainted with the import and export trade. There was no real evidence of the paperwork one would expect with the trade: no ledgers of accounts could be seen on the bare desk or empty shelves; no almanacs of shipping routes. Only a painted sign at the front of the tiny office declaring the proprietor. *John Wong – Importer of Oriental Wares*.

John shifted in the swivel chair and hunched forward. 'You go without backup to Central Station tomorrow you could end up dead if your suspicions about Granville White being behind the meeting are right,' he growled. 'You need me, Michael.'

'Not anymore, old friend,' Michael said mournfully. 'You have a wife and family to think about and I was stupid to even recruit you for the job here. I took advantage of your loyalty without thinking through the possible consequences the mission might have had to your safety.'

John's burst of laughter rolled around the tiny office, catching in the spider's web at one corner of the tin ceiling. 'Old friend, I was getting bored,' he said when the laughter had abated to a chuckle. 'I was almost missing the days you and I pushed our luck to the limit. I was growing fat on my missus' excellent noodle cooking and I was starting to question why the hell I had left you to have all the fun somewhere in the Orient. I often thought about raising the subject of rejoining you every time Horace came over for a chat.'

'It's different this time,' Michael warned with a sad smile. 'Here I have come the full circle of my life to confront the enemy who started me on the road to the hell that has been my life. I'm in his territory and he holds all the advantages.'

'Never much different in the past,' John grunted. 'You and I always seemed to be up against the odds. But somehow we survived.'

Michael stared at his friend. Yes. They had seen much together and had always beaten the odds. But this was different. Here, he worked under the shadow of the gallows, should he be identified and betrayed to the police. A warrant for murder did not cease in a man's lifetime. Here, his friend could be compromised by association with a wanted felon. A compromise that could ruin his business and life with his family. 'You leave tomorrow,'

Michael reiterated stubbornly as he bit down on the unlit Havana cigar he had retrieved from a box on the desk. 'What happens tomorrow is personal. It's got nothing to do with you.'

'All right, if you say so you bloody fool,' his friend answered with a tone of exasperation. 'I'll go, and leave you with your problems.'

Michael stared suspiciously at his friend as he leaned back in his chair. The damned inscrutableness of his Chinese half had come to the fore, he thought. 'Will you give me your hand on a promise to go?' he asked, as he continued to examine the expression of the man opposite and noticed a faint flicker of uncertainty.

But the uncertainty was quickly absorbed in the smile that came slowly as John thrust out his broad hand. 'On the lives of my family and my illustrious ancestors I promise I will leave,' he said and Michael took his hand.

'The lives of your family I believe,' Michael said with a wry grin. 'But your illustrious ancestors! I doubt that you have ever burnt incense for them.'

'I was talking about my Irish ancestors,' John retorted. 'And from what I've seen of barbaric Irish custom it seems you drink to them. Not burn incense.'

'Good idea. I suggest we share a drink for old times' sake and toast illustrious ancestors – Chinese and Irish.'

John nodded. An oath on the lives of his family was indeed a sacred blood oath and maybe he had forgotten to mention *when* he had promised to leave Sydney. At least not until he was sure his friend was not walking into a possible trap.

29

The meeting with the bankers dragged into the early evening. Lady Enid Macintosh hardly entered into the discussion on the merits of converting two more of the Macintosh ships with refrigeration engineering. Her hated son-in-law had taken most of the lead in the discussion with the grey men who would finance the enterprise.

She sat in the austere, dark panelled board room immersed in her grief and hatred for the smugness of the man who now sat at the head of the long, polished table. Granville had taken the chair as a gesture of his position within the Macintosh companies and Enid did not have the strength to comment on his assumed role as head of the financial empire that was, in reality, slipping from her rigid control.

The three other men who sat along the oak table represented the English financial institutions which backed the Macintosh companies. Granville had convinced them that the money needed to convert the ships for the Australia–England run would bring greater profit to the company with the addition of a meatworks in Queensland. Beef and lamb from the colony could be funnelled into the Macintosh abattoirs and then packaged for shipping direct to England. The revolution brought about by the invention of refrigeration meant Australian meat could be shipped fresh to English tables. No longer would the non-perishable clips of Australian wool be the only major product to be exported from the far-off colony. The finest cuts of Australian meat could grace even the Queen's table.

Cigar smoke curled in heavy blue clouds around the room as the bankers puffed and listened while the excellent port in crystal decanters made the listening even more tolerable. The men finally nodded as one and the plan was approved. Much as she hated and despised her son-in-law, Enid had to admit his plan to link the whole chain of meat production from the hardy Queensland pastures to the elegant tables of England, without a costly middleman, was sound. Theirs would be a monopoly.

'Thank you, gentlemen.' Granville smiled broadly as the men filed out of the smoke-filled room to go to their exclusive clubs in town or to their families in Sydney's more affluent suburbs. But his fixed smile melted once he was alone with Enid. She had not bothered to thank the men and remained seated at the table. Granville closed the door and turned to speak to her. His aristocratic good looks had faded with time and he now looked in appearance like a middle-aged bank manager or accountant. But his suit was the finest cut in the colony and had been tailored in London's Savile Row.

'I have been remiss in offering my condolences on your tragic loss, Enid,' he said with feigned sympathy. 'A terrible thing to happen to one so young.'

Enid stared listlessly at him. 'You may be able to convince the men who were here on the merits of the proposal,' she said in a tired voice, 'but you will never convince me you have any feeling except for power.'

'Oh, I have feelings for my daughters. *Your* granddaughters,' he retorted. 'Both will have reached their twenty-first years very soon,' he added as a veiled threat to Enid's tenuous control of the family fortune. 'I will probably give them coming-of-age gifts of substantial sums of money so that they may enjoy the fruits of their grandfather's legacy to them.'

'In return for their shares,' Enid replied, attempting to keep the rising bitterness from her tone. She did not want her hated son-in-law to see her distress at the statement about his daughters most likely selling their shares to him. He would then have an almost clear two-thirds share of the Macintosh companies. 'You give nothing away, Granville,' she said. 'Not even to your own flesh and blood.'

Granville glared with undisguised hatred at the frail woman who confronted him across the table. For so many years she had dominated the Macintosh family but her iron rule was coming to an end, he consoled himself. He suspected that she had only returned from England because she was paving the way for her beloved grandson, his own wife's bastard, to take a more active hand in the

Macintosh companies, should he leave the army as he had promised Enid. If so he would have returned to Sydney. But that was a moot point now that he was missing in action and most likely dead. 'It was *your* flesh and blood that gave me the opportunity to sit in this chair,' he sneered as he grasped the back of the chair he had occupied at the head of the table. 'A chair I doubt that you wished to relinquish in a hurry, dear Aunt Enid.'

'You have no right to the position, as you well know, Granville,' she replied as she walked towards the door. 'Until your daughters come of age we both hold the balance of decision making in the companies. And a lot can happen before then.'

'Not a threat I hope, Enid,' he said with mild surprise at his mother-in-law's statement. 'You don't have many friends left alive.'

'I will never believe my grandson is dead. Not until I see his body with my own eyes,' she replied with a steely determination in her statement. 'And from what I know of my grandson he is too much like his father to be killed that easily.'

At the mention of Michael Duffy's name Granville blanched. One of two recurring nightmares was to wake up and look into the eye of the man who he knew would one day exact his revenge on him should their paths ever cross again.

The other nightmare was losing everything to his mother-in-law. But there was also a third nightmare that visited him in the dark nights. A nightmare with no real substance, just a vague feeling of dread for a place he had never visited: a hill on Glen View Station surrounded by endless plains of brigalow scrub, a primitive place, sacred to a people long since dispersed by Sir Donald almost a quarter of a century earlier.

Enid felt a surge of pleasure at seeing the observable discomfort the name of Michael Duffy caused the despised Granville. Oh, if only she could turn back time. She had made few mistakes in her life but when she had they haunted her down the passage of years. They were mistakes that had commenced as ripples and ended as life destroying tidal waves. Bad decisions had lost Enid the love of her only daughter and turned her into a bitter and vengeful woman. Fiona had long cast her lot with Granville and the sale of her shares to him only proved further the lengths she would go to inflict the maximum damage on her own mother.

When Enid opened the door to the board room she saw Colonel George Godfrey standing in the hallway, an umbrella hooked over one arm. He stood admiring a painting on the wall and Granville, who had followed Enid into the hallway, paused when he saw the former army officer.

'Good evening, Lady Macintosh, Mister White,' Godfrey said politely as he turned from the painting. He was not in the corridors of the Macintosh building by accident; he had walked the same corridor many times on his way to the Macintosh offices to pass on information that would be converted to important intelligence. 'I pray I am not too late to see you.'

30

Steam and smoke swirled around the people waiting on the platform of the railway station. The chuffing iron monsters that trailed billowing smoke across the plains and mountains to the west of Sydney now trailed their smoky plumes into Sydney's Central Station.

The trains brought elegant ladies, rheumy eyed shearers, eagerly awaited mail, bales of wool and young men in search of work in the bright lights of the 'big smoke'. The railway lines joined the distant colonial capitals in a way only once dreamed of. Now a traveller could step aboard a train in Melbourne and cross the Murray River to change trains for the trip to Sydney, a feat made possible by the completion of the construction of a bridge spanning the river near the township of Albury.

Outside the cavernous structure of the railway station horse-drawn cabs, carriages, drays and buggies waited for fares, families or friends. Wealthy ladies wearing the awkward but fashionable bustled dresses of the day mingled with their poorer sisters who could not afford to be as uncomfortable and thus wore plainer, less voluminous dresses.

Adventurous or desperate young women from the country stepped off the trains in search of positions as maids and nannies in the homes of the colony's gentry. Young men in moleskins and the single shirt they owned left the station in search of a cheap flop house, and eventually a job working in one of the factories or building sites of the rapidly expanding prosperous city.

From an elegant horse-drawn carriage alighted a dignified older man in frock coat and top hat carrying an umbrella hooked over his arm. He searched the sandstone portal of the railway terminus for the man he had come to meet.

Michael Duffy doubted that he would need the small pistol he carried when Godfrey arrived to pick him up. It was unlikely Granville White would make his appearance in such a public place – or that he would do his dirty work personally. No, it was more likely he would be taken to a lonely place where men would be waiting for him. But Michael had decided to go along with the colonel and maybe he would have a chance to get to Granville. How? He did not yet know.

At least this time he was forewarned and partially prepared, unlike the many years earlier when he had confronted the vicious Rocks' thug, Jack Horton, and his equally dangerous half-brother. Both men had been hired by Granville to do his dirty work and dispose of Michael.

Godfrey approached him through the crowds of passengers and waved with his furled umbrella.

Michael moved towards him like a stalking cat. The colonel was aware of the Irishman's tense demeanour as he approached; he moved with the grace of a hunting cat ready to spring and the big man kept his right hand close to his side. He has a gun, Godfrey thought with mild amusement, realising Michael did not trust him.

'The carriage is just outside,' he said when Michael came close. 'It will take us to our meeting.' Michael nodded and followed.

The carriage was a fine piece of very expensive craftsmanship drawn by four beautifully matched greys. A well-dressed carriage man sat atop the seat with a long riding whip in his hand. He stepped up and into the carriage where he sat opposite Godfrey who sat facing the rear of the open carriage. The carriage man flicked the four horses into motion.

After half an hour of travelling it was dark. They had left the gas-lit streets of urban Sydney and were on a reasonably smooth dirt road that Michael knew led eventually to the south headland of Sydney Harbour. Shops and streets had given way to bush and the more luxurious homes of the colony's aristocracy and wealthy merchants.

Neither man spoke on the trip and even in the dark Godfrey noticed Michael's hand was never very far from the pocket of his trousers. 'Do you have one of those greased leather holsters, Mister Duffy?' he asked and Michael glanced at him with a mildly surprised expression.

'That's right, Colonel,' he answered. There was no sense in lying.

The colonel frowned and stared past Michael's

shoulder. 'And who may I ask is the person who has obviously hired a hansom cab to follow us?'

Michael's mildly surprised expression turned to a frown of puzzlement. 'I thought you might know that answer, Colonel,' he stated softly. 'One of Mister White's men, no doubt.'

'I most certainly hope not!' the colonel replied and Michael experienced a moment of confusion. If they were being followed, as the colonel had noted, then it was not likely he would have mentioned the fact.

'Where are we going?' he asked and Godfrey glanced around himself before answering, 'Not *where* we are going, Mister Duffy, as we are already there.'

The Irishman stared into the night and could see a huge home with a magnificent driveway bordered by mature trees. He knew immediately where he was.

'I don't think you will need to use your gun here, Mister Duffy,' he said lightly, smiling at Michael's confusion. 'I doubt that Lady Enid Macintosh will prove to be that much of a dangerous foe.'

Michael returned the smile with a sheepish one of his own. 'That remains to be seen. From what I have heard of Lady Macintosh's reputation . . .'

The colonel laughed softly. 'You could be right, Mister Duffy.'

The cab following them stopped just out of sight as Michael and the colonel passed through the intricately decorated wrought iron gates.

Michael glanced over his shoulder at the pin-pricks of the cab's light in the night. He shook his head and smiled. He now had a good idea who had followed them.

They had never actually met before. But Michael, whose life had been inexorably changed through her unyielding opposition to her daughter's future with him, felt he knew much about the matriarch of the Macintosh family. Nevertheless, he was taken aback by the woman. She appeared so frail, unlike the woman he had always imagined from Fiona's descriptions years earlier.

She sat in a chair with her hands joined in her lap. After the introductions George Godfrey stood protectively beside her chair in a manner that intimated a long and warm friendship.

A clock ticked unobtrusively in the background and sweet steam rose from the creamed coffee in Michael's cup. He was aware that Lady Macintosh was examining him closely with her emerald green eyes and guessed she must have been a stunning young woman. It was obvious from where Fiona inherited her own beauty. The intense appraisal did not cause Michael any discomfort. It was as if Lady Enid was looking for something.

Finally Godfrey broke the strange silence and cleared his throat. 'I'm sorry if you were under the misapprehension that I was working in the interests of Lady Macintosh's son-in-law, Mister Duffy.'

'Suspicion is something I have come to accept as part of life, Colonel,' Michael replied. 'However, I do not see why you did not tell me it was Lady Macintosh you wished me to meet.'

Godfrey shifted ever so slightly before he

answered, thereby disclosing to Michael his discomfort. 'I agreed with Lady Enid's opinion that you might not meet with her.'

'A lot of things have happened in my life,' Michael replied, without displaying any emotion. 'Some good, most bad. But your care and concern for my son in the last few years wipes away any animosity I may have held for you. I know now that you had no complicity in the matters concerning my reasons for fleeing the colony, Lady Macintosh.'

He could see an expression of gratitude flicker in her aristocratic features. Time had brought them together in a strange and unforeseen alliance; they both shared common blood in Michael's son.

'I know your life has been full of tragedy, Mister Duffy,' Enid said gently. 'I know my opposition to your acquaintance with my daughter those many years past has brought much of the pain that I see in your face. But I also know that I would make the same decisions today that I made over twenty years ago should the same situation arise.'

'I would expect nothing else from you, Lady Macintosh,' Michael replied with a rueful smile for her intransigence. 'From what I know of your reputation.'

'Thank you, Mister Duffy. We know where we stand with each other.' Enid appeared to relax slightly now that their mutual positions on old issues had been established. She took the coffee that Godfrey poured for her and continued, 'Patrick is so like what I see in you, Mister Duffy, that your presence reassures me that my grandson cannot be dead as the army has presumed. I was watching you when you entered the drawing room and what I felt was your power.' Michael raised his eyebrows in surprise as she continued. 'You are a rare man amongst men. I have been informed that you have survived many wars and carry the scars of each one. Your life has always been one spent in extreme peril and yet you have survived. I also believe that Patrick has inherited your power and that he is still alive. I will confess that until you entered the room I had intended to ask you to help me find and recover his body. But meeting you I now firmly believe Patrick is alive.'

Michael listened to the sincerity of her words and felt a strange liking for the woman. He placed his cup and saucer on a polished walnut coffee table. 'I would never believe my son was dead,' he said. 'He has the luck of the Irish.'

'He is also English – and Scots – by birth, Mister Duffy,' Enid reminded him quietly. 'I would like to think he has our luck as well.'

'That too,' Michael replied with a grim smile. 'He will need all the luck he can get if he is to be found safe and well.'

'I think if anyone can find him it will be you. His father.'

'You and the Colonel obviously have some plan for me,' Michael stated. 'If so, I am willing to be part of it, I assure you, Lady Macintosh.'

'Colonel Godfrey has valuable contacts in the army. His contacts extend even to the Sudan and he is able to arrange for you to carry letters of introduction. Those letters will assure you of all possible help from the general staff. To ensure that those in the Sudan comply with your requests I have purchased a newspaper. It has correspondents covering the campaign. I am sure my recently acquired employees will be more than willing to assist you by revealing any cases of tardiness or hindrance to your efforts from the army to me.'

That Lady Macintosh would purchase a newspaper company solely to ensure that the correspondents would make themselves available to help him impressed Michael. Then she spoke further.

'My son-in-law tried to oppose me on the purchase of the paper. But we compromised on another financial matter.'

'May I?' Michael requested politely indicating an empty chair opposite Enid. She nodded and he sat down. 'I am curious,' he said, 'to know why you didn't elect to choose someone else to find Patrick. You appear to have the means to hire your own army rather than just one man.'

For a moment Enid lowered her gaze and Michael could see she was deep in thought. She raised her eyes and answered, 'An army lost my grandson, Mister Duffy. But I believe the love of two people searching for Patrick will find him.'

Michael did not need to know more. She had answered his question in her simple recognition of his paternal love for a son whom he had only seen once in his life, although Patrick's photograph had been carried as his talisman over the years. On impulse he asked, 'Do you have any likenesses of my son, Lady Macintosh?'

She glanced up at Godfrey who excused himself

to leave the room. 'I have arranged with Colonel Godfrey for you to have bank drafts to cover your expenses,' she said. 'You will find they are generous. How you spend the money is of no concern to me, Mister Duffy. I know it is unlikely to be squandered when you are looking for my grandson.'

Godfrey returned to the room and passed Enid a framed photograph. Tears began to appear in the corner of her eyes as she gazed at it before passing it to Michael. While she dabbed at her eyes Michael looked down at the full-length sepia portrait of his son wearing the dress uniform of a Scots' Brigade officer. The face that stared back at him was his own of twenty years earlier. Although the likeness was not in colour, he knew the great difference was in the eyes. Patrick's were the Macintosh emerald green of his mother and grandmother, his own were the blue-grey of his people. 'May I keep this, Lady Macintosh?' he asked in a voice broken with barely concealed emotion.

'Yes. I have others. But I doubt that you would need a likeness of Patrick to recognise him now.'

Michael knew exactly what she meant and thanked her.

When she reached out with her hand to him she was helped to her feet by Godfrey and Michael guessed that she was telling him that their meeting was at an end.

'There is one thing I should say in parting, Mister Duffy,' Enid said as she paused at the door to the drawing room. 'I *may* have been wrong in my choice of husbands for my daughter. But knowing my grandson I fear he is very much like what you must have been like as a young man. And, knowing that, I doubt I could have let you marry my daughter.'

She turned and left the room with the regal grace of an empress and Michael grinned broadly after her. He had seen just a twinkle of merriment in her eyes at her parting rebuke and knew she was probably right.

'I will take you back to Sydney, Mister Duffy,' Godfrey said as he fetched his umbrella from a stand in the hallway. A pretty young maid in a starched apron showed them to the door.

'That will not be necessary, Colonel,' Michael replied. 'I already have a cab waiting for me.'

The colonel frowned and cocked his head questioningly. 'How is that, old chap?' he asked.

'I know only one person who would put his honourable ancestors' souls at risk. And my bet is that this person is lurking outside waiting for my safe exit.'

'I hope Mister Wong has had the sense to keep the cab waiting,' Godfrey said smiling. 'Because it is a long walk back to Sydney.'

John Wong *had* kept the cab waiting but at a high financial cost. Michael found him in the shadows of the sweeping driveway and greeted him with a warm growl. 'Thought you swore on the lives of your family, and the honour of your ancestors, that you were going back to Townsville?'

John grinned and slapped him on the back. 'I didn't say *when*.'

'No, you didn't, come to think of it.'

'So when are you returning home to Townsville with me?'

'As soon as I meet with Horace and settle some old business I have in Sydney,' Michael replied as the two men strolled down the driveway, the gravel noisily crunching under foot. 'Then I am going to find my son. Only after all that will I return to Townsville.'

Enid bade Godfrey goodnight and climbed the stairs to the library. She sat at her desk and removed an ornate, leather-bound journal from a drawer. The diary was used to record events she considered of some importance. It did not record such events as births, deaths and marriages which were penned in her copperplate hand in the great family Bible. But it did record the sinister side of her life: meetings in business matters that had very significant ramifications for the future prosperity of the family companies; information she received from her contacts about exploiting business opportunities; monies paid from time to time to grease the wheels of government.

In the latter category Enid found an entry for the payment of one hundred guineas cash paid to a detective of police by the name of Kingsley. It had been in 1874 and the detective had visited her with information he had obtained from a criminal by the name of Jack Horton. The dying man's last act on earth was to tell as much as he knew of the murderous connections of Captain Morrison Mort and her son-in-law, Granville White.

Horton's honesty had been motivated purely by a need to avenge himself on the captain who had deserted him in his time of dire need. Bleeding from a fatal slash to his stomach, Jack Horton also told the detective of Granville's complicity in hiring himself in an attempt on the life of one Michael Duffy. Duffy had killed Horton's vicious half-brother in self-defence.

At the time Enid had received the information she had dismissed the existence of a death-bed confession. Michael Duffy had been reported killed years earlier in the New Zealand campaign against the Maori. And even if she had known he was alive, it was doubtful that she would have used the information to help him prove his innocence.

Enid stared at the carefully compiled notes she had made just after the time of her conversation with the detective. Times, dates and names indelibly recorded in the pages of her journal.

She closed the book and walked across to the window of the library that commanded a view of the driveway below. Should she reveal what she knew of Jack Horton's confession? Was it in her interests to have Michael Duffy cleared?

Michael's existence posed a threat to her grandson's decision to renounce his Irish inheritance and adopt fully his Anglo-Scots blood. His father might well sway Patrick towards retaining his Papist religion. And a Papist controlling what was left of the Macintosh wealth was unthinkable! Even if he was her beloved grandson! No, better that Michael Duffy remain a hunted man in the colony. As such, his contact with Patrick would be seriously curtailed.

Enid thought the decision to conceal what she

knew of Michael's innocence was definite. But doubt nagged her conscience. What if Patrick came to learn of the knowledge she now had concerning his father's innocence? She felt a shiver of fear as she sat down behind her desk and placed her hand absent-mindedly on the cover of the journal. No, that would not happen! The consequences of such an exposure were too frightening to contemplate. For now she merely would allow the strange confidence she experienced when she first set eyes on Michael Duffy to warm her.

31

The expedition assembled on the scrub covered plain. In front of the rock strewn slopes of the craggy hill Gordon James sat astride his mount and a lone figure stood on the crest. Horses shifted under nervous riders; each and every member of the expedition had reservations concerning the wisdom of a frontal assault on the Kalkadoon hill. But the plan had been formulated and it was too late to make changes now.

Terituba could see the tiny figures on their horses form ranks below his position on the slopes of the hill. He crouched and fingered the selection of spears he had stockpiled behind his rock with nervous anticipation for what would happen next.

Wallarie stood alone on the rocky slope, gazing with fixed attention at just one of the tiny figures. The figure wore the blue jacket of the Mounted Police and did not carry a carbine. He could see the man gesticulating with his hands to bring his forces into the lines for what Wallarie knew was to come. The Black Crows had formed similar lines prior to attacking his people many years earlier when they were camped at the waterholes of his traditional lands.

When Gordon was satisfied his forces were in position he turned to survey the ranks. He had briefed them that morning on the tactics to be employed in the assault on the hill fortress of the Kalkadoon and would issue the legal challenge he was required to make. If the tribesmen did not respond accordingly they would charge the hill. They would ride as far as they could up the slope, then dismount and continue the attack on foot, using fire and movement tactics. Meanwhile, the grim faced bushmen sat astride their mounts, with rifle butts resting on hips; they stared up the slope to the lone figure.

Concealed halfway down the hillside Terituba also stared up at the Darambal man. Then a thin and distant voice drifted to them on a slight breeze from the plain below. 'What did the white man call?' Terituba asked Wallarie, knowing the Darambal man understood the white man's language.

'He said we must surrender,' Wallarie called back. It was the only translation he could think of for the call *Stand in the Queen's name!*

'Ahh!' Terituba spat at the earth and hefted his basalt war axe into his hand. 'I would like to see how he is going to make us surrender.'

Gordon stared up at the lone figure and frowned. Where were the warriors? Were they concealed amongst the rocks? He slipped his pistol from its holster, raised the weapon above his head, and with a sweeping movement of his arm initiated the charge. 'Forward!' he roared and the two lines of horsemen broke into a trot.

Then they picked up the pace to spur their mounts into a gallop. Bushmen and troopers alike whooped as they charged at full pace up the slope of the Kalkadoon hill. Commanche Jack let out an Indian war cry he knew from fighting the Apache. The red earth exploded into a cloud of dust as the hooves of the horses bit hard for leverage on the slope.

Wallarie had watched the impressive display of European tactics and could not help but be awed by the sight of the two lines of horsemen charging across the dusty plain onto the lower reaches of the slope. Awed though they were, the thundering charge of horsemen did not scatter the few disciplined warriors, who waited amongst the rocks of the lower slopes. As the only line of defence the cleverly concealed men would take the brunt of the attack.

Terituba could hear the thunder of the charge echoing amongst the rocks. It was not a sound he had ever heard before. It was fearful, not unlike that of the storm that brought the thunder and lightning.

For Wallarie it brought back distant memories of a terrified young man crouching in the scrub as the troopers swept past him to fall on the helpless men, women and children of his clan. He felt no fear this time. *This time he was ready*. He glanced down at Terituba and could see his body twitching with nervous excitement.

As the young warrior began to rise from his cover he heard the voice of the Darambal man shout, 'Stay down. Don't let the Black Crows see you until they are close enough for you to use your axe on them.'

Terituba sank back behind his cover.

Surely no myall would take on a full-scale mounted charge, Gordon thought optimistically as he spurred his mount onto the hill slope. From the corner of his eye he could see his troopers leaning forward in their saddles with their carbines. They surged forward like an unstoppable tidal wave, yelling and cursing. To scatter the Kalkadoon from the summit of the hill meant they could then ride them down and pick them off.

'Jesus!' Gordon swore when he saw about thirty painted warriors suddenly rise from amongst the rocks, spears notched in woomeras and heavy war boomerangs gripped in strong hands. 'They aren't going to run!' he heard himself explode above the thunder of the charge.

The mounted men reacted by firing from the saddle as they rode forward. Bullets smashed amongst the rocks and the ricochets whined around the slopes. Spears and boomerangs fell amongst the ranks of mounted horsemen and a horse whinnied in pain. A few of the wildly fired bullets found Kalkadoon targets as they attempted to retreat higher up the slope past Terituba's concealed position.

Gordon scanned the hill top as his men continued the charge. Where was the main body of the Kalkadoon? Just a handful of determined warriors on the lower slopes and a lone warrior standing at the top of the hill were watching their attack. Had the Kalkadoon changed tactics? The thought chilled Gordon as he imagined that somehow the main body of warriors were even now forming to attack his flanks or rear.

Horses reared in protest as the slope became too steep for them to advance any further and the attackers slid from saddles with their weapons. The horses, free of their riders, galloped back down the slope and sought the safety of the bush. A few of the fleeing horses had spears protruding from them and the bushmen and troopers could hear the derisive jeers of the black warriors taunting them from the summit.

Using the cover of the rocks, they cautiously moved forward. The blue sky above was full of rocks falling like rain as the handful of Kalkadoon defenders showered them from their stockpile of stones.

Gordon panted as he struggled up the steep slope and sweat stung his eyes. Around him he could see his men crouching behind any cover they could find to reload their guns, rise and fire, then duck again behind cover.

The momentum of the attack seemed to be wavering and the battle Gordon had planned for so long appeared to be falling apart against the determined resistance of a handful of Kalkadoon. He knew he could not afford to lose this decisive battle. Maybe thirty or so Kalkadoon opposed his larger force of heavily armed men. Where were the rest?

Terituba crouched ready to spring. He could hear the crunch of stones under a boot on the other side of his rock cover. The enemy was so close that he could hear him panting with ragged breaths.

Terituba rose and saw the startled expression on the white policeman's face. He swung his axe and the polished edge caught Gordon a grazing blow across his forehead. Blood splashed Terituba as the white officer toppled backwards. Gordon's forehead was split open and he crashed unconscious into the dusty earth of the slope. Seemingly from nowhere, a bullet struck the Kalkadoon warrior a smashing blow across the chest, breaking his ribs. The impact spun him around and he crumpled to his knees, gripping his chest.

Wallarie saw the Aboriginal trooper who had shot Terituba down on one knee reloading his smoking carbine. The shot had saved Gordon from certain death but the trooper also realised that his own safety was far from secure. He now had to confront the older warrior on the hill top who, in the meantime, had scooped up a spear and notched it to his woomera. With the carbine reloaded, the trooper took a hasty sight on the figure poised to fling the spear at him. The spear missed the trooper but it was effective enough to throw off his aim. He flinched and fired wildly and Wallarie would only remember that something struck him in the side of the head, nothing else.

'Get Inspector James!' Commanche Jack roared from the cover of a rock. 'He's down hurt!'

The trooper who had fired the shot that had struck Wallarie ran forward and was joined by three other frightened and sweating troopers. They grabbed their commander roughly by the arms and legs and dragged him unceremoniously down the slope under the continuous barrage of rocks.

From the heights, above the retreating attackers, a roar of triumph went up from the handful of defending Kalkadoon. But they had drawn blood against their attackers at a terrible cost to themselves. The rocky slopes were littered with their dead and wounded warriors.

The sky was a red haze of swirling black dots and his head thumped like a bass drum being played by an imbecile. Gordon James groaned and rolled on his side to vomit. The action caused even greater pain in his head. He was helped to sit up by a trooper who pushed a canteen of water to his mouth. Gordon gulped down the water but the nausea welled up in his stomach and the beating drum was drowned by the eerie sound of Aboriginal voices singing in the distance. 'What's happening?' Gordon groaned as he focused his blurred sight on the ring of grim-faced men around him. 'What's that noise?'

'Corroboree,' Commanche Jack answered, in a flat voice filled with disappointment. 'The Kalks are celebrating their victory.'

Gordon touched his forehead and was aware of a thick bandage that swathed his head. He vaguely remembered something hitting him. He thought that he saw Wallarie standing alone on the hill when the blurred thing struck him senseless. When he focused on Commanche Jack he saw the man's left arm below the elbow was at a strange angle. And when he glanced up into his face he saw the acute pain in the smoky eyes of the tough Indian fighter.

'Got in the way of a rock,' Jack explained. 'A

330

lot of the fellas got in the way of rocks and spears. We took a lot of casualties but no-one kilt yet.'

'Horses?' Gordon asked as he regained his senses. 'We get our horses back?'

'The boys rounded 'em up,' Jack replied, holding his broken arm with his good one. 'The boys are fit to ride out on 'em right now. They reckon the Kalks have given us a good lickin'.'

The young police officer struggled to his feet and swayed uncertainly as he surveyed the extent of his defeat. Bushmen and troopers with broken bones, split flesh and the occasional spear wound sat with their backs against the prickly bark of the arid land trees. They were silent and subdued and an air of defeat lay over the expedition like a heavy stifling cloak. The sound of rocks crashing and clattering on the hill slope, as the handful of victorious Kalkadoon celebrated their victory, drifted on the hot, still air.

The exhausted and demoralised men watched Gordon as he walked amongst them to examine the extent of his inglorious defeat against such a pitifully small force of determined men. 'Time to head home, Inspector,' one bushman said as he nursed his broken fingers. 'We'll need more than we got here to beat those blackfellas.'

Gordon did not answer him but walked over to Sergeant Rossi who was treating a man wounded by a spear. The man groaned in agony as the sergeant attempted as gently as possible to twist the barbed point from the man's shoulder. But the barb would not come out and it was obvious that he would require the services of a surgeon to remove it.

'Sergeant Rossi! I want you to get all able-bodied men together for a meeting in five minutes.'

Sergeant Rossi acknowledged his superior officer's order and left the wounded man. The able-bodied men ambled listlessly over to Gordon who stood staring up at the summit. He could see the distant figures of warriors exposed amongst the rocks of the hill top. He could not afford to be defeated by the Kalkadoon. To return to Cloncurry was not an option.

The bushmen and troopers who gathered around him were certainly a sorry sight. When Gordon addressed them his voice was full of confidence and the despondent men listened. But he was a born leader and could inspire men with the force of his personality.

The men listened as Gordon outlined a new plan; they would split the force and assault the hill from two directions. The main assault would be up the slope from whence they had retreated. A diversionary assault would take the Kalkadoon from the opposite side of the hill. It was a simple plan and its simplicity appealed to them.

The expedition was redeployed into two columns – one column under Gordon's command and the other under Sergeant Rossi. Gordon would lead the frontal assault on the hill and, although badly injured, Commanche Jack insisted on coming with Gordon. The American had one of the bushmen splint his arm and swapped his rifle for a revolver.

Sergeant Rossi and his column rode out to take up their position on the opposite side of the hill while Gordon waited in the sparse shade of the scrub with his own force. After an hour they heard the sound of gunfire. Sergeant Rossi had commenced his assault.

'Right, lads,' Gordon said calmly. 'It's time to go.' The remaining able-bodied troopers and bushmen rose to their feet and heaved rifles from the earth. They formed a skirmish line and advanced with guns blazing under a hail of rocks, spears and boomerangs against the lightly defended summit.

Again it was slow going as they moved from rock cover to rock cover, firing and reloading. But the attackers noticed a radical change on the summit. The defenders were no longer as organised and were running about in confusion as they moved to defend one side then the other. And, as they did, they were unwittingly exposing themselves to the guns of the attackers. One after another the Kalkadoon warriors fell as the bullets plucked away their lives.

Gordon fired his revolver until it was empty. On either side of him his men kept advancing steadily forward. He raised his revolver searching for a target. But the battlefield had fallen silent.

'Reload. And fall back to the horses,' Gordon ordered to break the eerie silence that had descended. 'See to the wounded.'

The men broke rank and straggled back in silence to the scrub where the more seriously wounded had been left.

'Goddamn Kalks!' Commanche Jack muttered as he walked and shook his head disbelievingly. 'Never knew when to give up!'

As weary men collapsed under the shade of the trees, Gordon wanted to seek a cool and dark place and crawl inside. He wanted to be alone and contemplate the enormity of what had just happened. But he knew he must stay on his feet and supervise the next stage of operations. His mission was not over – and would not be over – until the Kalkadoon ceased to be a people capable of ever waging war on the settlers of the Cloncurry district.

'Damnedest thing I ever see'd,' Commanche Jack said at his elbow. 'Bravest thing I ever see'd in all my years of fightin' Injuns.'

Gordon did not reply to the American's observation but simply nodded his head. Where was the main body of Kalkadoon when every sign had pointed to an inevitable final battle? Just a handful of courageous warriors standing against his superior force. Why?

When the answer came to Gordon he gazed up the hill. They had given their lives so that the women and children and the rest of the warriors could slip away. The realisation of the tribesmen's courage in their suicidal last stand humbled him and he bowed his head. They had denied him a victory and the story of their heroic stand would outshine his grasp for victory. Well, it was all over, he thought. The Kalkadoon had finally realised that they could not take on the might of the British Empire and he had done his job.

So why did he feel as if something terrible had occurred? Not only in the lives of the defeated Kalkadoon but also in his own. Was this hill a spirit place, like the spirit hill of the Darambal people? Was he forever cursed like his father had supposedly been cursed? With a superstitious shudder Gordon turned his back on the hill and strode over to meet Sergeant Rossi who was riding in with the second column.

In the late afternoon the troopers moved cautiously amongst the bodies of the Kalkadoon warriors to count the dead and shoot the wounded. Terituba regained consciousness and lay very still, feigning death, as the troopers stepped over him to advance up the hill. From the corner of his eye he attempted to see where Wallarie had fallen. But he was gone. Cautiously Terituba moved his head to scan the rocks around him.

Everywhere he looked he could see the enemy firing the terrible weapons that took the lives of his people on the hill. To run now would be certain death. So he lay his head on the earth and waited patiently.

When the sun was below the hill and the stars rose from the distant plains Terituba crept away from the battlefield. He wandered in the night until he came to the river where he knelt and slaked his thirst. His head throbbed and blood continued to trickle from the furrow of flesh opened up by the bullet.

He lay down in the sand of the river bank and fell into a deep sleep. In his dream he remembered the death song the Darambal man had sung before the battle and woke with a start. His acute hearing picked up the sounds of the wild dogs snapping and snarling over the feast they had found on the slopes. The pride of Kalkadoon manhood was nothing more now than food for the scavengers. Terituba fell back into his sleep.

As the sun rose the whistling flap of a flight of wild duck overhead woke the warrior. Much of his strength had returned. But he knew that his enemy would also have regained their strength. The leader of the white men had proved to be as ruthless as the Darambal man had warned. Terituba also knew that he would not leave the hills until he had hunted down the last of the Kalkadoon warriors. He knew that he must seek out any surviving bands of his people. But first he must find his wife and sons.

He waded into the shallows of the river where the cold water bit his naked flesh although he did not feel it as he washed away the blood-adhered feathers. In the washing away of the totem signs of his warrior people he was washing away forever a way of a proud and courageous people. As a warrior people the Kalkadoon had effectively ceased to exist.

In the gorges, and along the creek beds the troopers fired into the deserted gunyahs of the Kalkadoon. Smoke rose to mark the destruction to those survivors who had fled deeper into the sanctuary of the hills from where they watched in despair. Women wailed and the children joined their grief with tears of confusion for what had occurred the previous day. Surely in the long time reaching back to the Dreaming, no other catastrophe had ever been as devastating! However, had not the war chiefs listened to the Darambal man's advice not to pit the full strength of the tribe against the white man, then none would have survived. At least the women and children were alive and so too were a handful of the warriors.

Gordon James made a personal tour of the slopes before joining his force which was preparing to ride out in search of survivors. He walked slowly amongst the bodies that littered the hillside searching for just one man. But he did not find the body of the Darambal man amongst the dead. The old warrior was nowhere to be seen.

'What yer lookin' fer, Inspector?' Commanche Jack asked from astride his horse.

Gordon stared across the red plains that stretched east from the hills. Above the plains a majestic eagle floated gracefully on a thermal updraft with its great wings spread.

'I think I found what I was looking for,' he replied as he gazed at the eagle. Commanche Jack spat a long chew of tobacco onto the ground and reined away. It did not appear as if the inspector would have told him what he had found.

The American had guessed correctly. Gordon was not about to say that in the flight of the eagle he saw the spirit of the old Darambal warrior. He continued to watch the eagle until it drifted on the wind to blur with the distant horizon. Maybe Peter had been right. Wallarie was a spirit man who could never be caught.

32

The ferry trip across the harbour recalled bitter-sweet memories for Michael. Times when, as a young man, he and his cousin Daniel Duffy spent their precious leave roaming the secluded beaches and scrub covered headland of Manly. A time of innocence when Michael had dreamed of a career as a painter and Daniel of ambitions in law.

At least Daniel's dreams had been realised, as Michael knew from his sister Kate. He held a seat on the Legislative Council as the representative for the working-class district they had grown up in. Michael's dreams, however, had been shattered the night he killed Jack Horton's half-brother in a street fight. It had left him with two decades of living as a dead man to his family – with the exception of his sister – and two decades of constant danger to himself.

In many ways, he brooded, fate had cast his lot the day he and Daniel had stood on the pier of Manly Village waiting for the ferry as a violent thunderstorm brewed in the sultry summer after-noon. That had been the day he had first lain eyes on the beautiful young dark-haired woman whose hand had gripped his arm as a reaction to the close clap of thunder overhead. Meeting Fiona Macintosh had been purely coincidental. But as the circumstances of the deadly relationship between the Macintosh family and his own began to unfold, Michael no longer dismissed the chance meeting as coincidental. It was as if a powerful force brought them together – to punish either one, or the other, or both.

Kate was convinced that the slaughter of the Nerambura clan of the Darambal people had a definite link with the tragedies that had come to haunt both families over the years. At first Michael had dismissed her convictions. But he also had a respect for his sister's insights into the world that lay beyond the shadows of the night. Had the meeting with Fiona been ordained by a force beyond his understanding, he wondered again as he watched the pier crowded with people as the steam ferry approached the wharf. If so, was this yet another ordained passage in his life?

The gangplanks clattered from the wharf onto the ferry and the passengers disembarked. Michael breathed in the salty freshness of the air as he strode down the pier towards the picturesque village which nestled between the calmer waters of the harbour and the rolling breakers of the Pacific Ocean. The village always seemed to have a holiday air about it which had been intended by its visionary founder, Henry Gilbert Smith, who had arrived as an immigrant from England in 1827. His vision had been to make Manly the Brighton of Sydney.

Michael walked through the village along the Corso, named by Henry Smith after a street he had first seen whilst in Rome. He passed busy hotels and elegant little shops until he came to the end of the main street which terminated at the crashing waves. If what John had gleaned from his Chinese market gardener contact was correct, Fiona should be staying in the cottage this day.

It was mid-morning and the onshore breeze ruffled his thick, curling hair as he walked with the sand squelching beneath his boots. In the distance he saw the tiny figure walking away from him on the beach. She held a brightly coloured parasol to protect her from the sun and walked slowly in bare feet to savour the feeling of the ocean's crispness between her toes. Even at a distance Michael knew it was the woman he sought.

'May the angels protect you always,' he said softly when he approached her from behind. Fiona froze and for a brief moment Michael thought she might faint. But she steadied herself and turned slowly as if expecting to be frightened by the spectre of a ghost.

'Michael!'

His name came as a strangled whisper as she stared up at his face with an expression of utter astonishment.

'I thought you might remember those words,' he said gently, smiling sadly down on her. 'I knew you would be here. Don't ask me how, though.'

Fiona did not respond immediately, such was her shock at seeing again the face of the man she had once loved above all others. She had seen him once since their last moments together in the cottage not far from where they now stood on the beach. But the last time she had met him he was introduced to her as Michael O'Flynn, American gun dealer. She had thought at the time that he was the man she once knew, the man who had fathered her son. But his denials of his identity had been convincing, although not convincing enough to fool her cousin Penelope. Now he stood before her, years older. But he still had the slightly crooked nose, a legacy of his days as a bare knuckle fighter. She did not think his ruggedly handsome face was marred by the leather eye patch; his remaining blue eye sparkled with the spirit of humour and gentleness she had always associated with him.

'You are as beautiful,' he said gently. 'No, you are even more beautiful now than when I last saw you on this beach. Time has stood still for you.'

Fiona touched her hair self-consciously and her laughter was mixed with tiny tears. 'And you, Michael Duffy, have not lost any of that Irish charm of yours,' she said. 'My hair has the signs of age, as you can plainly see.'

'Only the streaks of silver that mark you as a lady,' he replied warmly, and his smile broadened for her benefit. 'Your beauty is ageless, like the blue of the ocean or the colours of the rose.'

'I know you are lying, Michael Duffy,' she said softly, and the tears welled behind her emerald green eyes. 'But I would believe anything you said because no man is as gentle and loving as you.'

The big man who had survived years of war and deadly intrigue looked away to the rolling waves that broke with a soft hiss on the yellow sands of the beach. He did not want her to see the tears that came to his own eyes, although her affirmation of that side of his nature that he had to deny to the world at large was touching. Very few people in his life outside his immediate family knew him other than as a battle-hardened soldier of fortune.

'I know about Patrick,' he said in choked words as he gazed across the sea. 'I am going to find him.' Then he turned to face her and the parasol fell from her hand as she reached out to embrace him.

She held him and deep racking sobs shook her body. She cried tears for the years they had lost; tears for the son they created but was now lost to them. Her pain found release in the arms she so vividly remembered. She clung to him and felt his big hand stroking her hair as if she was a child once again in the arms of her beloved nanny Molly O'Rourke.

As if they had gone back in time, Michael and Fiona sat together in the cottage and held each other's hands. But this time the passion was gone. Their love was different now as too much had happened in their lives.

'I know of all that which occurred between you and Penelope,' Fiona sighed. 'But I doubt that she shared your soul as I have, only your body.' He did not answer. But if he had it would have been to agree with her. 'Penelope and I . . .' Fiona seemed to struggle for words before she finally said, 'I love Penelope in a way you might not understand.'

Although Michael knew of the relationship that existed between the two women he did not reveal it. Better that she thought some things were secret from his dirty world of intrigue, he thought with a twinge of guilt. 'I think I understand,' he replied, and squeezed her hand gently. 'You need not tell me any more if you don't wish to.'

'I will always love you, Michael,' Fiona said softly. 'When I learned of you and Penelope I was hurt and angry but I remember Penny telling me she had not loved the same Michael Duffy I had once loved. So we have both been fortunate to have found the love of our own Michael Duffys.'

Michael laughed gently at her wide-eyed attempt to explain the situation. Her expression took on a puzzled crossness that was very appealing to him. 'What is so funny?' she asked him stiffly. 'I am being serious, Michael.'

He ceased his soft laughter and stared at her with a gentle smile. 'You know something. As a man I have been very fortunate in life to have known you both. But I pray to God that our son never learns that his mother and his aunt Penelope shared the bed of the two Michaels each of you knew. I suspect his English upbringing might not approve of the wanton ways of his mother and aunt.'

Fiona's stern expression melted with her laughter as she had a fleeting image of her son's shock. But the laughter died as she gazed gravely at Michael and said, 'You will find him. Won't you?'

A haunted look came to her emerald eyes as she pleaded for her son's life with the one man she truly trusted.

'I will,' Michael answered and held her hands tightly in his own. 'And when I do, I will bring him home to you.'

Fiona tried to smile at his confident, reassuring words. 'Even if you bring Patrick back, my mother has poisoned him against me,' she said in a whisper. 'He has been told by her that I sent him away to a baby farm and had it not been for Molly saving him he would have been killed.'

For a second Michael was stunned by the revelation and stared at her in horror. This was not an act possible by Lady Enid, he thought. 'Then I will tell him the truth,' he said. 'That your mother has lied to him.'

With a gratitude beyond mere words Fiona hugged Michael with all the strength in her body. 'Dear Michael, I know why I love you so much. You are able to see the truth.'

Neither noticed Penelope enter the room until she was standing before them. Then it was Michael who saw her first and he disengaged himself from Fiona's arms.

'Hello, Fiona,' she greeted politely, then turned towards Michael. 'I was expecting to see you earlier.'

Fiona's expression changed dramatically. She was caught between guilt and confusion. Although nothing had occurred between her and Michael the situation appeared compromising. She brushed down the front of her dress and greeted her cousin who returned her words with some coolness.

'What do you mean by "expecting to see me earlier"?' Michael asked and Penelope turned her attention to him after she received a quick hug and peck on the cheek from Fiona.

'Your return to Sydney is known to my husband,' she replied. 'I am afraid the men who work for Manfred report all contacts they make with strangers and my husband was not slow to realise that the big Irishman with one eye who spoke fluent German could be none other than Michael Duffy. You must be more careful, Michael my love.'

'Jesus, Mary and Joseph!' Michael swore. 'What else does he know?'

As Penelope took a chair Michael could not help but admire her beauty. Age had not dimmed the aura of her sensuality, he thought. She was no less sexually appealing than when he had shared her silk sheets a decade earlier.

'I'm afraid my husband fears you have been sent by that horrid Mister Brown to sabotage his mission,' she answered frankly. 'You know he has sworn to kill you if you attempt to interfere in his mission.'

'Claim New Guinea for the Kaiser?' Michael asked bluntly and she smiled mysteriously before answering, 'I never divulge what is spoken of in bed, Michael, as I hope you know and appreciate.'

Fiona glanced from Michael to Penelope.

'You can assure Manfred,' Michael said quietly, 'that I have no intentions of sabotaging his mission. Nor does Mister Brown.'

'I might believe you, Michael,' Penelope answered with genuine sympathy, 'but I doubt I could influence Manfred. He only knows you as a dangerous man capable of anything.

Unfortunately he does not know you in other ways, as Fiona and I do.'

'I mean it, Baroness. I am finished with working for Horace Brown and my life is my own.'

'I said I believe you, Michael,' Penelope re-iterated. 'But for your sake you should leave Sydney immediately so nothing will happen to you.'

'My sake, Penelope?' Michael asked with a grim smile. 'Or yours?'

Penelope was quick to seize on his intimation of her relationship with Fiona and she glanced at her cousin. She had come to comfort Fiona with her body and instead had found Michael in her arms. Never before had Penelope felt as uncertain of her cousin's love until now. 'Yours, Michael,' she replied, as Fiona's eyes met hers.

No words needed be spoken. Fiona knew from her answer to Michael that Penelope loved her with her body and soul and Michael now stood as an outsider, denied both of them and yet loved by them both.

Michael rose and bid them a polite good evening. His last recollection of the two women who had been so important to his life was of them holding hands as he closed the door behind him.

As he walked away from the cottage Michael realised that a part of his life had been reconciled with his meeting of Fiona this day. Other than the son they mutually shared they had very little else between them. Fiona truly belonged to Penelope and for that he felt no jealousy. What he had felt in the room between the two women was real love, although he had to admit he did not fully understand it. But then, he sighed as he stepped onto the yellow sands and gazed out at the big rolling waves of the Pacific, no man would ever understand the mysterious ways of women. It was an impossibility. Finding Patrick was at least possible.

33

Ben Rosenblum slipped from the saddle and led his horse to the stockyards. He passed Jenny's grave and slowed to glance at the little pepper tree struggling to grow. It would need more water, he thought as he walked to the yards. More water and attention.

Life on the property had not been easy for Ben. He needed stockmen who knew the bush and how to find the cattle in the scrub when the time came for mustering. At least with Willie they had been able to cope with the few head he owned. But labour was in short supply; men had been reluctant to ride the lonely tracts of scrub, deep in the heart of Kalkadoon territory, so long as the fierce warriors were still an active force in the district.

Ben looped his reins around a rail and his mount shivered. Myriad bush flies had descended on her sweating flanks. She stamped her foot irritably and Ben understood her bad temper all too well. His was not much better. The loneliness of his isolation was getting to him with each day that passed on his own.

'Whoa!' he said softly to his horse as he ran his hand down her flank to calm her. He raised her rear leg to check her hoof as she seemed to be favouring the leg when he rode back. And it was while he was bent examining the hoof that he saw the figure, standing at the edge of the scrub line.

Cautiously Terituba watched the white man he knew as Miben. What would his reaction be? Would he shoot at him on sight as had happened when he had fled with his two wives and two sons from the Godkin Range after the dispersal? The guns of the squatters had taken the lives of one of his wives and one of his sons since that terrible day of the battle. They had been shot down whilst attempting to flee from the mounted bushmen scouring the valleys and gorges of the hills north-west of Cloncurry.

The young warrior realised the hills were no longer a sanctuary and chose to escape east and into the vast tracts of scrub. He retraced the track which had taken him into the great gathering of clans and stumbled onto the Jerusalem property of Ben Rosenblum. And now he knew his only hope to keep his remaining wife and son alive was to befriend the white man. With Miben he felt there might be hope of such friendship; he was a white man who had a good spirit, a brave man who also had children. Terituba watched but made no move and knew that the white man was making an appraisal of him.

Ben straightened casually as his hand instinctively fell over the handle of his revolver. He squinted against the glare of the late afternoon sun. He could see the Aboriginal giant standing alone and very still at the edge of the scrub; the man was familiar. He was the same warrior who had accepted his gift of flour and sugar many weeks earlier. He noted that the Kalkadoon was not carrying weapons and appeared to have sustained a wound to his head. 'Come here!' he called to Terituba, and beckoned with a wave of his hand. 'Got some tucker in the hut.'

Terituba recognised the hand wave as a gesture to approach and grinned nervously as he sauntered across the dusty yard towards the bearded white man who stood with his hands on his hips. 'Miben,' he said when he was close. The white man broke into a beaming grin at the Kalkadoon's greeting.

Ben realised the joke was partly on himself. 'Yeah, Miben,' he responded, and thrust his hand out to the Kalkadoon.

The grasping of hands between the two men was a communication of spirit and Terituba knew that he had found a white man whose spirit was truly good. He thanked Ben in his own tongue for providing a sanctuary. Ben did not understand the language but understood from the grave tone that what was being spoken was something important.

Then Terituba raised his arm and Ben saw the figures of a young Aboriginal boy and young woman shyly emerge from the scrub. They were obviously hungry, he guessed from their thin appearance.

'Looks like I've got me a cook, gardener and maybe a stockman,' Ben chuckled as he examined the trio and led them to the hut.

Two days later a grubby and very weary young Saul Rosenblum stumbled home from his long trek from Townsville. He stood defiantly before his father who could only shake his head in wonder at how his son had weathered the perils of the arduous journey across the plains. Saul explained that he had befriended one of Kate's teamsters, and had promised his labour in return for a trip west to Cloncurry, where he was delivering supplies. The teamster had given him a job helping him with the oxen.

Needless to say, the poorly scribed letter Saul had left with his brother Jonathan would justify his sudden absence from the Cohen house. He had gambled on the fact that his uncle Solomon would understand why he had to return to Jerusalem to help his father with the property.

When Judith had read the letter she reacted by telling her husband that someone would have to ride after the teamster and fetch Saul back. But Solomon's response surprised her. 'He is a young man now,' he said firmly. 'And he must find his own way in the world.'

Judith glared at her husband angrily and sniffed. 'He is a boy and needs a good education.'

'He will,' her husband replied gently. 'He is a man like his father and will learn all he needs to mustering the cattle.'

Not completely satisfied with her husband's attitude Judith turned to Jonathan who stood quietly in the room observing the exchange of views. It was fine for Saul to want to be a cattleman like his father, Jonathan thought, with just a touch of guilt. But in Townsville he would learn and one day become someone important, like a doctor or lawyer, or even a bank manager. He was pleased when his Aunt Judith took him to her bosom and swore that he would be given the best education the Cohens could afford.

Ben Rosenblum did not know how he should react to the sudden reappearance of his son in his life. The boy stood before him without any sign of remorse for his act of disobedience.

'I ought to take the stockwhip to you,' he growled.

'Do that, Dad,' Saul replied. 'But don't send me away again.'

For a brief moment they glared at each other until the glare softened in Ben's eyes to be replaced with a moistness he did not want his son to see. 'Go and get something to eat,' he said as he turned away to stomp across the dusty yard. 'Terituba's missus will look after you.'

He stopped halfway across the yard and turned back to his son who had remained watching his father's back as if expecting either a whipping or a kind word from the gruff man he loved so much. 'It's good to have you back, son,' Ben added. 'But you're going to have to work hard if your decision is to be a cattleman and not get a good education in Townsville with your brother and sister.'

Saul wanted to run to his father and hug him with the love he felt for the tall man but knew that would be an admission of childish behaviour. Instead he let his heart skip a beat as he turned away to go to the bark hut where he would meet Terituba's wife and son.

As the days followed Saul found a friend in Terituba's son. Divided by language and race they soon bridged the gulf with their mutual love of the bush. And Terituba and his son were as good as any teachers, in terms of all that the boy needed to learn in order to live in a land which was hostile to Europeans from across the sea.

Ben would watch the two boys chattering happily together in a mix of English and Kalkadoon as they squatted in the shade of the trees near the hut after they had returned from roaming the bush in search of small game for the cooking fire. 'Maybe the young fella did the right thing in coming back,' he muttered to himself with a shake of his head. 'But I still have to make sure he can read and write proper.' To ensure that happened Ben realised that he would have to teach him the rudimentary rules of arithmetic and the alphabet. Saul needed more than a knowledge of the bush if he were one day to take control of Jerusalem Station.

34

The rain fell with a steady, drumming beat on the tin roof of the ramshackle eating house tucked into a corner of Sydney's Chinese quarter. Men with plaited pigtails sat around cramped tables playing mah-jong. Bamboo and ivory tiles clicked with the sound of twittering sparrows as they were turned and tossed on the tables. Other patrons of the eating house held bowls close to their mouths and tucked into steaming savoury noodles with chopsticks, occasionally glancing with curiosity at the two European barbarians who sat at a table tucked in the corner. Much to the surprise of the proprietor, a thick-set Fukien Chinese whose pale skin glistened with sweat from the heat of the tiny kitchen, the older of the two had ordered in fluent Chinese. The Chinaman's hostile expression changed immediately and he hurried away to prepare his best noodles for them.

When the noodles were placed before them Horace ate slowly but Michael ate with a ravenous appetite. It had been a long time since he had eaten Chinese food.

When Michael finished his third bowl of noodles, subtly flavoured with smoked red pork and vegetables, he wiped his mouth with the cuff of his shirt and sat back to ruminate on the pleasures of food. 'More, old chap?' Horace asked, but Michael shook his head. 'Enough for now,' he replied. 'Maybe later.'

Horace placed his bowl on the table and sighed contentedly. 'One misses the delights of Fukien cooking,' he commented, and wiped his mouth with a clean handkerchief. Napkins were not an item in the eating house. 'I could die happy at a Chinese banquet.'

'That bad?' Michael asked bluntly, and Horace nodded.

'That bad, old boy,' he replied sadly.

'Is that why you called off my mission here in Sydney?' Michael asked softly.

Horace stared at him. 'In a way,' he finally answered. 'But the proximity of one's own demise makes a man think on the importance of what he has done. Or is doing. When Godfrey telegrammed me the news concerning your son's reported missing in action I had cause to sit down and question my life.' He paused as the proprietor sidled over to their table and asked Horace if he would like another helping. Horace politely waved him off but praised his cooking. The man appeared pleased and when he was gone Horace continued speaking softly. 'I suppose if I was a religious man I might liken my experience with the telegram to that of Saul on the road to Damascus when he was struck down by divine revelation. I suddenly realised how inane all that we are doing is. For a lifetime I had tried to alert my colleagues in London that Germany was a real threat to Her Majesty's interests in this part of the world. But all I ever received in response was apathy. Here we were! A far-flung convict colony of no real consequence to England, except to rush to her aid with troops when the lion roars for help. And then there was your son. Colonial born, a sacrifice to the faceless grey men oblivious to everything except the grandisement of England.'

'Your talk is almost akin to treason, Horace,' Michael interrupted gently. 'You talk as if you were a colonial, rather than a true Englishman.'

Horace smiled sadly at Michael's chiding remark. 'I think I have been too long in the colonies, Michael. My loyalties are blurring . . . have blurred,' he corrected. 'I now see a people who desperately wish to impress Mother England with how grown up they are. But Mother England can be a callous bitch. She will use their misguided loyalty to fight her future wars. Her proud, tall Tommy Cornstalks will shed their blood to fertilise foreign fields where they will be quickly forgotten by the English public. That time will come. Mark my words. Maybe not in our lifetime. But the time will come. It will come as inevitably as von Fellmann claiming northern New Guinea for the Kaiser. And the first Australians to die will die fighting in the same territories the British government has given away in their blind and stupid apathy towards the interests of this land.'

'You feel what we have been doing is a waste of time then?' Michael asked. 'That my work over the last ten years or so comes to nothing?'

Horace reached over the table and patted

Michael's hand reassuringly. 'Not at all, dear boy,' he sighed. 'At the time it all made sense. And we tried to change things. But, in the end, it meant little to other people, though not you and I.'

'I never really worked for your interests,' the Irishman admitted bitterly. 'I suppose I got hooked like some bloody fish on the money and the only way of life I'd grown to know. An Irishman loyal to British interests. Hah!'

'Despite your personal feelings you risked your life on more than one occasion for us,' Horace replied. 'But now it is time that I went home to England's green fields and you went in search of your own life. George Godfrey has told me about Lady Macintosh's proposal to you concerning the search for your son in the Sudan. When do you leave?'

'Three days. I'm taking a ship to the Suez. From there I will travel down to the Sudan to meet with the general staff. The Colonel has letters of introduction for me.'

'Good old George. Not many people he doesn't know on the general staff,' Horace mused as he stared across at the mah-jong players. 'What will you do when you have found your son?' he asked. 'Return to the colonies?'

'When I've found my son, I will finish something I set out to do a long, long time ago.'

'Become a painter?' Horace guessed. And Michael nodded. 'You should always strive to use the little time you are granted in life to pursue a dream. Eventually dreams fade and we face the eternal dark sleep of death. I know.'

'I'll tell you something, Horrie,' Michael said

with the flash of a grim smile as Horace winced at the deliberate vandalism of his name. 'You might have been a cunning bastard with the Queen's interests at heart but I kind of got to like you.'

Horace blinked and accepted the compliment as the highest the Irishman could pay him. *True friendships had a way of transcending national boundaries and politics.* 'For that I thank you, Michael Duffy,' Horace replied, forcing himself not to choke on any display of emotion. 'But I feel we should part while we are saying these things to each other in a state of complete sobriety. Anymore said might embarrass us both.'

Michael grinned at the frail little Englishman sitting opposite him. 'You're right, Horrie,' he said mischievously. 'I guess your invitation to this god-forsaken part of town was not an accident.'

'No,' Horace said as they both rose from the table. 'I believe our Oriental host will be familiar with the places where I might purchase the fruit of the poppy. I have a need to dream the sweet dreams of the living.' He leant on his walking stick and thrust out his hand to Michael who took the fragile, veined palm in his, firmly but gently. 'You know something, dear boy,' Horace said quietly. 'If you ever call me Horrie again I will take this bloody cane to you.'

Michael laughed and his good eye twinkled. 'You are far from dead, Horace, when you can still make threats. I happen to know your cane has a sword blade concealed inside.'

Horace smiled. 'Damned right, dear boy. I'm not dead yet.'

* * *

Horace watched Michael leave the cramped eating house and step into the steady fall of rain on the dark street where he pulled up the collar of his coat and hunched his broad shoulders against the driving rain.

Horace was about to turn to the Chinese proprietor of the eating house when he noticed a furtive movement in the shadows opposite the shop. Through the wall of rain three men suddenly materialised and surrounded Michael. They gripped his arms before he could reach for his pocket Colt.

Horace frantically pushed past the smiling proprietor but was too late. The men were bundling Michael into a waiting coach drawn by two matched roans. He watched helplessly as the driver whipped the horses into motion. As the carriage clattered down the narrow, poorly lit street Horace instinctively knew who the men were and where they were taking Michael. The fear that gripped him was for Michael's last moments; he knew torture was inevitable before they killed him. But worst of all was the fact that there was little he could do to save the Irishman. The odds were too great.

35

The ship's hold reeked of oil and the three men guarding Michael were as miserably wet as himself. They had roped his hands to an overhead beam in the hold, the limited light from the kerosene lantern making the presence of the abductors even more ominous. The flickering beam cast their shadows on the rusty walls of the hold in a way that seemed to increase the Germans' physical size.

The crewmen guarding Michael were more than just simple sailors. They were crack marines of the Kaiser's army – tough men trained to sail with the navy and fight on land as soldiers. Their immediate leader was most likely an *unteroffizier*, the German equivalent of a British sergeant, Michael guessed.

Little was said in front of Michael as his captors knew of his fluency in their language, but Michael held out little hope of ever leaving the ship alive. Penelope's warning had proved all too accurate. Her husband was undoubtedly behind his abduction.

Michael's arms ached and his only relief was to stand on his toes like a ballet dancer. 'You wouldn't have a smoke would you, Gunter?' he asked in German with a grunt of pain. 'Man could die like this without a smoke.'

The brawny German was the oldest of the three marines and Michael had learned that he had once served with the French Foreign Legion in Mexico. Since Michael had also served in Mexico as a mercenary after the American Civil War, the two men had found some common ground.

Gunter stepped forward with a lit cigarette and pushed it between Michael's lips. He was not relishing his commanding officer's orders. 'It is regrettable, my friend,' he said sympathetically when he stepped back, 'that it has come to this. I have been told much of your military exploits and you are truly an impressive soldier.'

'Thanks, Gunter. I had a feeling there was nothing personal in all this,' Michael replied, as the cigarette bobbed in his mouth.

'You had us fooled, Mister Duffy,' Gunter said with a tone of admiration. 'You are very good at your job of spying.'

'Was,' Michael replied and took a puff on the cigarette. 'But I don't expect you to believe me when I tell you that I am no longer a spy for anyone.'

'No, Mister Duffy,' Gunter answered sadly. 'But I wish what you said was true. There is no honour in killing a brave man.'

Suddenly the three marines stiffened and glanced behind Michael in the direction of the tiny door of the hold. Michael guessed who it was.

Baron Manfred von Fellmann stepped in front of him. It had been almost twelve years since they had set eyes on each other and they both took in the changes. The Baron had not aged noticeably, Michael reflected. He looked every part the commanding soldier, even in the expensive suit of a civilian.

'I am sorry to have to do this to you, Mister Duffy,' he said, in the rich, educated voice of an aristocrat. 'I owe you a debt of honour for your part in killing Captain Mort those many years ago. But I suspect that you are not in Sydney for the fond memories that I know you have of the place. You see, I also know that you are wanted for murder by the police here.'

Michael spat the cigarette on the floor and strained to stand on his toes. 'I will admit that I know what you plan to do,' he answered quietly. 'But I will also tell you, on the honour of my true name, I have been ordered *not* to continue with my mission to stop you.'

They stared at each other and the Baron's unnerving blue eyes looked deep into Michael's good one. Manfred broke the silence. 'Under any other circumstances, Mister Duffy, I would tend to believe what you say. But these are not normal circumstances as you well know and I would require corroboration of what you are saying to feel safe enough to release you unharmed. Can you do that when, as far as I am aware, my old adversary Horace Brown is in Townsville?'

They were in the dark about Horace meeting him in Sydney's Chinatown, Michael thought. Careless work on the part of the Baron's men. 'I suppose you do not have the time to telegraph Mister Brown in Townsville to confirm that I am telling the truth?' he asked with an edge of bitter irony.

'Sadly, no,' Manfred answered, shaking his head. 'Time is short and I cannot afford delays. So this brings me to an unpleasant choice. I must subject you to a rather brutal interrogation in order to ascertain who else knows about my mission.'

'I could easily lie to you under torture,' Michael said, trying to sound calm. 'I know you are going to kill me anyway.'

'I will know if you are telling the truth, Mister Duffy, I assure you.'

The Baron stepped away from Michael and nodded to Gunter who moved forward to rip Michael's wet shirt from his body. Then Michael saw the silver flash of a knife in his hand.

Gunter's face was expressionless apart from a tic twitching at his eye. He did not like inflicting pain but in his time as a Legionnaire he had learned much of interrogation techniques from the Mexicans, as crude and bloody as they were. He stood and waited for the command to begin.

'Sergeant Klaus will inflict pain on you, Mister Duffy,' Manfred said. 'Then I will ask a question and expect a truthful answer. Believe me, I will know if you are lying. If I am satisfied that you are telling the truth the torture will not continue and you will be granted an honourable death befitting a man such as yourself. Do you understand?'

Michael nodded, praying that he might be able to withstand the pain. He had so little to tell them but was most afraid that he might break and volunteer the information that Horace Brown was in Sydney. He knew that revelation would be Horace's death warrant.

Manfred nodded and Gunter slid the sharp point of the knife under the skin of Michael's ribs. Slowly he thrust up and the sharp blade slid over the bone and cartilage without penetrating the lung cavity.

Michael arched in agony as the blade severed raw nerves. He gagged on his scream and blood splashed the deck as Gunter withdrew the blade and turned his back on Michael.

'Who else in Sydney knows of our plans?' the Baron asked quietly as he stared into Michael's face, searching for the flicker of truth he might see in the man's eye.

'Just me. And your wife!' he gasped. *Thank God John Wong had left.*

'Penelope?' Manfred asked in a surprised voice. 'Have you seen my wife on your visit here?'

Michael hoped that he could unnerve his tormenter who could well get angry and become impatient with keeping him alive. Death might come early to relieve his agony.

But Manfred only smiled when he realised what Michael was attempting to do. 'I know you have had an affair with my wife, Mister Duffy,' he said softly into Michael's ear so that his men could not hear him. 'My wife is a very unusual and depraved woman. She likes to inflict pain. It makes her excited in a way that I am sure you know about. When I recount how you died she will fantasise for a long time about your death. She may even express her regret to me that she was not able to torture you herself. So do not attempt to make me angry at the mention of my wife's name.'

Manfred was about to let Gunter resume the torture when he stared disbelievingly across Michael's shoulder.

'You and I should talk,' Horace said, leaning on his cane staring back at him. 'In private.'

Manfred nodded and gestured to Horace to accompany him to his cabin.

When they were gone Gunter lit a cigarette and placed it between Michael's lips. 'I regret what is happening, my friend,' he said apologetically. 'But I must obey orders.'

'I know. Nothing personal,' Michael answered bitterly. 'Just doing your job. I only wish you weren't so bloody good at it.'

The brawny German snorted a bitter laugh at the other man's ability to find humour in the situation. *He was a truly tough and brave man!*

'It has been a long time, Mister Brown,' Manfred said. He settled down behind a table in his cabin and Horace took the chair offered to him. 'Cooktown and French Charlie's excellent restaurant if I remember correctly. A time when your man Michael Duffy set out to avenge the deaths of his bushmen on the *Osprey* and inadvertently killed the murderer of my brother.' It was a remembrance of a more pleasant night that the two men had shared when they had met in a rare truce between spy masters.

'But I was informed that you were currently in Townsville,' he added.

'Your intelligence needs reviewing, Baron,' Horace mildly rebuked. 'I have been in Sydney for at least twenty-four hours and you did not know. Not very professional, old chap.'

Manfred frowned. 'You are here to rescue Mister Duffy from us,' he said curtly. 'I doubt that you have involved the authorities in your plan because it would, as you say, be a case of out of the frying pan and into the fire for him if the police were involved.'

'No, I have come alone,' Horace replied, leaning forward on his cane. 'I have come to reason with you for his life. As one gentleman to another.'

'I will listen,' Manfred replied, with polite respect for the Englishman who had risked his own life by coming to him. 'But I doubt that anything you say will help Mister Duffy,'

'Why kill him when you very well know that your mission to seize New Guinea is known to me and suspected by others in my government?'

'Because you *may* suspect, but only Mister Duffy has the ability to seriously interfere. Or have you forgotten that you used him to sabotage the *Osprey* on my first mission?'

'Captain Mort scuttled your mission, not Mister Duffy,' Horace gently reminded his old adversary. 'It was Mister Duffy who saved your life when you were in the water.'

Manfred shifted uncomfortably in his chair. Had it not been for Michael Duffy keeping him afloat in the tropical waters of North Queensland Manfred would not be alive today to kill the man. The irony was not entirely lost on the normally inflexible man. He owed Michael Duffy a very powerful debt. But his own life meant very little in relation to the interests of his country and the Kaiser. He was, after all, a soldier and such sentimentality had no place in decision making. 'I am grateful for Mister Duffy saving my life. And I wish I had a way out of this situation. But you must realise I have a mission to complete and I know that if you were in my place you would do the same.'

Horace nodded. 'I don't know if he has told you, but I cancelled his mission a couple of days ago,' he said. 'You *really are* wasting your time torturing him.'

'He told us he was no longer working for you,' Manfred replied. 'But I cannot risk releasing him while you are in Sydney. Together you are a dangerous team.'

'What if you cut off the head of the animal?' Horace asked quietly. 'Then you would have nothing to worry about.'

Manfred stared at the Englishman and smiled. 'You and I know that I have no intentions of harming you, Mister Brown. That is not the done thing, old chap, as you English would say.'

'But what if I were dead? Would you give your word to me as a gentleman of honour, that Michael Duffy would be released with no further harm to him?'

'In that unlikely situation, naturally I would release Mister Duffy,' Manfred replied in a puzzled tone. 'I would give my word to you on that.'

'Good!' Horace replied and smiled enigmatically across the small space of Manfred's cabin. 'Do you have a chess set by any chance, Baron?' he asked.

Manfred returned the smile with a grim realisation of what was transpiring in his cabin and recovered a finely carved ivory chess set from a sea locker. He placed the board on the table between them and scrounged a bottle of expensive port wine whilst Horace set up the game. The wine was one of two bottles Manfred had been saving to toast the Kaiser's claim to northern New Guinea. But he felt that this special occasion warranted a claim to his precious stock.

When the colours were decided and thus who should move first, Manfred raised his glass. 'A salute to courage,' he said gravely and Horace accepted his tribute in silence. *No speeches of recognition for what was to be done ... just a toast from an erstwhile enemy.*

'A toast to Michael Duffy,' Horace responded quietly. 'Reluctant servant of Her Majesty and father of Captain Patrick Duffy who is a relative by marriage to one of the Kaiser's most honourable soldiers. To you, Baron von Fellmann.' Horace's convoluted toast uncomfortably reminded Manfred of his distant relationship to Michael's son.

'You have my word, Mister Brown,' Manfred reiterated his promise. 'But for now we shall see who is the master at chess, and drink this fine wine.'

'A longstanding and perverse ambition of mine,' Horace said as he sipped at the port, 'has been to beat you at chess.'

When the game was over Manfred left the

courageous English agent alone in the cabin. Although Horace had taken the Baron's queen, he had lost the game of life.

Gunter released the tension on the rope that was still holding Michael's arms stretched painfully above his head. The action caused pain to shoot through the upper part of his body and he winced as he reached for a sailor's shirt to replace his own, which had been torn from his back by Gunter.

'Where is Horace?' Michael asked, as he massaged his aching muscles.

Manfred did not answer the question but dismissed his marines and turned to Michael once they were alone. 'Mister Brown has died by his own hand.' Michael knew that the Prussian was not lying; he had no need to under the present circumstances. 'He wrote a letter saying he was taking his own life as gesture of goodwill for the agreement we had between us.' The Baron spoke quietly and with respect for the death of his old enemy. 'But he does not write those words in his final letter. He has written that he has taken his life because of the pain he suffers from his illness. I will notify the authorities of his death and ensure that he gets a decent burial. You are free to go, Mister Duffy. Horace told me that you were sailing for Africa this week to find your son and I wish you well.'

There was little else to be said or done, Michael thought, as he was escorted to the wharf by the brawny German marine sergeant. Horace was dead.

The rain still pounded the city and its chill bit into Michael's face and hands. Blood continued to ooze from his wounds and the shirt under his coat was stiff with it. But he did not feel the biting cold as he walked slowly away from the German ship. He realised he was still alive. *And that was enough for now!* Later he would feel the loss of an old friend whose courageous sacrifice had snatched him from the jaws of a certain and agonising death.

36

Gordon James was granted a dinner at Cloncurry's finest hotel to celebrate his glorious victory over the fierce Kalkadoon warriors. The speeches flowed – along with the copious quantities of beer and spirits – until the small frontier town was drunk dry.

But Gordon felt the unease of an imposter as the number of those who had opposed his numerically superior force grew with each retelling of the epic battle. He had wanted to explain that a handful of warriors had courageously sold their lives so that their people could escape from inevitable annihilation. But he was also a pragmatic man who realised that the exaggeration of his victory would enhance his reputation in the eyes of his superiors and the frontier people of Queensland. Who knew what prizes might be showered on him as a result of his final report?

But there was also Sarah. No matter how much his victory would enhance his career, he would lose her forever, should he choose to remain with the police. Just how much did he love her? He had brooded as the toastmaster droned on about his exploits. The answer was simple when he looked deep into his soul. He knew what he must do. But for now he accepted the standing toasts to himself and the men who he had led on his long expedition to hunt down the troublesome tribesmen.

With the celebration over and his patrol gathered together, Gordon asked around about Trooper Peter Duffy whose absence he had noted on his return to Cloncurry. Men shrugged their shoulders. No-one had seen him since his first day back in the town after he had accompanied the re-supply party. He must have continued on to Townsville, Gordon concluded angrily. He had not granted him permission to do so. Duffy had been ordered to remain in Cloncurry and oversee the re-supply for the expedition back out to the Godkin Range. He would chew him out when he got back to the barracks.

Weeks later Gordon was relieved to ride into Townsville where the exaggerated account of his victory was the accepted version printed by an enthusiastic local press. His superior officer, Superintendent Gales, lavished praise on the young police officer for bringing honourable mention to the Native Mounted Police. He immediately issued him orders to compile his reports for Brisbane and ensure that his patrol was squared away in the barracks. Pay was to be organised for his troop and all lost and damaged kit to be investigated and recorded.

Gordon accepted his orders with an outward

good grace but privately bridled at the interference his duties imposed on him. He desperately wanted to ride over to Kate O'Keefe's house to see Sarah Duffy. The long weeks on patrol had made him realise just how much he missed her and Peter's savage inference that he would use her and cast her aside for the sake of his career had forced him to confront what was more important in his life. He knew without any doubt that Sarah meant more to him than a career as an officer.

It took a day to square away all the matters for his patrol and meanwhile all discreet inquiries regarding Peter Duffy's whereabouts met with blank stares. No, Trooper Duffy had not been seen around Townsville. Concern now replaced anger but Gordon was too temporarily distracted by his duties to dwell on the matter of Peter's disappearance.

As he sat at his desk penning the last of his patrol report he felt decidedly uneasy at the sight of two of his troopers marching grim faced towards his tiny office. He moaned and swore when they rapped on his door. Gordon had good reason to feel apprehension. Any serious trouble in the barracks would delay his trip to Kate's house.

'Trooper Calder, what have you to say about the matter?' Gordon James asked, as the four men stood in the police barracks. Two European troopers had reported Calder to their commander.

It was hot and stuffy inside the bark and tin hut and Calder sweated even more under the searching interrogation from the young police commander. He stared at the small pile of coins and banknotes on his bed. They had been retrieved from inside the straw-filled palliasse of his mattress. 'I don't know how the money got there,' he replied.

'You stole it,' one of the other two troopers sneered. 'You low thievin' bastard. You stole from your own mates!' The trooper was only a small man and quivered like a fox terrier as he spat his words.

'Don't know what 'e's talkin' about, sir,' Calder replied defensively. 'They must 'ave set me up.'

'I don't think so, Trooper Calder,' Gordon said, as he bent to pick up the money from the bed. 'This will be held as evidence until an inquiry is held.' The two troopers who had caught Calder stashing the stolen money appeared disappointed; some of the money was theirs. Gordon noticed their reaction. 'I don't think the inquiry will take long. Sergeant Rossi will arrange for a hearing at the barracks first thing in the morning. I'm sure we will have an outcome over this matter before midday tomorrow.'

The two troopers brightened but given time on their own with Calder – and a little persuasion – they would have gained a confession from the thieving bastard. To steal from mates was the lowest crime on the frontier!

As Gordon did not like Calder he was not unhappy at the discovery of his crime. The man had boasted that he was going to 'do the half-caste darkie Duffy in' when they returned to Cloncurry but had been denied his opportunity. Peter Duffy had simply vanished. 'Trooper Calder,' Gordon said. 'In fairness to your record of service with my troop in the battle against the Kalkadoon, I will only confine you to the barracks until the results of the hearing tomorrow morning at ten o'clock. You are not to leave this building unless with my express permission. Do you understand what I am telling you?'

Calder glared at Gordon. He had no loyalty to the commander who was known to be friendly to the darkie Peter Duffy. Nor had he any intentions of hanging round to face an inquiry that, with no doubt, would find him guilty of stealing. 'I understand, sir,' he replied sullenly. 'And on my word I will remain in the barracks.'

'Good! Then I accept your word, Trooper Calder.'

The troopers who had confronted Calder in the barracks cast quizzical looks at each other. *Was Mister James mad?* Gordon indicated to the two troopers to follow him out of the barracks and Calder stood by his bed, watching the three leave the hut. Gordon James was added to the list of those he would one day settle with.

When Gordon and the two troopers were outside the smaller trooper could not contain himself. 'Sir, with all due respect, Trooper Calder will be gone before you get to your office.'

'I know,' Gordon replied calmly, and took the seized cash from his pocket. 'I respect what you are saying is true,' he said and handed the money to the man. 'And I may as well return the money to you now.'

The trooper accepted the money with an expression of disbelief and confusion on his face.

'But why, sir?' he asked as he accepted the money. 'Why let the bastard go?'

'Do you have enough evidence to say that Calder took the money from you and Trooper Davies?' Gordon asked quietly. The little trooper frowned and Gordon knew he was right in presuming they did not. But he knew both troopers well, knew that they were men who could be trusted on their words and actions. 'I would rather have Calder out of the Native Mounted than take the chance that an inquiry might find in his favour,' Gordon added. 'I trust nothing further will be said on the matter. I hope you are clear on what I am saying.'

The troopers grinned. Their respect for their commanding officer's leadership had just taken a great leap forward. 'What matter, sir?' the little trooper queried with a conspiratorial wink.

Gordon smiled. Now he could look forward to dining at Kate Tracy's house that evening – and more importantly to seeing Sarah Duffy so he could tell her the things that were in his heart.

James Calder was gone before nightfall as Gordon knew he would be.

When Gordon came to dinner Sarah Duffy wore the dress her Uncle Michael had bought her as a gift. She tried not to stare across the table at him in any way he might think was forward, especially in front of Gordon's mother Emma who had accompanied her son to dine with herself and Kate.

Emma James could see all the signs of a young woman smitten by her handsome son. 'I love your

dress, Sarah. Is it new?' she asked politely and
Sarah told her how her Uncle Michael had given
the dress as a gift.

Emma was one of the few people who knew the
true identity of the mysterious Irish–American,
Mister Michael O'Flynn. Her husband – Gordon's
father – had been killed while serving with him a
decade earlier. She felt no ill will towards Kate's
brother; Henry had volunteered to join the
expedition to hunt down Captain Mort. He had
always lived on the edge and the limitless horizons
of her husband's adopted country had seduced
him with the need to ride ever westward with men
like himself.

Sarah's frequent visits to Emma's house to
inquire whether Gordon had written left Emma in
no doubt of the young woman's interest in her
son. It was an interest that she approved of. Sarah
had been known to her since her arrival as a child
to Kate. When Kate was away on one of her business trips Emma would often take care of the three
orphans of Tom and Mondo and in many ways
Emma had always enjoyed a special place in
Sarah's affections, akin to that of a favoured aunt.

When dinner was over Kate and Emma retired
to the living room to fuss over Matthew. Both
women had sensed the tension that existed
between the young couple and they left Gordon
and Sarah on the front verandah.

Alone with Sarah for the first time since his
return from Cloncurry, Gordon was at a loss for
conversation. He did not want to talk of the battle
as the events haunted him. Nor did he want to
enter into a conversation that he knew must

eventually lead to questions concerning Peter, who was now officially a deserter from the Native Mounted Police.

Sarah sat in a chair while Gordon stood stiffly by the railing, staring out into the evening. 'What happened between you and my brother?' she asked, as if reading his thoughts.

'We seem to have grown apart,' he answered quietly. 'Your brother was not sure of his loyalties.'

'Loyalties? What do you mean by that?' Sarah asked, with a frown clouding her pretty face. 'Loyalties to who?'

'To the Queen.'

'You mean loyalty to the whitefella,' she scoffed. 'So he left because he felt that he was not accepted for being a half-caste darkie. I know all about Peter's so-called desertion.'

'How did you find out?'

'The bullockies who come through here stop off at Aunt Kate's store and tell her everything that happens out west,' she answered. 'They told her about Peter's desertion from your police and Aunt Kate said he should never have been a trooper in the first place. She said he was too smart to be a trap.'

'So I am stupid,' Gordon flared. 'Is that what you think?'

'I didn't mean it that way,' she replied apologetically. 'The police life suits you. But it was never for my brother. Not after what they did to my parents.'

'You can't blame the police for what happened to your parents,' Gordon replied quietly. 'Your father was a well-known bushranger who knew the risks of the life he led.'

'And my mother?' she asked, with a bitter edge to her question. 'She only stayed with my father because she loved him, despite the differences between them. Did she deserve to be shot down for loving him?'

Gordon shifted uncomfortably. The conversation was not going the way he had hoped. He wanted to talk of things that led to love between a man and a woman. 'Your mother was killed by accident, according to the old reports,' he said softly in an attempt to diffuse her rising anger. 'She was not murdered.'

'I was there, Gordon,' Sarah said quietly, and stared past him into the velvet blackness of the night. 'I can never forget the way she lay in the fire and burnt while we watched and could do nothing for her. To me she was murdered and I am glad my brother no longer rides with the same men who would do these things to others, like my mother's people.' Sarah's gaze returned to linger on his face. 'I love you, Gordon. I always have,' she said. 'And if you love me then you would have to resign your commission and find another job. I could never live with a man whose life is spent with the people who killed my parents. I would not even expect you to marry me. I love you enough to be your woman and ask little else.'

Gordon was stunned by the frank declaration and closed the gap between them by crossing the verandah to kneel by her chair and take her hands in his. 'I think I have always loved you, Sarah. Even when we were little and you used to follow us around like a real pest,' he laughed softly. 'You just got into my life and have never left.'

'Does that mean you would consider leaving the police and sharing our lives together?' she asked as she touched his face. 'Aunt Kate could give you a job working for her company I know, because I have asked her.'

'I also know your Aunt Kate would never allow her convent educated niece to live in sin with me,' he laughed. 'So I suppose I will have to tender my resignation.'

'Are you asking me to marry you, Inspector James?' she said and he nodded.

'Then I accept,' she answered softly.

He swept her into his arms and she feebly protested that he was crushing her new dress. He laughed and kissed her protests into silence.

'You really will resign from the police?' she gasped when she was eventually free of his kisses.

'Tomorrow,' he replied merrily as he swirled her around the verandah in a bear hug. You were wrong, Peter, he thought, as he swirled to a stop. Sarah means more to me than the Mounted Police ever did.

When Gordon had departed with his mother in her buggy, a very excited young woman babbled her news to her beloved Aunt Kate. Kate was overjoyed for her niece's happiness. Gordon was a fine young man. And yes, she did have a position for him in the Eureka Company. The news of the engagement would be released as soon as Gordon resigned.

There were so many arrangements to be made, Kate thought, as she gazed at her niece. Sarah looked as if she was almost exploding with her joy. The priest would have to be consulted on a mixed marriage as Gordon was an Anglican whereas Sarah was a Catholic. So much to do.

When Gordon told his mother on the ride home she congratulated him on his choice of wife. Although her congratulations were warm and well meant, she was disturbed, however, by his news that he was going to leave the Native Mounted Police to please Sarah. It was not a woman's position to tell a man what he should do with his life! She had accepted Gordon's father for the man he was. That her son had taken up his father's calling to be a police trooper was only to be expected and she wondered if her son's leaving the police would make him happy in the long term.

The following day, however, Gordon was true to his promise to Sarah. It had not been easy penning the letter requesting release from his duties as an officer in the Native Mounted Police but Gordon knew he must if he was to prove his love to her. He stood at the entrance of the super-intendent's office with the resignation in hand and knocked smartly on the door.

'Enter!' a voice boomed.

Gordon stepped inside where he threw a smart salute to the man sitting behind the desk. Superintendent Gales had been a lieutenant in the Native Mounted Police when Gordon's father had been a sergeant. He had first met Henry James when he was sent to Rockhampton to relieve the sergeant of his post at the barracks outside of town. There had been a disturbing rumour that the sergeant and his commanding officer

Lieutenant Morrison Mort had come to blows of sorts, as a result of which Mort had informally resigned by deserting his post and leaving the sergeant temporarily in charge. The authorities in Brisbane viewed the matter with a jaundiced opinion of the big English sergeant. Gales had found no fault with the likeable sergeant and was pleased to see the son of the same man calling in on him. He guessed it was to thank him for the commendation of service he had written for the splendid work against the Kalkadoon.

'Inspector James, good to see you,' the superintendent said as he rose ponderously from his chair. Time – and the duties of administration – had put a lot of weight on his once slim frame. 'S'pose you've heard the news about that trooper of yours. What's his name? Ah yes, Trooper Duffy!'

Gordon frowned as the superintendent stretched and shook his hand. He was a jovial man and well liked by his staff. 'What news is that, sir?' he asked.

The superintendent held up his hand with a gesture for silence as he bawled out of his office, 'Get two cups of tea in here, Jack!'

'Yes, sir, right away!' a distant voice replied, which Gordon recognised as belonging to Sergeant Jack Ferguson who was the barracks sergeant for Townsville's Mounted Police contingent.

'What news about Trooper Duffy?' Gordon asked again politely, and the rotund superintendent blinked at him.

'You don't know?' he asked with genuine

surprise. 'I heard about it yesterday meself.'

'I've been on leave last night, sir,' Gordon replied. 'Just came back on duty this morning.'

'Ah, yes. Well, it seems this Trooper Duffy has joined forces with a man we thought was long dead,' Gales said as he ambled back to his desk. He stared at a large wall map of the colony behind where he normally sat and shuffled the papers of his office. 'Had two reports that he has joined up with a blackfella by the name of Wallarie and they have done a couple of robberies whilst under arms. Also an attempted murder of a grog seller on his way west. Here, and here, we've had the reports from,' he added, pointing to positions on the map south-west of Townsville.

So Wallarie was with Peter! The thought did not come as a surprise to Gordon. Were there pre-destined events in men's lives? He stared at the points on the wall map. 'Were they on foot? Or did they have horses, sir?' he asked.

'Both mounted and well armed,' Gales answered. 'The reports concern me because both men together know the country, which could be a considerable problem in the future. That bloody old Wallarie was around when I was a young officer. He was wanted for murder then. And, if I remember rightly, he rode with this Trooper Duffy's father. What's his name . . . ?'

'His name was Tom Duffy, sir,' Gordon replied. 'My father helped hunt him down in Burkesland years ago.'

'Yes, I remember now.' Gales sat down as Sergeant Ferguson delivered two mugs of steaming sweet black tea.

'Thank you, Jack,' he said and dismissed the barracks sergeant. 'So, bad blood will always out,' he sighed as he sipped at the tea.

Gordon did not comment on the superintendent's opinion. 'What do you intend to do, sir?'

Gales fixed Gordon with an appraising stare and said quietly, 'He was one of your men, Inspector James. What do you think he is up to and where will we find him?'

Gordon walked over to the wall map with his mug of tea in his hand and ran his finger through the two points the superintendent had indicated. He continued in a line until his finger came to rest at a point mid-way down the Colony of Queensland. 'That's where they are going, sir.'

The superintendent peered at the name written in fine copperplate script. 'Glen View,' he read aloud.

'That's where you will find them both,' Gordon replied.

'How can you be so sure, young Gordon?' Gales asked. 'They could go anywhere in the colony. Just as Wallarie and Tom Duffy did years back.'

'I make my prediction based on personal knowledge about the Nerambura people,' Gordon said.

Gales cut across him. 'Never heard of the Nerambura.'

'Probably because they were so efficiently dispersed as a clan in my father's day,' Gordon sighed, 'that they have virtually ceased to exist. Except for Wallarie, who is the last full-blood, there are only Tom Duffy's kids, as far as I know, who have any Nerambura blood in them. I would

384

say that, from the direction they have taken, Wallarie intends to take Peter Duffy back to the traditional grounds, for something like an initiation ceremony.'

'Could be,' Gales mused as he stared at the map behind him. 'Blackfellas are a bit funny about things like that. Appears your Trooper Duffy was more blackfella than white from what I hear about him.'

'Appears so,' Gordon answered in a flat voice. He momentarily reflected on Sarah. She also had the last remnants of Nerambura blood and any children they might have would carry on a bloodline his father had assisted in attempting to wipe out. It was an eerie thought – and one with an uncomfortable echo.

'. . . *organise a patrol to ride south to Glen View* . . .'

'Sorry, sir,' Gordon replied. 'I missed what you said.'

'You recovered from that bang on the head?' Gales asked in a concerned voice when he noticed the pale, sweating face of his inspector. 'You look like you have some sort of fever.'

'I'm all right, sir.'

'Good! Because I want you to immediately organise a patrol to ride south and see if those two are at Glen View like you think they might be.'

'Yes, sir, will do so immediately.'

Gordon justified his decision to himself on the grounds that it was better that he should find Peter and Wallarie rather than strangers who could easily shoot first. That afternoon he visited his mother before returning to the barracks to ride out with a seven-man patrol.

Emma James listened to her son explaining his mission. It was only when he was gone that she sat and thought about the ironic turn of events; just as his father had hunted Tom Duffy, now Gordon hunted the son of Tom Duffy. A sad wheel turning in their lives and always coming back to the place where it had all started. All the threads had come together for a future tragedy: a Native Mounted Police patrol would once again ride armed into the lands of the Nerambura clan of the Darambal people.

The resignation letter remained in Gordon's hand. He would tender it as soon as he had found Peter and ensured that his best friend was safe. Surely Sarah would understand the importance of what he was doing?

Gordon did not ride over to see Sarah before leaving with his patrol. He sensed that in fact she would not understand why he would volunteer to hunt down her brother. How could he explain to her that it was more than his duty to find Peter and reconcile his differences with him before he could begin a life with her? To find Peter before he could get into any more trouble was paramount. He and Sarah would then be able to be free of the curse that seemed to dog their lives.

37

South-west of Townsville, and four days ahead of
the police patrol, Peter Duffy and Wallarie camped
in the thick tangle of dry scrub beside a waterhole.
There was a third member in their company: a
part-Chinese part-Aboriginal girl who had chosen
to join them when they had bailed up a drunken
shanty keeper.

Her name was Matilda and she had lived with
her mother until she had died. Matilda had then
remained with her stepfather until he sold her to
the travelling shanty keeper who had purchased
her from a prospector a week earlier for a considerable supply of good liquor. She was not of his
blood and the old prospector had little room for
sentimentality in his tough life roaming the
isolated regions of the colony.

Matilda's mother and father, a Chinese
shepherd, had lived together in a bark hut on a
squatter's property. Matilda's mother had
returned one day to the shack to find him
murdered for the little gold he had kept from his
meagre findings on the property west of

Townsville. She had fled with her baby daughter and was found by the prospector who took her in as cook and someone to warm his bedroll at nights.

Matilda had grown up in the company of the white miner and her mother until she was fifteen when her mother had died after a bashing from the cranky old man. He had turned to Matilda to take her mother's place but the young girl had threatened to kill him if he tried to touch her. He was afraid of the young woman but knew her exotic beauty – her slanted eyes and high-cheeked features – would help him fetch a high price with the right person. He was, after all, selling her into a decent employment – or so he convinced himself – at the sight of a crate of top shelf gin bottles offered for her 'indenture' into the grog shanty business.

The shanty owner had all intentions of offering her employment in his business – not behind the counter but in a cot in the back of his shop. She would fetch a good deal of money on her back, he had calculated, as he sized up the slim figure and firm young breasts and buttocks of the girl, as she leant over to serve her stepfather and the shanty owner a meal of curried beef and rice. The deal was struck between the grogger and prospector but on the track to his lonely grog shop Matilda had resisted his drunken approaches and he had beaten her.

It had been her cries of pain that had attracted Peter's attention as he and Wallarie rode up to witness the shanty owner straddling the young woman with his pants down around his ankles.

Peter and Wallarie's presence had cowed the would-be rapist and robbing the ranting man had not even required the threat of a gun.

Wallarie and Peter helped themselves to flour, tea and sugar as the grateful girl adjusted the cotton dress she wore, and helped them load the supplies into their saddlebags. Peter had reached down and with a powerful sweep of his arm lifted her onto the back of his mount and she rode with her arms around the young man.

Peter by now only wore the trousers and boots of the Mounted Police and a bandolier of ammunition, slung across his shoulder and broad chest. Wallarie by comparison wore an old shirt and trousers, but no boots, when he rode the horse he had stolen from the Cloncurry Mounted Police barracks. Peter had been stunned by his audacity when he had walked into the town dressed in the clothes of Aboriginal stockmen. He had arrived brazenly at the police barracks and asked to speak with the trooper who had returned with the re-supply party.

'How did you know I was here?' Peter had asked.

Wallarie had chuckled. 'Maybe I followed you on the wings of the eagle after the big fight out in the hills.'

Peter frowned at the old warrior's explanation but knew asking further questions would only elicit a nonsensical answer. 'You know the white-fellas will hang you if they catch you in town?' he cautioned.

Wallarie waved away the young man's concern. 'No whitefella smart enough to catch me,' he answered with a tone of contempt. 'Time you left the whitefellas' town and came with me to the Dreaming place to become a man of the Nerambura people.'

Peter reflected on the offer. He had been denied his rightful place in the European world. Had he not proved his ability at the European school? And why was it that Gordon should be an officer when he was not as smart? The answers were all too simple. To the whitefellas he would always be just another blackfella.

'We will need rifles and horses,' Peter said, with an unwavering stare into the smoky eyes of the mighty Darambal warrior.

'Just like the old days when I rode with your father,' he smiled. 'We will show the whitefellas we aren't beaten yet.'

And that was how it happened.

It all seemed so simple but in due time the grog shop owner had lodged his complaint with the police headquarters in Townsville. Embellished by his fury, the man added attempted murder and robbery whilst under arms to his story.

No-one questioned the word of a white man under the circumstances and, unfortunately for Wallarie, the shanty owner remembered his name being used by Peter. He also remembered the legend of the Aboriginal bushranger who once rode with the Irishman, Tom Duffy.

From the first night of their meeting Matilda and Peter had shared a bedroll. Before long she had fallen pregnant. For two weeks Matilda rode with Wallarie and Peter and for two weeks she had ridden with a life growing in her. Now she also carried the remnants of Nerambura blood with hers, a fact that did not go unnoticed by the old Nerambura warrior.

Not that she appeared different. But even so, Wallarie knew she had a spirit in her. He did not confide to Peter his knowledge. He would learn soon enough! When Matilda herself realised that she carried a spirit.

As Wallarie sat chuckling by the campfire, luxuriating in the beauty of the night sky and drinking cups of sweet black tea, he poked at the fire. A dingo howled in the distance and the old warrior suddenly lifted his bearded face to stare north. It was on the wind and in the mournful howl. Gordon James was riding south to find them and time was short. The old prophecy was soon to come true. Either Peter or Gordon was destined to die at their next meeting.

Wallarie stared morosely at the young couple curled together a short distance away under Peter's blanket, blissfully unaware of his dreadful premonition. Would all he had attempted to teach Peter prepare him for the meeting? Or would the son of Henry James prevail? Only the ancestor spirits knew the answer. It was told by them long ago in the stories of his people's Dreaming.

Instinctively he glanced across the brigalow scrub towards the craggy hill silhouetted by the night sky. Once again they were in the traditional lands of the Nerambura clan and the sacred hill beckoned to him with its ancient power. In the morning Peter must leave Matilda and go with him to the cave to be initiated as a Nerambura man. Only then could he face Gordon James.

38

Lieutenant Alexander Sutherland scanned the flat plain of broken rock and arid sands. In the distance beyond the shimmering plain he could see an endless sea of sand and broken rock. Behind him rose the craggy mimosa covered coastal hills and the busy military port of Suakin. Onwards was hell itself. Only a return to Suakin from the long and dangerous patrol would give a chance to return to heaven. To bath once again in cooling waters, he thought wistfully, and loll around the bazaars of the white stone city. A chance to buy exotic gifts for his family back home in Colchester.

The young officer scratched at his grimy face and dry skin peeled away under his dirty finger-nails. His sunburn had long disappeared and under the peeling dry skin his once-peach complexion was tanned a nuggety brown. Constant exposure to the fierce African sun had left him a mottled colour. As a former officer, in command of a troop of Her Majesty's horse cavalry, the transfer to the Guards' Camel Regiment had come as somewhat of a blow. The glamorous image of the dashing cavalryman was long lost to working with the huge ungainly looking animals. But time – and the remarkable endurance of the huge and often quarrelsome beasts – had converted him to the merits of the creature. They were unsurpassed on the long-range reconnaissance patrols into the burning, broken lands of the Dervish.

The lieutenant scanned the wasteland of rock and sparsely scattered scrub with his binoculars but there was nothing of worth to note. No camps of bedouins or concentrations of Dervish warriors. No tracks or trails left by the enemy roaming the land on the same mission as himself: to reconnoitre for their respective armies and collect information to be converted into intelligence. Behind him, two escorting troopers sat on their camels scratching at the tiny insects that itched their sweating bodies. They had removed their goggles, issued to keep sand out, and rubbed at their sore eyes with the backs of grimy hands.

'Blimey, Harry,' one of the men grumbled to his companion. 'Mister Sutherland looks like 'e might want to go further south.'

Harry stared across at the young officer who had advanced fifty paces in front of them to a tiny rise in the sand.

'Gor blimey! You could be right,' his companion answered. But he noticed that something had gained the attention of their patrol leader.

Lieutenant Alexander Sutherland leant forward and fiddled with the focus on his binoculars.They brought into sharper outline the blurred image of a solitary man who plodded towards the patrol.

Although the man was at least a quarter of a mile away, Sutherland could see that he was big, with broad shoulders and he appeared to be wearing what looked like the tattered uniform of the British army. 'Trooper Krimble, Haley. Up here,' he called back softly and the two cavalrymen urged their camels onto their feet. 'Out there, to my front, 'bout four hundred and fifty yards, there is what appears to be a man wearing what looks like a British uniform,' Sutherland said. He pointed with his binoculars across the sand at the shimmering figure which twisted and turned in the heat haze. 'At least what is left of one of our uniforms. Do you see the man?'

Trooper Harry Krimble squinted, his hand held to shade his eyes. He could just see the outline of a man. He brought his camel down into a kneeling position, dismounted and slipped his Henry carbine from across his shoulders, laying the barrel across the saddle. It was loaded and he slid the rear sight back for a long shot so he could drop the fuzzy wuzzy while he was well out, just in case he had any mates with him. Harry raised the rifle to his shoulder and used the saddle of his camel as a prop to steady his aim.

'Don't shoot him just yet,' Sutherland cautioned. 'Wait until he is at least a hundred yards from us before you fire, Trooper Krimble. It looks as if he has seen us, and the chap does not appear afraid to take us on.'

'Sure you want the crazy bugger that close, sir?' Krimble questioned from behind his rifle, as he kept the blade of the fore sight on the target which was steadily drawing closer. ''E might 'ave some of 'is fuzzy wuzzy mates with 'im out there.'

'No, I doubt that,' Sutherland answered. 'I have a good view of the terrain to our front and he is well and truly alone. Possibly got separated from one of his Dervish patrols and has decided to get to his Moslem heaven by attacking us. Only right we grant him his wish for salvation.'

'Right you are, sir,' Krimble answered with a grin and slid the rear sight of his rifle back to one hundred yards.

They waited patiently under the blazing sun as the figure advancing towards them came on steadily, if erratically. At one hundred yards Krimble had the man well and truly in his sights and was squeezing the trigger when he heard his officer bark at him, 'Check your fire! Don't shoot!'

Lieutenant Sutherland dropped his binoculars and leapt from his camel as the two puzzled soldiers glanced at each other. They were confused by their young officer's sudden concern for the fuzzy wuzzy staggering towards them but neither of the camel men had the advantage of the officer's binoculars. They had not seen the green eyes of the sun blackened man.

'Captain Patrick Duffy,' the sunburnt man gasped through cracked lips as he stumbled into the arms of Lieutenant Sutherland. 'Of the Scots' Brigade. And lately, of hell . . . out there.'

Patrick returned with the camel patrol to Suakin from where he was sent to recover from his three-week ordeal on the *Ganges*. She was a hospital ship anchored off the white-washed port city of

395

Suakin on the Red Sea and his removal from the missing in action list brought a flurry of newspaper reporters to his bedside.

Amongst the correspondents was one who worked for the paper now owned by Lady Enid Macintosh.

39

George Godfrey greeted the maid who took his hat and coat and returned the greeting with a warm familiarity born of his frequent visits to Lady Enid Macintosh's house. He shook off the outside cold of the early winter weather as he stepped into the large living room where he was pleasantly assailed by the heat of the log fire burning with a gentle flame. Enid greeted him with a vibrancy that Godfrey had not seen in her in a long time. The telegram that had arrived two days earlier proclaiming that Patrick was alive and well had rejuvenated her and her eyes were alight with the flame of assertiveness that had always marked her life. Once again she was ready to fight her son-in-law for control of the family companies as she now had an ally in her grandson who soon would be returning to her.

Enid swept across the room with a radiant and triumphant smile to greet Godfrey.

'I knew that he must be alive,' she said, as she took his hands in hers. 'He is recovering at Suakin.'

Godfrey clasped her hands with a gentle squeeze and led her across to a couch where they sat together. 'Your grandson certainly has inherited the luck of his Irish father's people,' he said.

Enid glanced away guiltily to gaze into the fire. Godfrey realised that the indirect mention of Michael Duffy had caused her observable shift in mood from bubblingly happy to considerably sombre. 'Michael Duffy should be arriving in Suakin in the next couple of weeks,' he added. 'There is more than a good chance that he will meet his son.'

'I know,' Enid replied as she continued to stare at the fire. 'I fear he will.'

'It was bound to happen sooner or later.' He tried to comfort her with a gentle and reassuring squeeze. 'You must have realised that would happen. What could concern you about the boy meeting his father? It was, after all, your idea for him to find Patrick in the first place.'

'I did so when everything appeared so desperate,' she replied. 'But now that I know my grandson is alive, I have had time to reflect on my rather foolish haste to employ Mister Duffy.'

'I would not say that your decision to employ Michael Duffy was a foolish one, Enid,' Godfrey said gently. 'He is an extremely capable man.'

'He is also capable of swaying Patrick away from his inheritance and of convincing him to keep his Papist religion.'

Godfrey rose and walked across to the open fireplace where he stood with his back to the flames and gazed back at Enid. 'Is it *that* important that Patrick renounce his religion in favour of yours?' he asked.

She nodded. 'The very Macintosh name carries the defence of English and Scottish Protestantism in its utterance.'

As simple as that, George thought. Nothing in Enid's life was simple except her unwavering adherence to her religion. 'Then I can take steps to prevent Mister Duffy ever meeting his son,' he replied with a sad sigh. 'If that is what you desire.'

'That is what I desire, George.'

The former British army officer accepted Enid's request reluctantly. He had a grudging admiration for the Irishman he had last seen at Horace Brown's funeral. The little Englishman had been laid in the earth of the country he had grown to love – to the point of shifting his final loyalties to its interests over those of England's perceived strategic interests. Godfrey was aware of the ultimate sacrifice Horace had made for Michael Duffy's life. The Irishman had mourned for his friend and employer of the last decade. No tears, only the twisted pain in the big man's face, which said it all.

The Baron's expedition had long sailed to fulfil its destiny and Germany now claimed a half of the second largest island on the planet. The hoisting of the imperial flag on the Gazelle Peninsula caused a minor crisis in Anglo–German relations. Bismarck had been careful to hide his intentions in the Pacific from the English and the British Admiralty was abruptly informed by telegram in December. Spurred by the easy annexation, German traders pressed for further claims of the region. German territorial ambitions in the Pacific were beginning to prove Horace right.

Manfred von Fellmann had personally attended the funeral of his erstwhile adversary before he sailed, his attendance bringing the total of mourners to three. The tall Prussian had stood on one side of the grave whilst Michael and George Godfrey had stood on the other. They had acknowledged each other's presence with courteous words and a handshake.

And now Enid was asking Godfrey to stop Michael Duffy from meeting with his son! He could do what she wanted. The means to do so were within his long reach that extended across the Indian ocean to Africa.

'Are you able to stay for supper, George?' Enid asked.

'Yes, I will stay for supper,' he replied, bemused by her easy shift. It was as if nothing of importance had occurred in the last few minutes. But that was Enid's essential nature, to be able to shift alliances as quickly and as effortlessly as events dictated.

Not all persons related to Captain Patrick Duffy welcomed the news of his rise from the ranks of the dead. Granville White fumed alone in his library as he read the brief account of Captain Patrick Duffy's miraculous feat of survival behind enemy lines, the heroic account colourfully recorded in the newspaper Enid had recently purchased in her expansion of the Macintosh companies. But what galled Granville even more was the fact that the paper ran a front page article portraying the hero of the Scots' Brigade as a native-born son of the Colony of New South Wales and revealing him as grandson of the Lady Enid Macintosh of philanthropic fame.

When Duffy returned he would be waiting and fully prepared for him. There could only be one left to inherit the Macintosh companies at the end of the day! The deal struck with his estranged wife had curtailed any hope of challenging Patrick's right to inheritance – but there were many other ways of discrediting a man. If only Captain Mort had been successful in his conspiracy to have the Duffy bastard murdered years earlier, then all the energy required to plot the man's downfall would not be required now.

The ticking of a clock marked the silence in the library. Granville sat behind his desk and brooded. His attention was drawn to the collection of spears, nullahs and boomerangs fixed to the wall and he experienced a feeling of dread for not the first time. He knew it was purely superstition. But the dread of the unknown had an unshakeable quality about it which sometimes haunted his dreams with images of a place he had never visited but knew well enough about: the pride of the Macintosh properties, Glen View in central Queensland.

Granville rose from the swivel chair and walked to the trophy wall where he snatched at a spear and snapped it across his knee. It shattered with a brittle crack. He flung the broken spear aside and scattered the other Nerambura weapons from the wall. And so he would scatter Glen View! Rid himself of the awful nightmares that haunted him, he thought savagely. And rid himself of the damned name of Duffy once and for all.

40

The station dogs barked up a fury as Duncan
Cameron, the manager of Glen View, stood on the
wide verandah of the main house and watched
the seven men of the Native Mounted Police ride
into his yard. The pack of dogs yapped furiously as
they danced nimbly around the big mounts until,
on a command from Duncan, the dogs reluctantly
slunk away from the troopers to return to the cool
shade under the tank stands and shearing shed.

Glen View had taken on an air of staid
permanence since its establishment thirty years
earlier by the tough squatter Donald Macintosh
and his eldest son, Angus. Both men now lay
buried in the red earth on the property, slain by
Wallarie's spears. Despite their violent deaths, the
property survived and was managed by a man
appointed by Lady Enid Macintosh who, a Scot
himself, was every bit as tough as his predecessor,
Sir Donald. Improvements had been made to the
main house and its outbuildings that would have
pleased Sir Donald.

Duncan's young, Isle of Skye-born wife

provided the female touch to the house itself. Mary Cameron now joined her husband on the front verandah to watch the dusty and weary patrol file into the yard. Visitors were a rarity and a welcome respite from the lonely isolation of the frontier, especially for a woman who had grown up in the close knit community of her Scottish village where regular visiting was a part of life. The tough looking mix of European and Aboriginal police certainly provided some colour to the day, Mary thought, as she stood by her husband watching the leader of the patrol, a young and handsome inspector, dismount.

'Inspector James, sir,' Gordon said as he strode across the dusty yard. 'At your service. We have ridden from Townsville the past week in search of two darkies I suspect may be on your property.'

The Glen View manager took the extended hand. 'Duncan Cameron and my wife, Missus Mary Cameron,' he replied. 'Might explain the tracks one of my boys picked up around the hills in the south paddock. Tracks of three myalls, he said they were.'

'Ahh. It sounds like it might be why we have travelled here,' Gordon said, slapping down his trousers to brush away the dust. 'Probably still got the darkie girl with them who they took just south of Townsville some weeks back.'

'Inspector James, you said?' Cameron mused as if remembering something. 'Not the young police-man who dispersed the Kalkadoon up north? Inspector Gordon James?'

'That would be me,' Gordon smiled, a little embarrassed at his spreading fame.

'Read about your battle with the myalls only yesterday,' Cameron said. 'Bloody fine effort you and your laddies put on.' He turned to glance at Gordon's weary men slouching in their saddles under a blazing sun. 'Best we organise some tucker for your men and horses, Inspector. I'll get my gardener to show your lads where they can toss down for the night. I presume you will be staying the night?'

'Yes, thank you, Mister Cameron,' Gordon answered gratefully. 'We've ridden pretty hard the last few days and the boys need a break. But we will be rising before dawn tomorrow and I will have to impose on your hospitality to provide a guide to take us to the hills. That is where you said your boy picked up tracks?'

'Not far from the hills,' the manager replied. 'But my lads are a little shaky about riding too close to the hills when it comes on dark. They say the place is haunted by the spirits of the dead blackfellas old Sir Donald had dispersed back in '62. Even my white stockmen believe the stories! Knowing its reputation as I do now I doubt that you would find any blackfella hanging around the hills.'

'I don't know if you have heard of Wallarie, a Darambal man from around these parts,' Gordon said.

'I've heard of him all right,' Duncan replied nodding his head. 'It was said he killed young Angus Macintosh during the dispersal of the Nerambura clan near the waterholes and later speared old Sir Donald himself. I thought the man was some kind of blackfella myth.'

'Wallarie is real enough,' Gordon said grimly. 'He has gone back to his old tricks of bushranging. Except now he has a partner, a former member of my troop by the name of Peter Duffy.'

'Duffy? The same name as the bullocky who the myalls killed just after the dispersal?' Cameron remembered the stories passed down to him by the old hands of the station. 'Any relation to the bullocky?'

'His half-caste grandson,' Gordon replied in a tired voice. 'But it appears the Nerambura didn't kill the Irish bullocky. It may have been Lieutenant Mort, who was in command of the detachment which carried out the dispersal.'

Mary Cameron listened in silence to the exchange of stories surrounding the mysterious hills south of the homestead. She had found Sir Donald's old journals when she had been re-decorating and had read with revulsion his brief description of that terrible day. She also remembered something else.

'It is rather strange, Inspector,' she said quietly, and Gordon turned to her. 'There was a sergeant Henry James who was second-in-command of the Native Mounted Police the day you and my husband speak of.'

'My father, Missus Cameron,' Gordon replied softly.

'When one puts all the pieces together,' Mary Cameron said, casting him a strange look, 'it almost looks as if history is repeating itself in a queer sort of way.'

'I hope not,' he said firmly. 'I certainly hope not.'

'Well, I think we should go inside,' Duncan Cameron said politely. 'No sense standing out here all day. Ah Chee!' he roared, and an old Chinese with a pigtail down to his waist hurried from behind the house.

'Yes, masa Camerwon.'

'Show the troopers where they can bed down for the night over in the shearers' quarters. And tell the cook to prepare extra meals to feed 'em.'

The gardener made a quick bow from the waist and in an authoritative manner rounded up the police troopers to shepherd them to the empty shearers' quarters.

When Gordon was satisfied his men were well provisioned and comfortable he strode across to the main house to have afternoon tea with the manager and his pretty wife. Gordon noticed that she was showing the first swelling signs of a pregnancy and for a fleeting moment had an image of Sarah carrying a baby in the future. It was a gentle and warm image that caused him to smile.

He reached the verandah and wiped his boots clean before knocking and being invited inside. An Aboriginal maid took his cap while Gordon unbuckled his gun belt to hang it on a coatstand in the hallway. The house was not luxurious by city standards, but it was at least spacious and clean. The original bark hut that Donald Macintosh had built was now used as a shed to store hay for the horses.

Gordon joined Duncan and Mary in the back-yard under the shade of a rotunda-like building where grapevines struggled to enclose the shelter.

Tea and scones were served by the Aboriginal maid as the three chatted about the latest prices of wool and beef transport costs and the news from the far-off Sudanese war.

South of the Glen View homestead from the summit of the old volcanic plug, Wallarie gazed across the plains at the orange ball slowly being swallowed by the scrub. No sound of the children's laughter or the old people's bickering at the end of the day, he reflected sadly. Just the gentle sounds of the bush lying down to rest for the night, the sounds of the earth as they'd been even before the coming of his people way back to the Dreaming.

The warrior tugged absent-mindedly at his long beard now shot with grey streaks. His thoughts were on times long past when he and Tom Duffy sat side by side gazing out across the same bush-land. That had been the time of the walkabout into the channel country and back with the small party of survivors from the dispersal. *So long ago!*

And the squatter's shepherds had killed the old man and boy who had been with them on the trek. They had shot the old woman and taken Tom's woman for their own. But he and the Irishman had tracked the killers and exacted a bloody vengeance on them. That was when he had been taught the killing ways of the white man he remembered. How to ride and shoot and talk their language. But now he sensed that Gordon James was close at hand.

The sun was almost gone and the hush of that time between day and night settled on the hill. The old warrior eased himself to his feet and scooped up his odd mix of weapons: a Snider rifle and stone axe.

He would find Peter at the bottom of the hill by the campfire and retell the stories of the Nerambura. He would explain the meaning of the sacred tableau of painted figures on the wall of the cave and they would feel the spirits of the sacred place come to them. In the morning he would prepare Peter for his initiation into manhood. Granted it would not be a true initiation, the Darambal man admitted to himself. But it would be better than no initiation.

He found Peter sitting cross-legged before the fire in the cave. The young man had left his woman, Matilda, at their campsite down on the waterholes below the hills. Not in the place of the slaughter – that was taboo land – but further up the creek line. She would wait for Peter's return to her as a true Nerambura man.

41

Captain Patrick Duffy reported back to brigade headquarters. His three-week ordeal wandering in the Sudanese wastelands had left him gaunt and haunted. He had said very little to anyone of his experiences and when he did speak it was only to say that he had been lucky.

Luck and an inherent toughness of body and spirit had kept him alive when he had stumbled on the Dervishes in the night. He had survived where lesser men would have despaired and died. The ragged remains of his uniform, now stained black with blood, said it all. No-one was about to closely question the captain who seemed to have genuinely blocked from his mind all that had occurred before he had been found by the camel patrol. Time might make him less reticent about his experiences, but for now he was silent and brooding.

On the night of his ill-fated mission he had fired blindly into the shapes looming out of the night and then escaped in the dark. But instead of attempting to make his way towards his own lines he had chosen to use the darkness to escape deeper into enemy held territory. He had guessed correctly that the Dervish would automatically assume that he would make a dash for the Zareba.

The following morning, as the sun rose over the tortured land of stone, sand and thorny scrub, Patrick lay hidden amongst the rocks of a small hill deep in the heart of the Dervish patrolled land. He watched helplessly as the roving bands of heavily armed Dervish warriors patrolled between him and the withdrawing army of khaki clad soldiers of the British force. He had been right in not attempting to head for his own lines.

Nor could he make contact with the patrols of mounted lancers whom he could see only as tiny figures on the horizon. They were obviously searching for him. Dervish snipers and ambush parties lay concealed and would welcome the lancers with bullet, spear and sword should they be foolish enough to stray too far from the main force of the British square. Any attempt to attract the attention of the roving patrols could possibly lead them to their deaths. By sunset, thirst drove Patrick from his well-concealed position where he had watched with despair the tiny cloud of dust marking the withdrawing British army.

Patrick knew he must first find a source of water and he was fortunate to stumble on an old well in the hills that had been overlooked by both the Dervish and British forces. It was not poisoned and he drank the cool and muddy water as if it were the finest of champagnes.

For the next three weeks he lived the life of a nocturnal beast of prey, hunting for supplies from the unwary Bedouin in the vast fortress which was the Sudanese desert. Using stealth, and the razor edge of his knife, he accumulated a small but adequate store of dates and unleavened bread. It was enough to give him the strength to live to see the burning sunrise each following day.

His lethal and stealthy forays into the camps of the desert people caused an unprecedented terror that outweighed the previous presence of the British army. At least they had been able to see the British infidels. But this nightly visitor was like some demon of the desert! An evil spirit that came when the sun lost its heat and the desert was as cold as a corpse. A devil that left the throat cut of the restless camel driver and was never seen in the day – which only proved he was not human.

Patrick always travelled a little further northeast each night but not in a direct line as he knew the Dervish patrols would expect him to do so. Patience and caution became his principles of survival as he made slow but sure progress towards the port of Suakin.

Living like this, Patrick was stripped of everything but his cunning and instinct to survive. No longer did he have thoughts of whether he should renounce his religion and accept the Macintosh name; no longer thoughts of fox hunts or fancy balls of his past English life. Just thoughts of where his next hiding place would be and finding a camp to raid when the night came.

Near the end of three weeks he had reached the end of his endurance. Time had become a meaningless blur and his tattered uniform was stiff with the blood of the uncounted men whose throats he had cut in his quests for supplies.

At times he would sit in the shade of a thorn bush on sunset and stare westwards across the plains softened by the disappearing sun. And sometimes in the lonely stretches of his three weeks he thought about Catherine. But they were thoughts for the pain she had caused him by letting him think she would be waiting for his return, only to taunt him with her cruel silence.

Still, Patrick knew that beyond the horizon was the place of Celtic mists. A place of magic and the home of the Morrigan. And often his thoughts would turn from pain to a bitterness fed on the despairing hate that gave him the desire to live and eventually confront Catherine with one question, one word: *Why?*

Then the day came when he watched the three figures mounted on camels shimmer in blurring outlines against the horizon. His first instinct was to bury himself deeper in the sand under the mimosa tree. But the flash of light caught his attention. Were they possibly a British patrol? Had the flash come from a set of binoculars or a telescope? As far as he knew the Dervish did not use the ocular aids in the desert. But he was almost beyond caring whether he lived or died. If they were Bedouin then let it be he went down fighting, he thought as he forced himself to his feet. And with the last of his strength he staggered towards the patrol.

Major Hughes greeted Patrick with a display of genuine delight. His decision to send Patrick on the reconnaissance mission had weighed heavily on him and when he had received the report that he was missing in action it had become a crushing weight on his conscience. *Had the aim of the mission been worth the price of one of the brigade's finest young captains?* Days earlier he had privately celebrated Patrick's return to Suakin by uncorking and consuming a bottle of his best port wine as soon as the news came through. It had been an almost miraculous survival.

Now Patrick was invited to sit in a cane chair draped with a tiger skin that the brigade major had acquired whilst he was in Burma. It now travelled with his mess kit wherever he served as a soldier of the Queen – a personal idiosyncrasy not confined to the B.M. as other officers also carted exotic, and sometimes bulky, items with them on active service.

Patrick looked more relaxed than when the B.M. first had seen him brought in from the desert. Then he had been a bearded giant with the dangerous, staring eyes of a hunted wild animal. But even now that Patrick appeared relaxed, the hunted look was not completely gone. A shadow of what he had experienced in the three weeks of his ordeal remained as a haunting spectre behind the eyes.

The B.M. had the task of briefing him on his duties. He was back on active service and his mess bill was overdue for payment. Missing in action did not exclude him from three weeks of rates levied for the food and wine he was denied the opportunity of consuming. However, there was something more important to discuss first.

Major Hughes fingered the letter Patrick had tendered to him through the routine army channels by way of the orderly room. Although the letter was directed higher than himself, it still had to pass through his hands. 'Do you really wish to resign your commission?' he asked.

Patrick shifted slightly in the cane chair. 'Yes. I think it is time I returned home, sir.'

'You are a damned fine officer, Patrick. And in my lengthy time of soldiering I dare say one of the finest soldiers I have ever had the privilege of serving with.'

His frank praise made Patrick feel guilty. But service in the army had only ever been a temporary stage in his life, an interlude to allow himself to sort out his future aspirations. 'I will not be leaving the army altogether,' he said. 'I hope to parade with a colonial militia unit when I am back in Sydney.'

'You have probably heard the rumours circulating that we are about to pack up and leave here,' the B.M. said quietly. 'If that is so, then I might be able to arrange that you ship out with the New South Walers. Would that suit you?'

'I was planning to take my discharge in London,' Patrick replied. 'I have some business in Ireland before I return to the colonies.'

'A young lady?' Major Hughes questioned with a raised eyebrow.

'Yes, sir, a young lady,' Patrick confirmed.

'Well, I will put my recommendation on your request for discharge from your duties to become effective upon our return to England. But remember, you can still reconsider your resignation before we reach London.'

'I know, sir. It is not a decision that I can say I enjoy. I have a lot of friends around me here. A lot of good memories.' He winced at the last statement and continued, 'And a lot I would rather forget.'

'If there is nothing else then, I should stand you a drink in the mess tonight, Captain Duffy. I'm sure your brother officers will do likewise when they learn that you will be leaving us.'

'As I'm not leaving until we return to England I doubt that my mess account could stand farewell drinks,' Patrick said with a rueful grin. 'Possibly when we are back at the regiment.'

'Yes, you could be right, Captain Duffy. No announcements until we return.'

Patrick stood, saluted and left the brigade major's tent. He stood in the blazing midday sun and pondered his future. First he must find Catherine and end the tortured thoughts that plagued him. To at least learn *why* she had ignored the flow of letters he had sent her. He had steeled himself to the possibility that she had found someone else and forgotten him. At least, he tried to convince himself, he was prepared to accept such. But a disquieting voice whispered in the depths of his mind that such an outcome was too horrible to contemplate. Time and distance had not tempered his desire for her.

He stood for a moment as thoughts flooded him and he felt absorbed by the vastness of the desert that lay beyond the British army encampment of Suakin. Living day to day beyond the hills, he had seen in the wilderness the bare meaning of life, the simplicity of survival when nothing more than the spirit gave him a reason to live, the omnipotent feeling at the end of his knife as a man's life ebbed from his body and the blood flowed from the severed jugular vein. What use was money and power when a man had only his physical and spiritual strength to survive? Was the man he had met in himself out there all that there was to his life?

Soldiers stripped to singlets sweated and toiled under the same blazing sun as they went about their military chores. The sounds of an army at rest drifted to him: the sharp clanging of a black-smith's hammer on iron at his forge as he shaped the shoes for the horses; the barking bawl of a drill sergeant on a dusty patch of ground as he re-inforced the need for men to act as one; the querulous voices of the army cooks arguing over rations being prepared in the big stewing pots. Such sights and sounds had become as familiar to Patrick as had the jangle of horses and carriages in the cold, wintry streets of London.

He stumbled to his tent where he slumped into a chair behind the tiny table covered in the dust of the desert. Tears welled from his eyes as the empti-ness of his life overwhelmed him. He was a man with no real family other than his grandmother. He wondered about the man who had been his father. *If only he had known him!* To be able to have met with Michael Duffy whose persistence even in death had given rise to a living legend.

Patrick's melancholic thoughts were distracted by a small object wrapped securely in a clean rag and he stared with a puzzled expression on his suntanned face at the parcel. But he did not need to unwrap the little goddess to know she lay within the folds.

'Private MacDonald! You wonderful devious bastard!' he exclaimed with a joyous hiss of relief. 'You disobeyed my orders!'

Gently he unwrapped the little stone icon and stared at her primitive lewdness as she smiled back up at him. The Morrigan was still with him!

On the hospital ship *Ganges*, Private Francis Farrell lay between sweat stained sheets and stared into the darkness as he listened to the men tossing and moaning in the vile grips of the enteric fever. Sleep was the blessed release that did not come to the former Irish policeman of Sydney Town as he watched the iron ceiling floating in nauseous waves above him. He cursed the debilitating disease that ravaged his body. Only three days earlier he had been on top of the world and had congratulated himself on surviving the campaign.

But now he lay helpless, ravaged by the deadly bacteria in his bowel. He knew they would be going home soon as the news had travelled through the ward and back. Loading of supplies had already begun.

Private Farrell feared that his illness might exclude him from transport on the troopship assigned to steam to Sydney with the Australian volunteer contingent. He had heard rumours that those soldiers too ill to transport would be left behind to recuperate and already a colonial soldier had died from the same disease that gripped Francis Farrell.

He felt the burning thirst spread through his body as the disease continued to dehydrate him in bouts of uncontrollable diarrhoea. The milk and rice diet he had been put on did not seem to be working. The tough former policeman who had walked the beats of some of Sydney's most dangerous areas felt as helpless as a child.

Tears splashed down his face. If he died now he would be denied the opportunity to tell young Patrick Duffy that his father was alive. 'Water!' he croaked feebly, and a shadow appeared beside his bed.

A gentle hand touched his brow and the soothing accent of an English voice came to him. 'There, Paddy, I'll get you a drink.' The medic on duty brought the water to his lips and helped prop him to drink. Francis had trouble swallowing and much of the liquid dribbled down his chin into his bushy beard. He could not see the medic's face but felt his aura of caring concern. 'Try and get some sleep, Paddy,' the gentle voice crooned, and Francis reached out to grip the man's hand in the dark. The grip was strong enough to tell the medic that the Paddy would get well.

Sleep did come to Francis Farrell. A deep and fevered sleep with strange and unexplainable visions of a craggy hill that shimmered with flames. It was a place of death and Francis felt himself drifting on the wings of an eagle over its fiery turrets. Was this hell, he wondered as the hot thermals of the surrounding desert buffeted him into helplessness high above. Or was this a recollection of the craggy hills where the New South Wales contingent had toiled under the blazing Sudanese sun to cut the line for the railway track for the British army from Suakin on the coast to Berber in the west?

The orderly's major concern that long night was for the big Irish colonial who was teetering on the verge of death. His temperature had suddenly soared and he was in the stage of delirium where the door opened to the next world. He sat by the bed of Private Francis Farrell and swabbed his fevered brow. There was little else he could do. He hummed a tune his mother had long ago sung to him when he was a child growing up in the slums of the Liverpool dock area. It was only right that a man hear the gentle sounds of a loving mother before he died. He wondered at the strange ramblings of the soldier. What did he mean when he called out 'Patrick, your father is alive and I know where he can be found'?

42

The horsemen were soft shadows in the piccaninny dawn. The expectation of the sun rising brought forth the sweet sounds of nature as the spirits of the night fled to the caves and crannies of the sacred hills of Glen View.

The weary horsemen let their mounts pick their way through the scrub. Not much sleep and an early morning rise still hung over them as the single file of troopers of the Native Mounted Police followed the Aboriginal stockman guide riding in front while Gordon James rode directly behind.

'Place baal up there!' the Aboriginal guide hissed and pointed.

Gordon followed the man's finger to see the craggy summit of a hill rising just above the thick scrub crowned with a tiara of the last stars in the early morning sky. He wondered how such a peaceful piece of geology could be a bad place. So this was the sacred place, he mused, as he reflected on the stories his father had told to him of its eerie power. Although his father had scoffed at the Aboriginal beliefs it had occurred to Gordon that his father had always seemed uncomfortable when relating the stories of the Nerambura hill.

'On your guard,' Gordon warned. 'Trooper George to me,' he called softly, and was joined by one of the Aboriginal policemen. 'Scout down the waterhole. If you see anything, come straight back to me with your report.' The trooper nodded his understanding and reined away. The order was passed along the file of horsemen to 'stand easy'. In many ways Gordon hoped that he had been wrong in his presumption that Wallarie would be taking Peter to the Nerambura. The two men might elude him, then he could return to Townsville and resign. A tiny fear nagged Gordon. It was a fear of indefinite substance and one of those bad feelings Kate Tracy might call a premonition.

His troubled thoughts were broken when the police scout returned within minutes. His expression was grim and Gordon felt a knot in his stomach.

'Found something, boss,' he said and led them along the creek line.

Although Gordon did not unholster his service pistol his men had rifles ready. They moved quietly and broke into a small clearing set amongst the big river trees where they caught Matilda curled in a deep sleep by the dead embers of a log fire. Gordon signalled to one of the troopers to dismount and take her prisoner. She awoke to find herself looking up into the barrel of a police carbine levelled at her by an Aboriginal trooper. Behind him in the slowly strengthening light of day she could see other uniformed police. They sat astride horses, gazing down at her with a mixture of curiosity and in some cases undisguised lust. She was aware of her fear but refused to cringe before them.

'What name you girl?' the Aboriginal trooper asked gruffly. 'You name Matilda?'

Matilda could not see any reason to deny it and nodded. The revelation of her identity seemed to please the trooper who turned to call over his shoulder to the white officer, 'This lubra Trooper Duffy's woman.'

'Not *Trooper* Duffy anymore,' Gordon corrected, and gazed curiously at the young woman. She was quite beautiful, he thought.

'Where is your man?' the trooper asked with a menacing growl. 'He nearby?'

Matilda's grasp of English was excellent but she suddenly appeared not to understand the question asked. The trooper realised she was deliberately ignoring him and raised the butt of his rifle menacingly.

'No sense in roughing up the girl,' Gordon said to protect her from any harm. 'We will find him.' He turned to the guide. 'Do you know where there is a cave in the hills that the Nerambura considered sacred?'

The guide shifted uncomfortably in his saddle and would not look the police officer in the eye. 'Place up there, boss. My word!' he answered softly. 'No good blackfella go there.' Gordon guessed the stockman meant the largest of the hills in the range.

'Where up there?' he asked further.

The stockman looked at him.

'Alonga hill down alonga place alonga black rocks.'

Gordon gazed up at the face of the hill now slowly taking on shadows and lines as the sun's rays crept into crevices and shone off rocks. He could see a small cliff face of granite-like rocks and a deeper shadow that might indicate a cave. 'That place?' he asked, and the stockman nodded. He did not want to say the name because it would bring bad luck!

'Put the girl in irons,' Gordon ordered. 'And guard her well. Under no circumstances is she to be harmed. Do I make myself clear?'

The troopers reluctantly mumbled their under-standing and Matilda was manacled under a coolabah tree. Gordon then issued further orders to set up a base camp by the creek, just down from where they had captured Matilda. While the troopers went about establishing a camp he quietly slipped away. He would go to the cave alone and attempt to find Peter.

'Wallarie said you would find us,' Peter Duffy said as he sat cross-legged on the floor of the cave before a smouldering fire. His near naked body was stripped of all European trappings and he was painted with the ochre of the earth. 'He said you would come to this place.'

Gordon gripped his revolver and scanned the gloomy interior of the cave. 'Where is Wallarie?' he asked quietly.

'Around,' Peter answered vaguely, and poked at the fire to stir new life into the embers. 'He is not far away.'

'I have your woman as my prisoner,' Gordon said defensively. He felt the cold exposure of a man vulnerable to sudden ambush. 'She will not be harmed,' he added. Peter did not comment but stared into the fire. 'You have to return with me,' Gordon said. 'You will have to answer charges of robbery whilst under arms and possibly a charge of attempted murder.'

'I won't be going anywhere with you, Gordon,' the young man finally answered. 'You would have to kill me first.'

'You are not stupid, Peter,' Gordon pleaded. 'You must know I didn't just come here on my own. You must also realise that I came after you and Wallarie because I was concerned that any other patrol might just shoot you down on sight.'

'You could just as easily leave here and say you never found me,' Peter replied. 'But you won't do that. You won't leave well enough alone because your duty to Her Majesty is more important than old friendships.'

'I was going to resign my commission before I came on this patrol,' Gordon said as he slipped his revolver back into its holster. 'Sarah asked me. So that I could marry her.'

'*You* . . . marry Sarah?'

Gordon squatted on his haunches opposite Peter. 'Yeah. This is my last patrol.'

'You're really going to marry my sister,' Peter repeated and shook his head. 'That matters. But I won't be going back with you. Wallarie and I have other plans.'

'I have your woman,' Gordon reminded him. 'She will probably be returned to her employer who I know you have met in your travels.'

'Drunken bastard. Probably said we tried to kill him. Did he?'

'Yeah. But from what I heard he doesn't have much evidence.'

'We didn't,' Peter scowled. 'If we had wanted to kill him he wouldn't be alive now.'

'I know. That's why I didn't believe his story.'

The slight smile that crossed Peter's face marked a recognition of his old friend's faith in him. He stared through the veil of dim light. 'Maybe I will come with you,' he said. 'But I need you to do a couple of things first.' Gordon nodded his agreement. He would listen. 'You do your best to get Matilda a job here on Glen View. She is smart and speaks good English. Not much she can't do around the main house for the manager's missus.'

'That's fair enough,' Gordon granted, and Peter continued, 'Second thing. You call off any further search for Wallarie. You take me, but leave Wallarie here. This is his land and he doesn't have anything else in the world. He's not a young man anymore and no future threat to the white man.'

'You ask a lot when it comes to Wallarie,' Gordon replied painfully. This second request put his duty in conflict with his sense of fairness. 'The old bastard has a lot to answer for.'

'That's how things stand,' Peter said stubbornly. 'Look after those two things and I will go with you.'

A silence fell between the two men. Gordon rose to his feet and Peter could see that he was battling. His own choice to surrender had been made long before Gordon's arrival. He had made his decision upon learning of Matilda's pregnancy. Wallarie had told him that the spirits of the sacred rocks of the hill had entered her body. The consideration of his life as a wanted man in light of his responsibilities to Matilda and the child that she carried in her, brought the realisation that he should take his chances in a court of law. Better to go to a gaol than lose forever the chance to see his children grow into adulthood. Besides, he thought with a wry grin, he had outsmarted his old friend. He had always known that he would have to face Gordon eventually and by surrendering he would break the spell of the dreadful premonition. Neither need die.

From the first moment Peter had stepped inside the sacred place of the Nerambura he had felt uneasy. It was as if some terrible tragedy was brewing, like the anvil thunderhead clouds of the fierce electrical summer storms over the brigalow plains. Whatever it was, he knew that there was some kind of cycle that he must break.

'Do you believe in all this?' Gordon asked as he gazed upon the ancient painted figures on the back wall of the cave. 'All this blackfella stuff?'

'I don't know,' Peter answered. 'I think I do. But the nuns who taught me at school said it was all superstitious nonsense. Maybe it all depends on who taught you first. Like Wallarie teaching me now about the Nerambura stories. I might have thought all the Christian stuff was superstition and all this real. But here it's real enough.'

'I think I know what you mean,' Gordon said as he found his attention focused on a tiny stick-like warrior painted in white poised with his spear searching for a target. A faded scratch mark severed the figure as if a knife blade had been used in an attempt to desecrate the ancient art work. 'It's like you and I are being forced to do things that have been done before.'

Peter glanced up sharply at Gordon. He was staring with rapt interest at the cave wall. The sun was now at such an angle that it briefly flooded the gloomy interior with a golden glow and the figures seemed to come awake and take on a life of their own. Hunts continued as the stick-like figures pursued forever the giant kangaroos; corroborees danced and an eagle soared against a black sun over the red earth. 'You feel that, too,' he said softly. 'Like a force guiding our actions in ways we are not aware of.'

'Like I had a fear I might end up killing you,' Gordon answered quietly. 'Or you me. That's why I had to come to you alone and prove to myself we could break the power of the spirits.'

'You are starting to think like a blackfella,' Peter chuckled softly. 'You sound like you believe in blackfella magic.'

'Maybe I remember the things Wallarie taught us when we were kids,' Gordon said, as he turned to glance over at Peter sitting by the fire. 'And I'm not a blackfella like you,' he added with a wry grin. 'You come with me and I'll do as you say. Wallarie can keep his freedom.'

Peter rose from the earth and walked over to where his clothes lay in a heap with his rifle. He dressed quickly and handed his rifle to Gordon who asked sardonically, 'Why is it that I have the feeling you outwitted me from the moment I set foot in this place?'

'I was much smarter at school than you,' Peter replied with a grin.

'I suppose that could be true.'

The two men emerged from the cave into the brightness of the early morning sunshine and they walked side by side through the scrub, chatting as they had when they were growing up together. Gordon even discussed how Kate might be able to get the best lawyers from Brisbane to represent Peter at his trial. And Peter talked on about the coming wedding between his best friend and his sister.

As they walked down to the waterholes they were once again the two boyhood friends who had sworn eternal friendship by the campfire of the Darambal man. They laughed together for the first time in many years.

But their laughter was short lived as they walked into the camp. With blood on his face Wallarie lay on the earth surrounded by the troopers who greeted Gordon with the announcement that they had caught the infamous Aboriginal bushranger attempting to free Matilda.

Then it all happened so fast!

Gordon James would be forever haunted with the dreams of those fateful seconds. Peter snatched a rifle left leaning against a tree by a careless trooper and yelled for Wallarie to run. The old warrior rolled to his feet and grabbed a revolver from the hand of a trooper who had been distracted by the sight of Peter pointing a rifle at them. Each second seemed like a minute.

A trooper raised his rifle and Peter swung round to point the rifle directly at the man. Gordon instinctively snatched at his own holstered pistol and found it pointed at his boyhood friend. 'No!' he screamed as he noticed Peter squeezing the trigger for the lethal shot. 'Peter, no!' he screamed again, and in the blink of an eye, he fired. He was hardly aware of the kick in his hand as the weapon discharged. In his horror he was vaguely aware of the shattering impact of the bullet striking Peter in the side of the head and his friend's blood spattering his outstretched arm. Peter crumpled and the unfired rifle fell from his lifeless hands.

Wallarie was gone.

But Peter lay dead at Gordon's feet as Matilda wailed her grief. With the fury of a wild animal she flung herself on his body and wrapped her manacled hands around his bloody head. Stunned by the speed of the events, Gordon stood frozen, his pistol dangling at his side whilst the troopers scattered in a desperate attempt to get to their horses. But the wily Darambal man had cut them loose and run them off as he escaped on one of the police mounts.

The gun fell from Gordon's hand as he reeled away. He staggered like a drunken man until his legs gave way and he collapsed to the hot earth where he sat staring back at the woman who smothered Peter's body. Around him troopers cursed as they ran after their horses in the scrub.

Something unexplainable had reached out and touched them with its bloody hand. Just as it had years earlier to touch their fathers' lives. It was an unrelenting curse on their lives that was at its strongest at the source itself. Sick with the terrible realisation of what had occurred in the beat of a heart, he was barely aware that something hard and smooth lay under his hand. He sat transfixed. He forced himself to look down. He gasped at what he saw. The skull of a child lay in the sandy earth. *They had camped on the site of the original slaughter of the Nerambura clan.*

Duncan Cameron was warned by the yapping of the station dogs that the police patrol was returning. He met the men riding in and noticed that a body was strapped over the front of the saddle on the horse ridden by Inspector Gordon James and guessed that the police had found one of the men they had gone in search of. But there was a sombre mood hanging over the returning patrol that Duncan had not expected. Behind a trooper rode a girl whose features indicated that she was of mixed race.

Gordon reined his horse up to the front gate to the homestead yard but did not dismount.

'See you got one of them,' Duncan commented and the young inspector nodded. 'You taking him back with you?' he asked, as he stared at the body slung over the horse in front of Gordon's saddle.

'No. I want to bury him here. At Glen View,' Gordon replied. 'The place where his grandfather Patrick Duffy is buried. I'll need to borrow your man to show me where his grave is located.'

'I can't see any harm in your request, Inspector James,' Duncan said. 'Seems only fit he lie with kin under the sod. What is going to happen to the girl?' She had an intelligent look about her that impressed him.

'I was hoping you might be able to use her around here when we're gone. She speaks good English and I've been told she's pretty handy at cooking. She lived with an old prospector and looked after him. Think she might be expecting a kid to Peter Duffy. That a problem for you?'

'That's not a problem,' the Glen View manager replied. 'Missus Cameron is expecting and we might have need of the services of a wet nurse in the future. She can stay on here and generally help my wife out during her confinement.'

'Good!' Gordon grunted, and issued orders for the girl to be released into the manager's employment. At least Peter's child would be born on Nerambura land, he thought bitterly. And Cameron appeared to be a fair man who would look after her.

Before he left Glen View Gordon was taken to the place where Patrick Duffy and his faithful Aboriginal friend Old Billy were buried. The graves were hardly discernible in the clearing. Time and the elements had reclaimed the once freshly turned earth and covered the ground in wild grasses. Only the small piles of stones gave a true indication as to the graves of the two teamsters – murdered by Morrison Mort years earlier, and buried by Tom Duffy.

A grave was dug a few feet from where Patrick and Old Billy's bones lay in the earth and Peter Duffy was laid to rest beside a paternal grandfather he had never met. The tragic irony was not lost on the young police officer.

Nor did his order to call off the search for

Wallarie come as a surprise to his men. They also began to realise the terrible coincidences of their hunt. Whispered stories by the campfire embellished the power of the curse. It was concurred that it would be extremely unlucky should they persist in going after the old Darambal bushranger. *Let some other patrol finish the job*, they said amongst themselves.

When the burial was completed Gordon led his patrol north to Townsville, where he now had to confront Sarah and tell her that he had killed her brother. As he rode with his men he did so with little conversation except to issue orders. He was racked with grief for what had occurred – and for what was to be with Sarah.

Wallarie came in the night. He did so with great trepidation as he knew he was breaking the taboo of being in the presence of the dead. He sat a distance from the freshly dug grave and chanted a death song to see Peter's spirit on its way into the Dreaming. At least he would go as an initiated Darambal man, he consoled himself as he sat cross-legged in the dark.

Soon the sun would rise and the old warrior knew he must once again trek from the lands that had been his people's hunting grounds. The safe places in the colony were shrinking as more and more Europeans settled the far places of the horizon. Where would he go? The spirits of the Dreaming no longer spoke to him. Where would he be safe to live out his years? Never before had he felt so alone.

The sun rose over the plains and Wallarie rose

to face the hill towering over the scrub. Was it a whisper on the breeze that spoke to him? 'Whitefella not catch old Wallarie,' he swore to the ancestor spirits. The spirits of his people had called to him from a long way and he would go where he would be safe. He would go, where an old promise had been made, to a spirit man of the white man's religion.

Maybe this would be the last time he would know the freedom of his traditional life, he thought. Or maybe not. Scooping up his spears he took the first step to seek out a man who had come from over the seas.

43

The library of her mother's home held sad and bitter memories for Fiona. Here she had experienced the terrible confrontation with her mother, almost a quarter of a century earlier, when she had been a girl in love with the handsome Michael Duffy.

Once again she stood in the sombre light of the library, confronting her estranged mother. The two women had lost little of the venom they held for each other. They exchanged poisonous glances across the room.

'You may sit if you wish,' Enid said coldly as she took a chair behind the big wooden desk. 'I will have Betsy bring us tea.'

'Thank you,' Fiona replied without any sign of emotion. She could not bring herself to add *mother*.

Enid rang a tiny hand bell and Betsy entered the room. Enid issued her desire to take tea in the library. The maid bobbed her head and when she was gone Enid broke the icy silence. 'Your desire to see me is somewhat unexpected, Fiona,' she said. 'Has there been a death in the family?' she questioned sarcastically.

'I no more desire to be here in your presence than you desire mine,' Fiona replied, facing up to her mother. 'I requested this meeting because of recent events that I am sure affect you as much as they affect me.'

'From that I presume you mean the news of my grandson's safe return to his regiment?'

'*Your* grandson?' Fiona spluttered with a short and bitter laugh. 'You mean *my* son.'

'You gave him up when he was born, Fiona,' Enid retorted. 'Or have you forgotten?'

Fiona fought to keep down her bitter rage but paled visibly as the blood drained from her face. Not only had she lost her baby boy but also her beloved nanny, a woman who had been a mother figure to her. She composed herself and the blood returned to her cheeks. 'I know the lies you have told my son, *Mother*,' she replied. 'I know that you have convinced him that I never wanted him. As much as you never wanted me in your life. Oh, I know you have told him of how I plotted to have him sent to one of those dreadful baby farms so that I could marry Granville.'

'And did you not agree to get rid of Patrick?' Enid countered triumphantly.

'It was not that way,' she whispered in a choked voice. 'I was young and confused. And *you* took advantage of my confusion. *You* convinced me of how important it was to dispose of my son to a good family, for his benefit as much as mine. You know I would never have let him go if there was the slightest chance he might be sent to a baby farm. *You* know that, Mother! So long as God is my witness, and yours!'

'I do not know that,' Enid countered and Fiona detected just the slightest quaver in her mother's voice.

Enid was puzzled by the strange expression that had crept into her daughter's face. Had she given away the guilt that had haunted her for so many years? The guilt that was hers every time she looked into the emerald green eyes of her grandson and saw a part of her own daughter there. The eyes of the man whom she had come to love more than any other human alive? How ironic life was when the object of shame became the subject of pride!

'I have the means to rid you of your guilt and shame, Mother,' Fiona said softly, as if reading Enid's thoughts. 'That is why I have come here.'

'I have no guilt for anything I have done in my life,' her mother replied stiffly. 'I have nothing to be ashamed of.'

'Well, if that is so, then I have come here with an offer that I know will at least appeal to the high price you put on the Macintosh name. I may be in a position to give you the majority holdings in the family's estates. All I ask in return, is that you tell my son the truth of those years past.'

'How can you?' Enid scoffed dismissing her daughter's appeal. 'How can you when you treacherously sold your shares to your husband? Or has that slipped your mind?'

'Has it slipped your mind that my daughters

hold two-thirds of a third share in the estate?'

'I suspect your husband also knows that,' Enid replied facetiously. 'And, knowing his penchant for dubious business dealings, I also suspect that he is poised to use his position to buy out Helen and Dorothy's shares at the first possible opportunity.'

Fiona smiled grimly and Enid could see that her daughter had already thought of this. 'He is currently unable to raise the money to buy out my daughters' shares. But I have the capital from my transfer of shares to him and that allows me to make an offer to my daughters that I am sure they will accept.'

Enid gazed across the dimly lit room with just the glimmer of a growing respect. But she was confused as to why her daughter had sold her one-third share to her husband in the first place. 'It has always bewildered me why you would give your husband so much power. Did you do so to hurt me further or to destroy the Macintosh name?'

Fiona smiled sadly and shook her head. 'I did so to protect my son's inheritance, Mother. I did not make the decision lightly. But by doing so I was able to stop Granville from taking you to court to dispute Patrick's birthright. We came to an agreement. That is the *only* reason I sold Granville my inheritance.'

The revelation left Enid drained of any response. In the simple explanation a bridge was thrown across the gulf that separated mother and daughter. But it was not in Enid Macintosh's nature to express love in words. 'When Patrick returns we will *not* need your help,' she replied to her daughter's offer. And the bridge came crashing down between them.

Fiona shook her head despairingly and tears flooded her eyes. *What more could she do?* She rose from her chair just as Betsy returned to the library with the cups and saucers on a silver tray. 'I cannot believe any person could be as heartless as yourself, Mother,' she said, as if being strangled. 'I asked only that you tell my son the truth. Tell him of my love for him. Nothing else. And for that you could have had the majority control of your precious companies. Is there no pity in you? Cannot you feel human pain?'

Betsy glanced from one woman to the other and realised wisely that she should not remain in the sea of raw emotion engulfing the confines of the room. She quickly placed the tray on Enid's desk and mumbled an apology as she retreated tactfully. But she was only a couple of steps ahead of Fiona who brushed past her, weeping in great sobs of despair.

Enid remained at her desk as she stared at the open doorway. A part of her struggled to call after her daughter and say that she would consider the offer. But her voice was frozen into silent rejection. To accept her daughter's offer would mean exposing herself as a liar to Patrick as over the years she had reinforced his mother's supposed total lack of feelings for him as her son.

Then her voice came to her as she tried to rise from behind the desk. It came as a hoarse and strangled cry of despair. '*Fiona. My daughter! I'm sorry.*'

But her daughter was already at the step of her carriage and her own sobbing grief drowned all sounds except the agonised beating of her own heart. The time for reconciliation had come and gone. Only the gulf remained.

44

Patrick stood in the early morning sunshine on the Suakin waterfront watching the troopship make her way out of the harbour into the Red Sea. Drifting from its decks he could hear the colonial band playing 'Home Sweet Home'. He had come to see the troopship carrying the New South Wales contingent steam out of Suakin harbour because the men who sailed on her were not unlike himself. Like them, he knew his home was the far-off ancient, sun-drenched continent of Australia.

Where the sun touched the ripples on the calm seas the blue waters sparked in flashes of shimmering silver, bringing back dim memories of the magnificent harbour of Sydney. His Uncle Daniel and Aunt Colleen would take him and his cousins on ferry trips across its beautiful expanse bordered by tree-lined shores of tall, majestic eucalypts.

Patrick knew that when he had found the answers to his troubling questions about Catherine in Ireland he too would sail for Sydney and take his place beside his grandmother in the family enterprises. He gazed at the grey-black smoke of the departing funnels until the ship was out of sight and then walked slowly away to rejoin the brigade preparing for its departure from the Sudan.

Although the Dervish had not been defeated, revenge for the death of General Gordon of Khartoum had been seen to be done. The public in Britain had been placated by the sterling efforts of the commanding general, Lord Wolseley, who had inflicted heavy losses on the infidel Moslem and had taught them a lesson in British might.

Patrick's resignation from the army had been accepted by the War Office in London – but with a provision that he spend three months on staff duties in Cairo before it became effective. He had bridled but also accepted that as a commissioned officer he had duties to Queen and country.

Still, he had another very important duty before he departed the shores of Africa. The brigade boxing championships were soon to be held and Private Angus MacDonald clearly had his sights on Patrick's title for the heavyweight division. Friendship forged in war had little to do with how they would face each other on the dusty arena before their peers. No quarter would be asked nor any granted. It would be a gruelling battle between two fighters and he knew that he must resume training. The slow walk turned into a loping run. No sense in wasting time.

On the deck of the departing troopship Private Francis Farrell gazed back at the wharf and noticed a tall, broad-shouldered young British officer amongst the clusters of soldiers who bid them farewell.

Although he could not discern the facial features of the officer standing alone and watching them depart, he sensed he was seeing Patrick. He shook his head, muttering, 'Patrick, I failed. Something was keeping me from telling you about your father.'

Beyond the cluster of tiny figures on the wharf was the white stoned city of Suakin and beyond the city the craggy coastal hills of the Sudan. For some inexplicable reason Francis had a vague recollection of a fevered dream and a fiery hill. The thought went from his mind, however, as the troopship cleared the harbour and left in its wake the hills, the deserts and the white stoned city of Suakin.

'I'm sorry that you have travelled so far for little reason,' the captain said apologetically. A tall, broad-shouldered civilian sat in a chair in the corner of his office wearing a fashionable white suit and vest and holding a Panama hat in his lap. 'But your letters of introduction have been cancelled, Mister Duffy.'

Michael stared hard into the face of the staff officer sitting opposite him behind his ornately carved wooden desk. Overhead a fan stirred the languid air of the room. Outside the general staff headquarters, street traders babbled in Greek, Arabic and Sudanese as they went about the business of buying and selling in the bazaar. Their voices drifted to the window of the second storey office, a cacophony of humanity battling for financial survival.

Somehow Michael was not surprised at the captain's pronouncement on the invalid status of his letters of introduction. When he had arrived to inquire as to the fate of his son he found himself shuffled from one office to another until he reached the captain. He was a man about Michael's own age and, from the many ribands on his khaki uniform jacket, a battle experienced soldier of many campaigns.

'Captain French, I have come a long way. And I am sure you are acquainted with the influence of the signatory to the letters I have presented,' Michael growled ominously. 'This rather unexpected resistance to my attempts to contact Captain Duffy makes no sense considering the letters you have before you.'

The captain glanced down at his desk and was obviously embarrassed by the question. But he was under orders to hold the Irishman and ensure he was put on a ship sailing for anywhere out of Suakin. 'I appreciate your question, Mister Duffy,' he said when he glanced up. 'But your letters have been rescinded by a telegram we received from Victoria Barracks in Sydney some days before you arrived. And, I may say, by the signatory.'

Why in hell had Colonel Godfrey counterordered his own letters? Why the sudden change of mind? Lady Macintosh! It came as a blinding and obvious answer. Enid now knew that his son was alive and thus Michael was no longer useful to her needs! 'Then I take it that I am not permitted to see Captain Duffy while I'm here?' he said, glowering at the British captain.

'That is about the sum of it, Mister Duffy,'

Captain French replied. 'We have orders to escort you to the first ship sailing from Suakin and ensure that you leave without seeing him.'

Michael rose from his chair and gazed out the open window to the busy street below. 'I gather that I am under some kind of arrest then,' he said as he turned to the captain.

'I would rather not call it an arrest, Mister Duffy,' he replied in a partly apologetic tone. 'Rather, that you are possibly a reluctant guest of Her Majesty's army's hospitality, for the moment. And under those circumstances you will be treated with the utmost courtesy.' The captain rose and extended his hand. 'We will endeavour to meet any reasonable request for your preferred destination when you leave,' he said politely. But Michael did not accept the gesture of goodwill and the captain dropped his hand to his side. 'As a matter of fact there is a mail steamer sailing for London via the Canal tonight. Would that be to your satisfaction?'

'As good as anywhere right now I suppose,' Michael replied grudgingly and the captain smiled with relief.

'You are more fortunate than I, sir,' the captain said with a sigh. 'I only wish we could trade places.'

Michael grinned ruefully at the captain who stood at the centre of the spacious cool room. 'Not I,' he replied bitterly. 'My days serving Her Majesty's interests are finished.'

His answer puzzled the captain but he did not inquire as to what the Irishman meant. 'You will be escorted back to your hotel to gather your personal kit. I doubt that I have to go into a long list of instructions that apply to your short stay. Except to say you will not endeavour to contact Captain Duffy in any way. Nor will you depart from your escorts until you step aboard the mail steamer tonight. Other than that, you are free to avail yourself of the sights of the city and its many delights.'

'Reasonable offer under the circumstances,' Michael grunted as he walked towards the open door where two burly uniformed sergeants stood outside waiting for him. 'I will bid you good day then, Captain French.'

The two sergeants fell into step beside Michael as they strode down a walkway that overlooked a spacious marbled room below. From their manner it was obvious they had no intention of their 'prisoner' getting more than one pace from them until he was put aboard a ship.

When they were on the busy street, thronged with street urchins hustling for a handout from the foreign visitors and robed merchants hawking for a sale, Michael turned to his guards. 'May as well buy you fellows a drink before I leave.'

They glanced at each other questioningly before the bigger of his two escorts replied, 'Now that would be against orders, sir, for us to partake while we are on duty.' He grinned. His Irish accent was unmistakable. 'But if we are to be hospitable, as Captain French has ordered, I can't see why we should refuse any reasonable request of yours to sip on just one or two little drinks in your company.'

'You know any place that is private enough

to indulge in a discreet drink or two, Sergeant?'

'Now that you would be askin' me I do know such a place in the Greek quarter by chance,' the Irish sergeant replied, licking his lips and grinning broadly. 'But don't go getting any ideas to get us drunk and slip away, Mister Duffy. Me an' Sergeant O'Day here have orders.'

'Now do I look like the kind of man who would even consider corrupting the likes of an Irishman serving Her Majesty?' Michael said with the easy blarney banter. 'Not two fine men as yourselves.'

The burly Irish sergeant laughed as they made their way through the bazaar.

'You would be, Mister Duffy,' he said, staring Michael directly in the eye.

Michael knew that the big sergeant was obviously a man who knew where his duty lay and dismissed any thoughts of attempting to give them the slip. Not that he had seriously contemplated doing so. His mission was to all intents and purposes over. His son was alive and no longer required finding as per the terms of the mission he had accepted from Lady Macintosh. The money she had paid for his expenses was generous and he knew that he now had enough to journey to Europe where he could hopefully eke out a living from painting. He had also accumulated enough over the years to see him through for a year or two and he sensed that it was not ordained that he should finally meet his son now, that the events in both their lives were destined to move forward until the winds of fate blew them together.

'Now where would this place be, Sergeant?' Michael asked and the Irish soldier guided them deep into the Greek quarter to his favourite place of wine, women and sad songs.

When Michael was poured aboard the coastal steamer out of Suakin that evening, he left with no other souvenirs of the ancient and exotic city than a bad hangover from too much cheap Greek wine. Ahead of him was Europe and his old dreams. No more the sights and sounds of war, he prayed, but the beauty of creation in the colours of his mind. Fate – and Lady Macintosh – had conspired to deprive him of the opportunity to meet his son. Fate was something Michael had come to accept as a guiding force in his life. When the time was right, he was sure that fate would eventually bring him and his son together.

45

Gordon James stood dejectedly at the bottom of Kate Tracy's verandah steps and she felt a momentary surge of pity for the forlorn young police officer. His red rimmed and sunken eyes reflected the effort of the trek north to Townsville and he had since learned of the sudden death of his mother from a massive stroke. Pain and exhaustion cloaked him in despair for all the events that had unfolded in the recent weeks.

But as much as Kate also felt his grief for the loss of her dear friend Emma James, she also felt the pain for the loss of her nephew Peter Duffy. He had, after all, Kate thought as she stared at Gordon, volunteered to hunt Peter down and the consequences must have been a consideration before he set out.

Sarah sat in a chair in her bedroom, staring with a stony face at the ornate wallpaper. She could hear her aunt's voice telling Gordon he was not welcome.

Gordon's shoulders slumped as he wearily resigned himself to defeat. He no longer had the strength to argue in his defence. He no longer doubted the power of the curse that had visited the son of the man who had first incurred the wrath of the powerful forces of the sacred place of the Nerambura people long before he was even born. He had no other way of explaining the unexpected death of his mother who had died at precisely the same time as he had killed Peter Duffy. Witnesses said she had been walking to Kate's store when she suddenly collapsed. She was dead by the time the doctor examined her.

From inside the house Kate could hear her baby son crying for her attention and she turned her back on Gordon. He walked back to his horse tethered at the front gate. There was nothing else he could do.

When Kate reached Matthew she found Sarah had already picked him up. The women exchanged grief stricken looks. Gordon's visit had only fuelled their pain. Sarah held the baby to her breast and rocked him.

'If you went to him to hear what he has to say,' Kate said, 'I would understand.'

Sarah shook her head. 'No. He has killed my brother,' she replied softly. 'And for that I could never forgive him. Ever!'

'But you still love him,' Kate stated gently

Tears welled in Sarah's eyes to burst like an explosion as she uttered one word. 'Yes!'

From the distance Kate was aware of the fading sound of a horse galloping away. Gordon was riding out of their lives. But for how long? Time inevitably weakened grief and when she gazed at her niece she could see that not all the hurt was reserved for her dead brother. There was also the terrible pain of a love lost and yet not forgotten.

There were so many reminders of his mother in the house, Gordon realised. Sudden death does not give one a chance to tidy up before it comes to take away the soul.

A book of poetry lay open on the kitchen table next to a mixing bowl. Gordon closed it. She must have been reading the poetry as she prepared to make a meal, he reflected. Then she had realised she was out of flour and had hurried to Kate's store. But death had taken her in the street.

He wondered what sort of woman his mother really was. He only knew her as a mother with her reason for living being to love and care for him. And yet she once had another life as a vivacious young woman who had the courage to cross the ocean to a far and foreign land. And, in the years when she was still young, to have loved and married his father. Had they experienced the passion of desire he did when he thought about Sarah Duffy?

'I am sorry for your loss, Gordon.'

He spun on his heel at the sound of the voice behind him. So absorbed in his thoughts of his mother he had not heard Sarah enter the house. 'Sarah!'

She stood hesitantly in the doorway of the kitchen. 'I did not mean to disturb you. I was watching you for a little while. You appeared to be deep in thought.'

'I just came back to tidy up before the house is sold,' he answered quietly. 'Make sure everything was in order. Will you stay a while with me?'

Sarah shook her head. 'No. I only came to tell you,' she replied sadly, 'that your mother was a very special person in my life too.'

'You won't stay and give me the chance to explain what happened?' he pleaded.

'There is nothing to explain, Gordon. You killed my brother.'

'Damn it, Sarah. I loved Peter as if he were truly my brother,' he replied sharply and realised he was growing angry. 'What happened was a terrible accident.'

'No-one forced you to hunt him down,' Sarah retorted bitterly. 'You must have known there was always the possibility that something terrible could happen when you met.'

'I made the mistake of allowing my concern for his safety to cloud my judgment. But I don't expect you to understand what I am saying. If I could go back in time I would not have elected to go after Peter. I swear.'

'It's too late for any explanations, Gordon. My brother is dead – and at your hand,' she said softly. 'I think I should go. Before you say something that might make me hate you.'

Gordon took three steps across the small kitchen to grasp her by the shoulders, before she could turn and leave the house. His grip was strong. 'You still love me, despite everything you say,' he said with fierce determination. 'Don't you, Sarah Duffy?'

She tried to shake off his grip – and his question. 'How I feel is irrelevant,' she answered as she struggled against his hold. 'Some things remain beyond my power to forgive. I have never thought about my heritage before now. But I know my brother would still be alive today if he had not been a half-caste darkie, as you would say. It must be the blackfella in me, but we have a belief in payback. It is stronger than you would ever realise. You can let me go, Gordon, because you and I can never be together. So long as we both live.'

Gordon could see the fire in her dark eyes as she snarled her last statement at him. He had never seen her like this before. Even when they were young and he and Peter had tormented her she would grow angry but never express her anger in the same raw way that she was doing now. Her payback was to deny him forever that which he desired most – her! Never before had he wanted her as much as now. 'If you want to act like a gin, then I'll show you how we treat gins,' he snarled, increasing his grip of her shoulders.

She winced with the pain but stared into his eyes with cold hate. Then she spat in his face and felt the back of his hand strike her a stinging blow across the cheek. 'Do what you like, Inspector James,' she hissed with a controlled hatred. 'Because I won't stop you.'

Suddenly Gordon felt his rage dissipate as he realised what he had almost done. Trembling, he released his grip and stumbled back against the kitchen wall where he slumped to the floor and covered his face with his hands. He burst into deep racking sobs as the loss and grief finally over-powered him.

Sarah stood uncertainly watching him. A part of

her so desperately wanted to go to him and hold him to her breast. But the memory of her beloved Peter welled up inside. The hand that had killed her brother had also struck her.

When he was finally spent of his tears Gordon hardly noticed that she was gone. He had lost more than his boyhood friend. He had lost everything in his life except his job. The only thing that kept him from taking the revolver from his holster and ending it all was a tiny but intense flame called hope.

The house was sold, Gordon's letter of resignation not submitted, and now he sat in uniform astride his horse gazing at Kate Tracy's house. He was alone and would soon ride out for Rockhampton to take up his new posting. Was Sarah in the house? His heart felt as if it would break. His mount shifted impatiently under him and he absent-mindedly patted her neck. 'I know,' he said softly to her. 'It's time to go.'

He reined away and rode with tears in his eyes. He could not remember the last time he had cried and self-consciously brushed away the tears with the back of his hand. 'That I could give my life to prove my love for you, Sarah, I would,' he whispered. 'If only you could see that.'

46

The sultry heat of the day was dissipating with the disappearance of the sun. The crowd of assembled men pushed and shoved to gain a better view of the dusty clearing where the two contenders stood toe to toe, bare chested and wearing tight, thigh-hugging trousers. The carnival atmosphere preceding the title fight for the heavyweight crown of the brigade was amplified by the worst kept secret in Suakin: that the army was leaving the desert to return to the milder English summer.

So here was an event under the rising con-stellations of the African desert to entertain men yearning for the balmy English summer eves at home. An event to take their minds temporarily from the tense anticipation of the waiting for the official word to pack up and board the troopships that lay in the harbour.

The spectators were fairly evenly divided in their support for both fighters. One section bet on Private Angus MacDonald because he was one of them, a soldier from the ranks. The other half gave their support to his opponent, Captain Patrick

Duffy, because he was an exception to the rule of class distinction; he was a man who had the ability to cross social lines.

The referee mumbled a few basic rules to the bare knuckle fighters and they nodded their understanding. This signalled to the enclosing ring of soldiers that the moment had arrived as to who would leave the Sudan with the title of champion. The odds were with the giant Scottish private as he was in excellent health and his supporters had a grudging sympathy for his opponent who, it was said, had barely recovered from his ordeal beyond the coastal hill range. But the sympathy ended with the wagers that were being surreptitiously made at the rear of the crowd. This was not only a fight but a means of making some money.

Patrick listened to the referee's mumbled words and stared at his former batman. He saw no animosity reflected in the dark eyes which caught the glint of the flames from the lanterns.

Angus's friendly grin as they brushed knuckles to signal that they were ready to fight was returned by Patrick who growled good naturedly, 'Watch my left hook, Mac, it will win the fight.'

Angus spat into the dust and retorted with a friendly jibe. 'Yor got a wee bit of Paddy in yer, sor, that makes you stupid.'

Then the fight commenced with a stinging blow from the brawny Scot that connected with Patrick's ear and brought on a rousing cheer from the Scot's supporters.

By the beginning of the ninth round both men were battered and bloody and the roar of the crowd was deafening as the two men swapped punch for punch. Their hands were bleeding and their knuckles swollen. Sweat streamed from them as they grunted with the pain each heavy blow inflicted and Patrick's ears rung like the chimes of Big Ben. But the original blurring speed of his punches was slowing, as was that of the Scot's punches. Both men reserved their strength for the occasional openings in their opponent's guard and the gruelling fight would only end when one man was able to muster the strength to deliver a flurry of damaging blows to his weakened adversary.

It was near the end of the ninth round when Patrick noticed the glazed expression in Angus's face and realised with a rising horror that something was terribly wrong with his friend. The battering had caused damage to his head and Patrick realised that a knock out blow just might kill the big Scot. The crowd had sensed that the end of the match was near, and roared as the spectators at the Roman games must have done with a thumbs down for the loser.

Angus reeled uncertainly and Patrick clasped his friend in a bear hug. 'Now Angus,' he hissed into his ear. 'Go for my head now.'

Angus turned his head to stare for a brief and confused moment at Captain Duffy. 'I canna do it, sor,' he gasped and Patrick thrust him away. 'Do it, you yellow Scots bastard,' he snarled as he dropped his hands.

With a final Herculean effort Angus waded into Patrick with grunts and furious blows. Patrick reeled under the barrage and felt his legs buckle. With a thud he hit the sand where he lay in a semi-comatose state.

The crowd went wild with cheers and hurrahs and surged forward to hoist the big Scot on their shoulders to parade him around the camp. Even those who had lost money on the outcome admitted the loss was worth it for the most entertaining fight they had witnessed in many a year. But one or two former fighters realised that the young captain had strangely left himself open to the delivery of the knock out. They shook their heads as they walked away and wondered at the stupidity of those with Irish blood.

Angus groaned as he soaked his battered, swollen hands in a basin of sun warmed water and only removed one hand to accept the silver flask of brandy Patrick passed him across the tent.

'Never again,' Patrick sighed through smashed lips. 'Never again am I ever going to fight you, Mac.'

'I didn't win the bloody title,' the Scot moaned before he swilled from the flask the fiery amber liquid. 'You let me win.' He gulped down half the contents and his eyes glistened through half-closed eyelids as the brandy hit his stomach. He sighed with pleasure and passed the flask back to Patrick.

'The right man won, Private MacDonald,' Patrick replied quietly. 'And the win should help you get those stripes you so much deserve.'

Angus accepted the gesture and both men sat in silence on empty ammunition boxes under a magnificent display of stars. They were alone for the first time since Patrick had been rescued from the desert and had much to talk about.

'Where did ye get the strength in the ninth

round?' Angus asked with a dumbfounded shake of his head. 'I thought I had yer in the eighth.'

Patrick grinned sheepishly and glanced down at his feet. 'I imagined you were someone called Brett Norris,' he said quietly. 'For just a moment you had his face.'

'He'd be having no face now,' Angus hooted. 'If he'd be a Sassenach gentleman you'd been hitting instead of me.'

Patrick looked up into the broad face of the Scot, broadened even more by the massive swelling of damaged tissue. Not that his own face was in any better condition. 'Ah, but that it had been him instead of you, Mac.'

They fell silent as they nursed their exhaustion and private thoughts. Patrick took a shallow swig of the brandy before passing the flask to Angus who gulped down the remnants and glanced apologetically at Patrick who only smiled, then laughed, and slapped the Scot on the shoulder. 'You earned it, Mac. For being Mister Brett Norris for just that moment.' The smile, and the laugh, faded as Patrick leant towards Angus. 'Why didn't you do what I asked,' he questioned quietly, 'before I went on that patrol, Mac?'

'I threw yor pouches in the sea like you asked me to. But there was this wee little thing I knew you would want when you came back to us.'

Patrick stared up at the heavens. 'Thank you,' he replied gratefully. 'I'll settle with the quartermaster.'

'No need, sor. He's my uncle and I've settled with him. He's written off yor kit.'

'I owe you a great debt for what you did.'

'No trouble, sor,' the Scot replied and ducked his head with embarrassment.

'I suppose I should retire to my tent,' Patrick said as he stood stiffly, feeling every muscle in his body scream out in pain. 'A lot to do before we go home.'

'You think that will be soon, sor?' Angus asked quietly, as he attempted to struggle to his feet.

Patrick waved him down and he sank back gratefully on the improvised seat. 'I hope so, Mac. I've had enough of this place.'

'Goodnight, sor, and God bless you.'

Patrick hoped that God would bless him. Or at least that Sheela-na-gig would still be with him when he finally went in search of Catherine. But first he had his duties in Cairo. He would have to wait another long three months before he could return to Ireland.

47

Little had changed in over a year. But then, little had changed in the last five centuries in the village.

Patrick hunched himself against the grey drizzle and walked quickly along the narrow cobbled street to the lichen encrusted church where he hoped to find Father Eamon O'Brien in residence. His reappearance in the village had caused him an uneasy feeling. People stared at him with more than usual interest and whispered behind his back as he passed them by. Although he had only just arrived and registered at Riley's tavern, he sensed his visit marked something out of the ordinary. It was in the expressions of disbelief on the faces of the villagers who turned aside when he approached them in the street. Even Riley himself had been reticent when he had registered at his hotel.

He reached the presbytery and rapped on the heavy wooden door. Eamon answered and his face lit up with delight at seeing Patrick. His broad smile warmed the chill of Patrick's soul. 'God bless me! Captain Duffy! Come in. It is good to be seeing you again after such a long absence.'

Patrick smiled with pleasure at the greeting and gripped the priest's extended hand, shaking off the cold drizzle as he stepped inside.

'Take off your coat and I will get something to chase away the chills,' Eamon said as he bustled around the kitchen searching for the bottle of whisky he kept for special visitors and particularly bad days in the parish.

Patrick took a seat at the old wooden table he had first sat at when he met the priest over a year earlier. When Eamon found the bottle he took two glasses and poured them both a stiff drink.

'Eamon, it is good to make your acquaintance again,' Patrick said as he raised his glass. 'I fear my appearance here seems to have caused somewhat of a stir amongst the local people of the village. I was hoping you might be able to tell me why.'

'Ah, yes. It is only to be expected,' he replied. 'But first, have you partaken of a meal?'

'The coach stopped at an inn for the midday meal only a few hours ago.'

'Well, you are welcome to dine with me tonight if you wish, Patrick. Nothing fancy. Missus Casey is away and will not be returning until late so I'm afraid I will be forced to reheat last night's supper.'

'Knowing Missus Casey's fine cooking I am sure that the supper would be as good as any I have had since returning to Ireland,' Patrick answered politely and took another swig of the whiskey. It tasted good and helped wash away the chill of the day.

Eamon followed his example with a good swallow and refilled their glasses even before they were emptied. 'You look different, Patrick,' he commented as he peered across the old table. 'As if things have happened in your life a man should not experience. Was the war bad?'

'Bad enough,' Patrick replied softly, and stared down at the table's surface where deep scratches and burn marks had accrued over more than two centuries. 'Worse when you live from day to day on nothing more than hope. Hope that the silence will be broken by even just a single word.'

Eamon took his spectacles from his face and polished them on the hem of his cassock. He knew what Patrick was alluding to and desperately sought a way in his mind to tell him the painful facts that he would soon learn in the village. 'George Fitzgerald passed away, God rest his soul, two months ago,' he said as he replaced the spectacles and looked Patrick directly in the eyes.

'I didn't know.'

'His passing was peaceful. He died in his sleep at the manor.'

'And Catherine?' Patrick asked softly.

'She is no longer in the village,' Eamon replied. 'The Fitzgerald place has been taken over by her sister-in-law who came back from the West Indies last week when Catherine left. No-one knows where she has gone. Not even her sister-in-law. She has a substantial inheritance from George's estate and is also still part-owner of the manor. I suppose she is travelling on the inheritance.'

'Do you have any idea where she might have gone? Dublin? London?'

'Initially, I suppose,' Eamon answered. 'But I suspect much further afield, under the circumstances.'

'What circumstances?'

'She left to be with a man,' Eamon replied, and wished he could be somewhere else when he saw the terrible pain in the young man's eyes.

Patrick took a deep breath to steady himself and the priest rose from the table, leaving Patrick alone for a brief moment. He went to his office adjacent to the kitchen and returned with a large pile of sealed letters. With a shock Patrick recognised his own handwriting on the envelopes. *They were all the letters he had sent Catherine!*

'When George died,' Eamon explained quietly, 'he left instructions in his will that I was to unlock his desk and take the contents without explaining to anyone what he kept there. I suppose I have broken a sacred trust in even showing you the existence of these. Catherine would haunt the post office after you left for the Sudan. Her grandfather had ensured that she was to receive no correspondence from you. He had his way. When she received none, she changed. She was heart-broken and, I suppose, presumed you had forgotten her.'

Patrick stared at the pile of unopened letters Eamon placed on the table. *No wonder the silence fell between them!* 'Now that George has passed on to his eternal rest,' the priest added, 'I suppose I can return the letters to you. They are rightfully yours.'

Patrick picked up one of the envelopes from the pile and immediately recognised the tiny dark spots at its edge. They were bloodstains. The letter had been written hours after the terrible battle at McNeill's Zareba. Although he had attempted to protect the precious envelope, the blood had run down his arm from the wound inflicted in the fighting.

Eamon resumed his chair at the table. He knew the worst was yet to come in the tragic story.

'You said she left to be with a man,' Patrick asked, with a deadly edge to his voice. 'Was it Mister Brett Norris?'

Eamon blinked as if hoping to blink away the question. He did not answer immediately but filled Patrick's glass with the remaining whiskey from the bottle. 'Get this inside you, Patrick, as you will need the strength of the Holy Spirit of the bottle to hear what I am about to tell you.' Patrick obeyed and swallowed his whiskey and waited for what Eamon was about to tell him. 'A man came to the village. Not this Mister Norris you ask about. But a man seeking peace for his troubled soul. I did not meet the man but the villagers talked long and hard about him. It was said his journey had been a sad one through life and he sought himself in the expression of art and to this end he was commissioned by Catherine to paint her portrait. You must remember ... she had despaired of ever seeing you again.'

'Who was the man?' Patrick growled ominously, but Eamon held up his hand to indicate he should be patient as there was much to explain.

'Oh, he was a man very much like you, Patrick. A grand style of a man who, it was said, did not encourage Catherine. In fact, he was a man old enough to be her father. But, as the villagers were quick to notice, she became infatuated by him. When he became aware of her feelings for him, he left, but she followed him.' Eamon fell into a short silence to gather the courage to tell the final part of the story. 'The man she followed . . . is your father.'

Patrick paled and the room swam before his eyes. His ears rang as if he had weathered a sustained volley of musketry. *His father! His father was dead!* He sat frozen in his utter shock at the revelation and the strangled words came barely above a whisper. 'My father was killed before I was born!'

'No, Patrick,' Eamon said gently, as he reached across the table to grasp his hand. 'Your father has been alive all these years . . . as the villagers have always known. He has been a man hunted by many enemies in his life and, I suppose, for that reason could never reveal his existence to you or anyone else in your family in Sydney.'

'Catherine has gone to God knows where . . . with my father,' Patrick echoed, and stared with a despairing plea at Eamon. 'For God's sake and my sanity, if you know where they might have gone, tell me.'

'If I knew I would. So help me on the office of my duties and before all that is sacred to the true Church, I would tell you if I knew, Patrick,' Eamon replied. 'But no-one in the village knows.'

Patrick's breathing came in ragged gasps as if he had run a long distance. *His father . . . Alive . . . And with the woman he loved more than his own life!* It was like some terrible joke on him. As if a malevolent force was laughing in the background of his life. 'No matter what it takes I will find them both,' he breathed. 'No matter what it takes.'

THE
STORM
1886

48

Catherine felt the kiss of the sun on her face and the rich scent of flowers. She stretched like a cat and opened her eyes slowly to savour the richness of the Aegean morning.

'Michael,' she murmured as she reached out to touch him. But her hand touched empty space and she sat up in the bed to glance around the hotel room. She saw him sitting by the window that opened to a panoramic view of the sea. His back was to her, and he seemed deep in thought and unaware of her presence.

'Michael,' she called again softly, and this time he reacted by turning to smile at her.

'Did you sleep well?' he asked as he left his chair to come to her bed and sit beside her.

'Wonderfully,' she purred and reached out to touch his face. 'But why are you dressed so early in the day?'

Michael seemed to wince at her question and he hesitated before answering. 'I had a lot to think about,' he replied. 'But nothing to concern you,' he added gently, as he felt the soft caress of her hand on his face.

'Why don't you come back to bed?' Catherine pulled back the sheet to reveal her naked body. It was an invitation that Michael disregarded and he stood and walked back to the window. Catherine felt hurt, but more than that, she felt a rising panic. Was it that he had tired of her and she was no longer attractive to him? But if that were so, why had the signs not been more apparent? Her question had no answer. They had lived a life of passion and adventure since she had followed him to London. She still remembered the shocked expression on his face when she plonked her bag in his hotel room and announced that she would be his lover. He had protested but she could see the longing in his eyes that contradicted his words – the same look she had seen when he had painted her portraiture at the Fitzgerald mansion in Ireland.

From that day on she had shared his bed and his life as he wandered through the great cities of Europe. It was as if he were searching for something. And as he roamed he stopped to paint landscapes although he was never happy with his efforts. She had witnessed the pain in his face as he stood back and examined his completed work, none of which he kept but instead sold for a mere pittance to anyone who might want a souvenir of the particular place.

The times that she had lain beside him she had wondered at the magnetism of the man old enough to be her father. He was like an old, battle scarred bear she had reflected: strong but vulnerable; dangerous yet none of his fearsome reputation for killing touched the gentleness in him. In those quiet times she often thought about Patrick and wondered what might have been. His long silence seemed to tell her that the son did not have the father's strength to commit himself to searching for what she had to offer. There had been times when she had wanted to tell Michael about her meeting with Patrick but sensed the mention of him could only cause pain to this already haunted man whose life had known little happiness. As far as she knew Michael had not been told by the Irish villagers of Patrick's visit over a year earlier. It was not in their nature to upset the man who was a living legend walking amongst them.

In Michael's arms Catherine found contentment and for the moment that was all that mattered. She sensed that in turn she also gave the troubled man a kind of peace. It did not matter that she was living simply for the day – that was her nature also.

Their travels across Europe had at length brought them to a little hotel overlooking the Aegean Sea. Michael had appeared happy in the warmth of the Greek spring and Catherine had marvelled at the way her man had fitted so easily into any culture they encountered. Sometimes he would tell her stories of exotic places in the Far East. He was her Marco Polo. He introduced her to the alien but exciting tastes of Mediterranean cuisine and Catherine soon acquired a taste for the peasant food he tended to eat and particularly developed a love for piquant olives, goat cheese and unleavened bread.

But it had been his lovemaking that was most

exciting of all. On their first night together he had taken her on a sensual journey with a mix of extreme tenderness and animal passion. Catherine had only suspected that lovemaking could be such a wildly fulfilling experience. She had never known a man before and the first time he had made love to her she felt that her body had always lived with the passion. He made the act both spiritual and physical, a kaleidoscope of colours in her mind and wild feelings throughout her body. To lose him was something she knew she could not bear.

'My little Irish rose,' Michael finally said when he turned from the view. 'I have things to do today. If you like you can go to the markets and buy us something for supper.'

Catherine frowned. He rarely did not invite her to be with him and his statement only caused her more consternation. I am acting like a foolish young girl, she chided herself. I must not let him see that I am upset. 'Cannot I come with you?' she asked, hoping it did not sound like a plea.

Michael selected a Turkish cigarette from a tin and lit the pungent stick. He looked so maddeningly handsome, Catherine reflected, as she watched him puff contentedly on the evil smelling cigarette.

'I will see you tonight,' he replied as smoke hung in the still, warm air. 'I have some business concerning money.'

'I have money,' Catherine quickly countered. 'I have my grandfather's legacy which can support us both for life.'

Michael puffed on the cigarette and smiled with tenderness. 'That is your money, Catherine, and that is how it is going to stay. I am a man and the first rule of any man is that he does not live off a woman. It's up to the man to look after his woman.'

The frown dissipated from Catherine's face. He had called her 'his woman' and she was quick to pick up on that. 'I will miss you,' she said, as he kissed her gently on the forehead. She did not see the pain in his face as he turned away and walked out the door.

Michael sat at a rickety table outside a coffee shop and watched the Greek villagers go about their lives. Occasionally some would cast a curious glance at the tall stranger with the black leather patch over one eye. Michael puffed on a cigarette and toyed with his glass of thick, black coffee without much thought for the villagers. His thoughts were troubled as he re-read the correspondence he had carefully concealed from Catherine.

Father Eamon O'Brien's letter had reached Michael through a tortuous route. The priest did not know where he was but suspected Michael's past had links with the murky world of international intrigue. On a gamble he had placed it in the hands of the British Foreign Office and they had tracked the Irishman to Greece.

The man who had delivered the letter to Michael now strode across the cobbled plaza to join him. Another version of Horace, Michael thought. But only younger.

'Mister Duffy,' the man said, as he sat down uninvited at the table. 'I hope you are well.'

Michael stared at the younger man, taking in his appearance. He had receding sandy hair, light blue eyes and a thin nervous face. Michael guessed him to be in his mid-twenties and judging by his white suit soaked with sweat he also guessed the man had walked a long way to meet him. Had he been someone of more importance he might have had transport provided.

'Mister Clark, I see you made it,' Michael said, with a slight smile of amusement at the man's dishevelled appearance. 'I hope my conditions were acceptable to your employers.' Clark took a handkerchief from his pocket and wiped his brow. 'There was only the matter of you signing the papers to say that you accepted that the ticket would be deducted from your payment. I have the documents with me, along with the ticket.' He reached in his coat pocket and placed a pile of papers on the table beside Michael's coffee.

Michael glanced at them. 'As your people felt free to read my mail before I received it, I feel that you can trust me when I say that I don't have to sign the papers to honour my word.'

Clark pulled a strained expression. 'Mister Duffy, a man with your past must have taken for granted that any letter delivered into our hands from a priest in that troubled land to you must have an interest to us. You were, after all, born in Ireland.'

'The letter was of a personal nature and had nothing to do with my work in the past,' Michael growled. 'I doubt that my family life is of interest

474

to the British Empire. At least your Mister Horace Brown respected my privacy in such matters.'

Clark's apologetic expression softened Michael's anger. He could see that the young man was merely the courier and not one of the faceless men in London who had indirectly ruled much of his life through Horace Brown. 'I am sorry, Mister Duffy, for the intrusion on your privacy. I was a great admirer of Mister Brown and agreed with his opinions on Bismarck's ambitions in the Pacific. Mister Brown held you in the highest of regard and even requested that your services to Her Majesty's government be recognised with an imperial award.'

Michael was mildly shocked by Clark's statement. He could never have imagined himself the recipient of a British award. He, an Irishman, who had made his feelings clear to Horace on the antagonism he harboured for British imperial ambitions around the globe. 'I work for money, not medals,' Michael replied, and could see that his pragmatism shocked the status conscious public servant.

'Well, as for your mission, I am sure that it pays well enough for you. You will also be doing a great service for Her Majesty where you are going.'

'Her Majesty, or Mister Rhodes?' Michael queried sarcastically. 'I read that there is a big grab for African land by British interests.'

'Better that we get our hands on Africa than the Germans,' Clark replied quietly. 'We, after all, play cricket,' he added with a crooked grin.

Michael smiled at the Englishman's statement. 'We Irishmen don't – and never will.'

'So much for cricket, Mister Duffy,' Clark said as he stood to leave. 'I will not concern myself that you have not signed the papers. If Horace thought so highly of you in his reports, then I can only be guided by his judgment.'

Michael nodded but did not stand to bid the English agent farewell. 'I will do the job and Her Majesty will get an honest day's work from me,' he said as he picked up the bundle of papers from the table and pocketed them. 'You can tell your boss that I will be leaving tonight.'

'Will you be telling Miss Fitzgerald of your assignment?' Clark asked.

Michael stared at him for a brief moment with his good eye before answering, 'Not that Miss Fitzgerald is of any concern to your interest, but I will tell you that she will not be coming with me to Africa.'

'Sorry, old chap,' Clark mumbled. 'But I had to ask. Secrecy and all that, you know. Well, I will bid you a good day and best of luck for your mission, Mister Duffy.'

Michael remained at the table. The coffee was strong enough to caulk a ship's timbers. Eamon had mentioned in his letter that Patrick had returned to Ireland to find Catherine. The news had stunned Michael as no-one in the village had mentioned his son's previous visit – least of all Catherine. The priest's letter intimated that Patrick was very taken by Catherine and that he would go to any lengths to find her.

When Michael had finished reading the letter his world was in turmoil. It was not that he was in love with Catherine. He was too practical to let himself become emotionally involved with any woman. He knew that the longer he remained with her the harder it would be to leave. She was everything a man could love in a woman. But he was also aware that his life was measured by the violence of his future. He had come to bitterly learn that he would never be a great artist. What he really knew was the life of a mercenary soldier. At least he could still earn a living working for Britain in those dangerous places that were not receptive to English accents. As an Irishman he was less suspect.

Along with the delivery of the letter had been a proposal for another mission for England. It was as if the faceless men knew that as soon as he read it he would opt to work for them. And they had been right. If nothing else Michael had his sense of honour. Had he ever known that his son was interested in Catherine, then he would have resisted her charms. It was too late to do that but not too late to make amends to a son he hardly knew.

Catherine returned later in the day from the markets with a basket of special treats. She had planned a romantic candlelit dinner on the tiny balcony overlooking the sea. And then they would make love on the big, sprawling bed.

The room seemed empty, she mused. She glanced around and with rising horror realised that Michael's single battered bag was gone. And there was a large envelope on the bed. Immediately her rising horror turned to outright fear.

'No,' she heard her strangled cry as the basket

spilled its contents across the floor. She stumbled across the room and tore open the envelope of papers. Inside was a ticket for a sea voyage and a letter. With trembling hands she held the single page up to the fading light. It said little other than that he had enclosed the ticket for her and that it was better their parting was this way.

Catherine swooned and collapsed on the bed. Racked by sobbing, she cried herself to sleep. When she woke in the early hours of the morning she felt truly alone for the first time in her life. Ending her life was an option she briefly considered until she remembered a sentence from Michael's short letter.

The ticket is more than a sea voyage. It is a ticket that will take you to your destiny with one who can truly give you the life you deserve. What we had together will keep us in the winter days of our lives as a sweet memory to cherish. I pray that one day you will understand why I had to leave without saying goodbye. I did so because I did not want you to see the pain that leaving you has caused.

By candlelight Catherine searched for the ticket. She read the destination printed on the slip of paper. Tears welled in her eyes. 'Oh Michael, I loved you,' she whispered. 'I truly loved you.'

Thousands of miles east of the Greek village another woman cried for the loss of the man in her life. Here, however, the warm sun was not shining and the constellation of the Southern Cross reigned in the heavens.

Kate Tracy sat in her Townsville office and sobbed alone, her only companions the feeble light of a kerosene lantern and the mournful hooting of a mopoke owl. She had worked late into the evening and whilst clearing a little used desk she had discovered Luke's battered tobacco pipe. Its pungent scent had caused the doors of her mind to swing open and flood her with memories. Although it had been over a year since his disappearance somewhere on the frontier she had lived every day in her well-concealed grief.

She cradled the old pipe in her hands and the racking sobs tore through her body as if they would never end. 'Oh Luke, I miss you so much,' she cried as the tears splashed the desk. 'I miss you with every ounce of my body and soul.'

'Aunt Kate?' the voice questioned gently from the door. 'Are you all right?'

Kate peered through the dim light to see Sarah standing hesitantly in the doorway. 'I came over to see if you were going to bed soon. You have been working too hard lately.'

'Come in,' Kate responded, making a feeble attempt to wipe away the tears with the back of her hand. 'I was going to finish anyway.'

'You were thinking about Luke,' Sarah stated, as she moved to stand beside her aunt and place her hand on her shoulder.

Kate nodded and took Sarah's hand. Such a simple gesture could mean so much. 'I am one of the wealthiest women in the colony and yet I would trade it all to just see his smile once more,' she said.

'You do, Aunt Kate,' Sarah replied softly. 'Every time you look at baby Matthew.'

Kate glanced up at her niece and felt a touch of pride for the young woman's wisdom. She is a remarkable young woman – with the proven resilience of both the Irish and the Nerambura, she thought. But she could not bring herself to tell Sarah that Matthew's grin was not the same as having Luke's protective arms around her or smelling the scent of his hard body, a scent that reminded her of the very country itself.

'What has kept you so long at the office?' Sarah asked to distract Kate from her melancholy thoughts. 'You seem to have been preoccupied with something the last few days.'

'I can tell you now,' Kate replied with a wan smile. 'I think there is a good chance that I may be in a position to purchase Glen View from the Macintosh companies. I have come into possession of information that my nephew Patrick has taken an influential position with the Macintosh enterprises, and I think that he would be sympathetic to any offer that I make for the property.'

Sarah caught her breath. Her aunt's obsession to own Glen View was well known – as was the Macintosh resistance to any Duffy stepping foot on the place.

'Do you really think that Patrick would accept an offer?' she asked.

'He is still a Duffy,' Kate replied, with the conviction of her ancestral clannish roots.

'He is also of Macintosh blood,' Sarah gently reminded her aunt. 'Time changes people.'

'So much wisdom for one so young,' Kate retorted. 'But not wise enough to choose to stay with me.'

Sarah looked away with an expression of hurt. 'You know why I feel that I must leave Townsville and take up a new position, Aunt Kate,' she answered. 'I am not leaving you or Matthew. It's just that I need to get away from the memories that are so strong around here.'

Kate felt a twinge of guilt for reproving her beloved niece who was as close as any daughter might be. She had raised the girl from a toddler and shared in her joys as well as sorrows over the years. Lately it had been sorrow that had dominated both their lives. Sarah's decision had been well thought out but still Kate could not help but feel that her leaving would be another loss in her life. 'I am sorry, Sarah, for my selfish comment,' she said gently. 'It's just that I will miss you so very much, and I know Matthew will too.'

Sarah wrapped her arms around her aunt's shoulders and kissed her on the forehead. 'And I will miss you both but Matthew has a good nanny and you are a woman who will continue to be absorbed by your work running the company – and all its prosperous enterprises, thanks to your brilliance.'

'Flatterer,' Kate laughed, and in that moment truly realised how close she was to her niece. 'Our brilliance,' she added. 'It only needs two women to take on the pompous might of the men in this colony.'

'You will come home now?' Sarah asked, and Kate rose stiffly to join her niece.

'I will go home now. And one day we will walk on Glen View land to visit the grave of my father and his friend Old Billy and place flowers on Peter's grave.'

Sarah made no comment. She knew that eventually her aunt would realise her dream. It would be good indeed to walk on the land that her natural mother had once walked with the tribeswomen of the Nerambura, the place where her mother had met her father. The land was sacred to them both.

49

The dust heralded the arrival of the police patrol at Ben Rosenblum's property. Ben squinted against the angry red fireball rising in the east and could see that the patrol numbered six horsemen, led by a tall officer who rode with the easy grace of a man born to the saddle. When they were closer he recognised Gordon James although it had been three years since he last had seen the young man in Townsville.

When they reached the bark homestead Gordon brought the patrol to a halt.

'Hello, Ben,' he said. Ben nodded. The troopers were covered in a thick coating of red dust and they stared listlessly at the bearded pastoralist standing by a wood pile of split logs.

'Suppose you're looking for that gang that raided the Halpin place last week,' Ben drawled.

'Yeah,' Gordon replied. 'Seems they have decided to head south. We were following them until my black tracker took sick. Had to leave him to make his way back to the Curry so I decided I might bring my boys this way to see if I could get your help.'

'Not much that I can do.'

'I was hoping you might lend me the use of the Kalkadoon I hear you have here,' Gordon said, glancing around the dusty yard.

'Terituba?' Ben replied with a frown. 'I need him here. He's shaping up to be a bloody good stockman.'

'You can probably guess what those murdering bastards did to Missus Halpin before they killed her husband,' Gordon said, leaning forward on the pommel of his saddle. 'I hear you were pretty good friends with the Halpins. I would have thought that counted for something.'

Ben winced at Gordon's obvious play on his past friendship with the Halpins. They had been good friends who had visited him after Jenny's death and he did owe a debt of gratitude for their unreserved help in his time of grief. 'You may as well get down and rest your troop,' he replied. 'And I'll call Terituba.'

'Thanks, Ben,' Gordon replied with a smile. 'I figured I could rely on you to help when it was needed.'

He turned and gave orders for his men to dismount. They had ridden all night in their attempt to close the distance between themselves and the four men they hunted. The Aboriginal troopers slid gratefully from their horses and when Terituba appeared from behind the hut they cast suspicious – almost fearful – looks at the former warrior of the Kalkadoon. Terituba stood proudly against their stares and sneered at the troopers. Tribal animosities ran deep and the Aboriginals recruited from the far away districts of the Colony of New South Wales had no love for the tribesmen of the north.

Gordon barely gave Terituba a glance. Had he done so he might have seen the Kalkadoon staring at him with an expression of surprise. The former warrior had seen the vivid scar across the white officer's forehead.

While the troopers led their horses to a watering trough Gordon followed Ben to the shade of the hut where he sat down on a bench made from a log. Ben disappeared briefly and returned with a jug of raw gin. It was the best he could afford until his cattle were mustered for sale in Townsville.

He took a seat opposite Gordon, placed the jug between them and wiped two battered enamel mugs. Gordon filled his mug and sipped gingerly at the fiery liquid as he gazed idly at his troopers chattering softly amongst themselves in the meagre shade of the stockyards.

'How long will you need my man?' Ben asked as he swigged the raw liquor.

'Maybe a month, no longer,' Gordon replied. 'If we haven't had a result in a month I will send him back to you. He will be paid a tracker's allowance while he is with us.'

'Good. You will be getting the best black tracker north of the Capricorn for your money,' Ben replied, noticing with interest that Terituba had kept a distance between himself and the troopers lounging around the stockyards. He knew the Kalkadoon had no love for the Aboriginals who had helped destroy his people the year before.

'I suppose you have heard that Kate and Sarah will have nothing to do with me,' Gordon said quietly. He knew that Ben was close to Kate Tracy and the news of his role in killing Peter Duffy would have eventually travelled west to Cloncurry.

'Yeah. I heard about Peter.'

'I didn't have much choice, Ben,' Gordon said. 'It all happened so fast. I still have nightmares about it.'

'Things happen,' the Jewish pastoralist grunted. 'Nothing much can change the past.' And in his simple reply Gordon could see that Ben was telling him that he did not hold the same animosity as Kate did. 'You know who the murdering bastards are?' he asked as if to tactfully change the subject.

'Know one of them,' Gordon said as he took another sip at the gin. 'From what we have been able to find out, he is a former trooper who I dismissed last year. A bad bastard called James Calder. We don't know the others in his gang except that they were stealing cattle before they decided to take to bushranging and murder.'

'This Calder fellow an experienced bushman?'

'Experienced enough.'

'You got your job cut out for you then,' Ben commented. 'But I doubt that he could lose Terituba no matter how hard he tried.'

'Hope you're right. The lads we are tracking are a particularly bad lot and right now haven't got a lot to lose. They will hang for sure when we catch them.'

'When are you planning to ride out?' Ben asked.

'Pretty well straightaway. At least as soon as your man is ready to leave with us.'

'I'll talk to him now. He'll be ready in about half

486

an hour,' Ben said as he stood and reached down for the jug. 'But, I don't think he is going to welcome working with your lot.'

'I suppose not. I doubt if he has much love for us. Considering what happened last year.'

'No, he won't,' Ben said with an enigmatic smile. 'Especially after what he told me about almost scalping some white trooper with an axe.'

Gordon glanced up sharply and instinctively touched the scar on his forehead. He gazed across the dusty yard at the big Kalkadoon who squatted in the dust. 'Jesus!' the police officer swore with shock.

'You still want him to track for you?' Ben added with a chuckle.

Gordon rubbed his forehead. He remembered with terrifying clarity how close he had come to death that day. 'Yeah. Maybe he might be the first to get to the bastards we're tracking,' he laughed softly. 'If he did, I wouldn't like their chances of ever getting to see the inside of a courtroom.'

Terituba listened to Ben outlining what was required of him and although he did not want to go he accepted what Ben asked of him. He trusted Miben, who had proved to be a fair boss and kind to his family. He had not attempted to take his woman from him as other white men might, and he treated his son with the respect that he would his own.

When Ben was finished Terituba went to see his wife and son and explained to them he would be gone for a while. They begged him to reconsider going away with the dreaded Mounted Police but he cut them short with a reminder that they would be well cared for by Miben. They accepted his final word and Terituba made his preparations.

Gordon stared in amazement at the transformation. Stripped naked to a belt of human hair with his war axe jammed at his waist and carrying his spears Terituba was once again the warrior who had confronted them on the hill. Gordon felt an uneasy twinge of fear for a spirit that refused to be defeated.

50

The office commanded a splendid view of the Quay. It had once been David Macintosh's and had then been occupied by Granville White. Now it was occupied by Patrick Duffy – since his return from Europe some months earlier.

Granville had relocated his own office to one further up the street – ever since a meeting of the Macintosh board of directors had recommended that Lady Macintosh's grandson learn the shipping side of the business. The brief meetings between the two men had been businesslike and cool and neither would allow the other to see any sign of disquiet at the uneasy arrangement in management functions.

Granville, however, had the upper hand in their meetings as he still managed the bulk of the company's transactions. But Enid knew that her grandson would eventually make his mark and impress the board of directors with his competence in the world of high finance. In doing so he would erode her hated son-in-law's hold over the Macintosh financial empire. In time Granville could be crushed. A wrong decision, costing the companies a large financial loss – or a scandal – would force him to step down. Whatever it would be, Enid knew she would find the right time to strike and discredit him. If Patrick thought war was a ruthless business he would soon learn that the financial world was just as brutal.

George Hobbs still screened the visitors to the office which he guarded as jealously as a dog guarding his master's yard from intruders. Others had come and gone in the company but George had survived on account of his devoted loyalty to Lady Enid. Granville had attempted to have him retired. His motivation had been prompted by his distrust of the secretary who knew too much for Granville's comfort. But Enid had vetoed it.

And now George Hobbs dutifully served Patrick. His intimate knowledge of the maze that was the financial structure of the Macintosh companies was invaluable and Patrick quickly became aware of George's astute abilities and was quick to acknowledge him with a pay rise, an act which further endeared him to the secretary.

With George handling the routine paperwork, Patrick had time to stand and stare out his window at the ships that lined the wharves. Elegant masts and spars webbed with rigging rode gently alongside the newer ships with funnels of lesser elegance. Months had passed since he had resigned his commission and returned to the Australian Colony of New South Wales, and since that time he had been tutored by the best people Lady Enid trusted in the management of the different components of the business. He proved to be a quick learner and the normally dour woman glowed with pride for the reports on his remarkable progress.

Patrick had a way with men, a legacy of leading some of the toughest troops in the Empire. The Scots were not a race who suffered fools easily and the young colonial had won their trust. Now he applied his leadership talents to those who came under his management, rather than adopting the autocratic rule of slavishly following regulations. He was not only liked by Macintosh employees for his easygoing manner but highly respected for listening to them as well. Enid's only concern were the reports of his great dislike for the routine of paperwork. At least there were people in the company she trusted to keep her grandson briefed on what he should know – and sign.

Patrick sighed when he remembered Granville's recommendation that they shed themselves of the clippers of their fleet in favour of the coal burning steamers. To do so was like putting down a beloved dog. As far as Patrick was concerned, the speedy clippers still reigned as the greyhounds of the open seas. But even he could see that their time was limited by the advances in modern technology. The majestic ships were slaves to the winds that blew with the unpredictable whim of a beautiful woman.

The recollection of Granville's recommendations for the conversion in shipping made Patrick uneasy. His influence was still strong with a handful of directors but Lady Enid had warned him that Granville might try and discredit him as the bastard son of a Catholic Irishman, not a desirable

491

pedigree in the staunchly Protestant world of colonial commerce. Nevertheless, his courageous record of service for the Queen had temporarily countered any move to discredit him.

Enid had also warned him – somewhat pessimistically – that the press loved scandal and would happily wait until people forgot all that he had done for the Mother Country. Only the fact that the paper she had purchased the previous year was keeping his name alive as a hero of the Suakin campaign kept the rival tabloids quiet. She hoped fervently that her grandson would be able to establish himself to a point where the other papers would not dare attack his heritage.

As Patrick stood by his window gazing at the sea of masts he waited with some amount of nervous anticipation. He had received a calling card the previous day and had not hesitated in cancelling all other scheduled appointments to meet his Aunt Kate.

Would she be as aloof as his Uncle Daniel, he wondered as he stood with his hands clasped behind his back, the uncle who had refused to meet with him because of his renouncement of his Catholicism? Or would she, the sister of his father, be more sympathetic to his adoption of his maternal grandmother's Protestant religion? In a matter of minutes he would know. He heard the muffled voices from the annexe. 'Missus Tracy to see you, sir,' George Hobbs said as he poked his head around the corner.

'Bid her enter, Mister Hobbs.'

The first impression Patrick had of his famous

aunt was that she did not look like the image he had harboured of an austere businesswoman. She was downright beautiful. Her large, grey eyes were soft and he could see depths of an infinite love in them. Her long, dark hair was splashed with streaks of grey but it also was soft and luxurious. She wore her hair piled in a neatly set bun and her long satin dress of dark green rustled when she moved across the room to greet her nephew.

Patrick took her extended hand and felt the firmness of her grip. 'Aunt Kate, it is both a pleasure and an honour to meet you after all these years,' he said with sober intensity. 'You must be the most beautiful Duffy woman in all the colonies – or even in Ireland itself.'

Her merry burst of laughter was like the tinkling of a bell. 'Patrick Duffy. You are as big a liar as your father,' she replied with a broad smile of pleasure. 'God knows where you Duffy men get your blarney when you were born here in the colonies and not dear old Ireland. But I love your flattery all the same. You make an old woman feel young again.'

'Old!' Patrick exploded with mock anger. 'You could grace the palaces of Europe and men would be fighting duels to the death for the honour of your smile.'

'If that was only so,' she sighed as he released her hand and invited her to sit in one of the comfortable leather chairs in the office. 'But your opinion of me may change after we have discussed what I have come to speak with you about.'

'By that I presume you mean you have come

493

about the possible purchase of Glen View,' he replied grimly. 'Regardless of the outcome of any discussions we have, I would still consider you the most beautiful Duffy woman alive.'

Kate sat with her hands clasped in her lap and smiled. 'I pray you retain that opinion of me, Patrick. I have always intended to meet you at the first available opportunity. I suppose we should clear the air before we talk about more pleasant matters. Will you sell Glen View to me? I already own Balaclava Station adjoining Glen View and it makes sense to my business interests to unite both properties.'

Patrick sat up in surprise at the bluntness of her question. 'If it were in my power to do so, I might consider your offer,' he said. 'But the sale of Glen View is solely in Granville White's hands. You see, when my grandfather died he left the property to my mother. When she transferred her inheritance to her husband he automatically acquired the property.'

'And you have no say in the sale?'

'Sadly, no,' he replied. 'Lady Macintosh is furious at his proposal to sell Glen View. As you know my grandfather and uncle are buried on the property. It means a great deal to the Macintosh name to retain the property for that reason alone.'

'Both your grandfathers are buried on Glen View,' Kate reminded him softly. 'And lately your cousin Peter Duffy.'

'You are right,' he corrected himself. 'Both my grandfathers and my cousin Peter who, I regret, I did not have the opportunity to meet. I read in the newspaper of the tragic circumstances surrounding his death. Uncle Daniel did not even have the courtesy to inform me himself,' he added bitterly.

'You cannot blame your uncle for his silence, Patrick,' Kate stated, defending her cousin. 'It is not every day a Duffy renounces his heritage.'

'Then why is it that you deign to speak to me?' he asked bitterly. 'Was the offer on Glen View the only reason?'

'No, Patrick,' she replied gently. 'I do not hold the same views as your Uncle Daniel. I have always been considered somewhat of a non-conformist in the family. I married my first husband against the wishes of my Uncle Frank and Aunt Bridget. Unfortunately their reservations on his character proved all too accurate. But even if I had known that then I would still have married Kevin O'Keefe. No, I came to meet you because you are the son of my brother and part of my blood.'

Patrick glanced down at the floor and felt shame at his peevish manner. 'I'm sorry for my outburst,' he said. 'It's just that I have no family on my father's side anymore.'

'You will always have me and your father,' she corrected softly. 'No matter where he is. I know he holds a great affection for you.'

'I wish I could believe that about the great Michael Duffy but he has never made any attempt to find me in all the years that have passed.'

'That is not true, Patrick,' Kate said, interrupting his bitter rebuke. 'He even travelled to the Sudan to search for you when you were reported missing in action last year.'

Patrick stared at his aunt with an expression of utter surprise. 'What do you mean? What are you talking about?'

'I thought you must have known,' Kate frowned. 'Your father wrote to me from Italy last year that Lady Macintosh hired him to search for you. But it appears that by the time he reached the Sudan you had been found already and the authorities there refused to let him see you.'

'Are you sure of what you are saying?' Patrick asked, leaning forward in his chair with his hands extended as if he was begging for information like a beggar would alms. 'That my grandmother hired my father to search for me.'

'I am sure. Your father would not have written those things to me if it wasn't the truth. Apparently a Colonel Godfrey counter-ordered his letters of introduction sent to Suakin.'

'Godfrey!'

'Do you know this Colonel Godfrey?' Kate asked.

'Yes. I know Colonel George Godfrey,' he replied with a growl. 'I am sure he will tell me what I would like to know.'

Patrick rose and paced the office. He was tense with a disquieting concern. The revelation concerning his father's search for him had repercussions that would surely echo in the library of his grandmother's house.

'I am sorry that my news has caused so much obvious grief to you,' Kate said. 'I presumed that you would have known.'

'I returned to Sydney because I hoped I could use the considerable resources of the Macintosh name to search for my father, and one other. I have a need to meet him, at least once in my life. I am not sure I would even like him if I did. But I do know that I will never be able to truly know who I am until I confront him. Do you have any idea where in the world he is?'

'If I knew where your father was I would tell you. But his last address was Rome and that was over ten months ago. Knowing your father as I do, he could be anywhere now.'

'What was he doing in Rome?' Patrick asked with an edge in his voice that puzzled Kate. 'Was he with someone?'

'He didn't mention anyone else in his letter. He was writing to tell me that he had returned to painting and that he was attending some of the art studios in Rome.'

Patrick fell into a brooding silence. Was Catherine still with his father? If so, was she his lover? How would he react to finding both his father and Catherine together? 'Aunt Kate, thank you for telling me all that you have,' he finally said. 'I would very much like you to dine with my grandmother and myself tomorrow tonight at Lady Enid's residence.'

'Thank you for the kind invitation, Patrick, but I will decline,' Kate said as she rose from her chair. 'I am afraid, as much as I hold no animosity to you as my brother's son, I will never step foot in any place that belongs to the Macintoshes. As it is I have a passage booked for Rockhampton the day after tomorrow and I have a need to see to business interests first.'

'Your declining is my great loss,' Patrick said

gallantly. 'But I feel that we shall keep contact in the future no matter what should happen in our lives.'

Kate leant forward impulsively to kiss her nephew on the forehead. 'Oh, if only you could meet your father,' she sighed. 'He would be so proud of you.'

'I hope you are right, Aunt Kate,' Patrick said, as he escorted his aunt to the street where he hailed a Hansom cab and helped her to board.

He stood on the busy city street watching the cab join the stream of carriages, drays and horse-drawn omnibuses that displayed advertisements on their sides for whisky and tobacco products. It was a warm winter's day and big black clouds boiled up in the smoke filled sky, almost as dark as his own thoughts. He would first confront his grandmother and ask her why she had not told him of her meeting with his father. He would also ask her why it was that Godfrey counter-ordered the letters of introduction as he knew he would not have done so unless she had insisted. Then he would question Colonel Godfrey. He suspected that the former soldier knew a lot more about his father than he had ever let on.

Granville was not happy in his new office, nor was he pleased at losing his control over the shipping line to Patrick Duffy. Exporting the colony's produce was the key to the country's future and shipping the main means of reaching the lucrative markets in far-off England. He had lost control to a man who was nothing more than a mistake on the part of his estranged wife during an impressionable time of her life.

498

He paced the office and for a moment felt an almost wistful loss for his former employee, Morrison Mort. If he still retained the services of the vicious sea captain he might be able to discuss the means to dispose of his rival for power. But Mort was no longer of this world. The lurid stories that had filtered down from the northern frontier of Queensland years earlier described his death as particularly gruesome. It had been rumoured he had ended his life in a myall cooking fire as part of a heathen feast.

Granville shuddered. It was also rumoured that Mort's untimely demise was partially the work of that Irish soldier of fortune, Michael Duffy, father of his current hated enemy.

He plonked himself in a chair. Deep in thought he steepled his fingers and reassured himself that violence was not the sole means of destroying a man. He could take a page from his mother-in-law's book on the more subtle means of causing irreparable damage to a man's reputation. He sensed that even now Enid was playing her game of attempting to discredit him by the move to the new office.

The company ledgers lay open on the desk before him. They had been routinely delivered from David's office for his scrutiny without any fuss. It was purely a matter of good business to examine the big leatherbound books that recorded profit and loss for all the Macintosh companies.

Just for a moment Granville remembered his dead brother-in-law. Seventeen years earlier Enid's son had been an obstacle to Granville's ambitions as David stood ahead of him in the line of inheritance. But Mort had carried out his orders faithfully and the young man's bones were buried in an unmarked grave in the sands of a tropical island in the Pacific. David's death had been attributed to hostile natives but Granville knew his estranged mother-in-law did not believe the official account rendered by Mort when he returned to Sydney aboard the blackbirding barque *Osprey*.

Two could play the game and even the hero of the Sudan would not be safe. He would no longer need to use extreme violence to discredit Patrick Duffy in the eyes of the world. He had at his fingertips the most reliable and unscrupulous means of destroying an innocent man's reputation. Did not the Macintosh companies include the ownership of a newspaper?

A plan had formed in Granville's astute scheming from the moment Patrick had taken possession of his office. Now it was time to execute his plan. Execute, he mused. A good word to be used in destroying Patrick Duffy and his chances of controlling the assets of the Macintosh companies.

For the first time all day Granville smiled. The neatly written rows of figures in the ledger columns were his ammunition. He had on hand a master forger who could transcribe in Hobbs' hand the figures to the blank pages of newly acquired ledgers, albeit with some telling additions – additions which would be corroborated with suitable bank receipts on hand for an audit.

The pen was indeed mightier than the sword, he smirked. And men like Mort not always required to destroy a man.

51

Barcaldine was the name of the town. It was little more than a few pubs with their sprawling shady verandahs and stores that held the bare essentials for life. There were also one or two houses and a police lockup to hold the rowdy drunken shearers after they had blown their pay on drink.

Gordon James sighed with relief at the sight of the iron roofs that shimmered across the line of low scrub under the blazing midday sun. His patrol had trekked south for two hundred miles across a vast, flat expanse of miserable scrubland and the first real vestige of civilisation now lay before them.

Often on the trek he had questioned his decision to remain with the police. Without Sarah he realised he had little else in his life that held any meaning. Astride a horse on the sweeping plains he could lose himself in the loneliness of the great wide country of limitless horizons. But never was Sarah far from his thoughts. No matter how much he attempted to lose himself in his job he would often find himself thinking about her. The memories seared his soul worse than the midday sun of the harsh Australian summer. At least hunting men with his patrol helped divert such thoughts of her. As the leader of his band he was responsible for their welfare.

Gordon spurred his mount forward to follow the big Kalkadoon tracker through the bush. Terituba seemed tireless. Day after day he had followed the faint trail of the four bushrangers – a trail that was visible to him alone. At least until they were fifty miles north of Barcaldine when the tracks had disappeared after a series of destructive small, tornado-like winds whipped through the scrub. The willy-willies obliterated the delicate signs of the tracks and, puzzled, Terituba had wandered in search of them.

Gordon had lost a day in his hunt for the four men as he waited for the Aboriginal tracker to pick up the tracks again. He consulted his map and shot a bearing along the line of the pursuit with his compass. He deduced that the tracks had been leading them south to Barcaldine and remembered that Calder had once worked in the district as a shearer before joining the Native Mounted Police. It appeared that the wanted killer was leading his gang back into familiar territory.

Gordon had put away his map and issued orders to the patrol to ride south until they reached the tiny township. It was a hard ride, with only a few hours' sleep in the two nights preceding their approach to Barcaldine.

But now they were within sight of the township and he issued orders to his troopers to be on their guard as they rode in. According to Gordon's reckoning they were very close on the heels of the fugitives and his first stop would be at the local police lockup.

Sergeant Johnson adjusted his heavy blue uniform jacket as he strolled out of his one-room office to greet his unexpected visitors. He was a gruff man with a pock marked face that sweated considerably.

He stood in front of his office and eyed the young inspector with some curiosity and contempt. The Native Mounted Police allowed blackfellas to join the ranks and carry firearms. It was not a good thing. Sergeant Johnson did not feel he was required to salute the officer who he viewed as less than a real policeman. But nor was he discourteous. 'Want to get down and come inside, Inspector?' he invited. 'Your boys can water their horses 'round the back if you want.'

'Thank you, Sergeant,' Gordon replied, and slid from his saddle with an easy grace.

The local sergeant also eyed the giant Aboriginal who stood beside the stirrup of the inspector's saddle. 'Not a local blackfella by the looks of him,' he commented as Gordon tied his horse to a hitching rail.

'Kalkadoon, from up north,' Gordon replied.

The sergeant raised his eyebrows with surprise. 'I thought you blokes wiped them out last year, north of the Curry?'

'Not all.'

The sergeant shook his head and chuckled. 'He looks like he hasn't taken much to the white man's civilisation. Looks a bad one to me, if you ask.'

Gordon was annoyed at the police sergeant's

tactless observations as Terituba had proved himself invaluable to the mission, even though he had no real reason to help the men who had slaughtered his people. 'He has a pretty good grasp of English, Sergeant,' Gordon said. 'So I wouldn't be too free with any insults or you might end up getting a taste of the axe he has tucked in his belt. I can assure you, from personal experience, that he is very good with it. That's how I got this,' he said, pointing to the scar on his forehead.

The sergeant blinked and cast the Kalkadoon a new look of respect. 'He did that?' he said in an awed voice, and Gordon nodded. 'Then you must be Inspector James . . . sir.' The local policeman had read much about the fierce battle with the Kalkadoon. 'Sorry if I appeared a bit disrespectful.'

'No offence taken, Sergeant,' Gordon replied.

Terituba gazed around at the tiny town with an expression of curious interest. This was the first white man's town he had ever been in and the way these people lived was a fascination to him. Why would they go to so much trouble building structures of permanence when the harshness of the land dictated that they might have to go walkabout in search of water and game thus leaving all their hard work behind to be reclaimed by the land?

'You come with us, Kalkadoon man,' one of the troopers called to him, and he followed obediently to go with the horses to drink from the trough. At least the trough was useful.

Gordon followed the sergeant inside and

plumped himself down on a chair. The office contained little furniture other than a noticeboard plastered with wanted posters, a cheap government issued desk and two chairs.

The sergeant sat down behind the desk. 'What brings you to Barcaldine, sir?' he asked.

'We've been tracking four men from the Curry. One of them is called James Calder. Do you know him? Or have you seen any strangers around here lately?'

'Four fellows camped out along the creek just south of here – or so I've been told by a couple of shearers passing through.'

'How long ago?'

'Still there as far as I know. 'Bout an hour's ride from here. They haven't caused any trouble that I know of, though.'

'Could be them,' Gordon mused. 'Don't suppose you could guide us to where they are camped?'

'Yeah. What are they wanted for?'

'Murder, rape and robbery whilst under arms. They killed a selector and raped his missus in the Cloncurry district a few weeks back. The murdered man's wife gave us a pretty good description of them. At least the two who raped her. Unfortunately, they struck at night and she didn't get much of a look at the two who stayed outside.'

'Who did the killing?'

'Calder.'

The sergeant rose from his chair. 'I'll grab a few supplies and saddle up. Might be we could be out a few days if the lads have upped camp and left already.'

'I gather you will be joining us then,' Gordon said as he rose from his chair.

'Looks that way, sir. With all due respect for your tracker I know the country around here and I know where the properties are. If these boys are as bad as you say, I wouldn't like them calling on any of the homesteads uninvited. I've got a lot of friends in this district.'

'Fair enough, Sergeant . . . ?'

'Sergeant Johnson, sir,' the man said, as he withdrew his service revolver from a drawer and slipped it into his holster.

'Do you have a spare mount?' Gordon asked.

'Yes, sir. You be needing it for the tracker?'

Gordon nodded.

'I'll throw a saddle on then,' he answered as he retrieved a Snider rifle from behind the door and dropped a box of bullets in the pocket of his trousers.

The two men stepped outside and the sergeant walked across to the house adjacent to the lockup. As Gordon waited patiently for the sergeant to arrange his departure he gazed idly down the street at the bushmen and few townspeople who were staring at him with a mixture of curiosity and apathy. They lazed under the shady shelter of the wide verandahs of the hotels, gripping glasses of beer or spirits. Not much happened at midday in Barcaldine and even the town's dogs kept off the streets when the sun was at its zenith in the azure blue sky.

'I'll be damned!' Gordon swore. 'Hey, Willie!'

He walked quickly down the dusty road towards one of the hotels where he noticed the young man stepping onto the verandah. He was carrying a bottle of rum in one hand and at the sound of his name he froze.

'Willie!' Gordon called again.

Willie waved. 'Mister James. When did you get here?' he asked, thrusting out his free hand.

'Just rode in a few minutes ago. What are you doing in this part of the world?'

Willie glanced across the inspector's shoulder at the troop of Aboriginal police who were in front of the station adjusting the straps on their saddles for the hard ride their boss had promised them. 'I'm doing a bit of prospecting around these parts,' he answered as his eyes settled on Gordon James again. 'Just come to pick up some supplies.'

'You on your own? Or you working with a partner?'

'On my own,' Willie answered. 'What are you doing in Barcaldine?'

'Tracking four men wanted for questioning about a murder,' Gordon replied. 'You probably knew them, Jack Halpin and his missus. They had a selection not far from Jerusalem.'

'Yeah, I knew them,' Willie answered softly and shifted his gaze nervously back to the troopers of the patrol. 'What happened? Someone kill Jack?'

'Yeah. It was pretty bad. Really messed up his missus as well. The four we are looking for are camped about an hour's ride from here. You wouldn't have come across them in your travels?'

'Have, as a matter of fact,' Willie replied. 'Four fellas south of here. About an hour's ride, like you said. Still there as far as I know. Saw them this morning when I was riding in.'

'That's good news. With any luck we will be able to catch up to them and see if they are the ones we want.' Willie shifted from one foot to another and Gordon was vaguely aware that the young man appeared nervous. 'It looks as if Sergeant Johnson is ready to go,' Gordon said as he noticed the local policeman lead his horse and a spare onto the street. 'So I had better join the troop. It was good seeing you again, Willie.'

'You too, Mister James,' Willie said as he extended his hand to the policeman once more. 'Probably see you around if you are in these parts for a while.'

Gordon walked back to his men who were standing by their horses. He turned once to see Willie swing himself into the saddle of his own mount, a huge animal with a good bloodline.

'Ready to go, Sergeant Johnson?' Gordon asked as he swung himself into the saddle.

'Ready, sir,' the sergeant answered. Gordon turned to tell Terituba to mount the spare horse. But the Kalkadoon was squatting in the dusty road, examining the earth.

The tracker frowned and stared down the road as Willie disappeared into a line of scrub beyond the town's limits. He glanced up to meet Gordon's eyes. 'That fella white man he go longa there,' he said, pointing to where Willie had disappeared into the scrub. 'He riding one horse Terituba track.'

'You sure?' Gordon gaped. 'You sure that you have the right horse?' But even as he questioned Terituba he knew with sickening certainty that the tracker was right. Willie Harris was one of the four wanted men! He did not want to believe that the young man whom he had known since the day Kate brought him and his mother to Cooktown was now in the company of killers. 'After him!' Gordon bawled to his men.

He spurred his mount into a gallop with the troop following. Sergeant Johnson was caught unawares by the sudden order, however, and followed a good hundred yards or so behind as the troop charged the scrubline in a desperate attempt to catch Willie Harris. But Willie had a good start on his pursuers and as soon as he felt that he was out of sight he had spurred his big mare into a gallop. The troopers' mounts crashed through the scrub but it was obvious that they were no match for the pace of the horse they pursued.

'Rein in!' Gordon bellowed as he pulled down on his own reins bringing his mount to a panting halt.

Sergeant Johnson caught them as they milled in confusion. 'What's up? We still have him in sight.'

'He'll lead us away from Calder and the others,' Gordon bellowed over his shoulder as he realised that Willie was riding north, and not south, where his companions were last reported camped. 'We have to get to the creek where they're camped before he gets to warn 'em.'

The sergeant realised the inspector was probably right and, with a yell to urge his mount on, swung her head south. The troop galloped after him.

Willie kept his mount at a flat gallop until he knew she could take no more. The horse crashed through the scrub and he glanced over his shoulder. He could no longer see his pursuers and slowed his mount to a walk as the mare's great lungs heaved and foam flecked her mouth. 'Good girl,' he whispered as he leant forward to pat her affectionately on the neck.

He slid from the saddle, let the reins fall from his hand and sat down with his back against a tree. He had always known that it would only be a matter of time before his role in the murder of the selector would be discovered even though Jack Halpin and his missus had not seen him standing guard outside their hut. Then he'd be tied in with those who had committed the horrific crimes. He had hoped that he could have at least reached Sydney before that had happened so he could realise his vow to his dying mother. Now it seemed he would not fulfil his promise. Within days his name would be circulated to all the colony's police forces, via the telegraph line.

Around him was only the silence of the bush, and above him the sweeping blue skies. He slipped the bottle of rum from his pocket and removed the top. With a great swallow he threw back a deep draught of the dark liquid. It did not quench his thirst but it did help to quell the despair that welled up in his spirit, threatening to drown him. *How had it all gone wrong?*

He knew the hollow echo in his soul was the answer to his question. It had all gone wrong the day he had fallen in with the former trooper and his two shifty companions. Cattle stealing was one thing – but murder, rape and robbery another.

His guilt for leading Calder and his men to the

isolated homestead of the Halpins burnt his stomach as the rum's intoxicating effects took hold. Calder had promised that they would only bail up the selector and steal the stores they required.

But Jack Halpin had stubbornly resisted the hold-up attempt, as Willie should have known he would. Calder had become enraged by the brave selector's efforts to hold them off with an ancient muzzle loader which was no match for the combined fire power of the four men. Calder had shot him, and while Halpin lay dying he had been forced to watch as Calder and his equally psychotic lieutenant, Joe Heslop, raped his wife. Calder finished off the wounded selector with a bullet in the head and then turned the gun on the hysterical woman. They had left her for dead, although Willie was relieved now to hear that at least she had survived. The four men had taken what they had needed and rode hard to put distance between themselves and the Cloncurry district.

Willie had decided to take the long trek across the burning plains north of Barcaldine. And he would desert his companions at the first possible opportunity. They were madmen who talked of restocking their supplies with a similar raid on another isolated homestead. But meanwhile he had needed them to survive the trek to Barcaldine and they had not suspected his intentions to desert them. Indeed, they had trusted him enough to ride into town to buy alcohol.

Running into Gordon James in Barcaldine had been the most nerve-racking moment of his life.

He had kept his nerve until he was able to ride out of sight and then break into a hard gallop. He was not leading the police away from Calder and the others but simply fleeing for his own life. Calder and the others could go to hell, for all he cared. But he did not want to take the trip with them.

With half the bottle emptied Willie felt his head swim and he leant over and vomited the contents of his stomach onto the ground. He groaned as he wiped his mouth with the back of his sleeve and cared little if the troopers caught him. He had failed to keep his promise to his mother. Falling in with the wrong company had made sure of that!

52

When Patrick arrived at Enid's house he found Colonel George Godfrey and his grandmother taking afternoon tea in the vine entangled rotunda in the garden. Despite the ominous threat of a storm hovering over the city, Enid had opted to take in the magnificent view of the harbour below the garden as she chatted with the colonel. Silver salvers were spread with delicate sandwiches of salmon and little cream tarts. They sipped tea from fine china cups and Lady Macintosh expressed her surprise at seeing her grandson home so early.

'Hello, Lady Enid,' Patrick said stiffly when he joined them in the rotunda. 'Colonel.' Enid was disturbed by the dark expression that clouded his face and quick to note that he did not give her the usual peck on the cheek.

'Rather a pleasant surprise, old chap,' Godfrey said as he rose from his chair to greet Patrick.

'I'm rather glad that I have found you both together.'

'Is something wrong, Patrick?' Enid asked in a concerned voice. 'You appear to have much on your mind. I will call Betsy to bring us more tea.'

'I doubt that my stomach is up to even tea at the moment,' Patrick replied as he stood facing his grandmother and the colonel. 'I have a matter of great importance to discuss with you.'

'Would you like me to leave?' Godfrey asked politely, placing his cup on its saucer. Patrick shook his head.

'No,' he frowned. 'What I wish to discuss very much involves you, Colonel. I would prefer if you stayed.'

Godfrey cast a quizzical look at Enid. She nodded, feeling a rising trepidation for what was to come. She had never seen the strange tenseness in her grandson that he now carried like a heavy cloak.

'Why didn't you tell me that you met with my father last year and hired him to go to the Sudan?' Patrick's bluntly delivered question caused Enid to catch her breath. Why had she ever thought that she could keep the matter a secret? It had been hard enough concealing from him the fact that she had known for some years that Michael Duffy was alive.

'How did you find out?'

'I met with my Aunt Kate this morning.'

'Your father's sister,' Enid replied, using the relationship of his aunt to his father rather than himself in her reply.

'My aunt by family blood,' he corrected.

'I did not tell you, Patrick,' she answered calmly, 'because your father is a man who is wanted on a charge of murder in this colony.'

'Is that a reason, or an excuse, Lady Enid?' he

asked angrily. 'Or was it that you hoped I would never learn he was alive and endeavour to find him?'

'It would not do your name well to be associated with a felon,' she answered him. 'Your father has not even revealed himself to his family in Sydney, as far as I am aware. From what I can gather, he wishes to remain anonymous to all. Even you.'

'I doubt that to be true when he was prepared to search for me.'

'You may doubt what I am saying but you must consider the fact that at no time in the past has he ever attempted to make contact with you.'

'He may not have been able to,' Patrick replied. 'I was halfway around the world for the last twelve years. First, in England, then in the army. He may have wanted to see me but was unable for that reason alone.'

'I doubt that, Patrick,' she scoffed. 'Not *if* he loved you as a father would a son.'

In her retort he found an element of truth. Why had he not attempted to contact him?

The tiny doubt threatened to grow like a cancer. He turned his attention to Godfrey who stood protectively alongside his grandmother with his hand resting gently on her shoulder. 'And you, Colonel,' he said, fixing the man with brooding eyes. 'Why did you counter-order the letters of introduction when he went to the Sudan?'

Godfrey returned the stare with the ice-cold disdain of an officer being questioned by a sub-ordinate. 'You should realise, Captain Duffy,' he bristled, 'that I am not answerable to you. I think you should reconsider your question.'

'I am not under your command, Colonel Godfrey,' Patrick answered with a cold anger. 'I ask the question without retraction.'

George Godfrey was not a man to be intimidated. He had faced the enemies of the Queen many times in battle without flinching and had even faced mutinous Indian soldiers bent on destroying the British power in their country. A mere captain held no fear for him.

Enid could see the friendship that had blossomed between the two most important men in her life rapidly unravelling. She realised that Godfrey would never betray her trust. Not even to death itself. 'George, I think I should answer my grandson's question,' she said quietly, and looked up at Patrick. 'I told the Colonel to counter-order the letters. He was reluctant to do so at the time – but I insisted. I thought I was doing right for all concerned. But I see now that my decision to do so was wrong.'

Patrick was taken aback by his grandmother's sudden repentance. Lady Macintosh had never been known to bend in any matters.

'Your father is a fine and courageous man, Patrick,' she continued. 'And, I suppose, in many ways I have been responsible for much of the misfortune that has been brought upon his life. No-one can recover the fragments of the past and put them back together again. If I could do so then I might have reconsidered many of my past decisions. But there is one I would not have changed. The decision to allow your father to marry your mother.'

'Because my father was Irish?' he asked.

'No. Because of his Papist religion. No Papist could ever inherit the Macintosh name. Not even you.'

A short silence fell between them as Patrick pondered on the importance his grandmother placed on religion. He had renounced his Catholicism for no other reason than he was an atheist. He only paid lip service to his grandmother's staunchly Protestant beliefs.

Thunder rumbled in the dark skies and great drops of rain plopped amongst the trees and shrubs. 'I think we should go inside,' Godfrey said, breaking the silence. 'I fear we are in for a drenching.'

He assisted Enid to her feet as the maid hurried outside to recover the linen table cloth and salvers of uneaten sandwiches.

On an impulse Patrick then asked quietly, 'Colonel, do you know where my father is now?'

He cast Enid a questioning look and she nodded. They had developed such a close contact over the years that communication between them did not always require words. 'Your father is presently working in South Africa, on vital matters for the Empire,' he replied. 'His exact whereabouts is not known to me. But I do know that he is somewhere in the Cape Colony.'

'What is he doing there?' Patrick asked as a cold fear rose in him. If Catherine was with him she might be in danger.

'I can only surmise from what I know of his past that your father is spying on the Boers. As you probably know your father is rather fluent in the German language and I believe he has ingratiated himself as a gun dealer. There are some in England who believe that the Dutch farmers will rise again, as they did in '81 and your father has the task of collecting intelligence on them for the Foreign Office.'

'God almighty!' Patrick said in a strangled voice. 'The Boers are no fools. He is bound to be uncovered in his mission.'

'Sadly, I must agree with you, Patrick,' the colonel said gently and with true sympathy in his voice. 'Your father is a tremendously brave man. But his uncanny luck cannot last forever and the Boers are not very forgiving of spies in their ranks.'

'I have to go to the Cape at the soonest possible time to find him.'

'You may be wasting a trip,' Godfrey said. 'Every day your father deals with the Boers is a day off his life, one way or the other.'

'Patrick is right, George,' Enid interjected softly. 'I think he should try. And if I remember correctly we have a clipper carrying a cargo of wool for England. It sails tonight and is sailing via the Cape. If you are able, you could just make the ship before she sails. It's the *Lady Jane*, our fastest clipper.'

Patrick glanced at his grandmother and felt a sudden respect and affection for her assistance. 'Thank you, Grandmama,' he whispered as he bent to kiss her gently on the cheek. It was the first time he had ever called her this and she felt the tears well in her eyes for his impulsive and loving gesture. She was too proud to let him see her cry, however, and excused herself as soon as they reached the house.

Only Godfrey had noticed the tears welling and wondered on the dramatic changes he had seen in her that afternoon. If only she could reconcile herself with her daughter, he thought sadly. Then she might find the love that she had denied herself for so many bitter years.

Enid went directly to her library. She needed time alone to consider the consequences of her sudden change of heart. Was it that the lie had to be exposed? She could only trust in her God that Patrick could forgive her. If she was guilty of anything, it was growing to love him, and doing all in her power to keep him by her side. Surely he would be able to understand an old woman's weakness to protect the only flesh and blood who stood with her. She prayed fervently to her God that He would show the way.

George Hobbs hardly noticed the torrential downpour on the roof above his office. He was a man absorbed by the mystery confronting him in the columns of his ledgers. A simple error in his bookkeeping had caused him to refer back to the accounts commenced when Captain Duffy had taken over the office. Now George ran his finger down a column of payments and noticed that mysterious and large sums of payments had appeared that he had no prior knowledge of. The handwriting was so much like his own. But it was not!

He frowned and flipped the heavy book shut to examine the cover. It appeared to be one of his books, but still the payments recorded in the columns were a mystery to him.

He gasped as the thought of forgery crept into his mind. Someone had altered his books so cleverly that the forgery would have gone unnoticed, until an audit revealed the extent of payments.

George rose from his chair and rubbed his face in his consternation. The rain pounded the building and only now was he becoming aware of the storm outside as he stood to stare out his window at the ships at anchor below. Had Captain Duffy arranged for a forger to alter the books? The answer resounded as a definite 'no'. Why would Captain Duffy so blatantly pay a well-publicised Fenian supporter in the colonies such a large and regular sum of money? The Fenian was a rabble rouser, preaching that guns for Ireland be used against the Crown in a bloody rebellion and his radical views reported by the colonial press.

But a tiny doubt nagged the clerk. Had not Lady Macintosh's grandson spent a long time in Ireland before returning to Australia? Had he succumbed to his Irish heritage and was now using the Macintosh finances to commit treason?

The very thought of treason caused George Hobbs to shudder. What a scandal any such revelation would cause to Lady Macintosh and the family name. But the fact that he knew that the entries were blatant forgeries would crush any attempt to discredit Captain Duffy who had well and truly established his loyalty to the Queen with his illustrious service in the army.

Hobbs knew that he must bring the matter to Captain Duffy's attention as soon as possible to avert any whiff of a scandal. Whoever had conspired so cleverly must be stopped. But who would do so?

Mister White!

George slumped in his chair and despair was clearly written in his face. If Mister White was behind the conspiracy then the matter had taken a perilous turn. The clerk had always feared his former employer. There were stories whispered in the streets of Sydney that he was not a man to be crossed. George noticed that his hands were trembling when he attempted to flip open the great ledger. What was he to do? He felt like his head was in a steel trap poised to snap shut.

When he finally locked the office and stepped out into the rainswept street, he was not in the least surprised to find two very burly men waiting for him. George Hobbs sensed correctly that his very life was in mortal danger if he did not listen to what they had to say.

Granville had anticipated that David's clerk may have become suspicious of the books when they were returned to his keeping. He had never underestimated the man – or his loyalty to Lady Enid's interests. Either way, Granville decided insurance was best applied before any bleating by George Hobbs.

53

The troop rode hard. What was normally an hour's journey took only half that time. As they were approaching the last known campsite of the gang, Sergeant Johnson signalled to slow down. The horses panted and foam flecked their mouths while sweat streamed from their bodies. Gordon reined his mount alongside Johnson's horse.

'Just up ahead along the creek behind that clump of trees,' the sergeant said as he pointed to a copse of large coolabah trees where they could see a thin plume of smoke.

'If it's them,' Gordon said, 'we had better arrive before they get a chance to saddle up.'

The sergeant grunted his agreement and with a final desperate effort the troopers spurred their exhausted mounts into a gallop. As they rode hard at the campsite they slid rifles from saddle buckets. Gordon's revolver was in his hand as he led the charge.

Calder was first to hear the drumming of horses' hooves on the plain while he was snoozing under the shade of one of the big coolabah trees, his hat over his face. He sat up and peered in the direction of the sound and saw the dust rising through the shimmer of the early afternoon heat.

Instantly he was on his feet and as he snatched up his rifle he screamed a warning to his companions who were further along the creek fishing in one of the deeper waterholes. They dropped the lines and snatched their rifles.

Calder dashed for his horse and desperately released the hobbles around its legs. He flung himself on the bare back and, with one hand gripping the mane, urged the horse into a gallop. But his effort was in vain as the troopers descended as a wave over the campsite.

'That's them!' Gordon yelled when he recognised the former trooper attempting to ride out. 'Stand in the Queen's name,' he bellowed above the whinny of horses and whoops of his own men.

A rifle crashed from close at hand and one of the trooper's horses whinnied more loudly as the bullet found a mark. The horse toppled forward, throwing the trooper into the hard earth. The fight had begun.

Calder's horse reared and hurled him against a tree trunk where he lay on the ground, winded for a short time. In the long dry grass he was able to roll into a sitting position as his breath came in ragged gasps. Bullets ploughed the earth around him from the troopers who were unable to steady their aim from the backs of their prancing mounts. Despite their cursing to bring their horses under control, the agonised whinnying from the trooper's critically wounded horse frightened them. Gordon leapt from his horse with his pistol in his hand and, crouching, he dashed for the cover of a tree.

Calder had regained enough of his breath to raise his rifle as he sought a target. He was determined not to be taken by the police as he knew the penalty for his crimes was certain death by hanging. He had nothing to lose by holding them off.

For a fleeting second he saw the crouching figure of Gordon James diving for the cover of the tree and his snapped shot plucked bark from the tree just above Gordon's head. 'James, you bastard. You aren't taking me alive,' he screamed defiantly as he quickly reloaded and dropped back to the ground out of sight without waiting for a reply. He wriggled away through the grass for the creek bed which provided a chance to find better cover behind the high banks of the meandering stream of sluggish water.

Gordon cautiously peeked from behind the tree trunk at the disposition of his troopers. They were dismounted and had also sought the cover of trees to return fire. He could see a puff of smoke when one of the wanted men fired on them from the other side of the creek; he had waded across to take up a position amongst the tangle of exposed roots of a river tree. The shot was answered with a volley of fire from the troopers who kept him pinned in a hopeless situation. He had no hope of escaping.

Sergeant Johnson snapped orders to the troopers to fire and move on the trapped man. Gordon was glad that Johnson had elected to ride with them; the troopers tended to get dangerously enthusiastic under fire and needed the cool guidance of an experienced police officer.

Gordon had noticed the third member of the gang disappear up the creek after he had fired the shot that had brought down the trooper's horse. But he could not see where Calder had gone after he had fired wildly in his direction.

He took a deep breath as he gathered himself for an attempt to rush forward to his next piece of cover. Hopefully it would give him a view of the men he hunted. He let out his breath and in a crouching sprint dashed for a large tree further along the creek line, acutely aware that by doing so he was dangerously stretching the distance between himself and his troop.

With a gasp for breath he flung himself down on the ground and waited in the grass. Nothing! Cautiously he peered above the grass at the thicket of trees to his front and saw the flash of a red shirt.

Calder was running as fast as he could away from the campsite and Gordon stood, steadied himself and fired on the fleeing man. Two shots whined through the trees, clipping leaves from branches and causing Calder to swerve and go to ground.

Gordon was not sure whether one of his bullets had found its mark. The second shot had not been his and the bullet that had plucked at the sleeve of Gordon's jacket came from his flank. Suddenly he realised that he had exposed himself to the third unseen man. He spun and saw the thin haze of gunsmoke from the thicket of trees to his left.

'You get him, Joe?' Calder called in a voice that

was muffled by the trees ahead of Gordon. But the blast of Gordon's pistol in the direction of the curling wisp of smoke soon answered his somewhat optimistic question. Behind him Gordon could still hear the ragged volleys of shots being fired at the man in the tangle of tree roots. He was certainly putting up a brave – but foolish – stand against the overwhelming odds stacked against him.

Gordon was down on his belly and, using the grass as a cover, crawled forward so that he could reach the thicket of river trees. Another shot from the third man kicked up dirt in his face. The bastard knew where he was, Gordon thought, with a terrifying realisation that he was in a crossfire. He had three shots left and knew that to load his pistol took precious time – time that could cost him his life. He would have to make his three shots count.

He tensed and sprang forward like a spring uncoiling and his action took the third man unawares. He fired a wild shot that found only an empty space where Gordon had been. From the sound of the gun firing Gordon knew that it was a single shot Snider, which gave him the chance to make the cover before the man could reload.

He flung himself into the thicket and went to ground where he wriggled forward to the protection of a fallen trunk of an old tree and paused to listen. He did not hear the telltale snap of twigs or the swishing sound of grass being disturbed.

Gordon's hands sweated and he trembled uncontrollably as if he was in the grip of a fever. The bush around him seemed to have narrowed to a long tunnel and his heart pounded. Maybe he had made a lethal mistake in chasing Calder alone, he thought despairingly. And he had foolishly placed himself well away from the support of his troop which continued to exchange fire with the bushranger stubbornly holed up in the tree roots.

Calder, however, had not seen Gordon make his dash for the thicket of scrub that grew profusely in places along the creek line. The former trooper slithered on his belly to the edge of the creek and onto the barrel of his lieutenant's rifle.

Joe Heslop's eyes bulged with fear and his lips were curled back from his yellow stained teeth. His expression was that of a trapped animal as he pulled down the rifle a mere second before he was about to fire at the figure slithering towards him. 'Jesus, I thought you were that bloody trap,' he snarled. 'You know the bastard out there shooting at us?'

Calder dropped down beside him behind the bank of the creek. 'The bastard was my boss once,' he said. 'Inspector James is the mongrel's name.'

'Same bloke who did the Kalkadoon in?' Heslop asked.

Calder nodded as he checked his revolver that had been tucked in his belt. 'How much ammo you got?' he asked Heslop.

'Not much. Left it all behind at the camp. Three rounds left for the rifle and only what's in my pistol. How about you?'

'Rifle ammo's gone. Just six rounds for the pistol.'

'That's not enough to hold the bastards off,' Heslop spat. 'Maybe we should give up.'

'You can if you like,' Calder snarled. 'But I'd rather take my chances, while I'm free to.'

Heslop fell silent as he stared across the top of the grass. He knew the fearsome reputation of Inspector Gordon James in getting a job done. If only half of what they said was true, their chances of getting away were about as good as nothing. Maybe it would be better to surrender now. At least he would be granted an extension on his life until he met the hangman. 'I'm going to throw it in,' he said softly. 'No sense in dyin' out here.'

'Your choice, Joe,' Calder snarled. 'But leave us your guns and spare ammo.'

Heslop shook his head as he handed over his pistol and rifle ammunition. 'You won't get out alive,' he said.

But Calder flashed him an evil and enigmatic smile. 'I have a plan,' he answered. 'All Mister James has to do is show himself for a second.'

'What are you going to do?' Heslop frowned.

'That's my business.'

Heslop shrugged and raised his head. 'I'm comin' out, Inspector James,' he called out uncertainly. 'Don't shoot!'

Gordon heard the voice call to him but dared not reveal himself. At the same time he knew that he must give away his position behind the fallen tree if he was to accept the man's surrender. He was at least protected from gunfire behind the thick trunk so long as he kept his head down. What worried him most was the unknown whereabouts of Calder. 'Show yourself and walk towards the sound of my voice,' Gordon yelled back, peeking very carefully from the end of the tree trunk until he saw the bushranger at the edge of the creek. 'Put your hands in the air where I can see them,' he added, and the man obeyed. 'Where's Calder?'

Heslop was about to answer when he heard a warning hiss from the bushranger behind him. 'Keep yer mouth shut Joe or I'll send yer to hell.' Heslop knew that his threat was not an idle one and his mouth clamped shut as he began his slow walk towards the sound of the inspector's voice.

Behind him Calder slipped the rear sight setting to fifty yards – the distance he calculated he was from Gordon James. He propped himself against the lip of the creek bank and scanned the ground between himself and the thickets. All the bastard had to do was show himself for a second, he thought, and James was a dead man.

Gordon watched Heslop walking with his hands in the air uncertainly towards him. He appeared to be unarmed but the policeman was taking no chances. The man approaching him had nothing to lose by attempting to pull a concealed gun at the last moment. But where was Calder?

The firing from further up the creek had ceased. Gordon could hear the jubilant voices of his men chattering and guessed they had finally subdued the bushranger.

All he had to do now was call to them and bring them up as reinforcements to flush out Calder. The third bushranger could wait where he was until it was safe to manacle him. 'Halt! And stay where you are with your hands raised,' he called to the man who was now only ten paces from him. Heslop obeyed.

Calder cursed softly. The bastard had out-guessed him. Or had he? He had hoped, in the arrest of Heslop, James might expose himself. Drastic situations called for drastic solutions! 'Get him now, Joe!' he yelled and the bushranger half-turned. What in hell was he talking about?

The heavy Snider round took him in the back between the shoulder blades with a thwacking sound and Joe Heslop pitched forward with a thud as he hit the ground.

Gordon was stunned by the seemingly senseless killing. Without thinking, he rose from his hiding place, as if to catch the man falling towards him, and stood fully exposed with his pistol half raised searching for Calder.

The bushranger sucked through his teeth in his triumph and ejected the empty brass cartridge. After reloading, he flung the butt of the rifle into his shoulder. Gordon was in his sights. So occupied was he, however, that he was not aware of the stealthy, black shadow rising from the murky water of the creek behind him. Nor was he aware of the axe descending on the back of his head in a deadly blurring arc. His sight of the exposed inspector exploded in a sheet of red. With a grunt he dropped the rifle from his nerveless fingers and the Snider clattered down the bank of the creek where it sank out of sight.

Gordon saw the giant Kalkadoon raise the axe again and realised immediately what its intended target was. 'No!' he screamed and his order was immediately obeyed.

The sun glistened on the water that ran from Terituba's muscled body as he stood over the unconscious body of the bushranger. Now Terituba was confused. Did he not have the right to kill an enemy they had hunted?

'Sergeant Johnson! Over here!' Gordon shouted as he heard the voices of the troopers calling to each other as they approached his position.

Terituba stood patiently over his victim and watched the troopers burst from the cover of the scrub with their rifles pointed forward. They lowered their weapons, however, when they saw the two bushrangers lying on the ground.

Sergeant Johnson holstered his pistol as he came to Gordon and stared at the dead bushranger face down in the dry grass. 'We got the other one,' he said.

'Dead?' Gordon asked.

'Shot to pieces,' he replied in a flat voice. 'You shoot this one?' he asked, and Gordon shook his head.

'Calder shot him.'

The sergeant frowned but made no comment. It made little sense for a man to shoot his mate.

As the two policemen gazed down at the body of Joe Heslop the Aboriginal troopers hauled the unconscious body of Calder onto the bank with little consideration for his injury. Calder groaned as he fought to regain his senses and his groan was answered with a savage kick to the ribs by one of the troopers. Gordon called on his men to leave the prisoner alone. He wanted him in a reasonably good condition to escort him to Rockhampton.

Sergeant Johnson and Gordon walked over to

where Calder lay on his back in the grass. Blood welled from the severe cut to the back of his head. When he finally opened his eyes they were glazed. His lips curled in a snarl which bared his teeth. 'James . . . You murderin' bastard. You had no cause to kill poor old Joe,' he sighed before he lapsed into blissful unconsciousness again.

'He's lying,' Gordon snapped. 'He killed Joe. Shot him in the back for no apparent reason.' The sergeant nodded his agreement but Gordon could read the doubt in his eyes. 'You got a doctor in town?' he asked, dismissing the accusation of murder.

'No. Nearest thing to a doctor around here is Missus Rankin at the Balaclava run,' he replied. 'She was a nurse before she married Humphrey.'

'I know him,' Gordon said. 'He's the manager. Also just happens that I know the owner of the property.'

'You know Missus O'Keefe?' Johnson asked.

Gordon nodded. 'She's not Missus O'Keefe anymore. Got herself married to a Yankee, by the name of Luke Tracy some years ago.'

'I got a message last year to keep a lookout for him,' Johnson stated. 'Appears he went missing somewhere up in the Gulf Country. I doubt that he would be still alive if he hasn't turned up by now.'

'Missus Tracy holds the same opinion. I suppose we better get Calder over to Balaclava, and see what Missus Rankin can do to keep him alive until we get him to Rockhampton.'

'Bit of a waste of time if you ask me,' Johnson growled. 'Considering what he's done. The bastard looks like real trouble.'

'Yeah, well by keeping him alive for a bit longer, he gets the chance to sweat about hanging.'

'Suppose you're right, sir,' Johnson agreed. 'We'll bring him around and put him on a horse. What about the fourth? The one that we started chasing back at Barcaldine?'

Gordon frowned. Poor Willie Harris, he thought. The news of his involvement in the Halpin murder would break Ben's heart. 'I will organise for another patrol to come out and search for him once I get to Rockhampton,' he said. 'But he's probably halfway to South Australia by now the way that horse of his could gallop.'

Gordon arranged for the items at the bushranger's camp to be gathered up. Amongst the items collected was evidence of the bushranger's raid on the Halpin homestead at Cloncurry. He also arranged with Sergeant Johnson to ride back to Barcaldine with Terituba and take Heslop's body to be buried there.

Terituba was now released from his duties and the young inspector instructed the sergeant to supply the Kalkadoon with a horse and supplies for his journey north. He wrote out a personal requisition to cover the costs and handed it over, with a promise that the formal paperwork would follow. Then Gordon approached Terituba who stood watching the proceedings of keeping the bushranger alive. None of it made much sense to him.

Gordon fully realised that had not the Kalkadoon tracker intervened when he did he would not be alive to extend his hand in gratitude.

'Thank you, Terituba,' he said. 'What you did was a brave thing. You could have easily been killed and your actions will be duly noted in my report.' Terituba accepted the extended hand and at the inspector's words of praise glanced down at the ground shyly. 'I do not understand why you did what you did when God knows you have no reason to risk your life for mine. For whatever reason, I am eternally grateful.'

Although Terituba's knowledge of English was limited he understood the emotion in the officer's voice. Nor could he understand why he had risked his life to save the whitefella except a spirit voice had told him to do so.

And so they parted – Terituba riding out with Sergeant Johnson for Barcaldine; Gordon riding east for the Balaclava property with the wounded Calder sitting groggily astride a mount, jammed between two troopers.

The irony of Terituba's courageous act was not lost on the young inspector as he rode east with his troop. Only a year earlier they had met in a struggle to kill each other. Now the same man who had permanently marked Gordon with his axe, had used the same weapon to save him.

Gordon's patrol was not alone in riding east. When Willie Harris came to from his drinking binge he found his horse grazing nearby. He pulled himself into the saddle and through a haze of rum fumes sought sanctuary from those who would search for him. He remembered Kate Tracy's stories of the hills of Glen View Station. Hills where very few people visited because of a supposed curse on them.

Willie turned east for Glen View where he would lay low until he could figure out a safe way to reach Sydney. He had very little left to do in his life except to meet the man who was his father and kill him. He had nothing to lose anymore. He fully knew that he was most probably facing the gallows should he ever be captured.

54

Granville smirked as he held up George Hobbs' statement to allow the ink to dry. 'You have done the right thing, Mister Hobbs,' he said to the frightened man sitting opposite him on the other side of Granville's desk. 'I know that you have a high regard for Captain Duffy but there are more important issues at stake than your misplaced loyalty.'

Hobbs did not reply. He felt that he would rather answer for his act of treachery in the next life than face the devil in this one. What matter that the rich fought their battles, when he was but a mere pawn in their games? At least Mister White had also provided a large sum of money to sweeten the treacherous act. He knew that his statement corroborating Granville's forged entries was damning. He could imagine the headlines of any newspaper that might run an article on the supposed allocation of monies to an organisation viewed by the government as hostile to the peace of the British Empire: HERO OF THE SUDAN A TRAITOR TO THE EMPIRE . . .

At least, Hobbs consoled himself, the news-papers would not be told of the entries. Mister White would probably just confront Captain Duffy with the false evidence. Captain Duffy would realise how a public disclosure of the accusations would bring a terrible scandal down on Lady Enid, even though he would know that the accusations were fabricated. But the captain was an astute man and his commonsense would prevail. Mister White had given his word as a gentleman that Captain Duffy would simply be asked to resign his position as head of the shipping department and be provided with a stipend so that he could pursue his interests in the colonial militia. The army was still his love and so drafting the document was probably the best thing he could do for the captain in the long run.

'You may leave, Mister Hobbs,' Granville said without looking at him. 'Just remember that your support on this matter will benefit not only you but also the future of the company. I am sure that under my management you may expect promotion.'

'Thank you, Mister White,' Hobbs mumbled as he rose and headed for the door. He closed the door and noticed a slight and nervous man stand-ing in the annexe with his hat in his hand. 'Mister Hobbs, isn't it?' the man said by way of greeting. George remembered who the man was. The realisation sickened. With his head down, he pushed past the man who stepped aside. Was Mister White's power so great in Sydney that he could induce Lady Enid's own newspaper to be part of the sickening conspiracy to besmirch the name of a true hero?

* * *

'Mister Larson, please take a seat,' Granville said as he rose and indicated the chair that had only just been vacated by George Hobbs. 'I wish I could say it is a pleasure to meet with you again but I am afraid that under the circumstances I have requested this meeting there is little pleasure in what I must tell you.' Larson took the seat and Granville felt a twinge of fear. Getting George Hobbs to cooperate he had known would be easy. He had known the man for many years and as such was aware that he was basically a weak man, easily swayed by the power of his betters. But the editor of Enid's newspaper was a different matter. In his late forties Mister Larson was a man with a reputation for integrity – an unusual characteristic for a newspaperman. But he was also known for his zeal in pursuing stories that might discredit the upper classes. It was this combination of integrity and zeal that Granville most wanted to work for him against Patrick Duffy.

'I received a message that you have a story for me concerning Captain Duffy?' Larson said bluntly. 'You do realise that I work for Lady Macintosh?'

Granville forced himself to appear calm. 'It is for that reason I decided to call you in rather than have any other journalist be the first to break the story.'

'What story, Mister White?' Larson asked.

Granville detected just the hint of a journalist's sudden interest in the scent of something worth a headline and began to relax. He knew how he would manipulate the meeting and win

Enid's own editor on his side.

'I am afraid the story concerning Captain Duffy is one that, no matter how much we would attempt to conceal the facts, would eventually get out. Knowing this I decided that you should be the first to know and somehow break the story with as little damage as possible to the reputation of Captain Duffy.'

'Any damage to Captain Duffy's reputation will also reflect on Lady Macintosh,' Larson replied with a frown. 'My position as chief editor with the paper won't be worth a penny.'

'I am aware of that,' Granville said. 'After the story concerning Captain Duffy is out I am sure the board of directors will insist on me taking charge of all the enterprises. And that includes the newspaper. I think you know what that will mean for your future.'

He could see that Larson was thinking very hard but not entirely convinced. It was time to tell the story.

'Recently George Hobbs brought a matter to me of grave importance. It seems he could no longer bear to be party to what appears to be Captain Duffy's rather treacherous acts.'

'With all respect, Mister White,' Larson scoffed. 'It's well known that George Hobbs has always been loyal to her ladyship. I find it hard to believe that he just suddenly decides to mention something that might embarrass her.'

'Would this convince you?' Granville said, sliding the now dry statement across the desk. Larson read the statement and Granville could see from the sagging of the newspaperman's jaw that he was almost convinced. 'Hobbs would corroborate these words?' Larson asked, holding up the paper.

'You can question him yourself,' Granville replied. 'As a matter of fact, I can have one of my men fetch him here, to do so if you wish.'

Larson shook his head.

'Hobbs mentions John O'Grady as the recipient of the payments,' Larson said quietly, as if chastened by what he had read. 'How does he know about O'Grady's subversive activities against the Crown?'

'I suppose he reads your paper to know that, Mister Larson,' Granville replied with a wry smile. 'We have all read about that Fenian's rabble rousing activities in Sydney to raise funds for his treacherous compatriots back in Ireland.'

'And Hobbs has dutifully recorded the payments, supposedly made by Captain Duffy?'

'Duffy underestimated Mister Hobbs' loyalty to the Crown,' Granville countered when he noticed a doubt cloud the astute newspaperman's face. 'He made a presumption that Hobbs's sense of loyalty to the family would be greater than his loyalty to the Queen.'

'It's all a bit circumstantial,' Larson said, toying with the hat in his lap. 'But I have a duty to investigate the story and publish the truth.'

'That is all I ask, Mister Larson,' Granville said with a smile. 'An act of treason cannot be dismissed – no matter who is involved.'

'I will talk to O'Grady,' Larson said as he rose to leave. 'If he confirms that he has been receiving regular amounts from a benefactor – amounts that correspond with those recorded in your ledgers – then I suppose I have no choice.'

Granville knew that the Fenian would unwittingly implicate Patrick. The payments had been made, at a financial cost to Granville, and duly appeared as from the mysterious benefactor only known as 'The Captain'.

Granville trusted the editor to have the ability to get at least that much out of the Irishman. Newspapermen were good at that sort of thing.

'Should I find that your accusations are founded in my investigation,' Larson said in parting, 'I will not publish the story until Captain Duffy returns from Africa. It is only fair that I hear his side of the story.'

'I would expect no less,' Granville replied, trying to hide his disappointment. 'I am sure that Captain Duffy will naturally refute his role in the affair.'

Larson did not reply but closed the door behind him. As much as he disliked White, from the knowledge that he had obtained over the years concerning the man's reputation for dabbling in seamy deeds, he had to admit the evidence would stand up in a court of law. Even if the courts were to find the man innocent, the mud would stick, and the conservative members of the Macintosh board insist on Granville White taking full control. Duffy would be out and her ladyship could not live forever.

Besides, being a man of integrity he was also a practical man, who knew that he would do his job, and let the facts lead where they may. At least he had granted Captain Duffy a chance to defend himself. Larson had been perceptive enough to note the bitter disappointment in White's face when he had informed him of the delay to any headline. That was at least a little satisfaction to the newspaperman who happened to like his boss, Lady Macintosh.

He left Granville White smirking at how easy it had been to discredit his hated enemy. With Duffy out of the business Enid had lost her most powerful ally against him. All it took was a little money and a reputation for absolute ruthlessness to achieve his aims.

Granville's smirk slowly evaporated as his carriage rattled along the streets bound for his sister's house. Despite his clever scheme to discredit Duffy he might still be thwarted by letters that had been brought to his attention by his solicitors this very day. It was a matter that must be sorted out if he was to consolidate his share of the Macintosh companies and only one person was standing in his way. The one person who had in the past denied him a son and heir.

The carriage rattled to a stop outside the darkened house. Granville stepped from the vehicle and glanced around nervously. Although the alcohol consumed at his club had fortified his courage he was skittish that Fiona might not be alone. He feared that his sister Penelope might be with her and Granville had long learned – and with good cause – to fear her. It did not take brute strength to be a dangerous adversary, just a fertile mind for plots and counterplots. Penelope had inherited that ability as had he.

When he rapped on the door he was met by a

sleepy and surly maid in her nightdress who was about to chide him for the unexpected and late visit. 'I am Mister Granville White,' he said arrogantly. 'And I have come to visit with my wife. So stand aside woman and allow me to pass.'

The sleep addled maid attempted to bar him but he brushed past her and in the process handed her his hat and cape. Confused, she accepted the items and he was gone before she could react any further. She glanced out the door to the carriage-man waiting patiently on the driver's seat. 'It's all right, love,' he said with a grin. 'Mister White is married to Missus White.'

She shrugged and shuffled back to her room. It was obvious from his means that the man was not some street ruffian and if he was visiting his wife then it was no concern of hers. Missus White was a guest of the Baron's house and her duty was to the Baron and the Baroness.

Granville found his wife in her room and she sat up as the door swung open. He was framed in the doorway against the light of the hall and instinctively Fiona drew the bed sheets around her chin. He entered and sat in a chair beside a chest of drawers in a corner of her room.

'What are you doing here, Granville?' she asked in a frightened voice.

'Oh, I thought you could guess the reason for my very rare visit to your boudoir,' he said with a slight slur.

She knew immediately he had been drinking. He was most dangerous when he was drunk! 'I want you to get out immediately,' she hissed.

But he only chuckled as he proceeded to light a

thin cigar. For a moment the flare of the match framed his sweat glistened face in the dim light of the room. 'You may be under my sister's roof, dear wife, but I am legally your husband with rights I can take any time I so desire. Remember that well.'

Fiona tightened her grip on the sheets and felt a wave of nausea well in her throat. Dear God! He had come to force his unwanted attentions on her!

'I have come to ask you why my daughters have turned against me,' he said in a menacing tone which did nothing to allay her panic.

'I do not know what you mean,' Fiona answered honestly. 'How can you say your daughters have turned against you when you haven't seen them in years?'

'Because both have rejected my offer to buy out their shares in the Macintosh companies. I received a letter today from Germany.'

Now Fiona was fully aware of her husband's reason for visiting her room. 'They are old enough to know what is best for them, Granville,' she replied. 'If they wish to retain their shares in the companies, then that is their prerogative.'

'You know damned well that they would have sold to me as their father. Unless they were advised otherwise.'

'I do not know what you mean,' Fiona lied.

'Damned liar of a whore,' Granville hissed back savagely. 'Dorothy has already written that she and Helen were advised by you not to sell to me.'

Fiona did not reply. She wondered if he was bluffing in an attempt to make her admit her lie. She had advised her daughters not to mention that she had requested them to retain their shares. Denial now would be fruitless – and silence less incriminating.

'Or did your mother write to them?' he pondered as he sucked on the cigar, filling the bedroom with the acrid smoke. 'I wouldn't put it past her.'

He had been bluffing, she thought with a rush of relief. Dorothy had not broken her confidence.

'No matter,' he brooded. 'I will take a trip to Germany after I arrange the sale of Glen View, and put my case to them.'

'You cannot sell Glen View,' Fiona said with a shock. 'The place is very special to my family.'

'Your family!' he exploded. 'Ha! You despise your mother and always told me you would do anything within your power to hurt her.' It was then that the thought crept to him that Lady Enid was not the only family she had. 'You mean that bastard son of yours, Patrick Duffy. Don't you? Is it that you plan to buy my daughters' shares yourself?'

Fiona felt the bile rising again in her throat. 'My protest is in regards to you selling the place where my brother and father are buried, Granville. Nothing more. But you would not understand a woman's sentimentality for such things.'

'My sister would,' he snarled. 'Do you discuss sentimental things when you are in bed together, dear wife? Or do you cry out with pleasure for the things she does to your body?'

Fiona felt her face burning as her husband suddenly turned on the most precious bond she had formed outside that for her children. A bond she did not expect anyone other than her gentle and passionate lover of many years to understand. 'What do you do to each other when you are in bed together?' he asked savagely. 'Do you . . .'

'Shut up, Granville,' she snapped. 'Shut your filthy mouth. As if you can talk. You with your penchant for young girls. Oh, I know all about your depraved ways. I know all about the girl, Jenny Harris, and how she bore you a son when she was only thirteen.'

Granville blanched at the mention of a subject he had thought she was unaware of and regretted goading her into the revelation. The ever-occurring thought of his wife in the arms of his own sister had almost driven him to the point of madness many times. 'Does your precious son know that his mother is a whore who sleeps with another woman?' Granville countered.

But Fiona was determined not to let him black-mail her. 'I doubt that anything else said about me could make him hate me anymore than he does now,' she retorted as Granville shrugged his shoulders. 'You might as well know,' she continued, 'I have made arrangements to take a passage to Germany at the end of the year to live permanently with Penelope and my daughters. Oh, and before you ask what Manfred thinks of the arrangement I can assure you he fully approves. You see, he is a real man.'

At the intended slur upon his manhood Granville rose from the chair and advanced on his wife. She tensed with an eruption of naked fear for the unbridled hate that filled the room and which threatened to explode in violence towards her. But he hesitated just as he was about to hit her. A mask-like smile loomed over her, an evil cunning emanated from her husband's face. 'You are not worth all the pain you have caused me,' he said in a controlled voice. 'I have ways of hurting you that you could not imagine in your worst nightmares.'

He backed away and turned for the open door. Fiona watched him leave, slamming the door after him. She lay in the dark too petrified to release her grip on the sheets around her chin. She knew her husband too well. His threat was not an idle one. Somehow she knew that his parting statement involved Patrick.

In the Great Australian Bight the *Lady Jane* fought the giant rolling black seas chilled by the currents of the Antarctic Ocean. Patrick Duffy stood on the deck, just as he had as a child sailing via the Cape of Good Hope for England with his grandmother many years earlier. The cracking of the hemp rigging securing the huge expanse of square canvas sails brought back many memories.

The bow of the graceful ship rose on a wave and slid with a terrifying falling speed into the trough below. She wallowed for just a moment as she fought off the seas which threatened to crash over the stern while the wind howled with an eerie banshee cry that reminded Patrick of his ancient Irish heritage. The furious winds soaked him in a fine mist of salty water but he cared little for the discomfort as he stood gripping the rails. For here in the vast loneliness of the ocean he could reflect on all that was his life. And in his pocket was the tiny stone goddess Sheela-na-gig.

The captain of the *Lady Jane* had informed him at dinner that night they would be docking in Port Elizabeth, God willing and the winds prevailing, within four weeks. Not soon enough for Patrick who had never thought he would return to Africa. And what would he do when he finally confronted his father who was now his competitor for the love of Catherine?

But the howling winds of the southern ocean gave him no answers and he turned away from the ship's rail to make his way cautiously down the rolling deck of the clipper. He would share a game of gin rummy and a bottle of whisky with the captain.

55

The last person Gordon believed he would ever see again was Sarah Duffy. She stood on the verandah of the Balaclava homestead staring at him with an enigmatic expression.

Astride his mount, and with his troopers and his prisoner in tow, he felt confusion race through his weary body like currents of electricity. His and Sarah's eyes met and he was aware of neither happiness – not that he would expect such a reaction – nor bitterness as he would also expect. Just an unfathomable depth to her eyes that said nothing.

'Dismount!' he ordered and the troopers slid gratefully from their saddles to stretch their tired bodies in the dusty yard that surrounded the homestead which was far grander than that of Glen View.

Sarah said nothing as she watched the troopers yank roughly at the white man who still remained in the saddle of his mount. His hands were manacled and he looked very ill. A bloody bandage was wrapped around the crown of his head under his hat.

Calder barely resisted the rough handling. He was indeed very ill from the blow to his head inflicted by Terituba's war axe and often over the two days that it had taken to reach the Balaclava property Gordon had thought that his death might cheat the hangman.

'Troopers here, Missus Rankin,' Sarah called inside the house.

Adele Rankin bustled onto the verandah to greet the visitors. She was dressed in similar manner to Sarah: a long dress caught tightly at the waist and plumed at the back with a bustle. Adele Rankin was in her late thirties although the desiccating effects of the Queensland sun had wrinkled her skin prematurely, but she had a pleasant and not unattractive face. 'I see you have an injured man, Inspector,' she called to Gordon as she recognised his rank. 'Bring him around the back to the kitchen.' Injured and wounded men, Aboriginal and European, were a regular sight at Balaclava and her reputation as a nurse was akin to that of a local doctor.

An Aboriginal trooper prodded the manacled man forward as Gordon opened the creaking gate and led the way down the narrow footpath of hard packed earth. As he walked towards the house he was aware of Sarah's eyes following him.

'The man is obviously your prisoner, Inspector,' Missus Rankin said as she poured water into an enamel basin by the tank stand at the back of the house. 'What has he done?'

'Killed a couple of men,' Gordon replied, without elaborating on the rape of the selector's wife as it would not gain anything to upset the kindly woman.

Calder leered at Sarah who had joined them. 'Get your eyes off her, you bastard,' Gordon growled.

'You planning on getting some of the darkie later, Inspector James,' Calder retorted crudely.

Gordon was sorely tempted to smash the man in the face with his fist but refrained. He did not want to risk injuring the man any further. *Better he lived longer to reflect on his fate at the end of a rope.*

Adele Rankin glared at Calder.

'Sorry, Missus,' he said with the flash of an apologetic grin.

'Sarah, fetch some clean rags from the house and bring me the medical chest,' Adele ordered as she peeled away the dirty bandage from the injured man's head to examine the wound. Very carefully she probed the hair matted with blood. 'Skull seems to be intact, not fractured.' Calder winced and swore as her probing fingers caused a fresh flow of blood. 'I'll stitch the wound. And that should keep him alive for you.'

'That's all he needs?' Gordon asked, somewhat surprised. 'Just stitching up?'

'That's all I can do,' she replied as she waited for Sarah to return with her medical chest. 'By the way, Inspector, you haven't introduced yourself,' she added with a frankness gained from working most of her life around men.

'I'm sorry, Missus Rankin. My name is Gordon James.'

'Gordon James,' she repeated and a look of hostility suddenly appeared in her expression. 'From Townsville way?'

'I was. But I'm stationed at Rockhampton now.'

'You're the man who was responsible for the killing of all those poor blackfellas up north last year. And I believe you know my governess, Miss Sarah Duffy.'

'Yes,' Gordon mumbled. 'To both your observations.'

'Then if that is so, you are no more welcome here than this man,' she said, indicating Calder.

'We had no intention of staying, Missus Rankin,' he replied politely. 'Just imposing on your skills as a medical person. We will leave as soon as you stitch up my prisoner.'

Sarah returned with a small wooden chest and refused to look at Gordon. Adele Rankin proceeded to clean the wound by cutting away at his hair. He complained bitterly but she told him to act like a man and shamed him into silence.

When she had completed her preparation work with the scissors she produced an evil looking needle from the chest and some cotton thread. 'Hold him,' she ordered the Aboriginal trooper who stood to one side, watching the proceedings with some curiosity. 'He's not going to like what I'm about to do.'

The trooper grasped Calder by the arms and hissed a threat in his ear. Between his strong grip and the whispered threat, however, the prisoner did not struggle and with great skill the former nurse stitched the wound. Tears of pain streamed from Calder's eyes but to his credit he did not attempt to struggle against the sharp point of the needle.

'There!' she said triumphantly when she had

finished. 'Almost done. I will just apply a clean bandage and then you can go, Inspector James.'

'Thank you, Missus Rankin. For what you've done.'

Adele repacked her medical chest and stared at Gordon. 'Nothing to thank me for. I would have even done the same for you, had you needed treatment,' she replied pointedly.

Her meaning was not lost on Gordon who guessed that Kate had informed Missus Rankin of him in some detail. It was no wonder she was so hostile, he thought morosely.

Missus Rankin then closed the lid on the medical chest and strode towards the house without further ceremony. For a brief moment Sarah stood uncertainly as Adele departed.

'Sarah,' Gordon choked, knowing it was he who must break the silence between them. 'Could we talk for a moment.'

'Gordon, I . . .' Sarah answered softly. 'I do not think we have anything to discuss.' She turned to stare at the house. 'I think I should see if Adele needs my help.'

'Please,' Gordon begged as he took her arm, aware that his troopers were staring curiously at their boss and the pretty half-caste girl. 'I would like you to just give me a couple of minutes . . . away from here,' he said with a nod of his head in the direction of his troop and steering her to the shade of a big gum on the far side of the yard.

Sarah did not resist and looked directly into his eyes without turning away. 'I came here to take up this position as Missus Rankin's governess so that I would be far away from the bitter memories that you caused in all our lives. It was Aunt Kate's suggestion that I take a position here. She thought I might be able to care for others and forget the pain that you brought to my life when you killed my brother.'

'I did not mean to kill Peter. You must know that,' Gordon said with a note of despair. 'I loved Peter as I would my own brother but the day it all happened events occurred beyond my control. I swear that if I could go back in time, I would have chosen to be the one who had to die, not Peter.'

Sarah felt his grip on her arm and saw the pain in his eyes. 'What do you mean "had to die"?' she asked. 'No-one "had to die" if you had not sought to continue with the Mounted Police.'

'It was always meant to happen,' Gordon answered with a plea for understanding in his eyes. 'Peter told me years ago what the ancestor spirits had told Wallarie. That he and I could never be friends in this life because of what my father had done to Wallarie's people before even your brother and I were born. That a blackfella destiny said one must kill the other in the future.'

For a moment Sarah felt as if she should tear herself away and scoff at his idiotic explanation, but she felt the intensity of his words. Did not Aunt Kate say that there were things beyond the world of light unexplainable to mortals? The good nuns who had taught her the catechism had also explained that some things in religion were mystical in their existence. So why could the beliefs of her mother's people not be equally accepted? Were they not older than the Christian beliefs of the white man? 'Do you truly believe that?' she asked. 'Do you believe that there is a power in the spirit of my Aboriginal heritage?'

'I do, Sarah,' Gordon answered sadly. 'I don't know why but I have come to believe that this land is different to anywhere else. It has a strange power that I think only the blackfellas know about.'

'And now you,' she said softly as tears welled in her eyes. 'I wish I could forgive you, Gordon James, and know that you accepted that part of me is rooted in the same soil as my mother's people. I could accept your grief for those things that live in the shadows of our lives if you could accept that I live between two worlds.'

'Sarah, I have always loved you,' he choked. 'But I was a fool and let my ambition cloud my feelings. I meant all that I said to you on the eve I rode out looking for Peter. What happened after that was beyond anything I could do to stop.'

The young woman's expression softened with her tears. 'It does not matter anymore,' she said bitterly. 'You and I can never be . . . even if we wanted to.'

'Why can't you and I be together?' Gordon asked in his confusion. 'I love you more than I have ever loved before.'

'Because I am betrothed to another and will be married within the month,' she sobbed as she broke away and ran to the house.

Stunned, Gordon watched her stumble away. To have killed Peter had been bad enough but to lose Sarah to another man felt worse. This was a living death for him.

* * *

Sarah did not bid Gordon farewell as he and his troop rode out of Balaclava. Instead she sat in her room and stared at the wood panelled wall. Why had life been so cruel as to allow her to see Gordon a month before she was to wed the young station manager from Penny Downs, the handsome, educated young Englishman Charles Harper esquire, who had wooed her and accepted her exotic beauty?

They had met when she had accompanied Adele Rankin on a trip to the property six months earlier. The courting had been gentle, his love declared and the bitter, sad memories of Gordon almost gone from her mind. But now Gordon had returned and she could see the love and pain in his eyes. What would it take to end the confusion she felt?

Gordon returned to Rockhampton with his prisoner. True to his word he drafted a letter of resignation and admitted to himself that he would miss the adventurous life of the Mounted Police. But he also consoled himself that the woman he had left behind at Balaclava Station was worth the sacrifice.

The ink was dry on the paper and Gordon marched smartly across the dusty parade ground to his commander's office. He stood outside the door and took a deep breath before knocking.

'Enter,' the voice boomed from within, and Gordon stepped inside to snap a salute to the seated officer. 'Inspector James,' Superintendent Stubbs frowned. 'I was just about to send for you.'

Gordon felt a touch of uneasiness from the

expression he read in the officer's face. Stubbs was unlike his compatriot in Townsville, Gales. Stubbs was an intense man in his late thirties with a face that never knew a smile. His frown was as close as Gordon could remember to the man ever changing expressions.

'You wanted to see me, sir?' he queried and Stubbs stood up. He was also a tall lean man who seemed to bow in the middle.

'That man Calder you brought in yesterday,' he asked. 'Did he make any implications to you that he was going to make a formal complaint, that you shot down his companion when he surrendered to you?'

Now it was Gordon's turn to frown.

'No, sir.' But Gordon hesitated and remembered something he thought was of no consequence at the time and added, 'He did babble something about me murdering his mate. But it was just nothing more than a malicious slur against me by a bitter man.' Stubbs now had another expression on his face. This time it was akin to pain. He turned away from his junior officer and seemed deep in thought as Gordon stood stiffly with the letter of resignation in his hand.

'Were there any witnesses to his accusation at the time?' Stubbs asked, without turning to face Gordon.

'The sergeant from Barcaldine was with me.'

'Was the sergeant with you when you captured Calder, and this dead man, Heslop?'

'The sergeant was with me when I took Calder, although he did not see Calder shoot Heslop.' As Gordon answered the question he felt a sick knot of bile rising up in his throat. He had been a policeman long enough to know what the superior officer was alluding to. 'I didn't kill Heslop, sir. Calder shot his own man, either by accident or deliberately.'

Stubbs turned and met Gordon's eyes directly. 'You realise that a formal complaint of murder has been made against you by Calder, and that I will have to make a full investigation of the matter.'

'Sir?'

'I do not relish the task and have no doubts that the man is lying,' Stubbs continued in a reassuring tone. 'I have not known you for long, but what I have seen of your service to the Queen, I am sure you are a good police officer. I will require only that you remain at your post and that you do not leave the Rockhampton district until I complete my report on the matter.'

'I was going to tender my resignation,' Gordon said, holding out the paper to the superintendent. 'I was hoping to give my notice and return to Townsville.'

Stubbs eyed the offered paper. 'I am afraid that if I accept your resignation at this stage, Inspector James,' he said, without making any attempt to accept it, 'it would appear that you were looking for a way out of this rather distasteful matter.'

Gordon withdrew his hand. He knew that his superior was right. 'My reasons for resigning have nothing to do with Calder's accusations,' he said. 'My reasons were of a personal nature, sir.'

'The reasons are irrelevant. What is relevant is that you must remain, until we satisfy a magistrate that you did not shoot down an unarmed man surrendering to you. Until then, you will remain a policeman.'

'Yes, sir,' Gordon dutifully replied. 'Is there anything else, sir?'

'No, Inspector,' Stubbs said dismissing the young police officer. 'Just keep your head low and do your job.'

Gordon saluted and left the office. Why had Calder killed his own mate and accused him of the crime? The answer was simple. Because Calder wanted his company in hell, after he'd been duly hanged. Some men were prepared to sell their souls for revenge and Gordon was acutely aware that the matter could very easily go against him. If so, then Calder would have his company on the gallows.

56

Almost a quarter of a century had passed since Kate had set foot on the muddy banks of the Fitzroy River at Rockhampton. Much had changed in those intervening years. The town had lost its raw, frontier atmosphere and now had a feeling of staid conservatism. Banks, shops, schools, churches and even a hospital had been established in the town to cater for the families of the second wave of settlers who had followed in the wagon tracks of the first pioneers.

Gone were the ironbark slab hotels where thirsty shepherds came to drink and forget the fear and isolation their lonely occupations entailed. And gone also was the sight of the Kennedy Men, the tough, bearded young bushmen of the wild frontier, who had once ridden their horses recklessly down the dusty or muddy – depending on the time of year – streets of the settlement. Rockhampton was now a vital commercial town, catering to central Queensland's well-established cattle and sheep industry.

Kate noticed the changes with a mixture of

nostalgia for things lost and pleasure for seeing the settlement turn into a town where young families could find a permanency in their lives, a way of life unlike her own tragic early years of loss and transition. Rockhampton held many memories for her. It was here that her first child was buried. It was in Rockhampton too that she had met the strong and gentle American prospector Luke Tracy. And it was here she had cemented a lifetime friendship with the Jewish storekeeper, Solomon Cohen and his wonderful wife, Judith.

Kate sat in the office of the man who had once been her lover. But he had betrayed her to the financial interests of the powerful squatter Sir Donald Macintosh. Hugh Darlington's office had changed very little – but Hugh Darlington had. Gone was the suavely handsome young lawyer and across the desk sat a fat, balding man, hardly recognisable to Kate as the man she had once known. His rising career in Queensland politics as a member of the colonial parliament along with the wealth he had accrued representing the interests of squatter clients had put a lot of good food on Hugh's table.

Kate also knew he had married and had five children. She could not help comparing him with Luke who had remained at the peak of physical condition to the end of their married lives. Seeing Hugh Darlington now she truly appreciated the choice she had made in marrying a man whose lean and hard body had taken her to the heights of sensual ecstasy countless times.

Hugh Darlington's continuing unabashed

admiration of Kate was evident in the way he stared at her. Her slim waist and beautiful face had remained despite the years that had intervened in their respective lives. And her eyes still had the same magic appeal he first remembered. *Ah but that he had the time over again!*

'Kate, you haven't changed a bit,' he said with a sigh.

She smiled. 'And your charm is still there, Hugh,' she replied diplomatically.

'I'm just glad you haven't got a glass of champagne in your hand,' he said with a grin. 'If I remember rightly, you have a habit of spilling good champagne on people who upset you. When was that? '74, '75?'

'I think it was '75,' Kate answered as she recalled the incident.

It had been in an elegant restaurant in Cooktown during the Palmer River gold rush. French Charley's, the restaurant had been called, and she had just learned that the man she had thought was working in her legal interests was, in fact, working for her arch enemy Sir Donald Macintosh. The revelation had sparked her fiery temper and she had poured a flute of expensive champagne over him.

'I'm sorry events turned out as they did,' he said, with a touch of sadness in his voice. 'I think my ambitions for power lost me something far more valuable.'

'Time and lost opportunities go hand in hand, Hugh,' she said softly. 'But time is also a healer of old wounds.'

'You are dangerous when you are nice, Kate,' he

said teasingly, the old Hugh Darlington still living in his words and the way he delivered them. 'You must want something more than my company.'

She smiled at his perceptiveness. 'I must admit, I made the appointment to see you for reasons other than idle curiosity,' she replied. 'I believe you are still the legal representative here for the Macintosh interests.'

'I am,' he answered. The Macintosh companies extended from central Queensland with Glen View to the coast at Mackay with its sugar plantations and meatworks. They also included coastal shipping which reached out to the Pacific islands. 'And I have a pretty good idea that you have heard Glen View is on the market.'

'Yes. As you're the solicitor for Mister Granville White, I thought that I might approach you and tender my offer to buy the property.'

'Before you go any further and waste your time I should inform you that while he was alive Sir Donald made it very plain that no Duffy would ever own his property.'

'Sir Donald is dead,' she countered. 'Surely business is business.'

'Is it business for you to be buying Glen View, Kate?' he cautioned. 'Or is the purchase motivated by emotion for what the property means to you personally?'

'It should not matter to the vendor the motivations of the purchaser,' she answered, without addressing his question directly. 'I would have thought any generous offer would be considered.'

The solicitor pursed his lips and steepled his fingers under his chin. The woman was right about business being business. Possibly the new owner of the property, Mister Granville White, may not hold the same prejudice as his deceased father-in-law. 'I cannot promise anything, Kate. But I will raise the offer at the appropriate time with Mister White, but not as your representative, as you must appreciate.'

'I fully understand. I can have my solicitors in Townsville draft an offer to be forwarded to you.'

'Then I think we can dispense with any further discussion on the matter and use our time to talk about more pleasant subjects,' he said as he relaxed and smiled.

Kate's unexpected reappearance in his life had brought with it a tension he had almost forgotten she could cause in him – a physical tension of heightened desire. Although he was a married man with a family, Hugh Darlington still retained his philandering ways and whenever he was in Brisbane attending parliamentary matters indulged himself in discreet dalliances with ladies willing to share his growing fame as a leading figure in colonial politics. He was a man tipped to be the future premier of the colony and power was an aphrodisiac women understood. But to Kate his power and wealth held little appeal. She was a woman who commanded an equal appeal when it came to power and wealth.

'It just occurred to me, Kate, that you might not be aware of recent dramatic events concerning an incident at Barcaldine some weeks ago,' Hugh said. 'Your friend Emma James' son, Inspector Gordon James, is currently under suspicion of wilful murder.'

Kate's eyes widened in surprise at the news. *Gordon under suspicion of murder!* 'What are you talking about?' she asked in a shocked voice. 'What murder?'

'It appears that he was involved in a rather violent attempted arrest of three men during the course of which two of the men were shot dead. The third has accused Inspector James of shooting down his unarmed partner in cold blood when the man attempted to surrender. Not that the man accusing the Inspector has much credibility in the opinion of most people. But since the publicity surrounding the Wheeler affair the Native Mounted troopers have made a lot of powerful enemies in the colonies. Not only down south but around here as well. A lot of well-intentioned, if misguided, people would like to see a conviction of any kind against an officer of the Native Police. It seems there has been some pressure to bring the young man before the courts.'

Kate knew of Frederick Wheeler. He had been an officer of the Native Mounted Police who the authorities had attempted to bring to justice for his barbaric crimes against not only the native tribes but also his own Aboriginal troopers. They had failed and Wheeler had disappeared as a free man.

'Gordon James is a lot of despicable things,' Kate said, 'but I doubt that he is a murderer.'

'I suspect that you are right,' Hugh agreed, 'knowing as much as I do about his courageous stand against the Kalkadoon last year at Cloncurry. And I also suspect that a coronial inquiry will find he has no case to answer. The matter will be seen for what it is: a grudge by a vexatious criminal against a fine young officer. Then the matter will be dropped.'

'I wish I could feel as certain as you,' Kate replied hesitantly. 'It is as if there was a curse on Gordon.'

'I doubt that the matter has anything to do with a curse,' the solicitor scoffed. 'More like the liberals looking for a scapegoat.'

Kate was not so sure. The events of Gordon's life had led him on such a path of destruction and she was well aware that forces existed outside the acceptance of most men. Strange forces, with the power to reach out and touch with a hand of vengeance those who would disturb the fragile fabric of the ancient land of the continent's original inhabitants. Gordon's father had been a party to waking the ancient spirits guarding the sacred places of the Darambal people and now his son followed in his father's footsteps, hunting the Aboriginal tribesmen. The unexplainable mystical forces seemed to touch them all in one way or another. They led back to the horrific dispersal of the Nerambura clan so many years earlier, the violent death of her father, the deaths in the Macintosh family and the many other untimely and violent deaths since then. No, the power of the ancient spirits was a real and ever-present curse, she reflected.

'There are some things one should not scoff at, Hugh,' she said softly. 'Things in this world we cannot explain with pure logic.'

'Like the mind of a woman,' he retorted with a smile. 'You are certainly creatures unlike us men with all your superstitious belief in the unknown.'

'We accept the unknown for the fact that it is just that. Unknown,' she answered seriously. 'But we women do not have to have you men accept our beliefs and hold them as our realities.'

'Very well put. I bow to your beliefs, even if they make little scientific sense to educated men of reason.'

'But I will accept that Gordon must be prepared to defend himself with your educated reason,' Kate said as she shifted her thoughts back to the world of courts, juries and judges. 'If Gordon does not have legal representation he could be facing imprisonment. Or worse. Death by hanging if the matter goes badly for him.'

'So you are going to fight your mystical curse with temporal logic and reason then,' Hugh said with a hint of sarcasm. 'To utilise a mere man to save Inspector Gordon.'

She flared at his cynicism but refused to be baited. 'I did not say that I do not believe in the powers of this world, Hugh,' she bridled. 'I realise that you have the means to prepare Gordon for an inquiry with your considerable expertise in matters pertaining to the law.'

'Thank you, Kate,' he replied. 'Your trust in my earthly abilities humbles me.'

'You and I may have had our differences, Hugh,' she said quietly. 'But I do know you are one of the best lawyers in the colony, otherwise Sir Donald would not have chosen you to represent his interests. If nothing else, Sir Donald was a very astute man.'

'You realise that I cannot approach Inspector James to solicit him as a client . . . ethical issues you know.'

'I realise that,' she replied. 'I will visit Gordon and suggest that he make an appointment to see you. That is, if he has not already approached anyone else in your profession.'

'There is a matter of fees,' the solicitor said, a reminder that his skills came at a price. 'And, I would think, they will be high, considering the case.'

'I will pay them, no matter what it costs,' Kate accepted. 'And I would expect you to spare nothing in ensuring that the matter goes no further than an inquiry.'

'No promises there, Kate. Except that I will do the best money can buy.'

When Kate had excused herself from the lawyer's office, she wondered why she had been so quick to assist the young man who had killed her nephew. But, after all, he was the son of her dear, departed friend Emma and as such it was only right that she help him. But the real answer came down to the intangibles of life: the love she knew Sarah still inexplicably harboured for the man.

Kate unfurled her parasol as protection against the tropical sun and walked back along the dusty street to her hotel. Admiring glances from men sitting under the shade of the wide verandahs along the main street followed the progress of the woman who carried herself with the regal bearing of a queen. A few who recognised her whispered that she was Kate O'Keefe who had once worked as a barmaid in the Emperor's Arms hotel. Kate had travelled a long, hard road with nothing more than a dream and the courage to challenge the traditionally chauvinistic world of business. And in the end she had won.

57

When Gordon James gazed out of the recently installed glass window of his office he could see the same dusty parade ground where his father had once drilled the Aboriginal police. It had been convenient for the local district superintendent of police to transfer Sub Inspector James from Cloncurry to Rockhampton and keep him in gainful employment around Rockhampton until the inquiry into the allegations against him could be dismissed.

The superintendent was in no doubt that Inspector James was innocent but he also realised that justice had to be seen to be done. The arrest of Calder had attracted too much damned publicity. It was no secret that there were powerful enemies of the Native Mounted Police who would dearly love to see the unit disbanded. There had been many accusations over the years of wanton killings carried out against the myalls.

The bleating sheep from down south, he had snorted. Europeans with no idea of how treacherous and vicious the Queensland blackfella was!

And the misguided fools pointed to the Native Mounted Police as the instruments of their systematic destruction. The superintendent was the darling of the handful of ruthless and powerful squatters who feted him as a hero for his efforts in defending their rights to clear the land of the black vermin. As such he had always supported his police against the accusations levelled against them of indiscriminate murder.

But there was an election scheduled and not all the squatters supported the actions of the police. Some of the misguided squatters actually lived in peace with the local tribesmen on their properties, and even went as far as attempting to bar the Native Mounted Police from entering their land. Their voice was being listened to by the bleating sheep down south and it fuelled the fire to have Gordon James face an inquiry. To make matters worse, that the accused inspector of police had a fine record of service mattered little to the newspapers.

Gordon had been formally informed of the allegations levelled against him and was also reassured that nothing would come of them. He was not so sure. Nothing much seemed to be going right in his life, although he appreciated the superintendent's unshakeable faith in him and accepted the temporary posting to Rockhampton until the outcome of the coroner's inquiry.

Gordon was standing in his office, staring out the window at the empty parade ground and pondering the events of his life when he heard a buggy rumble to a stop outside. A woman spoke to one of the Aboriginal troopers. She was asking his whereabouts and if he didn't know any better he would have sworn the woman sounded like Kate Tracy!

He opened the door and when he did he was astonished to see that it was in fact Kate.

'Gordon,' she said with stiff formality. 'I have come to see you.'

'Come in, Missus Tracy,' he replied, as he held open the door and allowed her to brush past him.

He followed her and pulled out a chair. Kate nodded politely and sat down gracefully. She could see that her unannounced visit had flustered him. He seemed ill at ease and confused at what he should do or say as he stood awkwardly behind his desk. 'You could get one of your men to bring us tea, Gordon,' she said quietly. 'I am rather thirsty from the trip out to your barracks.'

'Certainly,' he replied gratefully. 'Trooper Alma!' he bellowed.

'Mahmy.' The trooper who had been sweeping the verandah in front of his office replied and hurried to the door to stand stiffly at attention, awaiting his orders.

'Fetch Missus Tracy and myself a cup of tea quick smart. You hear?'

'Yes, Mahmy. Quick smart.'

When the Aboriginal trooper scuttled away to fetch a billy of tea from the barrack's communal kitchen, Gordon sat down. 'I am somewhat surprised to see you here, Missus Tracy,' he frowned.

'I happened to be in Rockhampton on a matter of business,' Kate replied coldly, 'when I was informed of your current circumstances. I was told that you have been accused of killing a man you were attempting to arrest.'

'I didn't murder him,' he replied angrily. 'He was shot in the back by that lying bastard Calder.'

'I didn't say you did,' Kate rebuked.

'I'm sorry if I sounded angry,' Gordon said quietly in his remorse. 'It's just that nothing much has gone right for me – as you well know.'

Kate appraised the young man's appearance and noticed that his uniform was crumpled. He usually had a smartly turned-out appearance, she remembered. He looked tired and washed out. She almost felt a twinge of pity for him. 'You are no doubt wondering why I have driven all the way out here to see you, when you know that my visit isn't motivated by any love for you. Or what you have done to Sarah and myself.'

'I was curious,' he answered in a tired voice.

'I came out to see if you have thought about legal representation for the coroner's inquiry.'

'No. I didn't think I would need any representation. Only my statement as to the facts.'

'Well, I think the way things are going in your life, you should consider approaching a solicitor for help. And to that extent I have one in mind. A Mister Hugh Darlington who has an office in Rockhampton.'

'I know of him,' Gordon said. 'He's the local member for the electorate. But I doubt that I could afford his fees.'

'I am looking after any costs,' Kate said.

Gordon looked at her sharply. He was stunned by her completely unexpected generosity and unsolicited help. 'You would help me? After all

573

that I have done to you?'

'Not for my sake,' she replied softly. 'But out of respect for your dear parents' memory. And for Sarah.'

'Sarah?'

'Yes, for Sarah's sake. It would devastate Sarah if you were hanged. I can see from the way your mouth is gaping,' Kate added, 'that my statement comes somewhat as a surprise to you concerning Sarah.'

'I . . . I . . . Yes,' he stuttered, as he tried to gather his thoughts and feelings into some logical form to answer. 'Why would Sarah be concerned about whether I lived or died? She is, after all, engaged to another.'

'Probably because she has never really stopped loving you, Gordon,' Kate answered with a sigh. 'She has always loved you and she could love no other man, as far as I can see. That love has been badly hurt by your actions but it still remains, although she does not speak of it.'

'Then how could you know?'

'I just do. I have known Sarah just about all her life and I know, as a woman, another's feelings for a man, even one as worthless as you. It's a weakness that afflicts women . . . to love a worthless man at some time in our lives.'

Gordon glanced down at his desk. Kate's statement, he guessed, was based on her first marriage to Kevin O'Keefe. He did not know that she also reflected on her affair with the solicitor she had recommended to him. His hands trembled and Kate was quick to see that her divulgence of what she instinctively knew of her niece's hidden feel-

574

ings for the young policeman had caused him an emotional reaction she had not expected. But she wondered if she could ever forgive him. It did not matter how she felt about Gordon James. What did matter was what Sarah felt for Gordon ... and he for her.

'I do not deserve Sarah,' he whispered, and Kate could see tears welling in his downcast eyes. 'I do not have the right to beg for forgiveness for all that I have done to you ... and Sarah. That I could give my life for Peter's, and still retain Sarah's love, I would.'

'I think you truly mean what you say, Gordon,' Kate said gently as she reached out to touch his clasped hands. 'I have never known you to lie.'

He glanced up at her and she knew she was right. His eyes were filled with tears and a terrible pain. Gordon reminded Kate of his father, so many years ago. She had been younger then and the big police sergeant had also begged for her forgiveness.

Trooper Alma was surprised when he peered into the office and saw the tough young inspector unashamedly weeping. Embarrassed and self-conscious for his mahmy's sorrow he crept away with the two steaming mugs of tea.

The following day Gordon sat in Hugh Darlington's office. Hugh made a sucking noise through his lips as he stared down at the statement of facts that the policeman had written outlining the events of the death of Joe Heslop.

'Tell me, Inspector,' he finally said when he

glanced up at the young man sitting very still in his chair. 'Where on the deceased's body did the bullet enter?'

'His back,' Gordon replied as if the fact was self-evident from his statement.

'And, at the time Mister Heslop was shot, what sort of firearm were you carrying?'

'A .45 calibre single action Colt, army model,' Gordon answered.

'And Mister Calder? What kind of weapon did he have when he was arrested?'

'A Snider .577 calibre carbine.'

'Did the bullet exit Mister Heslop's body when he was shot?'

'No,' Gordon replied and added hesitantly, 'I don't think so.'

'Where is the body of Mister Heslop now?' the solicitor asked, as if conducting a cross-examination in a court of law.

'He was buried at Barcaldine.'

Hugh leant back in his chair with a triumphant expression on his face. 'And what sort of bullet would we be likely to find in Joe Heslop's corpse if we exhumed him?'

'A .577 Snider round,' Gordon replied in an awed voice as the obvious dawned on him. 'A bloody carbine round!'

'I think Missus Tracy will be up for the costs of a trip to Barcaldine to start with. And the costs of a visit from Brisbane of an acquaintance of mine who just happens to be a former army surgeon major with a considerable wealth of experience in battle wounds and bullets.'

Gordon smiled for the first time in weeks.

58

So much of what Patrick Duffy saw of the countryside from the window of his carriage reminded him of the outback of his own country. Even the taciturn Boer farmers were like their *Rooinek* brothers in Australia – conservative men who lived by the unforgiving rules of nature's unpredictable moods and whose bearded faces concealed the disdain they held for the city people.

His journey had taken him through the fertile plains on the coast, over the range of mountains that ran as a craggy spine from Cape Town in the south-west to the Transvaal in the north-east, and onto the beginning of the veldt of the western province of the Cape Colony. He had marvelled at the similarities of the country that even shared the seasons with his own country. Not the cold, snow-bound Christmas season of the motherlands of Holland and England for the white inhabitants of southern Africa, but the hot, dry Yuletide Australians also experienced.

And even at the hotel in De Aar where Patrick now swigged on a cool beer, he felt that he could have easily been standing at the bar in Bourke or Walgett. Except that the European patrons spoke a guttural language, not unlike German which Patrick had a reasonable understanding of. He was the only non-Afrikaans speaking patron in the bar and was pleased that at least the publican was an Englishman. A big and burly man with a beefy red face, he appeared more than capable of handling any Boer who should take offence at his heritage as one of the perceived oppressors of the fiercely independent, Dutch descended farmers.

De Aar had been the starting point recommended by Colonel Godfrey for Patrick to commence his search for his father. It was the town where Michael Duffy was known to report to his Foreign Office contact from time to time.

The Boer patrons scowled at the tall young *Rooinek* amongst them and Patrick could feel their hostile eyes on his back as he stood at the bar. He had come from the railway station to the hotel he would use as a base for his search for his father – and Catherine. But he was beginning to regret his choice of accommodation. The mutterings from the patrons included a few derogatory words, particularly from five big, bearded men who sat around a table in the corner of the main bar room drinking gin.

'Might be an idea if'n you drink in the saloon bar, mate,' the beefy publican said quietly, as he sidled down the bar wiping the counter. 'These boys have been drinkin' since early this mornin' an' they're not real happy to see an Englishman here. This is what they consider their pub.'

'I'm not English,' Patrick replied, loudly enough

for the Boer patrons to hear him. 'I'm an Australian.'

'Don't matter to this mob, mate,' the publican warned. 'Anyone who speaks English is English.'

Patrick accepted the man's wise advice and retreated tactfully to the adjoining saloon bar. He had barely stepped into the tiny adjoining room when his attention was caught by a large painting on the wall. It was of a beautiful woman reclining naked on a couch. With stunned shock Patrick gaped at the face of Catherine Fitzgerald smiling back at him.

He called to the publican. 'That painting, how did you come by it?'

The publican gave him a suspicious look. 'Why do you want to know?'

'Because I would like to meet the man who painted it.'

'If you want to buy the painting you can,' the publican replied with a hint of mercenary cunning. 'Might help me recover the cost of the bar bill he still owes me.'

'How much?'

'Twenty quid. English,' he said quickly. 'Worth every penny. She's a beautiful drop of crumpet.'

'Twenty pounds, and you tell me where I find the man who painted her.'

The publican suddenly became evasive. The Australian was prepared to buy the painting for twice as much as what the big Irishman had owed. Come to think of it, he mused to himself, the Australian looked as if he could be the man's son such was the likeness between the two. 'You know Michael Duffy?' he asked quietly so that he might not be overheard by his patrons in the adjoining main bar.

'My name is Patrick Duffy. I'm his son,' Patrick replied as he attempted to restrain his rising excitement. *Of all the hotels he had walked into . . .*

'You got any proof of that?' the beefy man asked belligerently and Patrick realised with dawning certainty that the man was probably his father's contact. Why not? A man would not arouse suspicion dropping in for a beer in the very heart of Boer territory itself. From what he had learned of his father from others, it was in Michael Duffy's nature to suicidally push the limits of his luck. 'Look at me closely,' he growled softly. 'They say I'm the image of my father. Is that not proof enough?'

The man nodded and grinned. 'Yeah. Put an eye patch over one eye an' you could pass as 'im twenty years on,' he said. 'If yer lookin' for yer father you'll probably find 'im camped out 'bout ten miles from here on the track to Prieska. He's camped by a drift, I last heard. Has a wagon and supplies. That's about all I can tell ya.'

'Does he have a young woman, the one in the painting, with him?'

'As I said,' the publican reiterated, 'that's all I can tell ya.'

'Thanks. Now where do I get a horse and supplies around here?' Patrick asked as he counted out twenty English pounds from a substantial wad. The publican told him, licking his lips at the sight of the new notes placed in his hand. The publican called after him as Patrick was leaving,

'What about the painting you bought from me?'

'I'll pick it up when I return,' he called back over his shoulder. 'Keep it safe for me until then.'

Patrick had made only one mistake in his dealing with the publican. He had presumed the man was his father's contact. In fact, the publican did not particularly like the Irishman as he had a suspicion that the man was dealing in guns with the Boer patrons of his establishment. Not that he asked any questions.

'Hey, Englisher,' the oldest of the men who had expressed hostility at Patrick's presence in their hotel called to the publican. 'That *Rooinek*, he buy Katerina, ja?'

'Yeah, Lucas,' he answered. 'Paid off his old man's debts.'

'Herr Duffy! Das is the *Rooinek*'s father, ja?' the older Afrikaner asked. He glanced at his companions and said in Afrikaans, 'The Englishman who was just here has the smell of a soldier about him.'

Lucas Bronkhorst knew much about English soldiers. Five years earlier he had been in the final assault against the Scots' battalion occupying the rocky, treeless heights of Majuba Hill. The Afrikaner victory against the British that day had been an overwhelming success for Boer tactical skills.

His four companions nodded their agreement. Lucas Bronkhorst threw a handful of coins on the bar to pay for their drinks and the men at the table rose to join him. They would follow the *Rooinek* and learn more about him. To do so might tell them more about the Irishman who had sold them the German Mauser rifles. *Rifles that proved to be inherently faulty!*

It seemed to the Afrikaners that Duffy was in league with the British intelligence services active in the Cape Colony and the appearance of the young *Rooinek* seemed to confirm Bronkhorst's suspicions. First, they would question them both when the young *Rooinek* met with the older one. Then they would probably have to kill them.

Patrick was blissfully unaware of the interest his presence in the town had caused the Boer farmers. He was able to ride out of town with a horse of dubious qualities, and lead a pack horse of even less merit. He rode west along a track that was marked by the flattened grass of the sweeping savanna plains and undulating hills laden with seas of waving grass pastures. He passed only native families who trekked to their distant kraals and could not help but admire the proud bearing of the dark people he met as he rode along the track to Prieska. Tall, well-built men with jet black skins, wide-eyed children on their mother's backs who sucked thumbs and stared at the Australian high above them on his horse.

But the same people would stare with open fear as they passed the party of fifteen heavily armed men who rode as a column a mile behind the solitary horseman leading a pack horse. The Boer commando kept far enough back to remain out of sight of Patrick but close enough to keep him in sight from the rises in the land.

Just on sunset Patrick rode onto a rise and from his vantage point looked down on a meandering stream of muddy water that cut the grassy plains like a giant brown snake. He could see the tiny figures of two oxen grazing on the lush grass, a wagon and a man kneeling in the stony bed of the stream washing dishes. He appeared to be alone and without being able to distinguish the finer detail of the man Patrick sensed that he was seeing his father for the second time in his life. He remembered with a flood of memories a big one-eyed American who had given him a silver dollar when he was a young boy growing up in Sydney. The same man had sworn him to keep their meeting a secret from his Uncle Daniel.

With a gentle kick he spurred his horse down the gentle slope. The man rose to his feet and watched the horseman riding slowly down the hill.

Michael Duffy instinctively rested his hand on the butt of the big Colt pistol at his hip. *All visitors in his life were potential enemies.*

59

The sun was warming another hot day along the latitude of the Tropic of Capricorn and Kate kept her parasol near at hand as her luggage was loaded aboard the steamer. When she was satisfied that all her luggage was stored she turned her attention to Gordon James whose uniform, she noticed, was pressed and clean. Few people were present to see the coastal steamer depart for Townsville and only a few horse-drawn drays and the bearded men who tended them witnessed the departure.

A small huddle of Aboriginals were also present, dressed in the cast-off clothes of white civilisation. They squatted on the river bank, begging listlessly for tobacco or any spare coins. Kate cast the once proud Darambal people of the Fitzroy region a look of pity. She had an empathy for the people who bore the blood of her niece and to see them reduced to begging was upsetting.

'I suppose you will be looking forward to getting home to baby Matthew,' Gordon said when he saw Kate gazing wistfully at a naked Aboriginal toddler playing in the mud of the river bank.

'It seems such a long time since I last held him,' she sighed. 'And I wonder if he will recognise his mother when she returns.'

'I think so,' he replied with a gentle smile. 'Parents aren't forgotten.'

'Nor are children,' she said.

He understood her inference, and stared across the river at a flight of pelicans skimming the water. Kate could see that his attention was on other things than her departure and this was confirmed when he said quietly,

'After the exhumation at Barcaldine I will ride to Balaclava. I pray that you are right in what you say about Sarah's feelings towards me.'

'I am sure she will be able to forgive you, Gordon,' Kate said quietly, as she gazed into his face. 'Love is far more powerful than hate. Oh, I know that is easy to say. But it has been my personal experience that love will persist, despite all the hardships in our lives.' And with bitter-sweet memories she thought about the years that had separated her from the strong and gentle American prospector. Long and lost years, she regretted, during which she had not admitted her love for the man. 'Life is far too short to squander our time on worrying about what might happen,' she added with a simple philosophy.

Gordon hung his head then glanced away from Kate at the Aboriginals on the river bank. 'I have done a terrible thing to Sarah,' he finally said in a whispered voice. 'I really wonder if she can forgive me and I do not blame her for seeking another's love.'

'She loves you with her body and soul,' Kate answered softly. 'And it matters not that she is betrothed to another if you are prepared to fight for her love. I know Sarah needs you in her life and until I met with you a week ago, I might not have supported her unspoken love for you. But I saw in your eyes the depth of your pain – and that you have changed.'

'I'm leaving the police as soon as the inquiry is over, one way or the other,' he added with bitter determination.

'I doubt that you have anything to fear from the findings,' Kate said reassuringly. 'Mister Darlington has told me the facts of the case.'

'I owe you more than you will ever know, Missus Tracy,' Gordon said in a sad, distant voice. 'More peace than money can buy.'

'You will be owing me a considerable amount of money for the hefty legal fees I know Mister Darlington will forward to me, Gordon James,' Kate said with a broad smile. 'And I expect to see you with Sarah in Townsville at the first opportunity, so that you can work for me.'

'I even owe you my future prospects,' he said brightly. 'It will be a debt gratefully repaid.'

A deckhand on the steamer called final boarding as he prepared to haul in the gangplank. Kate took Gordon's hands in hers. 'Love is the most powerful force of all in the world,' she said. 'Never forget that. Empires come and go but love remains in our lives as a force greater than all else, even beyond death itself.'

She let his hands slip from hers. Gordon watched her go aboard, remembering her final words . . . *love remains in our lives as a force greater than all else, even beyond death itself*. For some inexplicable reason the words echoed in his mind. *Beyond death itself!*

He remained on the wharf until the ship had pulled out into the river where it built up steam for the open sea. He could see Kate, with her parasol unfurled, waving to him from the deck but soon both she and the boat were out of sight.

As Gordon James contemplated Kate Tracy's parting words, a man had arrived with a priority in Hugh Darlington's busy schedule of appointments. He sat in the same chair that only days earlier Kate had occupied. He was Granville White.

Hugh Darlington had never before met the man whose correspondence had occupied much of his time: deed transfers on the numerous properties along the Queensland coast; company registrations and contracts for construction of the meatworks, sugar refineries and for the employment of the indentured Pacific labourers – known as Kanakas – who worked the sugar plantations.

As the legal representative of the Macintosh financial interests in the northern colony, Hugh had an intimate knowledge of many of the dealings that flew close to the face of being unlawful. But Hugh was not a man to question such dealings; he had himself used similar tactics to further his own practice and political career.

'I pray you had a pleasant passage from Sydney, Mister White,' he said, as they settled down to the agenda of business Granville had scheduled for their meeting.

'Pleasant enough,' Granville replied. 'But the weather here is so damnably hot and unpleasant.'

'One becomes accustomed to the climate,' Hugh commented mildly. 'I fear that my blood has thinned over the years of exposure to the colony's weather.'

'To each his own.'

'Before we commence our discussions,' Hugh said, dispensing with social chatter, 'on the matters you have outlined in your letter, Mister White, I would like to raise the matter concerning the sale of Glen View.'

Granville looked sharply at the solicitor. 'That woman has made an offer on the property. Missus Tracy. Has she not?'

'You knew?' Hugh said with surprise.

'I guessed,' he replied. 'It was inevitable she would. She has been endeavouring to get her hands on Glen View for years.'

'She has informed me that she is prepared to make a generous offer.'

'She can burn in hell before I would allow any member of that damned Duffy family to get the place,' Granville growled. The solicitor was surprised; he had appraised White as a business-man first and a sentimentalist second. He was well aware of the animosity that existed between the Macintoshes and the Duffys, but did not know the animosity extended to Granville White.

But Granville was not as sentimental as the solicitor gave him credit for. It was only that Kate was the sister of the man whom he feared and hated most in the world. The disposal of Glen View was not based purely on monetary considerations. It was also a need to show Lady Enid he had the power to destroy that which she held precious. 'I already have a generous offer for the property from other sources,' Granville added in a way that did not invite further discussion on the matter.

Hugh accepted his conclusion. They would move on to the other issues for discussion.

When the matters were finalised Granville raised the subject of the family property again and stated that he would personally visit Glen View before it was transferred to an English company interested in getting a foothold in the beef industry.

Hugh was surprised at his client's desire to visit the property; it was not necessary to do so for the purposes of the sale. He stated this but Granville replied, 'I know what you are saying is correct, Mister Darlington, but I have my own personal reasons for visiting Glen View before it is sold. I have made arrangements with the stock and station agent and will travel with him from Rockhampton tomorrow.'

Granville did not feel the need to elaborate. *How could he tell anyone of his years of super- stitious fear?* Of a fear for the brooding presence in his life that was like some kind of curse. A fear that he had come to recognise as emanating from Glen View itself and which could, with an un-explainable power, reach out to him even in far-off Sydney. Discussions of such matters were not the grist of a sane man.

'Well, the matter is settled then,' Hugh said. 'I will have all the papers in order for you to sign upon your return.'

'Good,' Granville grunted. 'But there will be one proviso that the purchasers must agree to before I sign over the damned property.'

'What is that?' Hugh asked.

'That the property cannot be resold to any member of the Duffy family for at least ninety-nine years.'

Hugh raised his eyebrows at the request. 'It will be done, Mister White,' he replied. 'I am sure that the property will remain permanently out of reach of the Duffy family with such a codicil attached.'

Granville smirked with satisfaction. After all, Lady Enid Macintosh was not the only one in the family who was capable of using less than violent means to destroy her enemies. He too could play the game.

60

Patrick could see clearly that the big man had an eye patch. He scanned the immediate area for any sign of Catherine, but there was none.

The thought that he was about to meet his father caused Patrick a sudden feeling of panic. For reasons he could not fathom he wanted to turn around and ride away. What would his first words be? How did you address a man you had only met briefly once in your life? But Patrick did not have to concern himself with finding the words to introduce himself.

'Are they with you?' his father called to him from the river as he stared past Patrick to the grassy rise a half-mile behind him.

Patrick blinked in his confusion at the question and then turned in his saddle and caught his breath as he saw the commando of Boer horsemen fan out on the rise. They had rifles on their hips and it was obvious from their manoeuvre that they were preparing to carry out some kind of mounted attack. 'No, I haven't seen them before,' he called back.

His father hurried up the bank of the river and snatched a rifle from the wagon.

'English, are you?' Michael asked, as he took shelter behind the stout timber of his wagon.

'Australian,' Patrick replied, sliding from his horse. His reply caught his father's attention and he turned away from watching the Boers who were descending in a loose line off the rise. He stared into Patrick's face. For a long moment both men stared at each other without saying a word. Finally, Michael broke the silence. 'Bloody bad time to meet you, Patrick. I hope everything I've heard about your military reputation proves to be true, because right now I'm going to need all the help I can get.'

The advancing line of horsemen was only a quarter of a mile away. Patrick could discern the bandoliers of cartridges slung across the riders' chests and see the bearded Boer faces under floppy hats with the sides turned up. They were generally big men, with copper complexions burnt by long exposure to the African sun, and they rode as if the horse under them was part of their anatomy. 'What in hell is going on?' he asked, confused by the sudden appearance of the commando. They must have been following him from De Aar. He cursed himself for not being more vigilant; it was only to be expected that in his father's line of work he would have many enemies.

'It seems that Bronkhorst has discovered the Mausers I delivered him are a mite faulty,' Michael replied calmly as he rested the barrel of the Winchester on the edge of the wagon. 'And I don't think he has come for his money back. Grab one of these from under the blankets in the wagon,' his father commanded. 'I presume you know how to operate a lever action rifle.'

Patrick had never seen this model of the Winchester before but could see that it was not one of the lighter ones that fired a pistol cartridge. His observation was borne out by the packet of heavy brass cartridges on the tailgate of the wagon. They were a much larger cartridge. He hefted the heavy rifle from under the blanket. 'Loaded?' he questioned.

'Loaded,' his father confirmed. 'New rifle from my friends at Winchester. Invented by an old friend of mine, John Browning. Sent me a couple to test trial on big game here.'

Patrick took up a position at the wagon and rested his rifle against the timber. His stomach felt as if it wanted to turn inside out as he came to grips with what they faced: fifteen heavily armed horsemen advancing in a line that was capable of swamping them in a determined charge.

'Take out the horses only,' his father said softly as he drew a sight on the centre of the line. 'Try and not hit the riders.'

'Does the rifle have the range?' Patrick asked with a note of concern. He knew that every shot must count if they were to break up any deter-mined charge. And at a quarter of a mile the range was extreme for even the best of marksmen.

'It does,' his father answered softly and squeezed the trigger. His first shot had barely echoed off the gently rolling grassy hills around them when he had chambered a second round and fired again. Patrick saw two horses hit. One reared and dragged down its rider while the second crumpled, pitching forward. The rider leapt free and crashed heavily into the earth.

Michael rapidly fired and reloaded. Although many of his shots went wild, his hope for a disrupting effect was rewarded with the line of advancing horsemen suddenly milling in a confused melee. Riders desperately pulled down on reins to drag their horses around and retreat out of range of the deadly volley of fire coming from behind the stout wagon. Michael fired until the last spent round spun from the side chamber of his rifle.

Patrick continued to fire, amazed at the wonderfully smooth action of the repeating mechanism. Although he fired carefully he flinched when he saw a shot pluck a Boer from his saddle. The man threw up his arms and slid from his horse. The bullet that had gone high had taken the horseman square in the back. By the time he had fired his last round the Boers had deftly snatched up those men who had been unhorsed.

Michael reloaded and fired a couple of shots in the air over their heads to speed them on. Soon only the empty plain, dead and dying horses, and ringing in their ears from the blast of the Winchesters was left.

'What do you think they will do next?' Patrick asked in a hushed voice. 'Mount a charge?'

'Not likely,' his father muttered as he reloaded. 'More likely they will either wait until dark and close in on us on foot. Or encircle us and come at us from different directions on horseback. Either way these boyos are bloody good at fighting and are not going to be put off by a couple of *Rooineks* they have pinned down on the veldt.'

'I think they will attempt to take us out with a charge,' Patrick mused. 'They have the numbers.'

His father shook his head. 'My guess is that they will wait until dark, seeing as Bronkhorst is in command. He has a lot of experience in night fighting.'

Patrick sat down with his back to the wheel of the wagon and reloaded his rifle from a box of cartridges. His legs felt weak and his heart thumped in his chest, a reaction to the adrenalin that surged through his body. And he had been worried only minutes earlier about what he would say to his father when they met!

As Michael propped his rifle against the wagon and lit a cigar, Patrick marvelled at how calm his father was considering what they were up against. He seemed fearless. Or was it that, in his fear, Patrick had suddenly felt a surge of comfort at being in the paternal presence of his father? His father! 'What should I call you?' he asked as he gazed at the profile of the man puffing serenely as he watched the sky-line on the hill to their front.

Michael did not answer immediately. He felt as awkward as his son in the lull following the firing. 'An uncaring bastard,' he replied softly. 'If that makes you feel better.'

'Maybe. I have always wondered why you never attempted to contact me in all the years past.'

'I had my reasons, Patrick. Reasons I doubt that I could explain under the present circumstances.'

'Probably as good as any time to explain them,' Patrick said. 'Good chance we might not get out of these circumstances alive. Especially since it looks like I dropped one of them.'

'Yeah,' Michael sighed. 'That seems like a good certainty.'

'And where is Catherine?' Patrick asked, with a bitter edge creeping into his question. 'Is she still with you?'

'Do you see any sign of her around here?' Michael retorted angrily, 'And is your next question, were we lovers? Because if it is you are wasting your time asking me.'

'I was wondering,' his son replied mildly. 'But somehow I knew you would not tell me.'

Michael turned to his son and gave him a pitying look. He could see himself in the young man. The realisation of all that he had lost in his life stung him. It was obvious Patrick had travelled a long way to meet him – a long search that had exposed his son to the present, dangerous situation that he had created by his own hand. 'Maybe this isn't the time to play games with each other,' he said gently. 'I will try to the best of my ability to answer your questions . . . son.'

Patrick glanced at his father. His bitterness could not allow him to reciprocate with *father*.

Michael turned his attention to the distant horizon. He could just see the head and shoulders of a man surveying their position, no doubt scouting to plan a strategy. 'As for Catherine,' he said, 'I haven't seen her since Greece. She has an interest in archaeology. And when I left for the Cape she was about to leave for Constantinople to visit some ruins there. I don't know where she is now.'

'I saw a painting of her back at De Aar.'

'Ahh ... yes. Katerina I called that one,' Michael replied with fond recollection. 'I painted that one from memory.'

'She was naked!'

'Most artist's models pose naked at some time in their careers,' Michael answered. 'It does not mean that she was my lover.'

'But she allowed herself to be seen naked by you,' his son insisted. 'Surely one must come to certain conclusions.'

'You sound like a petty schoolboy, Patrick,' his father rebuked. 'You will learn in life that women are their own mistresses. And, *if* we were lovers, that is a matter between Catherine and myself. No-one else.'

'Then you admit you were lovers,' Patrick insisted.

Michael thought he could hear a whine creep into his son's voice. 'The biggest problem you have in your life is that you had no choice in who your father would be. Well, it's me and there is nothing you can do about that except understand that I am not a man who has much toleration for little boys in men's bodies. So, shut your infernal whining, or accept the facts as they are. She is no longer with me. And you and I have more to talk about than whether or not Miss Catherine Fitzgerald and I were lovers. If that is all right with you?'

Patrick glared at his father with an expression of contempt. 'You are a bounder of the worst kind. To allow a lady as young and innocent as Miss Fitzgerald to throw herself at you. She . . .'

'Jesus, Mary and Joseph!' Michael exploded. 'Where in hell did you get your ideas on the innocence of women? Eton, with all the other young men whose tiny minds are filled with romantic ideas straight out of books. And for that matter, Catherine was no little girl. Oh, she might have been young enough to be my daughter, as you have yet to express, but she was all woman when it came to satisfying her own needs. Believe me, son.'

'You bastard!' Patrick hissed as he rose from the ground and Michael swung on him defensively.

'Thought you might find a name for me sooner or later, other than father,' he said with a cold smile on his face. Patrick stood face to face with him as the two men eyed each other tensely like a pair of fighting dogs. 'You could try to hit me,' Michael said calmly. 'But I promise you I will hit you right back.' Patrick suddenly realised that his fists were clenched and ready to be raised. 'I hear you are pretty good in the ring. Old Max taught you well,' Michael added. 'But you have to remember, he also taught me.'

Patrick relaxed and turned away to resume his seat on the ground with his back to the wagon wheel. 'I didn't think it would be like this,' he said sadly. 'You and I almost coming to blows.' He gave a short and bitter laugh then continued, 'Here we are. We finally meet and I was terrified of what I should say to you. But right now we are up to our necks in trouble, and all I am worried about is whether you were Miss Fitzgerald's lover. I suppose it has something to do with pride.'

'There is nothing wrong in that, son,' Michael said gently. 'I did not know about you and her until we got to Greece.'

Patrick glanced up at his father. 'Is that why you parted company, because of me?' But the answer was an enigmatic smile from his father.

'Possibly,' he said.

In that simple answer and smile, Patrick saw his father in a new light. Maybe he was not the cad that he had first thought him to be. 'Anyway . . .'

Michael's sentence was cut short as wood splintered in his face from the side of the wagon. He flung himself on the ground and at the same time snatched his rifle from against the side of the wheel. A hollow rolling noise of a shot followed.

Patrick scrabbled to a position under the protection of the wagon. The shock of the sniper's round caused his heart to pound in his chest. 'Where did it come from?' he hissed across the space between himself and his father.

'The rise,' Michael answered as he lifted his head to scan the skyline. A faint puff of smoke lingered to mark the sniper's position. ''Bout five hundred yards out. Bloody good shot considering,' he added with a note of admiration for his unseen adversary.

'Think they will try and snipe us out?' Patrick asked.

'No. The range is too extreme. They will pot away at us until the sun goes down. Just keep us pinned here.'

'What do you think we should do then?'

'Wait until dark,' Michael replied as he rolled on his back to locate the cigar he had dropped. 'Then one of us will get out while the other keeps up a pretence that we are both still here. A trick I believe your Uncle Tom used to keep the traps occupied some years ago in Queensland. They had him and his blackfella mate Wallarie trapped in some hills in the Gulf Country. Worked for Tom. At least until they shot him.'

'I can remain,' Patrick volunteered. 'You have a better idea of this country than I.'

'Yeah. But I think you haven't finished your search yet,' his father replied gently. 'Better you get out of here while I hold them off. It's not the first time I've been in this kind of situation. You could say I've had a lot more experience than you.'

'If you mean my search to find Catherine,' Patrick said, 'then you are wrong. I've found all I need to know.'

Michael puffed on the stub of his cigar. 'No, I mean the search for yourself. That will take you a lifetime. Believe me, I know.'

Patrick felt a strange warmth in his father's words. How could this man know such deep, troubling thoughts that no-one else was privy to? 'Father?' Michael ceased puffing on the cigar. 'Tell me about my mother. Do you think she gave me up like Lady Enid said she did?'

The big one-eyed Irishman felt a strange peace settle over him. 'When we both get out of here I will tell you that your mother loves you with her whole body and soul. Always remember that, son.' And he turned away so that his son could not see the tears that welled in his remaining good eye.

Beyond the crest of the grassy rise the Boer commando prepared for the night. No matter how deadly the Irishman proved with his strange rifle the night would blind him. Lucas Bronkhorst had lost one of his men and that left a debt to be claimed in blood.

The firing from the rise continued throughout the late afternoon and the bullets claimed the lives of Patrick's two horses. Only Michael's two bullocks remained grazing on the lush grasses of the veldt.

Great, billowing clouds tumbled over the horizon. A storm was coming to the African veldt.

61

Exhuming a corpse is an unpleasant business. The square of canvas Sergeant Johnson had thrown between two trees for shade trapped the sickly, putrid stench of decomposition, making it even more difficult to bear.

Joe Heslop's body had been taken from his grave at Barcaldine's tiny cemetery and Sergeant Johnson attended as an independent witness to the autopsy carried out quickly and expertly by the former British army surgeon major, Doctor Harry Blayney.

Gordon and two Aboriginal troopers from his escorting party stood watching the grisly scene from a short distance away. The corpse lay on its back at the edge of the re-opened grave. The curious gravedigger stood to one side, watching the doctor perform the autopsy,

With a handkerchief soaked in cheap perfume wrapped around his face, the doctor probed the cadaver with forceps until he located the bullet. He dropped the lead projectile with the gore still attached into an empty tobacco tin. Then he handed the tin to Sergeant Johnson who duly recorded the fact that he had received from the doctor the bullet from the corpse of Joe Heslop. It was a recognisable .577 calibre round but Doctor Blayney continued to make a thorough search of the internal organs of the corpse to eliminate any other observable causes of death.

The lead projectile was worth more than a nugget of gold to the young inspector. The findings by Doctor Blayney had corroborated Gordon's version of the bushranger's death.

Satisfied that there could have been no other cause of death, the doctor rose from his knees and gave his permission for the body to be reburied. With little ceremony the gravedigger used his shovel to push the remains back into the ground. He would sell the cheap wood coffin to the mates of a stockman who had suicided after a massive drinking binge in town. After all, it had only had one previous owner.

The doctor, Gordon James and Sergeant Johnson retired to a hotel to celebrate the finding of the crucial evidence. Sergeant Johnson would ride to Rockhampton with the tobacco tin containing the bullet and thus be able to vouch for the unbroken line of evidence from body to the coroner's court.

The next day Gordon rode out of the town with the doctor and an escort of two police troopers. Two days later, when they were close to Balaclava Station, he left the doctor and his troopers at a camp they set up for the night. Gordon had to heal the pain in his spirit with the forgiveness and acceptance from the woman he loved above all others.

Although the tracks leading out from Rockhampton to the central west of Queensland were more clearly defined since the days when pioneers opened up the land to grazing, the going was no less arduous. Many times the city-born Granville White had regretted his desire to confront the place of his nightmares. Many times on the two-week journey to Glen View with the cheerful stock and station agent as his companion, Granville had been tempted to call off the trip.

But the agent kept telling him, in the indomitable way of the country-born man, that they were almost there and, finally, he was right.

A day after arriving at Glen View Granville stood in the front yard of the homestead. 'I feel you should postpone your trip to the hills, Mister White,' the manager said. 'Looks like quite a storm brewing on the plains this afternoon and I don't like the look of it. Not the time of the year for storms.'

But Granville had not come all this way to put off the last leg of his journey. 'I have to set out for Rockhampton no later than tomorrow, Mister Cameron,' he replied from the seat of the buggy. Beside him sat the Aboriginal stockman Cameron had assigned to guide Granville to the sacred hills of the Nerambura. 'Besides, you said it is less than a couple of hours from here.'

Cameron shrugged. It was not his place to tell the owner of the property where or where not he could go.

Mary Cameron watched her husband conversing with Granville White, aware that

Matilda was also watching as she stood shyly in the doorway holding her daughter in her arms. When Mary turned she was sure the young woman was scowling. 'What's wrong with you, girl?' she snapped irritably.

Matilda glanced up at her and mumbled, 'Nothing, Missus.'

Mary regretted snapping at Matilda but she was upset that the arrival of Granville White heralded her husband's demise as manager of the property. The city man had informed her husband that with the imminent sale of the property he should seek employment elsewhere as the new owners had their own man to manage the place. She brushed past the girl, scowling at their less than welcome guest. 'Man baal, I know Matilda.'

'Mister White, he baal all right,' Matilda replied as she followed Mary to a bedroom where her own infant son lay in his crib. 'He make Mister Cameron and you go from Glen View.'

'I'm afraid so, Matilda,' Mary confided. 'Probably within the month.'

She lifted her baby son from the crib and placed him in Matilda's arms to be wet nursed as Matilda undid the buttons on her cotton dress and placed the hungry baby on a fat nipple.

Mary sat down wearily in a chair while the girl nursed her child and reflected on the exotically pretty young woman who had briefly been the lover of Peter Duffy before he was killed. Matilda had proved everything that Inspector James said she would be. She was highly intelligent and keen to please and with the birth of their babies the girl was also a compatible wet nurse for her. The two

women had grown close in their time together –
the mutual bond of women who had participated
in delivering each other's babies.

'Why Mister White want to go long the hills,
Missus?' Matilda asked. 'Place baal.'

'I don't exactly know why,' Mary replied with a
sigh. The weather was so close that sweat
streamed down her body under her heavy clothes
and she envied Matilda for just the clean cotton
dress she wore. But an Aboriginal girl was allowed
such immodesty, as long as it concealed her female
charms sufficiently from the menfolk who worked
on the station. 'I suspect he has a need to see the
place personally,' Mary replied after some
thought. 'It has links with his wife's family.'

'Only bad spirits out there,' Matilda grunted as
the baby bit down with toothless gums. 'Baal
Nerambura spirits belong sacred hills.'

'Your son is part Nerambura,' Mary reminded
her wet nurse. 'How can you say that?'

'Baal spirits, Missus,' Matilda stubbornly reiterated. 'Mister White, he make the spirits of the
hill angry if he goes there. Make storm spirit
angry.'

'No, Matilda, just a storm, nothing more,' she
said with a weak smile of exhaustion. The weather
was oppressive and sapped her strength. 'And
when my son gets older, do not dare frighten him
with your stories about evil spirits,' she chided
gently.

'Not stories,' Matilda answered stubbornly. 'All
true.'

Over the dry brigalow scrub plains the
thunderheads billowed into massive castles in the

blue sky. In the brigalow scrub the creatures of the bush fell into a frightened hush as they gazed at the horizon with wide eyes. This storm had in its heart a destructiveness not seen for a long time on the plains.

The Aboriginal stockman had not wanted the task of taking Mister White to see the hills. Like all the employees of Glen View, European or Aboriginal, he avoided the small range of ancient volcanic rocks. It was well accepted that the area was haunted and bad luck befell those foolish enough to challenge the spirits of the hills that lived in the rocks, trees and waterholes of the region. Cattle that strayed into the area were often found dead from no apparent cause. It was a place to shun – at all times, by all men.

But he obeyed his boss's order to take the owner to the place that was baal. Within a couple of hours they arrived at the base of the hills and the stockman lurked by the buggy while Granville White stood a distance away, gazing up at the summit of the tallest crest in the range. 'Is the cave up there?' he called to the stockman.

'Yes, boss.'

'And where did the dispersal take place of the blackfellas who used to live here?' he asked as he walked back to the buggy.

'Don't know, boss,' the stockman lied, afraid the white man might ask him to take him to the killing grounds. As it was he had ensured they arrived on the opposite side of the hill to that of the spirit-haunted waterholes.

Granville flashed a broad smile of triumph

which the Aboriginal did not understand. He had faced the source of his nightmares and had only found a jumble of ragged, scrub covered rocks. He had finally exorcised the ghosts of his past. 'We can go back to the house now,' he said to the stockman who leapt into the driver's seat with a grunt of relief. He was more than happy to put the place behind them. Besides, the storm rumbling over the plains had an eerie feel which made the stockman's skin prickle.

The trip back to Glen View homestead was much faster than the trip out and Granville had cause on more than one occasion to rebuke the man for the reckless manner in which he urged the harnessed horse through the bushy scrub.

Wallarie did not know exactly where he was but he knew that if he kept heading in the direction of the setting sun he would eventually reach the mission station. There he would be safe; he could trust the white man and his missus whose lives he had saved years earlier.

Behind him was the place the white men called Glen View and the spirit of Peter Duffy. But from the west he could see the billowing clouds of a storm racing east. Wallarie grinned as he rattled his spears. The ancestor spirits had called on the storm to go to Glen View and visit its fury on those deserving death.

A gust of wind raised the red dust like dry blood around his body. They were here, he exulted. The ancestor spirits were all around him and he could hear their voices in the eerie shrieking whispers of a big storm full of lightning and thunder.

He felt like dancing that corroboree his old white brother Tom Duffy used to call an Irish jig. So he did, and he thought for a moment that he could hear Tom laughing with the ancestor spirits.

62

The sniping continued spasmodically, making sure Michael and Patrick were pinned down under the wagon throughout the remaining hours of light. The afternoon was shortened by the darkening of the sky by grey rain clouds. The fierce storm that had initially threatened, however, turned unexpectedly to a steady but gentle drizzle that brought with it a creeping chill to the men sheltering under the wagon.

Water dripped through the cracks between the floorboards and eventually soaked them as gusts of wind drove the drizzle sideways. The only consolation was that the weather was also making their enemies just as miserable.

The occasional shots fired in their direction had little effect other than to keep them aware that the Boer commando had not left. But they were sufficiently concealed and out of range to take comfort in the thought that their deaths would not be as the result of a well-aimed bullet.

Michael spent the hours talking to his son. He told him much about his life, including his work for the Foreign Office agent, Horace Brown. He also talked much about the battles he had fought, and the places he had been, in the last twenty years or so.

In turn Patrick related what he could of his own life, growing up first with Michael's own family in Sydney then his life under the patronage of Lady Enid Macintosh in England. Both men could not help but marvel at the strange parallels in their independent lives. Patrick was truly the son of his tough yet gentle father.

'It will be dark soon,' Michael sighed as he noticed the crest of the hills to their front begin to blur with the sky. 'Then they will come in full force, one way or the other.' As he spoke he checked the big Colt pistol by his hand which would be used as a backup to his Winchester. The gun was loaded and ready to be used should his enemy get that close to him.

'When should I leave?' Patrick asked reluctantly. He did not feel that it was right to leave his father alone to face the Boer commando. But Michael had reasoned with him; he reminded him that he was a soldier and should appreciate the importance of critical thinking at such times. Argument based on emotion was a useless tactic with his father; it only made him angry.

'Fairly soon,' his father replied as he peered out across the plain at the hill. 'As soon as we lose vision over fifty feet. Bronkhorst won't wait too long in this weather.'

'Then that will probably be in about ten minutes' time,' Patrick said as he peered up at the sky. 'According to my calculations.'

'You have all you need?' Michael asked as if talking to a son preparing to go to school rather than slipping out from a wagon under siege. 'You remember what I said about the kraal down the river?' Patrick patted a parcel of items he had collected and wrapped in canvas. The parcel was a life jacket of sorts that he would use in his escape attempt.

'Yes. Get to the kraal and ask for Mbulazi,' Patrick answered.

His father grunted, adding, 'Mbulazi is an old Zulu warrior and no lover of the Boers. He will get help from a British post in De Aar. But don't let yourself get into any drinking sessions with the old bugger. His people brew a mean drop of beer from maize. I should know.'

'You could come with me,' Patrick offered hopefully. 'By the time they get here we would both be gone.'

'No chance, Patrick,' his father replied sadly. 'The Boer is a first class fighter and he knows full well that we will try and use the darkness to slip past him. So long as they know I'm here they will concentrate their forces to rush me in the dark. I'm the man they want. You are only a bonus.'

'You hold out and I promise I will return with help,' Patrick said fiercely. 'So help me God! Or my name isn't Duffy.'

Michael laughed softly at Patrick's fierce determination. It was growing dark and he could barely see his son's features. He might as well have been the little boy he remembered from so long ago in Frasers Paddock in Redfern. 'Do you know, Patrick,' he said fondly, 'a long time ago in

Cooktown I thought I was going to die and your Aunt Kate told me about you. And I was able to fight off the grim reaper. So when I have you beside me now saying that you will get help, I know you will.'

Patrick heard his father's words of trust and fought back tears. It did not bode well that a son cry in front of his father! 'I think we still have a lot to talk about,' he said in a choked voice that he fought to control lest his father think he was crying. 'But we will do so when all this is over.'

'We will, Patrick. We will,' Michael answered softly. 'But now you get ready to leave because I feel they are making ready to come for us.'

Patrick crawled across to his father and reached out to take the big man's hand in his own. He held it tightly then he rose as his father grasped him in a brief bear hug.

'Tell your mother that you love her, son,' Michael whispered. 'That's very important to women, especially mothers.'

'I will. And I'll buy you a round of drinks at the first hotel we come across.'

'Good man,' Michael replied gruffly. 'And you can buy all the rest to follow with that Macintosh fortune of yours.'

Without another word Patrick turned and in a low crouch sprinted for the river. His father watched him disappear into the darkness of the veldt then turned with tears in his good eye.

He hefted his Winchester into his shoulder and fired off two shots, just to let the assembling Boer commando know he was still at the wagon. There was no returning fire. He knew there might not be as the commando was surely already advancing stealthily on him. 'Come on, you Dutch bastards,' he roared defiantly into the enveloping darkness that had been brought on prematurely by the drizzling rain.

He levered a third round into his rifle and waited. 'Come and see how an Irishman can die with the best of them.'

As Patrick splashed into the cold water with his boots tied around his neck he heard the shots from the wagon echo in the darkness. And he heard his father's last defiant words challenging the tough Boer commando. He waded out to where the river was strongest and the water caught at his legs, dragging him off his feet. With a splash he was swirled away from the wagon. The canvas wrapped parcel floated and Patrick held onto it with both arms to keep his head above the cold muddy waters. All he had to do now was drift with the current until he felt he was beyond the perimeter of the Boer commando. Then he would kick out and push himself to the shore. Nevertheless, it was going to be a long night. Patrick tried not to think of his father. To do so would have sent him mad with grief.

63

When Gordon rode out to the Balaclava homestead his less than welcome reception from the manager was to be expected. 'I only wish to speak to Miss Duffy briefly, Mister Rankin,' he said quietly. 'I promise I will then leave.'

'I know all about you, Inspector,' Rankin growled. 'My wife informed me of what you did to Sarah's brother last year.'

'I do not deny what has been said about me,' Gordon persisted. 'But I only ask five minutes of Miss Duffy's time.'

The manager stared at the young man standing at the foot of the steps with such an abject expression of sorrow that he could not help but feel a twinge of pity for him. He glanced questioningly at his wife and she nodded. 'I will speak to Sarah, Inspector,' she said and went inside the house.

A brief moment later she returned, with Sarah accompanying her. Adele and her husband made a tactful retreat.

Gordon stood forlornly in the blazing sun at the

foot of the steps with his police cap in his hand. 'Sarah, I love you,' he said in a choked voice. 'I always have and always will. There is nothing else I can do but speak these words.'

'I know,' she whispered and was barely audible. 'I wish I could not love you, Gordon, but I do.'

He stared up at her and his eyes brimmed with tears as he struggled for words to express complex emotions. 'I have done many bad things in my life but the only good thing I ever did was love you. I have come again to beg your forgiveness.'

'I can forgive you for what you have done to me but I cannot give my brother's forgiveness. For that you would have to ask him.'

'Peter is dead, Sarah,' he replied. 'I cannot ask a dead man to forgive me. I only wish that was possible.'

'In your own way you must find a way to be at peace with my brother,' she said with the wisdom of a spirit caught between two worlds. 'To do so is important for the future.'

They fell into a silence. There was a gulf between them of blood and spirits seeking peace. Would their love be strong enough to breach the gulf?

'I have to return to my camp on the waterhole north of here,' Gordon said. 'And then to Rockhampton to finalise some matters. I will be resigning my commission and will return to Balaclava for you,' he said. 'Will you wait for me?'

'Yes, Gordon,' she answered. 'I have always been waiting for you to return to me.'

He knew she had forgiven him. 'I have a job with your Aunt Kate when I leave the police,' he said. 'It will be a start where we could be together.'

She nodded and the tears splashed down her cheeks and with tentative steps he closed the distance between them. They stood weeping together as they embraced.

'I love you so much, Sarah, that I would rather die than ever hurt you again,' he said as he kissed her eyes. 'So help me nothing else is as important to me as you.'

He wanted the embrace to last forever as the love they had repressed for so long flowed but he knew that he must return to the camp before dark and with great reluctance gently broke away and held her at arm's length. He felt the gentle pain of boundless love. This beautiful, intelligent woman had loved him despite the tragedy that had occurred between them.

From a window the Rankins watched the touching scene. Humphrey Rankin gave his wife a puzzled look at the sudden shift in their governess's attitude to the police inspector. She merely returned his look with a smug expression of disdain for his ignorance of the ways of women. For Adele Rankin had always suspected that the young woman was in love with the inspector despite all that he had done to her. Life, she knew, was not ruled by absolutes but ruled by the heart.

They all waved to him as he rode away from the homestead. Sarah had shyly informed Adele that the matters between her and Gordon had been resolved. She would have to inform her suitor that she could not marry him and that she would be marrying Gordon instead upon his return from

Rockhampton after the coronial inquiry.

For Gordon, riding away from the homestead, life was suddenly filled with a meaning he had never truly experienced before. He rode into his camp an hour later with a smile across his face as wide as the plains. If a curse really existed then Sarah had helped lift the spectre from his life with her admitted love for him. Kate had been right. *Love transcends all!*

The following morning as Gordon and his troop prepared to break camp and leave for Rockhampton, Humphrey Rankin galloped to the waterhole. Gordon was puzzled at the set expression on the man's face as he reined in his horse beside them.

'You'd better saddle up quick, Inspector James,' he said without the ceremony of small talk. 'Sarah is very sick with a fever. She could be dying.'

Stunned by the manager's statement, Gordon gaped uncomprehendingly up at the man on his horse. 'But she was in perfect health when I left her yesterday. How could this be?'

'Some sort of blackfella stuff if you ask me,' the manager replied sadly. 'I've seen the same symptoms with the blacks who work on Balaclava when they think they have the bone pointed at them.'

'I'm a doctor. I will come with you,' Blayney said to Humphrey as he quickly rolled up his swag. 'I've never heard such nonsense before.'

Humphrey Rankin cast him a pitying look and shook his head. 'You obviously haven't lived in this country for very long, Doctor.'

'If the girl is sick with a fever, sir, I can assure you that her illness will have nothing to do with some native superstitious claptrap.'

But Gordon did not agree with the doctor's opinion. In his heart he knew what he must do to lift the curse from Sarah. Even if it cost him his life.

Doctor Harry Blayney shook his head as he stood by the bed and looked down at Sarah. The girl was very sick and lay in a comatose state in the tiny room with its curtains drawn to keep out the light. The once clean, crisp sheets were dank with her sweat and at times she would ramble on about unrelated things before lapsing back into her coma. Her pulse was at first rapid, then weak, and her temperature fluctuated between high and low.

Blayney's training told him that her illness had to have a sound medical basis, but just what that was he could not determine with the limited resources available to him. Nor was he impressed by Missus Rankin's diagnosis of some ridiculous Aboriginal spell cast on her. The woman had once been a nurse and as such should have known better than infer the illness was the result of such superstitious rubbish. 'I think there is very little we can do other than keep the liquids up to her, Missus Rankin,' he said with a sigh. 'And, I will admit, I cannot diagnose the cause of her fever.'

'I respect your credentials, Doctor Blayney,' she said as she bathed Sarah's fevered brow. 'But you must understand that out here I have seen many things that defy our understanding of the scientific world.'

The doctor washed his hands in an enamel basin of water beside the bed. 'Why are you so quick to diagnose a native spell if I may ask, Missus Rankin?' he questioned as he dried his hands on a clean cloth.

'I saw her earlier in the evening before she retired for the night,' Adele answered. 'She was perfectly well then. But later I heard her calling out, as if she was arguing with someone in her room. I was naturally concerned that one of the stockmen might have entered the house. When I entered the room . . .' She hesitated as she took the cloth from Sarah's brow to stare down at her. 'I know what I am about to tell you, Doctor, you will consider the opinion of a silly woman. But I will tell you anyway.'

'I doubt that I could ever consider you a silly and frivolous woman, Missus Rankin,' he said with genuine respect, having heard of her repu-tation for practical toughness in her dealings with the sick and injured in these parts of the country.

'Well, when I entered Sarah's room I swear there was a . . .' She groped for the right words. 'A presence . . . a ghost or spirit with us. I think it was her dead brother. I noticed that the girl was in an almost trance-like state and arguing as if her brother was as real as you and I.'

'What was she arguing about?' the doctor asked. He had to admit that he felt just the hint of primeval superstitious fear as she related her experience.

'Not so much arguing as pleading with him for

forgiveness. Forgiveness, I suspect, for admitting her love for Inspector James.'

'But why should she need her brother's forgiveness?' he queried, puzzled by the unexplainable events.

'Inspector James killed her brother on Glen View last year. He was in pursuit of him and an old blackfella called Wallarie at the time.'

'There is a school of thought around that the mind can suffer diseases like the body,' the doctor rationalised. 'I suspect Miss Duffy is under some kind of terrible delusion of guilt and in some way we do not yet understand this has manifested in her illness. I will admit that my premise on the matter is very thin but it's the only rational explanation I have at the moment.'

'You may be right, Doctor Blayney,' Adele replied but with a note of doubt in her voice. 'But the girl is half-Darambal and her people have their own explanations as to what causes illness. Who is to say that they are wrong?'

'The girl is also half-white,' he chided gently. 'I doubt that she would be subject to superstition. I am led to believe that she has had a very good European education. That should be reason enough not to succumb to the blackfella rot.'

'It all depends to whom her spirit belongs,' Adele said softly as she continued to gently stroke Sarah's long dark hair with her fingers. 'To us, or to her Darambal blood.'

Doctor Blayney gathered together his items of European medicine and packed them in the small bag he carried. They were obviously of no use in the current situation and he knew death lingering in the room when he saw it.

He left the woman tending to the sick girl to meet Gordon and Humphrey Rankin waiting anxiously in the adjoining room. The two men looked to him hopefully as he approached them. But he frowned and shook his head in answer to their unspoken question. 'I'm afraid all we can do is wait and see,' he said with a sigh as he accepted a glass of brandy from the manager. 'I do not hold with this native stuff you seem to believe in, gentlemen,' he said. 'But if they have a cure of some kind, I would recommend that you try it for no other reason than that I have no answers.'

Gordon excused himself and brushed past the doctor to go to Sarah's side.

He knelt and gently stroked Sarah's face with his fingers but she appeared oblivious to his presence and lay staring with vacant eyes at the dark ceiling. For long minutes Gordon stroked her face and held her hand in his and then he rose to leave. Without a word he left the house to go to his horse still saddled outside. Within minutes those in the house heard the horse gallop away.

64

The sun was hidden behind the blue-black horizon of seething angry clouds and lightning flashed in savage blazes across the dying day. Thunder rumbled ominously as Gordon dismounted and tethered his horse. Above him loomed the hill where he had found Peter the previous year in the cave. He stood gazing up at the summit where the sky had turned a deep purple and never before had he felt so alone.

He did not know what he must do but he did know that to save Sarah he must confront the invisible and unexplainable force that inhabited the heart of the cave sacred to the Nerambura. It was not that he was a deeply religious man, more that he recognised the force as a real entity in the lives of himself as well as others.

As he stood gazing up at the summit he felt the soft rustle of the wind in the scrub around him. Then the rustle turned to a low moaning as the winds swept before the thunderstorm's front, heralding its coming.

Fat plops of rain fell from the sky and were

quickly swallowed by the parched, hot earth. The pleasant earthy scent of freshly wet dirt reached him just as the storm hit the brigalow scrub, its fury pounding the bush with fist-sized balls of icy hailstones.

Gordon flung up his arms to protect his face from the chunks of ice that smashed into him. His panic stricken horse reared in terror, tearing away the reins from the bush to which it was tethered and in a mad gallop vainly attempted to flee the icy battering of the hail.

Gordon was truly alone now. On foot and in the open, his instinct was to gain the sanctuary of the cave above him. With his head down, he sprinted for the base of the hill to locate the track that led to the heart of the cave.

Willie Harris crouched in the cave beside the fire he had built and listened in awe to the roaring sound of the storm which was punctuated regularly with great white-blue flashes of lightning that arrived at the same time as the ear splitting cracks of thunder. A strange smell filled the air around him and every time the lightning flashed it illuminated the Nerambura figures painted on the back wall of the cave which came alive as garish, frightening spectres.

Willie averted his eyes from them. Never had he experienced a storm of such ferocity before and he was glad that he had decided to stay one more day before setting out to ride south. Although his supplies had dwindled and the hunting trips for wallaby and kangaroo had become less and less successful, he was still reasonably healthy. But to remain any longer would leave him with little choice than to raid a homestead for money and supplies – or surrender himself to the police.

He had no intention of doing either. His choice was to ride south in the hope that he might find more plentiful game to subsist on until he reached Sydney where he would find his father, Granville White.

He sat back on his haunches and hungrily watched the spiny anteater sizzling in the flames. He poked at the tiny carcass to turn it over in the coals and for a second he thought he heard a human voice scream out in agony immediately following a lightning strike nearby.

Willie's nerves tingled and he reached carefully for the Snider rifle that lay against his saddle. For a fleeting moment he wondered on the fate of his horse, corralled in a yard he had constructed from bush logs at the base of the hills. She would be frantic with fear.

With the rifle cradled, he nervously crouched, listening. Had the human-like scream been real? Or was it merely the result of his imagination stirred by the strangely heightened dread the storm had brought to the cave? But the words that accompanied the agonised moaning outside the cave were distinctly European.

Willie plucked a burning log from the fire and rose to his feet. He moved cautiously to the main entrance of the cave where he poked his head out-side. The howling storm snuffed out his torch, but he did not need it to see the figure lying on the track to the cave. Great flashes of lightning made the landscape stand out in electric hues.

Gordon had seen the flash of the burning torch before the storm had extinguished its flame. 'God help me,' he cried through the pounding rain. 'Help me!'

Then a figure was beside him and a voice queried, 'Mister James, is that you?'

'Willie,' Gordon gasped with stunned surprise as he recognised the young man's voice in the dark. 'I need help. I think the lightning got me. I can't stand up . . . My leg.'

Willie placed his rifle on the wet earth and took Gordon under the shoulders and with all his strength dragged the big man back into the shelter of the cave.

Gordon lay on his back, moaning from the pain that seemed to be all over him. He heard Willie gasp. Gordon knew that something was terribly wrong. The young man shook his head slowly. 'Lightning got you in the leg below the knee, Mister James. Your foot is gone. Blown clean off.'

Gordon heard the words from a long way away. He was falling into a dark vortex inhabited by spirits from other times and other places of his life.

Willie was glad that he was unconscious. He would at least feel no pain and the lightning had cauterised the stump where his foot should be. Even so, the rest of his leg below the knee looked pretty bad and Willie knew that the inspector of police was in dire need of medical attention.

Willie groaned in his despair as he realised that he had only one choice left to him. He would have to saddle his horse and ride for Glen View Station. But to do so would mean exposing himself not only to the terrible storm raging outside but also to possible recognition and subsequent capture. Why did the bloody inspector have to be a friend? What in hell was he doing on the hill anyway?

He stacked the fire before he left Gordon alone in the cave. With his saddle over his shoulder Willie struggled in the storm to find his horse. All the time he cursed Gordon James for being in the wrong place at the wrong time.

Alone in the cave Gordon again met Peter Duffy. They confronted each other in the unconscious world of the dying and dead. Theirs was a battle for the spirit of Sarah Duffy. This was the reason Gordon had come to the cave.

65

Overhead the storm raged with a fury of thunder, lightning and pelting rain that hammered on the corrugated iron roof with a continuous roar. The normally harsh land was filled with a spiritual beauty for those who knew that beneath the dust lay the seeds of life. For after the terrible storm an explosion of creation would spread across the plains.

'You were fortunate, Mister White, that you were able to return to the homestead,' Mary Cameron said loudly as she picked at a slice of beef, 'before this terrible storm arrived.'

Although Matilda had prepared a splendid joint for Granville's final night on Glen View, Mary's appetite was ruined by the thought that she was entertaining the man who had so callously decided to sell the property without consideration for her husband's future. Mister White had promised excellent references for Duncan for his work carried out managing the Macintosh property. But that was not enough. Glen View had become a home for Mary. When she glanced across the table at the man who ate her food oblivious to the sorrow he had brought, she felt anger that verged on sheer hate.

Granville ate sparingly although the roast joint of beef was indeed excellent. And he ate without any concern for the uneasiness he caused his hosts by his presence at their table. For such was the attitude of a man without a sense of morality.

'I must compliment you on the supper, Missus Cameron,' he said as he sipped at a goblet of claret that accompanied his meal. 'Your darkie cook prepares an excellent roast beef.'

'I am sure Matilda would be flattered to know that you approve of her cooking, Mister White,' Mary replied with an edge of sarcasm as she knew well that Matilda hated the man with a vehemence that not even she could explain. Any compliments by White would be wasted on the girl and Mary was in no mood to be polite towards Granville. 'I was surprised to see that you actually visited the Nerambura hills,' she added after she had consumed more wine than her husband could remember her doing before.

'And why would that be, Missus Cameron?' Granville asked mildly.

'I must confess that I know of the curse that is upon your family,' she said. 'I have read Sir Donald's journal which I found when Mister Cameron and I first came here. I did not mean to pry into his private thoughts but I decided to read the journal with a view of learning more about Glen View. I am surprised that you tempted the wrath of the Aboriginal spirits that inhabit the hills.'

629

Granville could see from the belligerent expression on her face that she was goading him. Only a woman's tongue could be as sharp as any rapier sword, he mused to himself as he placed his knife and fork either side of his plate. 'I must disappoint you, Missus Cameron, but such things as curses do not exist. Did he actually record the existence of a myall curse?'

'Not directly,' she grudgingly admitted. 'But it appears that some kind of evil extends to those who have come in contact with the Macintosh family. And you are, after all, married to Sir Donald's daughter.'

'I think that the talk of spirits should cease, Mary,' her husband interrupted. 'There are better things to talk about at the table.'

'Oh, I think it is rather suited to talk at the table, Duncan,' she retorted firmly. 'I believe it is all the rage in the best houses of England at the moment. Spiritualism, I believe the subject is called.'

'Yes, that may be, Mary, but it hardly applies to blackfella superstition,' Duncan replied. 'I'm sure Mister White no more believes in myall magic than I do.'

'To entertain the idea that only Europeans can believe in the existence of ghosts is nonsense,' she snorted and took another mouthful of red wine. 'The Aboriginal people have a greater affinity to this land than we could ever comprehend.'

Mary was an intelligent and very well-read woman and had become fascinated by the mania for spiritualism that had swept Queen Victoria's England. She had read about it in journals and the subject appealed to her Celtic roots. Such belief in the world beyond the earthly was easily accepted in her Scottish culture.

Granville smiled patronisingly at Mary. 'I must confess that up until a short time ago, I might have shared your belief, Missus Cameron,' he said. 'But today I visited the source of my fears and found nothing but a hill. And not a very impressive one at that. It was in confronting the unknown that I was able to realise that superstitious fear is born out of ignorance. I stood out there exposed to whatever demons might haunt the hills. But nothing jumped out to hurt me. I now realise that the only thing to fear is our imagination inflamed by the things we have not confronted. As you can see, the hill holds no fear for me as I am here dining on this excellent beef, hale and hearty.'

'Not all curses effect their power in direct and spectacular ways, Mister White,' Mary warned. 'Sometimes they are less direct, but certainly as dangerous.'

'If a bolt of lightning suddenly comes through the roof of the house and strikes me down now, I will believe you,' he said with a laugh.

'As you say, Mister White,' she agreed with grudging humour, and was about to continue with her argument from a different angle when Matilda appeared in the doorway of the dining room. She caught Duncan's eye and he excused himself and rose from the table.

'What is it, girl?' he asked Matilda, who appeared to be in a rather flustered state.

'A man has come to the door. He says he must talk to the boss.'

'What man?'

'A young man,' Matilda replied. 'He says a man called Inspector James is hurt bad.'

'I'll talk to him,' Duncan growled, hurrying to the door where he saw Willie Harris standing on the verandah.

'You the boss here?' Willie asked.

'I am,' Duncan replied, appraising the young man who was drenched to the skin and shivering from the cold. His skin had the blanched look of being in water too long. 'My name is Duncan Cameron.'

'There is a man, Inspector James, up in a big cave in the hills about an hour's hard ride from here. He's hurt pretty bad. Had his foot blown off by lightning. He's going to need a doctor.'

'How do you know this?' Cameron asked suspiciously. 'Have you been camped out up in the hills?'

Willie dropped his gaze. 'Doesn't matter about that for now, Mister Cameron,' he mumbled. 'More important Inspector James gets help pretty quick.'

'Matilda!' Angus roared back into the house. 'Get over to the stockmen's quarters and tell them to organise a party to go up to the Nerambura hills. Now! Tell them to take the buggy. When you've done that organise a meal for this young man, and lots of hot tea.'

Duncan's urgent call to Matilda reached Mary and Granville sitting at the table and when he joined them to apologise for the interruption to the meal, Granville said he understood. The meal was terminated as the homestead stirred into life for the rescue mission. Stockmen threw saddles on horses and a buggy was also prepared, although the rain had eased to intermittent showers and there were even occasional flashes of stars through the breaks in the clouds.

One of the stockmen volunteered that he had been told that a medical doctor was staying at the Balaclava homestead overnight and Duncan immediately singled out his best rider to gallop to Balaclava to fetch him.

Matilda led Willie to the kitchen where she sat him down at a table. She sensed his uneasiness. He sat poised in the kitchen as if ready to spring out the door at the slightest alarm. No doubt a fugitive from the authorities.

She poured him a steaming cup of sweet black tea and sliced slabs of beef from a joint. The boy wolfed down the meat and swallowed the tea without much consideration for the temperature of the hot liquid.

Duncan finally came to the kitchen when he was satisfied his men were ready to ride out. He stood in the kitchen with Willie who continued to stuff his mouth with bread and gravy. 'You ready to ride with us?' Duncan asked Willie who ceased eating to look up at the manager standing over him.

'I reckon you know where the cave is, Mister Cameron,' he replied quietly with a knowing look. 'You won't need me to show you where the Inspector is.'

'You're Willie Harris, aren't you?' Duncan stated calmly. 'I heard you might be hiding out in these parts. One of my blackfellas spotted your tracks not far from the hills and that's how you know about the cave.'

'What if I was Willie Harris?' the young man asked quietly. 'Would you turn me over to the traps?'

The manager fixed the young man with his eyes. 'That would depend on whether I was able to detain you,' he said in a deceptively soft voice. 'Wouldn't it?' Willie understood his meaning and drew a small pepper box pistol from under his coat.

'I'm sorry to do this to you, Mister Cameron,' he said as he pointed the small multi-barrelled derringer at Duncan. 'But I've done my bit for Mister James and now it's my turn to look after myself.'

'You ought to take the meat with you. And maybe some tea and sugar,' Duncan said, with just the slightest hint of a smile at the corner of his mouth.

Willie blinked in his confusion. But then the realisation dawned on him and he returned the smile gratefully.

'Get a sack for the young man to put some things in, Matilda,' Cameron said casually to the young woman who gaped at the sight of the gun. 'He might decide to take some flour as well.'

'I don't know why you are doing this, Mister Cameron,' Willie said as Matilda rummaged through the kitchen pantry for the items requested.

'Let's say that what you did by coming here to save Inspector James's life makes up for a lot of things. I suspect that you are not as bad as the others the police caught up with at Barcaldine.'

'I was there, Mister Cameron. And I'm guilty of being in the company of bad men. But I didn't do those things to Mister and Missus Halpin at Cloncurry. I swear on my mother's grave that if I'd known what they were going to do I would have shot the bastards myself.'

Duncan nodded. Willie's passionately delivered defence of his character and the risks he'd taken coming to Glen View had proved the boy had character. He might have strayed on the wrong side of the law but he was a boy any man might be proud to call son.

As soon as Matilda had piled into an empty flour sack the items that would give Willie a start on his trip to wherever he was bound, he took it from her with a grateful thanks. He turned and walked towards the kitchen door. The room seemed to suddenly explode, as if lightning had struck.

Willie pitched forward and the sack of provisions spilled along the floor as he lay crumpled on the kitchen floor, groaning in his pain. The acrid smell of a heavy charge of gunpowder filled the room. Matilda's scream swamped Duncan's explosive curse.

Granville stood with his arm extended towards the badly wounded young man on the floor. Smoke curled from the twin barrels of the carriage pistol. Its heavy load of lead shot had peppered Willie's back with bloody blotches which were staining the young man's coat.

'I got the young bastard!' Granville snarled triumphantly. 'That will teach him a lesson to come here and try to rob the place.'

He glanced at Duncan Cameron, puzzled by the expression of fury etched in the station manager's face. Not that it mattered anyway. What a story he would have to boast around his club when he returned to Sydney. He now understood the ultimate power of taking a man's life and experienced the rush he often felt when mounting the young girls at his brothel.

With a smirk he shifted his attention to the young man who lay at his feet in a rapidly spreading pool of blood. Whoever whelped the boy, he thought with grim satisfaction, would forever rue the name of Granville White.

66

The stockmen returned with Gordon James just before dawn. His condition was critical and Doctor Blayney did not have to carry out a lengthy examination to ascertain that he would have to amputate the inspector's right leg below the knee. The massive discharge of electricity in the lightning strike had destroyed the nerves and what remained of his foot was little more than a charred stump. Mary Cameron stood by the doctor's elbow to assist.

They lay Gordon gently on his back on the cleared kitchen table. He was semi-conscious and lost in a world of red waves that swept over him as a terrible wash of agonising pain. Doctor Blayney wondered at the man's courageous self-control. He had seen men with lesser injuries screaming in pain when he had been a surgeon with the British army, but the young man sweated tears rather than cry out.

In a guest bedroom of the homestead Willie Harris lay bleeding his life away. Doctor Blayney had examined him first while he waited for the

Glen View employees to bring in the inspector from the hill. There was nothing that could be done for him except to sit by his bed and hold his hand. The lead shot had penetrated the young man's lungs and he was slowly drowning in his own blood.

Matilda had volunteered to provide comfort to Willie in his last hours and she sat stroking the young man's forehead with a gentle hand and with soothing words for his spirit. Willie struggled to speak as tears ran down his cheeks. They were not tears of self-pity, but a frustration for an unfinished mission in his short life. Willie had a dying need to tell another soul about a terrible wrong that must not be forgotten by the living. And as he revealed his story to Matilda her eyes widened with shock. His words confirmed for her the terrible and awesome powers of the Dreaming. *Surely there could be no other explanation!*

In the kitchen the doctor called for the two Aboriginal troopers who had ridden with him and explained that they would have to hold down their boss when he started cutting the leg. He had no anaesthetic and his surgical saw would be cutting through live nerves.

They nodded and took a firm hold of the inspector whilst Mary ensured that there was plenty of hot water at hand. She was used to seeing animals slaughtered and prepared for butchering but the sight of the doctor poised with his knives and saw made her feel faint. This was a human who was to be cut and the pain would be excruciating.

'We will need something for the inspector to

bite on, Missus Cameron,' Doctor Blayney said quietly. 'A small but solid stick, or similar, would suffice.'

'The handle on a wooden spoon, Doctor?'

'I hope so,' he replied as Mary retrieved one of the large wooden spoons from a cupboard in the kitchen. She handed the spoon to the doctor who bent over Gordon and said, 'Clamp this between your teeth, old chap. I think you know why.'

Gordon nodded his understanding. His eyes were wide with fear but dulled by pain. He wanted the amputation to be over with.

'Sarah?' Gordon asked before he took the handle of the spoon.

'She is well enough,' the doctor replied. 'There has been no change in her condition since I last saw her a few hours ago.'

Blayney placed the handle between Gordon's teeth and straightened his back. He satisfied himself that the two troopers had a firm grip on the patient and cast Mary Cameron a questioning look. She nodded. 'I will stay, Doctor,' she said softly. 'You may need me.'

'It will not be a very pretty sight, Missus Cameron,' he cautioned. 'You do not have to remain during the operation.'

'Thank you, Doctor, for your concern. But I do expect the worst.'

'Very well,' he said, as he selected a sharp knife from the array of surgical tools that lay on a clean sheet of cotton on a sideboard.

When the first cut was made Gordon bit through the wooden handle of the spoon as if it had been no more than a thin twig and his drawn out scream of agony was heard at the stockmen's quarters.

Mary wavered for just a brief moment but regained her composure as the blood spurted in a red stream from the severed artery. With a deft expertise acquired on the battlefields of imperial England's colonial wars, Doctor Blayney clamped the severed artery. The former surgeon major of Queen Victoria's army had performed countless amputations and Gordon was fortunate to have a man with his experience undertaking the surgery. It was a small blessing, but still one that the inspector seemed slow to appreciate as the doctor went to work sawing through bone, cartilage and nerve endings.

Granville White also heard the scream as he sat on the verandah of the homestead puffing on a cigar. The rain had gone and the early morning was perfect. Butcher birds sang the sweetest song of the bush as they revelled in the beauty of a land that would soon come alive with flowers and green grasses. A magpie also warbled its song to the golden glow of the morning's light.

The scream brought a frightened but temporary hush to the songs of the bush birds and caused Granville to twitch with a start. He would be more than happy to see the last of the damned place! The stock and station agent who had accompanied him to Glen View was due to pick him up within the hour and he hoped that the man might be early.

The damned manager had reacted in a most unexpected manner to his shooting of the young man. He had since learned that the would-be robber was wanted for questioning on a murder anyway! One would have expected gratitude! Instead, he had received a torrent of enraged abuse! Cameron should have been grateful that he had happened to overhear the hold-up being carried out on him and grateful for the fact that he was able to get the better of the bushranger. He had certainly destroyed any aspirations he might have had for future prospects of employment as a station manager in the colony. Granville was determined that the man's surly manner would not be rewarded with any recommendation or references. No, the man could go to hell if he thought he could stand and abuse his employer in the manner that he had so insolently done. And he could take his damned wife with him!

The amputated leg fell from the table and hit the kitchen floor with a dull thud. Gordon was panting like a woman in labour. All through the operation he had remained conscious because he feared that in an unconscious state he might once again face Peter Duffy as he had in the cave.

'It's finished,' Mary whispered in his ear as she swabbed down his brow with a damp cloth. 'The doctor has done a grand job.'

'Please,' he whispered hoarsely, 'have my leg buried next to Peter Duffy's grave out there.'

She nodded. It was not an unreasonable request. 'I will get one of the men to do that for you,' she said gently as she continued to mop his brow while the doctor stitched his leg.

The sharp pricks of the needle seemed so

insignificant in their pain compared to what he had just experienced with the amputation. The two Aboriginal troopers stood away from the blood soaked table and glanced nervously at each other. Such a request to have the leg buried near Peter Duffy . . .

'You should take in some fresh air, Missus Cameron,' the doctor prescribed. 'I have just about finished here.'

'I will go and see Matilda, and the young lad,' she replied. 'I will organise one of the house girls to make us tea and Mister James can be moved to the room Mister White has vacated.'

'That would be good,' the doctor commented as he washed his saw in an enamel basin. 'The next couple of days are critical for the inspector. If the wound is clean he will live. I will see to the other young man before I return to Balaclava. If I stay in this country any longer I shall be able to come out of retirement. The number of patients seems to grow by the minute around here.'

Mary found Matilda sitting in a chair at Willie's bedside. The curtains had been drawn and the room lay in a twilight of gloom. Mary could plainly see that Matilda's job as a nurse was at an end; the doctor would not be needed to look in on his patient.

'His spirit is not at rest,' Matilda said quietly, glancing up at Mary standing beside her. 'His spirit roams searching for a man. A bad man.'

Then she told Mary all that Willie had told her before he gasped his last breath. Mary was stunned as the story unfolded.

* * *

Granville watched the stock and station agent's buggy drawing close to the house. The man waved to him cheerily and Granville was extremely pleased to see him. Now he could leave this infernal place!

He rose to his feet from the chair on the wide verandah and knew that within minutes he would be on the track to Rockhampton and thence by sea to Sydney. He doubted that he would ever have a need to visit Queensland again in his lifetime. The place was far too damnably hot for his liking anyway! The door to the homestead opened and Missus Cameron appeared on the verandah with a strange expression on her face.

'There is no need to see me off, Missus Cameron,' Granville said stiffly, He was fully aware of her animosity towards him. 'I fear such a display of concern by you would only prove a burden to us both.'

'I did not come out here to farewell you, Mister White,' she replied enigmatically. 'I came out here to see whether before you leave Glen View you would like to pay your respects to the young man you killed.'

'I think that won't be necessary,' Granville sneered. 'The man is dead and I hardly think his past criminal activities warrant any respect.'

'Matilda thinks his spirit will roam until he meets a certain man,' Mary said softly as she fixed the man she despised with a calculating look. 'And as such I would like to ask you just one question before you depart Glen View, Mister White.'

'You may ask,' Granville answered. 'Then I shall leave.'

Mary continued to stare directly into Granville's eyes. 'Did you ever know a young girl in your past called Jenny Harris?' She noticed nothing for a second and then she saw the flicker of fearful realisation cloud the man's eyes.

'I may have,' he replied in a tone that told Mary that indeed he did know Jenny Harris. 'How did you come by that name?'

'The boy. Before he died he told Matilda that the woman was his mother and that his only regret before he died was that he had not found his father in Sydney. He said his father's name was Granville White and I felt that, although the co-incidence was extraordinary, that man just might be you. I suppose if it were, you may have just killed your own son. I dare say that under those circumstances you might wish to pay your respects to the boy.'

The woman's words filled the space between them with an army of ghosts. Ghosts of his past that reached out as one to touch his heart with their deathly grasps. He felt the pain grip his chest.

'Mister White!'

He heard Mary Cameron's alarmed call reach out to him as he crumpled to his knees. The vice-like pain squeezing his chest spread rapidly to his arms, throat and back.

'Doctor Blayney,' she called back into the house. 'Please come quickly.'

Granville tried to rise to his knees but pitched forward onto the wooden planking of the verandah where he lay in a cold clammy sweat.

First came the unconsciousness that led him back in time to meet once again with those whom he had destroyed. He saw David Macintosh, bloody and battered, where the islanders' arrows had pierced his body and their stone axes cut his skin; and a tall, broad-shouldered young man stood over him with a smile of grim satisfaction. Was it Michael Duffy? Or was it his son? Finally in his journey he met Willie Harris holding the hand of a little girl who Granville recognised as Jenny, the boy's mother. But they all quickly faded into a deep and eternal darkness.

'I am afraid Mister White is dead,' Doctor Blayney said as he bent over the body. 'From what I can see he appears to have had a massive heart attack.'

'Lightning striking,' Mary said softly in an awed voice.

'I am sorry, Missus Cameron, but I did not hear what you said.'

'Oh, I was just remembering a discussion I had with Mister White last evening. It was just something he said.'

'We should get Mister White's body off the verandah,' Blayney said as he rose from beside the body. 'You, sir,' he directed to the stock and station agent who stood with his mouth agape and his feet rooted to the earth of the front yard. *One minute Mister White had been waving to him and then he was dead!* 'Help me get Mister White inside the house.'

The man came out of his frozen state to assist the doctor and grabbed the arms while the doctor grasped the legs. They carried the body to the room where Willie lay dead and Granville was placed on the floor beside his son.

The stock and station agent gaped at the body of the young man on the bed. 'God almighty,' he uttered. 'What's been going on around here?'

'I don't really know,' the doctor replied, equally bewildered. 'But if I was not a scientific man I would have said some kind of native curse.'

The stock and station agent cast the doctor a questioning look. He had heard rumours of a curse on the property but had dismissed the stories as bush yarns to frighten city people. Now he was not so sure.

But Mary Cameron was sure.

Gordon James had visited the sacred hills of the long dispersed Nerambura people and Granville White had also gone to the Nerambura hills. From those hills a strange and unexplainable power had reached out to wreak devastation on the lives of all who had defied the ancient spirits with their uninvited visits. And even the poor young man Willie Harris, who had inhabited the sacred cave, now lay dead in the house.

Mary shuddered and Matilda caught her eye with a knowing look.

On Balaclava Station Adele Rankin sat in the living room of the homestead, darning her husband's socks. She was alone but glanced up to see who had entered the room. But there was no-one. Just an eerie feeling of a presence.

She stood and walked to the window to gaze out across the brigalow scrub plains at the beautiful sunny day. The stockmen struggled with cattle branding in the stockyards. The bellows of the beasts being scorched with the red hot branding

646

irons was a sound she had grown used to, like so many others: the rifle-like cracking of the stock-whips as the men herded the cattle; the warble of the black and white magpies in the morning; the shrill chatter of apostle birds that flocked fear-lessly to the homestead for discarded scraps from the kitchen.

And there were more: the sounds made by the white man that filled the vast spaces of the bush and had driven out the gentler sounds of the first people to roam the land; the laughter of children around the campfires; the melodic voices of the young men and women engaged in flirting; the old people gossiping in the shade of the trees by the creeks.

But the white man had not completely driven out the people, she reflected. Their spirit still existed in the shiny black faces of the Aboriginal stockmen and their families living and working on Balaclava Station. The unseen spiritual forces of the land still existed alongside the white man's houses, sheds and stockyards.

And so it was that Adele Rankin was not surprised to see Sarah Duffy standing, drawn and haggard, in the doorway to the living room in her sweat-stained nightdress. Adele Rankin dropped her sewing and hurried across the room.

'My brother has been here.' Sarah's first words came as a hoarse whisper. 'But he has gone.'

'I know,' Adele Rankin said gently as she led Sarah back to her room and put her back to bed to rest. She could see that Sarah would recover.

67

On the desk of the library, between the two women, was a pile of letters neatly tied with a red ribbon.

'These are the letters that you did not receive from my grandson,' Enid said. 'And I wonder if you deserve them now.'

Catherine Fitzgerald was not about to be cowed by the formidable Lady Enid Macintosh and returned her steely gaze. 'Had I received those letters whilst Patrick was campaigning in the Sudan I might not have had to wait so long to be with him, Lady Macintosh,' she replied in a cool, calm tone. 'But as it is, Patrick and I have been fated to be together and your intervention is part of that fate.'

Enid raised an eyebrow at the young woman sitting across the library from her. She was certainly a stunningly beautiful young woman with her long red tresses and milky pale skin. But it was the eyes that Enid noticed most. They were emerald green and very much like those of her own family. In Catherine's eyes she could see a highly intelligent yet mysterious woman. She is strong, Enid thought. It was no wonder her grandson was completely taken with her.

'The intervention had more to do with Patrick's father,' she replied as she kept the young woman's gaze. 'It was a letter he sent from Greece last year that decided my intervention on your behalf, Miss Fitzgerald, not fate.' Her reference to Michael Duffy almost caused Catherine to lose her composure. So she had a weakness, Enid mused. And that was good, as the game between them was being played for stakes beyond even Catherine's imagination. 'I dare say that if the contents of Michael Duffy's letter should ever reach my grandson, then he might view his love for you in a different light.'

Catherine had regained her composure. Michael had been right about Lady Macintosh's absolute ruthlessness in pursuit of maintaining the family's name and fortune. But would Michael have ever mentioned their brief but passionate affair? It was not likely; he was not that kind of man. Lady Macintosh was bluffing and Catherine suddenly realised that she was in a game where the prize was yet to be decided. 'Would I be permitted to read Mister Duffy's letter?' she asked, although she already knew the inevitable answer.

'I am afraid the contents of Mister Duffy's letter are private,' Enid confirmed. 'I would rather destroy the letter than have any chance of it ever being viewed by Patrick.'

'In that case,' Catherine countered, 'I see that I have no other choice than to confess to Patrick my affair with his father and pray that he finds it in his heart to forgive me.'

For a brief moment Enid looked shocked but quickly gathered herself to parry the cleverly delivered thrust. The young woman was much wiser than she had given her credit for and this in its own right was a good sign. 'I doubt that will be necessary, Miss Fitzgerald,' she responded. 'I have no intentions of informing my grandson of your infidelity.'

'I do not wish to appear rude, Lady Macintosh, but infidelity can only occur in a marriage,' Catherine interrupted, with just the hint of a winning smile. 'Patrick and I are yet to be wed, but hopefully we will be upon his return from Africa.'

The damned girl was good. She reminded Enid of herself at the same age. Yes, she might prove to be Patrick's strong and guiding light in the future. All that was required was a tacit agreement between them that any future grand-daughter-in-law ally herself with her grand vision for the twentieth century. This woman could be the one, she thought, and she regretted less and less following the advice in Michael Duffy's letter to contact Catherine and invite her to stay in Sydney. It had been more of a pleading to help right old wrongs and allow two young people to find a lifetime of happiness together. There had been no hint of an affair between the two of them in the letter.

As such, Enid's invitation had arrived in Greece, and the telegram read by a completely puzzled Catherine. Somehow she had known that it had a connection with the sudden disappearance of Michael from her life. Only now the truth that Patrick had written to her in Ireland was evident. She had also learned that her grandfather had intercepted all Patrick's correspondence. Now it was time to seal the fate that had always intended that the Morrigan marry her Cuchulainn. It was time to win the formidable woman over.

'Lady Macintosh,' Catherine said softly and with feigned humility, 'I know that you may not approve of me as a wife for Patrick but I want you to know that fate cruelly divided us and yet has brought us near to finding each other again. But I would leave now if I felt that my presence in your house might cause dissension between you and your grandson. I love Patrick with all my heart and know that beside him and with your help we can make the Macintosh name even greater. I humbly leave that decision to you.'

'Are you a regular attendant of a Protestant church?' Enid asked.

'I am a member of the Church of Ireland,' Catherine replied, and was just a little confused when Enid smiled.

'That is just one step above being a Papist,' she said. 'And I fear that if you and Patrick have a daughter she may be inclined to perform on the stage like her mother.' Catherine made as if to protest but Enid cut her short. 'Oh, never fear, I will not ask you to leave, and I can see that you are confused by my acceptance. It has much to do with righting past wrongs that I must accept some responsibility. I think that you and I both have mutual interests at heart. I am now convinced that my grandson chose wisely.' She paused and reached for the letters on the desk. 'You may wish to read these when you move out of your hotel and move into my home to await Patrick's return.

I am sure that your presence is the best gift I can give my grandson when he arrives back in the colony.'

Catherine did not know whether to laugh or cry. Somehow she felt that she had been outwitted by the woman, but was not sure. *A gift* . . . the words had possessive overtones but for now that did not matter. She would be reunited with Patrick and knew she would become his wife.

As she accepted the letters handed to her, Catherine had a fleeting thought that in the future the formidable woman would become at the same time her best friend and worst enemy.

68

The wagon was burnt to its axles. Patrick stood staring at the scene of the final stand of his father against the Boer commando. Here and there in the long grass the sun glinted off the expended brass cartridge cases of the Winchester. It all seemed so unreal now that the sun was shining over the sea of waving grass of the African veldt. So peaceful, as if nothing had happened.

The patrol of ten mounted British soldiers behind him gazed about the plain with curiosity. They had been briefed on the situation at the De Aar outpost by their troop commander, Lieutenant Croft: one man standing alone against a party of heavily armed Dutchmen. The outcome was inevitable considering the time it had taken the Australian to get his message from the Zulu kraal of Chief Mbulazi to the British army outpost in the town.

'It appears that we have arrived too late, Captain Duffy,' the young lieutenant said sympathetically. 'I knew your father personally and he was a fine gentleman.'

Patrick did not answer but stared at the wagon. There were no bodies and very few signs, other than the expended cartridge cases, of a fierce struggle. Nor was there blood on the grass, he noted, as he scanned the area where most of the empty cartridge cases lay. But that was to be expected, considering that it had taken three days to contact and mobilise the British military patrol from the town.

'Naturally we will carry out inquiries,' the lieutenant said. 'But these damned mutinous Dutchmen are unlikely to even admit to leaving their farms. The bastards are a surly lot.'

'Possibly, you might make inquiries as to whether or not anyone has come across my father, Mister Croft,' Patrick replied as he stared at the distant horizon where the sun hovered. 'I doubt that he is dead.'

The officer nodded but with little conviction for the captain's wishful thinking. 'I will do that, sir,' he replied. 'But in the meantime there is little use hanging around here.'

Patrick returned to the mount the army had provided him. He swung into the saddle and the lieutenant gave the order to return to De Aar. There was little more he could do than file a report on the incident and hand the matter over to the local police to investigate. Maybe from their informants they would at least determine where the Irishman's body was buried. At least that would be enough to put him to rest. It was impossible for any man, the young English officer considered, no matter how good he was, to escape the determined assault of a Boer commando.

Tell your mother that you love her ... came softly to Patrick's thoughts as he rode on the track back to the town of De Aar. Why had he not asked his father whether he had loved his mother? But he had failed to ask a lot of questions. Maybe he was foolish in refusing to acknowledge his father's inevitable death up against such overwhelming odds. Why was it that when he left he had refused to admit to himself that he would never see his father again? They had not fooled each other with their bravely optimistic talk when they parted. They both knew that they were unlikely ever to meet again in this world of light and shadow. Was it guilt that he had survived and his father had died that refused to let him think of his father as dead? Had he not heard the distant, furious popping of rifles from the direction of the wagon as he floated down the river in the dark? Then the dreadful silence that descended on the veldt.

His father might be dead but the brief memory of a tall, strong man with one eye persisted. He would always be alive whilst he was remembered, Patrick thought, though not with the sad thoughts of inconsolable grief. He could not really feel this for a man he barely knew. His knowledge of his father had only extended to a brief and traumatic few hours under the guns of the Dutchmen.

He would return to Sydney via Greece at the first possible opportunity. Catherine lived some-where and wherever she was he would find her.

69

Very few people attended the burial of Granville White in Sydney. His body had been transported from Queensland on orders from Fiona. She did not want him to be buried in the same earth as her father and eldest brother. Such a gesture, she felt, would have been an insult to the memory of her father's work in establishing his beloved property which Granville had attempted to dispose of.

Only a handful of business acquaintances stood in the warm spring sunshine to listen to the minister drone on about the financial achievements of the man in the coffin. There was little else he could think to say about Granville without risking his own soul with fabricated good works.

Fiona had attended as the dutiful, grieving wife. She stood dressed in black with a veil to keep the buzzing clouds of flies from her face and one or two of the male mourners allowed themselves a sly and most disrespectful admiring glance at her. She was still a fine figure of a woman with a considerable dowry for any man who should be fortunate enough to win her hand.

But sharing her life with a man was not something Fiona even entertained for a moment. Before the sudden death of her husband she had arranged to travel to Europe to be with Penelope in Germany. There she would also be close to her daughters who had grown into beautiful young women and who revelled in the charming attentions of the young men of the European courts.

The death of her husband had actually been a god sent opportunity to sever her ties with Sydney. *No loose ends reaching back in her life!* Nor did she feel guilty for the lack of feeling other than relief that she experienced at the news of Granville's death. For the man had led an evil and destructive life that had probably included the murder of her beloved brother David those many years earlier. The only positive thing she could acknowledge was that he had been a good provider which had allowed her to maintain her elegant lifestyle. And the terms of his will, unaltered from better days between them, returned the third share of the Macintosh companies to her – a third share she had originally transferred to him to protect her son Patrick from Granville's intentions to discredit him.

Fiona was relieved when the final traditional words were intoned by the minister for the commitment of Granville's body to the earth. The few mourners attending the service paid their respects to her as they returned to their waiting carriages outside the cemetery. She did not linger at the graveside but walked slowly back to her carriage.

'Fiona!'

The voice that called to her from one of the carriages alongside the cemetery caught her unawares. She ceased walking and stared at her mother's fine carriage, distinguished by the thoroughbred set of greys in harness.

'Mother,' she answered. It was a word that came to her lips without thinking and Enid stepped from her coach. As she walked over to her, Fiona wondered at her mother's attendance at the funeral. Enid's face did not hold the hard-set expression she remembered from their last meeting in the library. Instead, she detected a gentleness she barely remembered. 'I did not expect to see you here,' Fiona said when her mother reached her. 'Considering how I know you felt about Granville.'

'I did not come to pay my respects to *that* evil man,' she answered softly. 'God will be his judge now and not I. I came to see you.'

'Me!' her daughter replied with bitter disbelief. 'Why should you wish to see me?'

'Do you think we could walk together, away from the curious stares of the people here?' Enid said, indicating the few remaining mourners who recognised her. 'I suspect our meeting will cause tongues to wag.'

'I see no harm in your request,' Fiona replied.

The two women walked aimlessly towards the rows of headstones where only the dead could listen to their words. When they had gone a short distance into the cemetery Enid broke the silence between them. 'Fiona, my daughter, I have done your life a great injustice over the years. I did so out of the sin of pride. A pride that was wrong because it has caused you so much grief. It has caused us both so much pain and I am here now to beg your forgiveness.'

Fiona stopped and turned to stare into her mother's face. Had she actually reached out to her with an apology for the two decades of alienating bitterness that had existed between them? She gazed into her mother's eyes as if searching for some sign of deceit. But she saw none and found her own emotions tumbling over each other like a leaf caught in the stream of a summer storm. In the rising heat of the early summer that had come to Sydney, she felt as helpless as such a dry leaf. Her mother's expression was that of a tormented woman seeking exorcism for the ghosts that haunted her past. The ghost of a love lost between mother and daughter that lingered even yet.

'You know that I am booked for passage to Germany,' she replied. 'And you must know why.'

'I know you will be going to Penelope,' her mother said quietly. 'Oh, I cannot say that I understand that which exists between you and your cousin, but I can say what exists in my heart for you. I know I have been a selfish old woman. That I did a terrible wrong in not telling Patrick of your love for him.' She hesitated in her words and glanced away at a lone gravedigger sweating to prepare a grave. Then she turned to face her daughter and continued. 'Patrick has telegraphed from South Africa to say that he is returning to Sydney. I expect that he will arrive home after you have taken passage to Europe. I just want you to know that when he returns I intend telling him of your love for him – and of my foolish complicity in concealing that truth from him over the years.'

'You would do that?' Fiona asked softly. 'Risk losing his love by telling him the truth?'

'I once met his father,' Enid said with a humility her daughter had not heard in the many years she had known her. 'I saw in him a strength and character I have never seen in any other man, except when I look into your son's eyes. The boy is his father's son and, as such, capable of great things. I trust I am right in hoping he can forgive me for the wrong that I have done you both. Had Michael Duffy not been a Papist I think he should have been your husband, despite his lowly station in life.'

Fiona reached out to take her mother's hands in hers. They felt so fragile and a surge of heart-breaking sympathy for her mother welled up in her tears. For a precious moment she was not the strong and stern woman, capable of ruthless manipulation of a financial empire, but a frail old woman who was her mother.

'You will never know what your words have meant to me, Mama,' she said with tears spilling down her face. 'No matter what should occur in our lives from now I will treasure your words, as if they were the most precious things ever said.'

Fiona suddenly became aware of a strange thing. It was something she had never seen her mother do before. Her mother was weeping!

'I know he will cross the ocean to see you,' Enid said between sobs. 'I know my grandson has a need to meet the woman whose blood is his. Just as much as he had a need to meet his father.'

They held each other in an embrace that

swallowed the years of bitterness as if they had never existed, the reconciliation of mother and daughter within sight of Granville's grave.

Enid gently disengaged herself from the embrace but continued to hold her daughter's hands. 'Will you dine with me tonight?'

'Yes, Mama, I would like that very much.'

'I have so much to tell you about your son, with so little time before you depart.'

'We have all the time remaining in our lives,' her daughter gently chided. 'As much as I long to go to my son I also know in my heart that Patrick will seek me out when the time is right for us both.'

'I wish that were true,' Enid said as she brushed away her tears with a little cotton handkerchief. 'But I fear my time in this world is limited. When I am gone Patrick will need the guiding hand of his mother to take our name into the next century.'

Our name! Fiona thought with a start. The Macintosh name!

'Our name,' she echoed. 'Father would have been proud of Patrick. If he only knew him as you have, Mama.'

The gravedigger stopped to ease his sweating body for a moment. He leant on his shovel and stared with idle curiosity at the two elegantly dressed women weeping and laughing together a short distance from him. Must be Irish, he mused as he watched them. Only the Irish could find humour in death. Probably going to a wake after the funeral. Lucky devils! Then he continued to fill the open grave with earth as the two women walked slowly away, hand in hand.

70

Patrick was awed by the sombre experience of standing in the cool gloom of the sacred place of the Nerambura and gazing at the ancient ochre paintings.

'It is all I imagined,' Catherine said softly as she stood beside her husband. 'A place of infinite sadness and yet a wonderful memory of those poor lost people.'

'Not all lost,' Patrick said softly in the hallowed place. 'I have heard that there is still one alive who would remember the rites that the Nerambura practised here before the time of my grandfather. An old warrior called Wallarie.'

'Where is he now?' Catherine asked with the amateur archaeologist's interest for a tangible link with the past.

'No-one really seems to know but one hears rumours from the blackfellas that he has been seen wandering the land. Then he just disappears.'

'That is sad,' his wife sighed. 'To be the last of his tribe and alone in our world.'

'I think he is not alone,' Patrick replied quietly.

'I think he must live with the spirits of his people.'

'Aha!' she said mischievously. 'Does the very practical heir to the Macintosh fortune believe in spirits, as I do?'

He turned to smile at his wife who in turn gazed up into his eyes with just the touch of a teasing smile. How beautiful she was, he thought with an overwhelming feeling of love. But she was not just physically beautiful; she also had a strange spiritual beauty he knew he would love to the day that he died.

A year earlier Catherine had been an unexpected guest of his grandmother when he had arrived home from South Africa – and she had not left his life since. The marriage to a good Protestant young woman of the Church of Ireland had been acceptable to Lady Enid Macintosh. The girl had an impeccable bloodline, even if she were of Irish birth.

True to her promise to her daughter, Enid had related to Patrick all that had transpired over the years concerning her concealment of the truth. He had accepted the confession without rancour, as she had prayed he would. Too much had happened in his own life to allow him the privilege of judgment.

One day he intended to travel to Germany where he would meet with his mother and ask her forgiveness for his foolish denial of the love she had always held for him. A love he so desperately wanted, just as he had wanted the love of the beautiful Irish girl he thought he had lost. The relationship Catherine had with his father was never raised between them.

'I think I understand how the old warrior feels from time to time,' Patrick said seriously. 'I experienced something similar when I was cut off from the army in the Sudan and was wandering in the wilderness. It is hard to explain.'

'You need not try and explain,' Catherine said gently. 'Some things defy our attempts to find earthly words. But I think, for now, we should not intrude upon the sleep of the spirits who live here, my love. I think we should return to the homestead and indulge ourselves in the Camerons' wonderful hospitality.'

'I think you are right,' he replied. 'But first, there is something we must do before we return to the homestead.'

Catherine nodded and held Patrick's hand as he bent to place the tiny stone icon in a slither of a crevice in the cave. They stepped back and Catherine smiled.

'She belongs here,' she said. 'This place and the burial mound of the old Celtic kings have much in common. They are places of magic and memory. Even if they are times and worlds apart.'

Patrick swept his wife into his arms and kissed her passionately. She did not resist his embrace but responded with her own rising passion as he fumbled with her clothing until she stood naked in the cool gloom of the cave. In turn he quickly stripped his own clothes away and they lay on the musty earthen floor to make love.

At first their desire was a fast and violent explosion of passion, a coupling of two young animals. But this was followed by a slower, more tender lovemaking that lasted until the shadows fell in the cracks and crevices of the ancient range of hills and crept with a golden glow into the cave itself.

As Catherine lay sleepily in Patrick's arms on the musty earth she remembered another time and place – a Celtic hill on the other side of the world and an older man who came to the village with paint brushes and canvas. He had arrived with his battle scarred body and she had experienced both pain and joy in his arms.

It was strange, she mused as the golden rays of the sun illuminated the Aboriginal figures on the rock wall. She had been the link between the two men, father and son, and now she had loved them both in the sacred places of their birth. For Michael Duffy had been born in sight of the ancient Celtic burial mound and Patrick born in the shadow of the Nerambura hills. In her own way she loved both men. One now but a memory and the other a reality in her life. Could it be that a woman could love two men equally, but differently? That question, she knew, she could not share with her husband.

When Patrick stirred they dressed and walked out of the cave hand in hand to emerge on the hillside. They gazed across the vastness of the brigalow scrub plains at the setting sun.

Glen View would always be Macintosh, Patrick thought, as he took in the view of the harsh but beautiful land. He had sworn his oath to his grandmother on the matter. His Aunt Kate would just have to accept that Glen View would never be hers; the property held just as much sentimental value to the Macintoshes as it did to the Duffys and she would have to accept that he was the link, fated to join the two families together, despite the bitterness that lay between them. Times had changed and the past was gone. *Surely the curse had run its course?*

They walked down the old path that had been trodden by thousands of bare feet and then by the boots of the new arrivals to the land. Behind them the hills sighed as a gentle breeze played amongst the tough clinging scrub of the rocks. The heart of the old volcano continued to beat within the stone core of the hill, whispering a warning to Patrick Duffy.

But Patrick did not hear the voices of the ancestor spirits. Only Wallarie could have understood their ancient words.

EPILOGUE

'That all happened a long time ago when I was young. Now you know how many whitefellas I killed.' (Wallarie chuckles.)

'But what can the police do to an old blackfella? The Native Mounted Police are gone. The government man got rid of the bloody buggers around the time you got a thing called Federation . . . Or it might have been when you got a twentieth century.

'You want to know how I got to sit under this bumbil tree on Glen View to tell you more about the two whitefella families? Some whitefella surveyors found Luke Tracy's bones up in the Gulf Country a couple of years back. They gave Missus Tracy a book he had written some words in and she read it every day, tracing the words with her fingers.

'You want to know about this pastor fellow I knew? Well, old Pastor Werner and his missus let me stay on their mission station up north. I think that time, when I went up north, was after cousin Peter Duffy was killed. I don't remember when that was. But it was a long time ago, before you whitefellas had that big tribal war over in some place called Europe.' (A silence as the blind old warrior reflects on something sad.)

'The pastor and his missus are gone to their Dreaming now. They got sick when the big fever came after the whitefella war. They were good people and I don't think the pastor would have liked this German fella, Hitler, I hear you white-fellas talking about.

'How did I get to Glen View? That is a long story and I can feel the sun going to sleep on my face.

'That means old Wallarie must go to sleep by the fire. But, if you come back in the morning with some 'baccy for my pipe, I might tell you what happened to the Duffys and Macintoshes.' (Wallarie chuckles again and stares with unseeing eyes into the setting sun.)

'Long time ago they think that the blackfella curse go away.

'But they were wrong.'

THE END

AUTHOR'S NOTE

The three central themes portrayed in this novel are all firmly based in historical fact.

The New South Wales military expedition to the Suakin Campaign saw an organised body of troops represent an Australian colony in one of the many British colonial wars of the nineteenth century. I have attempted to reconstruct the events surrounding the Tommy Cornstalks' advance on the Sudanese village of Tamai from K.S. Inglis' comprehensive account *The Rehearsal*. Needless to say, Captain Patrick Duffy's adventures in that campaign are purely fictional.

The guerilla war waged by the Kalkadoon warriors, who inhabited the territory in the Cloncurry district of central North Queensland, was one of the little known and heroic attempts by an Aboriginal tribe to quell the advance of white settlement. But they were not alone and many surrounding tribes of that region also bravely resisted the annexation of their lands. I have used author's licence to move the war from the early 1880s to midway through that decade for dramatic reasons of paralleling two colonial wars.

It should be noted that there is some conflict in accounts about whether the Kalkadoon made a final stand or were dispersed as a result of an ongoing campaign. I have portrayed something in the middle of the conflicting accounts.

Another interesting note on the warriors of central Queensland is their very different tactics – compared to other Australian tribal groupings – used in fighting their war on the frontier. To the reader interested in their culture most information can be found under the library search of *Australian Aboriginal Tribes – Kalkadoon*.

In my story Gordon James is a fictional character, and in no way does his character bear any resemblance to the real historical commander of the punitive expedition, Lieutenant Urqhart of the Native Mounted Police.

The covert German operation to annex the northern half of New Guinea and surrounding islands did actually occur in Sydney at the time portrayed in this novel. A good source of information on the subject can be found in Stewart Firth's book *New Guinea Under the Germans*. I have used licence to place the fictional intrepid English agent Horace Brown, and his somewhat reluctant ally the Irish mercenary Michael Duffy, at the centre of events. Needless to say the character of Count Manfred von Fellmann is also fictional. The actual covert operation which sailed from Sydney eventuated in German success. Its repercussions would be felt less than thirty years later when the first Australian troops to be killed in the Great War would die fighting German troops in German occupied Pacific islands and not at Gallipoli as many Australians would believe.

As for the colour and stories of the Queensland frontier I continue to thank Glenville Pike and Hector Holthouse whose books I recommend to any reader with an interest in Australia's northern frontier of the nineteenth century.

For the intrepid tourist, I can assure you that the spirit of Wallarie still roams the brigalow plains and camps by the lily covered billabongs of out-back Queensland.

A SELECTED LIST OF FINE NOVELS
AVAILABLE FROM CORGI BOOKS

THE PRICES SHOWN BELOW WERE CORRECT AT THE TIME OF GOING TO PRESS. HOWEVER TRANSWORLD PUBLISHERS RESERVE THE RIGHT TO SHOW NEW RETAIL PRICES ON COVERS WHICH MAY DIFFER FROM THOSE PREVIOUSLY ADVERTISED IN THE TEXT OR ELSEWHERE.

☐	14783 4	CRY OF THE PANTHER	Adam Armstrong	£5.99
☐	14812 1	SONG OF THE SOUND	Adam Armstrong	£5.99
☐	14497 5	BLACKOUT	Campbell Armstrong	£5.99
☐	14667 6	DEADLINE	Campbell Armstrong	£5.99
☐	14586 6	SHADOW DANCER	Tom Bradby	£5.99
☐	14587 4	THE SLEEP OF THE DEAD	Tom Bradby	£5.99
☐	14871 7	ANGELS & DEMONS	Dan Brown	£5.99
☐	14919 5	DECEPTION POINT	Dan Brown	£5.99
☐	14604 8	CRIME ZERO	Michael Cordy	£5.99
☐	14882 2	LUCIFER	Michael Cordy	£5.99
☐	14654 4	THE HORSE WHISPERER	Nicholas Evans	£6.99
☐	14738 9	THE SMOKE JUMPER	Nicholas Evans	£6.99
☐	13991 2	ICON	Frederick Forsyth	£6.99
☐	14923 3	THE VETERAN	Frederick Forsyth	£6.99
☐	14601 3	SET IN STONE	Robert Goddard	£5.99
☐	14602 1	SEA CHANGE	Robert Goddard	£5.99
☐	13678 6	THE EVENING NEWS	Arthur Hailey	£5.99
☐	14376 6	DETECTIVE	Arthur Hailey	£5.99
☐	14717 6	GO	Simon Lewis	£5.99
☐	14870 9	DANGEROUS DATA	Adam Lury & Simon Gibson	£6.99
☐	14797 4	FIREWALL	Andy McNab	£6.99
☐	14798 2	LAST LIGHT	Andy McNab	£6.99
☐	14838 5	THE GUARDSHIP	James Nelson	£5.99
☐	14843 1	THE PIRATE ROUND	James Nelson	£5.99
☐	14666 8	HOLDING THE ZERO	Gerald Seymour	£6.99
☐	14816 4	THE UNTOUCHABLE	Gerald Seymour	£6.99
☐	14391 X	A SIMPLE PLAN	Scott Smith	£5.99
☐	10565 1	TRINITY	Leon Uris	£6.99
☐	14794 X	CRY OF THE CURLEW	Peter Watt	£6.99
☐	14795 8	SHADOW OF THE OSPREY	Peter Watt	£6.99

All Transworld titles are available by post from:

Bookpost, P.O. Box 29, Douglas, Isle of Man IM99 1BQ

Credit cards accepted. Please telephone 01624 836000, fax 01624 837033, Internet http://www.bookpost.co.uk or e-mail: bookshop@enterprise.net for details.

Free postage and packing in the UK. Overseas customers allow £1 per book (paperbacks) and £3 per book (hardbacks).